Arthur William Moore

The Surnames and Place-Names of the Isle of Man

Arthur William Moore

The Surnames and Place-Names of the Isle of Man

ISBN/EAN: 9783337407025

Printed in Europe, USA, Canada, Australia, Japan

Cover: Foto ©Andreas Hilbeck / pixelio.de

More available books at **www.hansebooks.com**

THE

SURNAMES & PLACE-NAMES

OF THE

ISLE OF MAN.

BY

A. W. MOORE, M.A.

With an Introduction

BY

PROFESSOR RHŸS.

'As no impresses of the past are so abiding, so none, when once attention has been awakened to them, are so self-evident as those which names preserve.'— TRENCH (on 'The Study of Words.')

LONDON:
ELLIOT STOCK, 62, PATERNOSTER ROW, E.C.
1890.

PREFACE.

I AM at a loss what excuse to make for thrusting myself into the foreground of this work, except that I have
found it too hard to say 'nay' to its author, whom I
have known for years as a scholar who takes the
keenest interest in all that relates to the history of his
native Island of Man. Among other things I was aware
that he had singular facilities for studying everything of
the nature of documentary evidence bearing on Manx
proper names. Those who happen to have been
acquainted with the 'Manx Note Book,' edited with
such ability and such excellent taste by Mr. Moore,
will agree with me in this reference to him. It
always struck me as a pity that he should not place
on record the fruits of his familiarity with the official
records of the Island; and the expression, on my part,
of that feeling on sundry occasions, is the only possible
merit to which I could lay claim in connexion with
this volume.

The ground to be covered by the work is defined by
the geography of Man, and so far so good; but on the
other hand, proper names, whether of persons or of

places, usually present the most difficult problems of
glottology, which any country can suggest; and such
cannot help being especially the case with a people like
the Manx, whose home has proved the meeting place
for Ivernians, Goidels, Scandinavians and Englishmen.
Manx names are therefore a compromise, and where
one can fathom the history of a Manx name, it proves
of great interest, not only in its relation to its home,
but also in regard to the light shed by it on what may
have happened in the prehistory of other lands.

Mr. Moore has given the reader not only the results
of his reading in Manx documents, but he has also
added remarks and notes intended to help the general
reader with regard to the etymology of the names discussed. Celtic philology, however, has of late years
been making such rapid progress that it is the fate of
everyone who writes on Celtic subjects to have constantly to revise his views. As for me, I have had, alas!
more of this experience than I should care to call to
mind at the present moment; and Mr. Moore must not
be surprised if the same necessity should overtake him
as regards some of his derivations: it is the inevitable
condition of every man, except him who thinks that
he has done learning.

Apart from all points as to which difference of
opinion may be expected, the book teems with sugges-
tions which cannot help interesting the students of
archæology and anthropology. With regard to the
former, I need only mention the pages which abound
in allusions to tumuli, cromlechs, and cairns; and as
to the latter, I refer to such articles as that on *Chibber
Unjin,* ' Ash Well,' over which grew formerly a sacred

ash-tree, adorned with the bits of rags usually to be met with on such trees. Special mention may also be made of the article on *Chibber Undin*, ' Foundation Well,' apparently so-called from its position near the foundations of an old chapel, twenty-one feet long by twelve broad. ' The water of this well,' Mr. Moore tells us, ' is supposed to have curative properties. The patients who came to it, took a mouthful of water, retaining it in their mouths till they had twice walked round the well. They then took a piece of cloth from a garment which they had worn, wetted it with the water from the well, and hung it on the hawthorn-tree which grew there. When the cloth had rotted away the cure was supposed to be effected.' When I visited the place, a somewhat more elaborate ritual was mentioned to me ; but here, as in the case of other wells in the island, the patient is supposed to transmit his complaint to the rag, and as the rag rots the disease perishes. If he makes an offering it consists usually of a coin, which is dropped into the well. But why the folklore man chooses to speak of the accursed rag as the offering and to ignore the coin, is a question which I cannot answer. It may be, however, that he thinks coins are too modern for him ; but a few centuries, more or less, make very little difference in such matters, and the rags are no less a product of civilization than are the coins.

It is, however, to the student of history and glottology that the work appeals as a whole ; and one of the points of interest to both will be the traces of a sort of double tradition which some of the Manx names force upon their notice. This can be best explained by taking

an example. The mountain now called South Barrule
was formerly called Wardfell, so that a portion of it is
still known by that name, modified into Warfield.
Thus the actual forms in use are Barrule and Warfield,
and these can be shown to be two forms of one and the
same Norse name *Vörðfjall*, meaning 'Beacon Fell.'
Such a name is connected with the institution of
'Watch and Ward,' which was constantly enjoined on
the inhabitants. From the statutes respecting this
duty one finds that each parish had its warden, who
was responsible for 'the dutifull and carefull observance
of watch and ward,' and this went on till the year 1815.
The day-watch came to his post at sunrise, and the
night-watch at sunset; the former is supposed to be
commemorated by the hill name *Cronk-ny-arrey-Lhaa*,
believed to mean the 'Hill of the Watch by Day.'
Such were also, probably, the watch and ward held on the
mountain-tops called South Barrule and North Barrule.

But how, it will be asked, could such a word as
Vörðfjall become Barrule? It went through a series
of changes, the chief of which were the following:
according to Goidelic tendency, the stress would be laid
on the first syllable with the effect of curtailing the
second, so that the name became approximately 'Varfl.'
Similarly Snjófjall, which is now called Snæfell, meaning 'Snow Mountain,' became, probably Snjófl; and,
as Sartel is supposed to represent a Norse Svartfjall,
'Black Mountain,' here also a contraction to 'Sartfl'
probably happened. Then a further change took
place, resulting in 'f' being represented in modern
Manx by ŭ, as in *lout*, 'a loft,' in *carroo*, a carp,'
from Norse *karf-i*, and in *Calloo*, the islet called the

Calf of Man. Thus the three names would arrive at the stage *Varrul, Sn'oul,* and *Sartul* respectively. Now Sn'oul remains practically the Manx pronunciation of the name at the present day, though, more exactly, I should say that it is *Sn'aul,* with a German *au;* but, under the influence of Goidelic accentuation, *Sartul* could not well avoid becoming *Sartl,* which is, approximately, the actual pronunciation of *Sartel.* Similarly, *Varrul* might have been expected to yield *Varl,* but other influences came to play : thus no Goidelic word began with a *v,* which occurred initially as a mutation of *b.* So, according to a tendency well known in all Celtic languages, the name came to be regarded in Manx as *Barrul,* liable in certain positions to be mutated into *Varrul.* In other words, it would be regarded by a Goidelic Manxman as having no separate existence except as *Barrul.* Then popular etymology set in and found *Barrul* sounding like the words *barr ooyl,* meaning the ' top of an apple ;' and this is the popular notion now current as to the origin and meaning of the name. That there should have been two mountains called ' apple-tops,' in the island, though neither seems to resemble an apple, is not very easy to believe ; but this idea has had the effect of stamping the accentuation of the words *barr ooyl* on *Barrul,* which is pronounced *Barrule,* or *Barrool,* with the stress on the final syllable. That this was the history of the name is rendered highly probable by the occurrence of the form *Varoole* in the registers, in the name of a man designated Villy Varoole, or ' Willie of Barrule.'

The Goidelic tradition by which Vörðfjall came down as Barrule, requires, phonetically speaking, more explanation than that which made the same word into the treen-name Wardfell and Warfield; but, historically, the latter presents a greater difficulty calling for further investigation, as it suggests that Norse names became English without a break. In that case one would have to suppose that the Norse, once spoken in the island, was superseded, not by Manx, but by English. If so, it is to be compared with the transition from Norse to English in Orkney and the Shetlands. In any case the dual tradition is not confined to *Barrule* and *Warfield*; there are many other instances, such as the Calf of Man, which is in Manx called the Calloo, and Peel, which was Holme-town, called in Manx *Purt-ny-Hinshey*, meaning the 'Town of the Island.'

Even the same duality exists, after a fashion, between the word *Tinwald*, from the Norse Thingvöllr, 'a parliament field,' and the House of Keys, where *Keys* is possibly a word of Goidelic origin. Dr. Vigfusson, taking this for a Norse word, has left his opinion on record that it meant a house of *Keise*, or 'chosen' men. But shortly before his death—a loss, alas! which his numerous friends still deplore—I had a talk with him, in the course of which I asked him about the word *keise*, and found from what he said, that there was a difficulty in establishing the existence of such a form. Then I referred him to the house being called in Manx the *Kiare-as-Feed*, and any member of it a man of the *Kiare-as-Feed*. Then I explained that this, though literally meaning the 'Four and Twenty,' was used as a single word; that the first two-thirds of it were pronounced approximately Kĭārŭs or Kārŭs; and, further, that, though I had not heard it pronounced without the *r*,

the omission of that consonant was not at all uncommon in Manx Gaelic. My friend at once saw
that I was going to suggest that *Keys* was merely the
English pronunciation of *Kiarc-as*, and with his usual
candour he admitted that he thought it right : at any
rate, he regarded it as far more probable than the
etymology he had himself suggested. On a later
occasion he returned to the same question, and took
for granted that such was the origin of the word. As
for me, I do not consider it very satisfactory; but it
may, perhaps, be provisionally accepted, especially as
the folk etymology current in the Island is, that the
members of the House of Keys are the twenty-four keys
with which his Excellency, the Lieutenant-Governor,
unlocks the difficulties of the law.

Many a tedious talk pitched in this key have I had to
hear through in the Island, while inwardly burning with
impatience to be better engaged in ascertaining the pronunciation of a particular word, the gender of a noun,
the use of a verb, or something of interest to me concerning a language, which, alas! is daily dying away.
The same, however, is the case with Manx as with
languages more living : the information one seeks can
only be got copiously diluted with the informant's own
meditations. But, all in all, my attempts to learn
Manx proved predominantly pleasant to both the
teacher and the taught; and Mr. Moore's book has
the effect of enabling me to live over again the happy
hours I spelled away in Ellan Vannin.

JOHN RHŶS.

Oxford,
May 22, 1890.

AUTHOR'S PREFACE.

My aim in the following pages is to give a complete account of the Personal Names and Place-Names of the Isle of Man. With regard to the former, I can confidently state that no names which have continued in the island for more than a very limited period have been omitted; and with regard to the latter, which are more difficult to secure, as changes are going on every year, I believe that I have included all of any importance. No one has hitherto attempted to explain Manx Personal Names, though there have been several explorers into the Place-Names, among whom is Canon Taylor, who, in his most interesting book on 'Words and Places,' has correctly translated a few of them. The others, not being equipped with his knowledge, have made the most ludicrous blunders, some of which are so amusing as to be worth quoting: BALLAUGH—*bealach*, 'a pass;' CASSNAHOWIN—*Cassivelaunus* (a British chief). The following are some of a number supplied by an enthusiastic Welshman: SULBY—*Sul-dydd*, 'Sunday;' BEMAHAGUE—*benw-haig*, 'a multitude of women ;' BALLIG—*beddgw*, ' a hedgehog ;' BIBALOE—*pibawl*, ' squirting ;' BALLAKERMEEN—*Bala-cor-trefau*, ' a rising college in a small town ;' MAUGHOLD—*Machiad*, ' making secure an embankment ;' LONAN—*llan*, ' full ;' CONCHAN—*congyl*, ' a corner, an angle.' From such mistakes as these I have been delivered by having a knowledge of the topography of the island; but I am fully conscious that I also must have made many mistakes, though scarcely of so obvious a kind, in dealing with such a difficult subject and one in which ambiguities necessarily abound. I therefore cast myself upon the indulgence of my readers, and shall hope for their aid in pointing out any errors I may have fallen into.

I have to record my thanks to the rectors and vicars of the country parishes for their courtesy in permitting me to take notes from the registers under their charge.

I have also to thank the Commissioners of H.M. Woods and Forests for giving me access to the Manorial Rolls ; and to the Place-Names Committee of the Isle of Man Natural History and Antiquarian Society for the names collected by them. To Professor Rhŷs I am deeply indebted for his valuable preface, and to him, Canon Taylor, Mr. Henry Bradley, Dr. Joyce, whose excellent book on Irish Place-Names I have freely quoted, and the late Dr. Vigfusson for advice and assistance on various points.

A. W. MOORE.

CRONKBOURNE, ISLE OF MAN.

June, 1890.

CONTENTS.

CHAPTER   PAGE

INTRODUCTION - - - - - - 1

PART I.—SURNAMES.

I. SURNAMES OF CELTIC ORIGIN DERIVED FROM PERSONAL NAMES :

(PART I.) BIBLICAL AND HAGIOLOGICAL NAMES   23

(PART II.) NAMES OF PURELY NATIVE ORIGIN -   36

II. SURNAMES OF CELTIC ORIGIN FROM TRADES OR OCCUPATIONS ; FROM DESCRIPTIVE NICKNAMES ; FROM DESIGNATION OF BIRTHPLACE - - - 71

III. SURNAMES OF SCANDINAVIAN ORIGIN - - - 79

IV. EXOTIC SURNAMES - - - - - 93

V. NAMES OBSOLETE BEFORE WRITTEN RECORDS - 109

APPENDIX A: OBSOLETE CHRISTIAN NAMES - - 116

    „   B: NICKNAMES - - - - 118

PART II.—PLACE-NAMES.

A.—Celtic.

I. GENERIC TERMS FOR TOPOGRAPHICAL FEATURES - 129

(PART I.) SIMPLE NAMES - - - - 130

(PART II.) COMPOUND NAMES - - - 142

(PART III.) DIMINUTIVES - - - - 157

PART II.—PLACE-NAMES—*continued.*

CHAPTER   PAGE

II. NAMES OF DIVISIONS OF LAND NOT TOPOGRAPHICAL - 161

III. DISTINCTIVE AFFIXES :

    (PART I.) SUBSTANTIVES -   -   -   - 166

    (PART II.) ADJECTIVES -   -   -   - 231

B.—*Scandinavian.*

IV. GENERIC TERMS FOR TOPOGRAPHICAL FEATURES :

    (PART I.) SIMPLE NAMES -   -   -   - 250

    (PART II.) COMPOUND NAMES   -   -   - 253

V. NAMES OF DIVISIONS OF LAND, NOT TOPOGRAPHICAL 268

VI. DISTINCTIVE PREFIXES :

    (PART I.) SUBSTANTIVES -   -   -   - 272

    (PART II.) ADJECTIVES   -   -   -   - 300

VII. ENGLISH NAMES -   -   -   -   -   - 303

    INDICES :

      OF CELTIC ROOT WORDS   -   -   -   - 319

      OF SCANDINAVIAN ROOT WORDS   -   -   - 330

      OF SURNAMES -   -   -   -   -   - 332

      OF PLACE-NAMES   -   -   -   -   - 336

INTRODUCTION.

Iᴛ is now generally recognised that the study of
personal nomenclature occupies an important place
amongst the subsidiary sources of historical illustration. In modern Europe it is to the surnames rather
than to what we call the Christian names that this
illustrative value principally belongs. A complete and
accurate account of the family nomenclature of any
European country—an account including the etymology
of each individual surname, and the locality and ap-
proximate date of its first appearance—would tell us
not a little respecting the ethnological elements existing in the population of the country, the proportions in
which these elements were represented in different
districts, and the habits and occupations of the inhabitants during the period in which surnames came
into existence. In the case of any of the larger
countries of Europe, however, it is scarcely necessary
to state that no complete history of family names has
ever been written ; indeed, we may venture to regard
the accomplishment of such a task as an impossibility.
Many writers have attempted to treat partially of the

origin of the surnames of England and of other lands; but, from the want of documentary evidence, or the difficulty of consulting it, their statements are inevitably in great part conjectural; and the incomplete character of these attempts necessarily renders the general inferences which may be based upon them more or less insecure. The surnames of the Isle of Man have not, as yet, been systematically studied, but the small extent of the island, its isolated position, the comparatively stationary character of its population (before the present century), and the abundance of documentary material, are all circumstances which are favourable to the investigation of the subject. In the following chapters it is proposed, as completely as the means at the writer's disposal permit, to examine the surnames which are, or have been, in use in the Isle of Man; to determine their etymology, when practicable, by the aid of documentary forms; and to indicate the districts in which the names appear to have had their origin.

The study of place-names, generally speaking, affords even more pregnant historical illustrations than that of surnames; but in the Isle of Man they have been, for the most part, written at such a comparatively recent date as to be less valuable in this respect. Till the sixteenth century, indeed, when the Manorial Rolls began, there are not more than a hundred names recorded. Even the Manorial Rolls contain only the names of the *Treens,* or larger land divisions, and some few names of mills, no *quarterland* names having been entered till early in the following century, when Hooper's Survey was made. The coast, mountain, and

river names, when they do not describe taxable properties—and this is usually the case—are rarely found
till a still later date, as the maps of the island before
the present century were on a very small scale,
and consequently contained but few names. Not-
withstanding these drawbacks, an attempt will be
made to examine these names in the same way
as the surnames, and to illustrate them from other
sources.

The general results yielded by the analysis of Manx
family and place nomenclature are such as might be
anticipated from a consideration of the history of the
Island and of its geographical position. The history
of the Isle of Man falls naturally into three periods. In
the first of these the Island was inhabited exclusively
by a Celtic* people, identical in race and language
with the population of Ireland. The next period is
marked by the Viking invasions, and the establishment
of Scandinavian rule. The third period is that of the
English dominion, when the Island became open to
immigration from Great Britain.

With regard to the first of these periods, the Celtic,
it is well known that the Isle of Man has a share in the
legends that take the place of history in Ireland before
the Christian era, and perhaps for some time after
it ; and it is clear that its inhabitants were of the same
race as the Irish, for Orosius, who wrote early in the
fifth century, stated that the inhabitants of both countries
were *Scoti*, or the people who in the Celtic languages

---

* Whenever the word *Celtic* is used it is to be understood as
referring to the *Goidelic* branch only, not to the Cymric.

would be called *Gael* and *Gwyddyl*. It is also certain that, from the fifth to the eighth centuries, Manxmen were mainly Christianized by Irish missionaries, as some of these missionaries have left their names to our ancient *keeills* and churches.* There are also recorded in the same way a few names of missionaries belonging to the Gallwegian and Columban churches, which would tend to show a connection, though probably a much less intimate one, with Galloway and the Western Isles of Scotland. These Celtic influences, though weakened by the Norse incursions and settlement, did not entirely cease till the English connection was finally established under the Stanleys. So firmly, indeed, were they implanted, that as late as the end of the eighteenth century the majority of the inhabitants of the Isle of Man still spoke their native Celtic tongue.

With regard to the second period, we know that a great emigration from Scandinavia began early in the ninth century. It took two directions, one, mainly Danish, to the north-east of England, and the other, mainly Norwegian, to the coasts of the Shetlands, Orkneys, Northern Scotland, the Western Isles, Ireland, and the Isle of Man. The annals of Ulster tell us that the earliest incursion of the Vikings took place in A.D. 794, and that in 798 they burned INIS-PATRICK, probably identical with PEEL. These visitors seem at first to have mainly used the Isle of Man as a convenient centre for their forays upon the adjacent coasts, and as a depôt for storing their spoil till they conveyed it home before the winter set in; but in the

* See Chap. III.

year 852 the Norse Viking, Olave the White, reached Ireland with a large fleet, and founded a Norse principality at Dublin. At the same period the Isle of Man must also have received numerous Scandinavian colonists, but they do not seem to have been strong enough to subdue the native inhabitants till about the end of the ninth century. From this period till 1270, when the Isle of Man fell under the dominion of the Scotch, it was mainly ruled by the Norsemen of Dublin, though there were intervals of independence and also of close connection with Norway. These Dublin Norsemen were, as would appear from the local nomenclature of the east coast of Ireland, mainly of Norwegian rather than of Danish origin, though the latter formed a considerable minority. It must also be remembered, in judging of the influence of the surrounding nationalities on Man at this time, that there was a considerable Scandinavian colony in Cumberland, in which the Norwegian preponderance was greater than in Ireland. This influence, however, would have come to an end soon after the Norman conquest. In Man, therefore, lying midway between Ireland and Cumberland, we should expect to find traces of both Norwegians and Danes, with a preponderance of the former, an expectation which is justified by an examination of the test-words of each nationality. *By* is both Danish and Norwegian, and is very common. *Thorpe*, found only once in the Isle of Man, and which, though very common in Lincolnshire, is rarely found on the adjacent English coasts, is almost exclusively Danish. *Toft*, also Danish, which is as rare as *thorpe* in Cumberland, Lancashire, and

Westmoreland, is found twice. The Norwegian *thwaite*, so common in Cumberland, is not found, nor are *beck*, *with*, and *tarn*, which are more Norwegian than Danish. *Haugh* and *dale*, on the contrary, to which the same description applies, are common ; so are the purely Norwegian *fell*, *garth*, and *gill*, while the equally Norwegian *foss* does not occur. All the above words probably imply permanent colonization on the part of their donors, and are therefore more valuable than such names as *vik*, *vagr*, and *nes* in determining the nationality of the colonists. From the above instances we are justified in concluding that the Manx-Scandinavian nomenclature is one in which the test-words of the Dane and the Norwegian are intermingled more completely than in any other part of the British Islands. Less Danish than East Anglia and Eastern Ireland, the Isle of Man is considerably more so than Cumberland, Westmoreland, and the Western Isles of Scotland.

With regard to the third period, the English, which, commencing in the thirteenth century, had excluded all other influences by the beginning of the fifteenth century, it is only necessary to mention the fact that English names are now rapidly increasing at the expense of both Celtic and Scandinavian.

Each of these three historical periods, therefore, has left its traces in our surnames and place-names. Considering surnames first, we find, as might be expected, that those of Irish derivation form the largest class. The Scandinavian epoch is represented by a considerable number of surnames inherited from the Vikings. It is noteworthy, however, that in nearly every case these Scandinavian names are Celticized in form—that is to say, they have received the Irish prefix *Mac*, and have undergone the kind of phonetic corruption which was inevitable when they had to pass through Celtic-speaking lips. Nor is it difficult to show how this would take place; for the ancient records tell us that neither Danes nor Norwegians drove out the native Goidelic inhabitants they found in Man and the Sudreys, and as it was not likely that many Scandinavian women would accompany the men on their long and dangerous voyages, they would consequently marry native women. The mixed population thus formed was called *gallgoidel*, a name applied to *goidelic* people, who became subject to the *galls*, or strangers (*i.e.*, the Norsemen), and conformed to their customs.

Of these two facts, viz, the continuance of the natives in the Island and the intermarriage of the Norsemen with the native women, we have ample confirmation from the names preserved on our inscribed Runic crosses. The mixed *Scandio-Gaelic* composition of the Manx people has recently received a remarkable confirmation by the investigation into the physical anthropology of the Isle of Man by Dr. Beddoe,* who has pronounced that a very large majority of the present population distinctly bears this type. The language spoken by this mixed race was doubtless for the most part Gaelic, which in the Isle of Man gradually superseded Scandinavian, as in England the old Saxon tongue superseded the Norman, mainly, of course, in both cases, through the influence of the

* Manx Note Book, No. 9, pp. 23-33.

women, who would naturally teach their children their own tongue rather than that of their fathers.

The English rule introduced into the Island many surnames from Great Britain, and this process is still going on. Some of the older of these imported names underwent translation into the native language. On the other hand, the use of the English language in the Island has led to the translation of certain native names into English; and it appears that (as was the case also in Ireland) some families have been known both by their native Celtic surname and by its supposed English equivalent, the one or the other being adopted according as the language used was English or Manx. Amongst the indirect consequences of the English connection may be reckoned the partial colonization of the Isle of Man by the Anglo-Norman settlers in Ireland, which has given us the Hibernicized Norman surnames common in certain districts. The geographical separation of the Isle of Man from the mother-country, Ireland, caused the Manx dialect to become, in course of time, materially differentiated from the Irish speech with which it was originally identical. From the same cause many of the originally Irish surnames of the Island have undergone a degree of phonetic corruption that covers them with a disguise which can only be penetrated by a recourse to early documents. The prefix *Mac* has, in many cases, fallen away altogether; in other cases it is represented only by its final consonant. This is the explanation of the many names beginning with C, K, or Q, such as CALLISTER, CLAGUE, COOLE, KELLY, KILLIP, KEIG, QUIGGIN, QUILLIAM, QUALTROUGH, etc., the frequency of which is so striking to any visitor to the Island. Where the syllable *Mac* was prefixed to personal names beginning with *Giolla* or *Guilley* ('servant of'), the initial syllables have been frequently contracted into *Mylcy*, the surname MAC GILLEY CHREEST or MAC GILCHRIST, for instance, becoming MYLECHREEST or MYLCHREEST. Early in the sixteenth century the prefix *Mac* was almost universal; a hundred years later it had almost disappeared. The old distich says:

> 'Per Mac atque O, tu veros cognoscis Hibernos,
> His duobus demptis, nullus Hibernus adest.'

i.e.,

> 'By *Mac* and *O*
> You'll always know
> True Irishmen, they say ;
> But if they lack
> Both *O* and *Mac*
> No Irishman are they.'

O never took root in the Isle of Man, but *Mac* has left numerous traces of its existence.

Women had the curious prefix *inc*, a shortened form of *inney* ('daughter')* before their names. Thus, in 1511, we find DONALD MAC COWLEY and KATHRIN INE COWLEY. After the middle of the seventeenth century *inc* is not found, though *Inney* survived as a Christian name till about a century later.

In Europe generally surnames may be divided, with regard to their derivation, into four classes: (1) Those derived from the personal name of an ancestor; (2) Those derived from trades and occupations; (3) Those

---

* Cf. Irish *ni*, a contraction of *inghin*.

which originally indicated place of birth or residence; and (4) Those which were originally nicknames descriptive of a person's appearance in character, or residence, or containing an allusion to some fact in his history. The Celtic and Celto-Scandinavian surnames of the Isle of Man, however, belong almost exclusively to the first and second of these classes. The evidence of early documents shows that nearly all of them at one time contained the prefix *Mac* followed either by a Christian name or by a word denoting a trade or calling.

The native portion of the nomenclature will, there-fore, here be discussed under two heads: surnames derived from Christian names, and surnames derived from words significant of occupations, nationality, and other personal characteristics. Although in the Isle of Man descriptive nicknames scarcely ever became hereditary, and therefore have contributed in very slight degree to our list of surnames, they have been and still are quite as largely used as in other countries as a means of distinguishing between namesakes. A considerable number of these distinguishing epithets may be found in our Parish Registers and other early documents, which, as they may be fairly regarded as so much unused raw material of family nomenclature, will be given in an appendix.

It has already been stated that an attempt will be made in these pages to assign the etymology, so far as it can be ascertained, of the Celtic or Scandinavian names discussed. Many of these are derived from Biblical or Hagiological Christian names which are the common property of Europe. In these cases it will be

sufficient to give the ordinary English form of the
Christian names in question. When surnames are
derived from personal names of purely Celtic or Scandinavian formation, the original forms of the personal
names will be quoted from Irish or Icelandic documents. To translate a compound name as if it formed
a significant whole is generally a mistake; but the
meaning of the roots from which the names are formed
will usually be stated. Out of about 170 surnames
which were in use in the Isle of Man at the beginning
of the present century, about 100 or 65 per cent. are of
Celtic origin, and about 30, or 17.5 per cent., of Scandio-
Celtic origin. The place-names of the Isle of Man, like
the surnames, clearly demonstrate the Scandio-Celtic
character of its population, with a strong preponderance of the latter element. For an analysis of these
names shows that out of about 1,500 names in use in
the Island at the present day, rather more than 1,000,
or 68 per cent., are purely Celtic; about 130, or 9 per
cent., are purely Scandinavian; while about 90, or 6
per cent., are of mixed Celtic and Scandinavian origin.
There are about 80 English names, or 5.4 per cent.;
about 50 names, or 3.3 per cent., of mixed English and
Celtic, and about 20, or 1.3 per cent., of mixed English
and Scandinavian names; while the remaining 100
names, or 7 per cent., can only be classed as of doubtful, though probably mainly Celtic, origin. It can be
shown, too, that the distribution of the Celtic and
Scandinavian names is remarkably regular throughout
the Island. For, taking the *treen* and *quarterland*
names, we find that there are 310 Celtic and 66
Scandinavian names in the northern parishes, and 286

Celtic and 70 Scandinavian in the southern—a very similar proportion.

The origin of the place-names being, as stated above, for the most part comparatively recent, has had, with regard to the Celtic names, the effect of rendering them easily explainable, as they were understood till recently by most of the people who used them, and their forms are in accordance with the pronunciation of the present day. They resemble the Irish place-names more closely than the Scotch, though, owing to the later connection with Scotland, the Isle of Man having been under Scotch rule during the end of the thirteenth century, the language approaches more closely to Scotch than Irish. With regard to the Scandinavian names the case is very different, for, having been for centuries in the mouths of people speaking a totally different language, they became in many cases hopelessly corrupt. To show this we append an account of the ' Limits of the church lands in the Isle of Man,' given in the *Chronicon Manniæ*, which was probably written about the end of the fourteenth century. The spelling of both Johnstone's* (1786) translation and of Munch's (1874) are given, and the modern names, which, it will be observed, are mainly of Celtic origin, are also appended in brackets.

1. This is the line that divides the king's lands from those belonging to the Monastery of RUSSIN: It runs along the wall and ditch which is between CASTLETON and the Monks' Lands; it winds to the south between the Monks' Meadow and M'EWEN's Farm or MAC-AKOEN's Farm; ascends the rivulet between GYLOSEN

* Johnstone's names are given first.

or GYLOZEN (Glashen), and the Monks' Lands; turns to
HENTRAETH, goes round HENTRAETH (Rhenshent) and
TROLLO-TOFT or TROLLA-TOFTHAR,(Slieu-ny-clagh) along
the ditch and wall; descends by the ditch and wall to the
river near OXWATH; turns up the same river to a rivulet
between AR-OS-IN or ARYEUZRIN, and STAINA or STAY-
NARHEA; goes down to the valley called FANC (Nank);
mounts up the ascent of the hill called WARDFELL or
WARZFEL, (South Barrule); descends to the brook
MOUROU; ascends from the brook MOUROU along the old
wall to ROSFELL; descends along the same wall between
CORNAMA (Cordeman) and TOT-MAN-BY (Tosaby); descends obliquely along the same wall between OX-RAISE-
HERAD or OXRAYZER (Lhergy-clagh-Willey) and TOT-
MAN-BY (Tosaby) to the river called CORNA.   CORNA is
the boundary between the king and the monastery in
that quarter to the ford which lies in the highway
between THORKEL's farm (Kerroo-kiel), otherwise KIRK
MICHAEL, and HERINSTAD or HERINSTAZE (Kerroo-
moar); the line then passes along the wall which is the
limit between the above-mentioned THORKEL's estate
and BALLY-SALLACH or BALESALAZC (Ballasalla); it
then descends obliquely along the same wall between
CROSS-IVAR-BUILTHAN or CROSY-VOR-BYULTHAN (Crossag or Balthane), and so surrounds BALLY-SALLACH; it
then descends from BALLY-SALLACH along the wall and
ditch to the river of RUSSIN or RUSSYN, as is well
known to the inhabitants; it then winds along the
banks of that river in different directions to the above-
mentioned wall and ditch, which is the limit between the
abbey land and that belonging to the castle of RUSSIN.

2. This is the line that divides the lands of KIRKER-

CUS or KIRKCUST (Kirkchrist Lezayre), from the abbey lands: It begins at the lake at MYRESHAW or MYROSCO (Ballamonagh), which is called HESCA-NAPPAYSE or HESCANA-AP-PAYZE (Glenduff); and goes up to the dry moor directly from the place called MONENYRSANA MUNENYRZANA (Ballameanagh); along the wood to the place called LEABBA-ANKONATHWAY or LEABBAAS KONATHAY; it then ascends to ROSELAN or ROZELEAN (Claddagh), as far as the brook GRYSETH (Kella); and so goes up to GLENDRUMMY or GLENNADROMAN, and proceeds up to the king's way and the rock called CARIGETH or KARRACHETH, as far as the DEEP-POOL or DUPPOLLA (Nappin), and descends along the rivulet and HATHARYEGORMAN or HATHARYGEGORMAN, and so descends along the river SULABY to the wood of MYRESHAW or MYRESCO; it incloses three islands in the lake of MYRESHAW (Ballamona); and descends along the old moor to DUF-LOCH, and so winds along and ends in the place called HESCANAKEPPAGE (Balla-karka).

3. This is the line which divides the king's lands from those of the abbey towards SKEMESTOR or SKYNNESCOR (Skinscoe): It begins from the entrance of the port called LAX-A (Laxey), and goes up that river in a line under the mill to the glynn lying between St. Nicholas Chapel and the manor of GRETA-STAD or GRETA-TAZ (Grettest); it then proceeds by the old wall, as is known to the inhabitants, along the winding declivities of the mountains, till it comes to the rivulet between TOFTAR-AS-MUND (Follit-e-Vanninn) and RAN-CURLIN or RYN-KURLYN (Glyncoolieen); it then descends to the boundaries of the manor called ORM'S-HOUSE or ORUMSOUZ

and TOFTAR-AS-MUND (Brough-ny-soo), and, as is known to the country people, descends to the sea.

It will be observed from the above that there has been a gradual process of substituting Celtic for Scandinavian names, which continued till the beginning of the present century. In the earliest manorial rolls there are 146 *treen* names, which can be definitely assigned to either the Goidelic or Scandinavian languages; and of these 83, or considerably more than one-half, are Scandinavian. During the sixteenth century, however, the Scandinavian predominance had completely passed away, for early in the seventeenth century we find that of 585 *quarterland* names (the *quarterland* being usually one fourth of the *treen*) which now appear for the first time, 533, or more than nine-tenths, were of Celtic origin. Yet, though many Scandinavian names have become corrupt, some have escaped this fate by having fallen out of popular use during the last three centuries, and a considerable number have remained practically unaltered in form to the present day, such as SNÆFELL, FLESHWICK, LANGNESS, LAXEY, GRENABY, TROLLABY, etc., and several Scandinavian words, such as *ghaw* (*gja*), *sker*, *stack*, *how* (*Haugr*), *ooig* (*ögr*), have been adopted into Manx. 'And,' says Munch, 'very remarkable is the fact, that although so early severed from Norway, and with a population more Gaelic than Norwegian, the Isle of Man has preserved until our days the outward form, at least, of the legislature peculiar to Norway in former times, and organized by the Norwegians wherever they formed settlements. Even the name of the place where the annual meeting is held, the TINWALD, is the old Norwegian denomination of þingvöllr (field of the Thing, or Parliament), only slightly modified.'*

In treating of this subject of Manx place-names, the writer has the advantage of an intimate personal knowledge of the Isle of Man, without which the most learned etymologist would assuredly often go astray. He has in every case obtained the earliest recorded form of each name, and has interpreted it in accordance with the laws of phonetic change, tempered by a due regard for its applicability to the locality which it describes, and for the various causes of corruptions, such as ignorance of the language and carelessness in spelling. He has taken for granted that those who gave the names considered them to be accurate descriptions of the localities to which they are applied, and that they are never mere arbitrary sounds, but have a rational significance. Acting, therefore, on these principles, he has carefully avoided etymological guesses, or, if in a few cases he has not done so, he has stated that they are not to be relied upon, and in order to substantiate the correctness of the words given, he has, in all cases where they could be discovered, quoted the corresponding words in cognate languages. With regard to the Celtic words, he has invariably called attention in doubtful cases as to whether they are (1) in common use, (2) used colloquially, (3) occur in Irish or Gaelic, (4) mentioned by one Manx lexicographer only, and, if not found in a Manx dictionary, proofs are, if possible, given of their genuineness. Scandinavian words not being in colloquial use could not receive identical treatment.

* Introduction to *Chron. Manniæ*, Manx Society, Vol. XXII., p. 31.

It remains to give an account of the documentary aids which have been employed in the present inquiry.

First, with regard to the surnames: There are a few names found, before the time of written records, engraved on stones in the Ogam and Runic character, which will be discussed separately in Chapter VI.

The earliest of the records is the *Chronicon Manniæ* (A.D. 1017-1376), kept by the Monks of Rushen Abbey. It contains but few names, and is, consequently, of but little use for our purpose. There is no record of surnames worth mentioning till A.D. 1408, the date of the ' Declaration of the Bishop, Abbot, and Clergy against the claim of Sir Stephen Lestrop.'* From 1417-1511 our chief authority in the Statute Law Book of the Isle of Man, wherein ' ensueth diverse ordinances, statutes, and customes, presented, reputed, and used for Laws in the Land of Mann, that were ratified, approved, and confirmed, as well by the honourable Sir John Stanley, Knight, King and Lord of the same Land, and diverse others his Predecessors, as by all Barrons, Deemsters, Officers, Tennants, Inhabitants, and Commons of the same Land.'† The *Libri*

---

* Oliver's Monumenta, Vol. II., p. 247.—Manx Society. Vol. VII.

† The Statutes of the Isle of Man, edited by J. Frederick Gill, 1883, p. 3. The spelling of the personal names in this edition has been adhered to, except that the names in 1417 have been taken from the *facsimile* of the copy in the Rol's Office, given as frontispiece to Vol. III. of the Manx Society's publications. The full lists of the ' Commons of Mann' in 1429 and 1430, and the names of the members of the ' Quest taken at the Castell of Rushene ' in 1521, and of the Jury in 1570, as they are not given in the Statute Law Book, have also been taken from the Acts in this volume, which have been printed from the MS. copy in the British Museum.

Assedationis, and *Libri Vastarum*, or Manorial Rolls, which commence in 1511, and have been continued at intervals since that time to the present day, form the chief source of our information till the beginning of the seventeenth century, when we have the Parish Registers to refer to.* The earliest Parish Register, that of Ballaugh, commences in 1598. Our Registers are especially interesting from the way they show the distribution of the various names. Thus, on the low sandy coast of Bride, Jurby, Ballaugh, and Michael, where the Vikings of old could easily run their flat-bottomed ships on shore, Scandinavian names are most common. On the south-west coast, adjacent to Ireland, we find a predominance of the Hibernicised Anglo-Norman names, borne by the descendants of the MAC WALTERS and the MAC WILLIAMS; while in the centre and on the east coast the names which came from Ireland at an earlier date and those of purely native formation are most frequent. It is remarkable how very seldom people moved from parish to parish before the present century. Names quite common in one parish were hardly known in the next.

The documentary aids employed for elucidating the place-names are the same as the above with the addition of a few ancient charters published by the Manx Society in their Volumes IV., VII., IX., XXI., and XXII. Wood's Atlas and Gazetteer, Brown's Gazetteer, and the 25-inch Ordinance Maps have also

---

* It must be remembered that the earlier records in the Isle of Mann are written in Latin, and that, consequently, many of the proper names are corrupted by being Latinised. In the Registers the different forms of a name frequently arise from careless spelling, as correct orthography is quite of a late date.

been made use of;* and a considerable number of field-names have been rescued from oblivion.†

Indices are given (1) of all the surnames, whether obsolete or not, the former being indicated by italics; (2) of all place-names; and there is also a glossary of Manx root-words with their cognates in Irish, Gaelic, Welsh, etc.

Our information respecting old Irish personal names has been chiefly derived from the following sources: (1) The Annals of the Four Masters, edited by O'Donovan (Dublin, 1856), which were mainly compiled by Michael O'Clery, a Franciscan Friar, between A.D. 1632-6, from the then existing Irish MSS. They extend from fabulous antiquity to A.D. 1616. (2) *The Chronicon Scotorum*, a chronicle of Irish affairs from the earliest times to A.D. 1150, edited by W. M. Hennessy (London, 1866). (3) The Topographical Poems of *O'Dubhagain and O'Huidhrin*, edited by O'Donovan (Dublin, 1862). For the original forms of the Scandinavian names to (1) The *Landnáma-bóc*, which is a record of the colonization of Iceland (*Clarendon Press*, Oxford). (2) Cleasby and Vigfusson's great Icelandic Dictionary (*Clarendon Press*, Oxford, 1874). (3) The *Flatcyjarboc* (Copenhagen), the *Sturlunga* and other Sagas (*Clarendon Press*, Oxford, 1878). For the explanation of the place-names, in addition to the above, and for purposes of illustration and comparison, refer-

* The spelling of the names in each of these three last authorities, which are all of recent origin, is frequently very corrupt.

† The field-names in the parishes of Braddan and Onchan have been collected by the writer, and in the parishes of Maughold, Lezayre, Ballaugh, and Michael by the Place-Names Committee of the Isle of Man Natural History and Antiquarian Society.

ence has been made for Celtic names to (1) Kelly's Manx Grammar (Manx Society, Vol. II.); (2) Kelly's Triglot Dictionary, in MS. (1808); (3) The Manx Society's Dictionary, edited by the Revs. W. Gill and J. T. Clarke, from Kelly's Triglot (1859); (4) Cregeen's Dictionary (1835). These Manx Dictionaries are all very incomplete and unsatisfactory: Cregeen's being the most trustworthy. (5) The Manx Bible (1772); (6) O'Reilly's Irish-English Dictionary (Dublin, 1877); (7) Macleod's and Dewar's Gaelic Dictionary (Glasgow, 1870); (8) Irish Names of Places, Joyce (4th edition, and 2nd series, Dublin, 1875); (9) Studies in the Topography of Galloway, Sir Herbert Maxwell (Edinburgh, 1887); (10) A Glossary of Cornish Names, Dr. John Bannister (1869); (11) Words and Places, Canon Isaac Taylor. For Scandinavian names to (1) Glossary of Shetland and Orkney Dialect, Thomas Edmonston (London, 1866); (2) Glossary of Scandinavian Names in the Hebrides, Capt. Thomas (Scottish Antiquarian Society); (3) Lincolnshire and the Danes, Streatfield (London, 1884); (4) Words and Places, Canon Taylor; (5) Jamieson's Scottish Dictionary (Edinburgh, 1867). The information given about objects of antiquarian interest has been partly taken from the *Report of the Archæological Commissioners of the Isle of Man*, 1878, and from additional MS. notes appended thereto.

EXPLANATORY NOTE.

The surnames are in small capitals and their derivations in italics. All words in any language but English are in italics. The dates in square brackets are the earliest, as far as can be ascertained, at which they are found in the insular records. The date (1511) is to be considered to stand for both 1511 and 1515; the former being that of the earliest rent-roll of the sheadings of

Rushen, Middle, and Garff, and the latter that of the earliest rent-roll of the remaining three sheadings. No dates are given after the end of the eighteenth century. The following abbreviations are made use of in Part I. : vc, very common ; c, common ; u, uncommon ; w, wanting, which refer to the comparative distribution of the various names in the respective parishes before the present century. [For this purpose a careful analysis of all the parish registers (17) has been made.]

O.N.—Old Norse, or Scandinavian.

Four Mast.—For Annals of Four Masters.

Chron. Scot.—For Chronicon Scotorum.

O'Dubhagain and *O'Huidhrin.*—For the topographical poems by those authors.

O'Donovan Introduction.—For the introductory account of Irish surnames given by the editor of the above poems.

All place - names are likewise in small capitals, except the Scandio-Celtic and Anglo-Celtic names in the Celtic text and in the index, the Scandinavian and English portions of which are indicated by italics.

The following abbreviations are made use of in Part II. : E, English : F, feminine ; C, Cregeen ; Cl*, Clarke ; G, Gaelic ; Gi*, Gill ; I, Irish ; K, Kelly ; M, masculine ; N, neuter ; Ob, obsolete ; S or O N, Old Norse, or Scandinavian ; W, Welsh ; ?, doubtful.

---

* When Cl and Gi are quoted it means that the word is given by them only.

MANX SURNAMES.

CHAPTER I.

SURNAMES OF CELTIC ORIGIN DERIVED FROM PERSONAL NAMES.

Part 1.—Biblical and Hagiological Names.

IN treating of the surnames derived from personal or 'Christian' names, it will be convenient, though not quite in accordance with the order of historical sequence, to begin with those which are formed from the Biblical and Hagiological names imported by the early Christian missionaries. These names were in very frequent use in Ireland and the Isle of Man. It is important to observe that while the names of saints were themselves given in baptism, they more frequently gave rise to secondary Christian names formed by prefixing the Irish word *Giolla*, 'servant'; or, in the Isle of Man, the Manx form *guilley*.* Thus the name

* Feminine Christian names were often formed in a corresponding manner by the use of the prefix *cailleach*, 'a nun, or female servant,' which is usually corrupted into *calli*, as CALLIVORRY, 'Mary's nun;' CALLICHRIST, 'Christ's nun.'

of JOHN (*Eoin*) became a common Christian name amongst the Celts, but its derivative *Giolla Eoin*, 'servant of St. John,' was still more generally used. Both these classes of names have contributed to the list of Manx Surnames. For instance, while the descendants of Eoin were called MACEOIN, and ultimately KEWIN, the descendants of GIOLLA-EOIN are known by the corrupted surnames GELLING and LEWIN, and, as has been already stated in the introduction, the combinations *Macgiolla* and *Macguilley* have been in many cases contracted into *Myley*. In other instances it has disappeared altogether, so that it is sometimes uncertain whether a particular surname is derived from a primary Christian name or from the secondary name formed upon it. In the following list we shall endeavour, where documentary evidence is forthcoming, to distinguish between these two modes of derivation, and the family names formed from a secondary Christian name will be placed after those formed from the corresponding primary name.

LUCAS, the same name as LUKE, was formerly common in the Isle of Mann, but since the middle of the seventeenth century it has been almost entirely superseded by Clucas.

LUCAS [1429].

CLUCAS, contracted from *MacLucais*, 'Luke's son,' is a purely Manx name.

MACLUCAS [1511], CLUCAS [1643], CLUGAS [1655].
> Jurby, Marown (vc), Braddan, Maughold, Malew, Santon, Rushen (c), elsewhere (u).

KISSACK, contracted from *MacIsaac*, 'Isaac's son,' is rarely found except in the Isle of Man. GILBERT McISSAK was one of the twenty-four " Keys of

Mann " in 1417, and in 1422 HAWLEY M'ISSACKE " was arraigned for that he felloniously rose upon John Walton, Lieutenant of Mann, sitting in the Court of Kirk Michaell."* Compare—(Gaelic) M'ISAAC, M'KISSACK ; (English) ISAACS, ISAACSON.

McISSAK [1417], M'ISSACKE, McKISSAG [1422], MacKISSAGE [1429], M'ISACKE, M'ISAACKE [1430], M'ISAACK [1504], KISSAGE [1586], KISSAK [1599], KYSSAGGE [1601], KISSAG, KISSAIGE [1610], KYSAIGE [1629].

> Santon (vc), Ballaugh, Lezayre, Michael, Braddan, Malew (c), elsewhere (u).

KEWIN, contracted from *MacEoin*, ' John's son.'

'In the province of Ulster the English family of Bissett, seated in the Glius, in the County of Antrim, assumed the Irish surname of MacEoin, MaKeon, from an ancestor HUAN, or JOHN, Bissett.'†

PATRICK McJON was one of the 24 ' Keys of Mann ' in 1417. (This name is wrongly spelt McGON in the Statute Law Book.)

In the Charter of the Bishopric of Man, A.D. 1505, we find ' Confirmation of Churches, Lands and Liberties, given, granted, and made by the most noble Lord Thomas, Earl of Derby, Lord Stanley, Lord of Mann and the Isles, to HUAN, Bishop of Sodor and to his successors.'‡ Compare—(Irish) KEON, McKEON, McKEOWN, and McKEOWIN ; (Gaelic) McEwen ; (Welsh) BEVAN.

McJON [1417], McJOHN [1429], M'KEWNE [1504], McKEWN [1511], KEWYNE [1540], KEWEN [1609],

---

KEWN [1671], KEWNE [1672], KEWIN [1700], KEON [1715], KEOIN [1732].

Jurby, Patrick, Andreas, Lonan (c), elsewhere (u).

GELLING, contracted from *Giolla Eoin*, 'John's servant.' ' Death of Niall, son of GILLAN, after having been thirty years without food or drink.' A.D. 856.* 'MAG-GELAIN, Bishop of Kildare,' A.D. 1222.† Compare —(Gaelic and Irish) MACGILLEAN, MACLEAN, and MACKLIN. It is a purely Manx name. MAC GILLANY (?), MACGILLEON, MACGILEWNE, GELLEN [1511], GELLYNE [1540], GELLIN [1622], GEL-LING [1626].

Braddan, Onchan, Marown, Malew (vc), German (c), elsewhere (u).

LEWIN has precisely the same origin as GELLING, but the *Giolla* has only transferred ' l ' to *coin* instead of Gill. It is a purely Manx name. MCGILLEON, MACGILLEWNE [1511], LEWIN [1627], LEWNE [1628], LEWN [1629], LEWEN [1698].

Braddan (vc.), Onchan (c), elsewhere (u).

QUANE, contracted from *MacShane*, ' Johnson,' ' MAC-SHANE,' A.D. 1542.‡

It may possibly be a contraction of *MacGuane* from *Macdubhaine*.

' MACDUBHAINE who has spread stories over the bright fine Cinel-Euda.'§ It is a purely Manx name.

Compare (Irish) QUAIN, (Gaelic) MACQUEEN. This latter is very common in Galloway.

MACQUAINE [1429], MACQUANE, MACQUENE [1511],

---

* Chron. Scot., p. 155.   † Four Mast, Vol. III.
‡ Four Mast., Vol. IV.   § O'Dubhagain, p. 43.

MacQuayne [1540], Quaine [1629], Guane [1680].

> Andreas, Bride, Patrick, German (c), elsewhere (u).

Killip, contracted from *MacPhilip*, 'Philip's son.'
Compare (Gaelic and Irish) McKillop, (English) Phillips, Phipps.

M'Killip [1430], McKillip [1511], McKillop, Killop [1540], Killip [1604].

> Ballaugh, Lezayre, Malew, German, Lonan (c), elsewhere (u).

Quark, probably contracted from *McMark*, though it may have been the same name as Quirk originally; it was the commoner name in the Isle of Mann 200 years ago, but now Quirk has almost entirely superseded it.

Markeson [1408], McQuarke [1511], Quarke [1616], Quark [1649].

Cammaish and Comish, contracted from MacHamish, 'James's son,' or possibly from *MacHomase*, 'Thomas's son.' Commaish looks more like the former, Comish the latter. Compare—(Irish) MacComas, (Gaelic) MacOmish.

The form Commaish is more common in the North and Comish in the South of the Island, but the name is not so often met with as formerly. MacComish [1430], MacComis, MacComais [1511], Comish [1650], Camish [1676], Camaish [1704], Cammaish [1704].

> Andreas, Bride, Maughold, Arbory (vc), Jurby, Santon, Malew (c), elsewhere (u).

Shimmin, from *McSim-een*, 'little Simon's son.' 'Dermot MacSimon slain,' A.D. 1366.*

> * Four Mast., Vol. III., p. 633.

Fraser, Lord Lovat, who was born in 1666, was called MacShimi Baldu, 'the black-spotted son of Simon,' from a black spot on his upper lip. Excepting Maughold the name is almost confined to the Southern parishes.

Compare—(Gaelic) McSymon ; (English) Symonds, Simmons, Symons, Simpson,* Symondson, and Simpkinson which latter exactly corresponds with it.

MacSheman and MacShemine [1430], Symyn, Hymyn, and McSymond [1511], Shimin [1614], Shimmin [1653].

> Malew, German (vc), Maughold, Arbory, Santon, Rushen (c), elsewhere (u).

Knickell, contracted from *MacNichol*, 'Nicholas's son.' It was formerly a common name in the Isle of Man, but has now almost disappeared. Compare —(Gaelic) McNichol; (English) Nicholson, Nicholls.

MacKnaykyll [1429], McNaykill, McNakill, Mc-Naikell [1430], Knacle [1648], Knickell [1650], Knickall [1653], Kneacle [1674], Kneakil [1730], Knackle [1757], Knicol [1758], Nicol [1771].

> Formerly, Patrick (vc), German, Lezayre, Maughold, Malew, Lonan (c), elsewhere (u).

Martin, originally *MacGiolla Martin,* 'the son of Martin's servant.'

St. Martin of Tours was St. Patrick's uncle. He died A.D. 448.†

MacMartyn [1429], MacGilmartyn, MacMartyn,

---

* Four Mast., Vol. III., p. 633.   † Four Mast., Vol. I., p. 129.

MacMarten [1511], Martinsone [1521], Martin [1668], Martee [1672].

> Andreas (vc), Lezayre, Patrick, Santon (c), Bride, Jurby (u). Hardly found elsewhere.

COSTAIN and COSTEAN contracted from *MacAustcyn*, a shortened form of *MacAugustin*, 'Augustin's son.' (Augustin is the diminutive of Augustus.) The fame of AUGUSTINUS of Hippo, and his namesake, the missionary of the English, would cause this name to be a favourite among Christian converts. Magnus Barfod, King of Norway, who died A.D. 1103, had a son OSTEEN and a grandson, son of Harold Gyllie, OSTEEN.

COSTAIN and COSTEAN are purely Manx names.

COSTEANE [1507], MacCoisten, MacCosten, Coisten, Costen [1511], Causteen [1687], Costain [1715], Costean [1747].

> Maughold (vc), Rushen, Arbory, Santon, Lonan (c), elsewhere (u).

STEPHEN and STEPHENSON, from the protomartyr, are, in the Isle of Mann, very frequently the translations of COSTAIN, which, however, has quite a different origin (see above).

STEAN, which has now disappeared, if not a shortened form of Stephen, may be from (O N) *Steinn*, 'stone.' Compare—(Dutch) STEEN.

In A.D. 1334, GILBERT MAKSTEPHAN was one of the commissioners appointed by Edward III.* 'to seize the aforesaid Island (Mann), with its appurtenances into our hands.'

MAKSTEPHAN [1334], STEPHEN [1408], STEVENSON [1417], STEPHAN [1598], STEPHENSON [1643],

* Manx Society, Vol. VII., p. 181.

STEVEN [1676], STEANE [1598], STEAN [1640], STAI [1665], STEEN [1722], STEON [1726].

STEPHEN—Ballaugh (vc), Jurby, Lezayre (c), else-where (u).

STEPHENSON—Arbory, German (c), elsewhere (u).

STEAN—Ballaugh, Jurby, Braddan, formerly (c), now extinct.

MYLECHREEST and MYLCHREEST, contracted from *MacGiolla* or *MacGuilley Chreest*, 'the son of Christ's servant.'

'*Giolla*, especially among the ancients, signified a youth, but now generally a servant, and hence it happened that families who were devoted to certain saints, took care to call their sons after them, prefixing the word *Giolla*, intimating that they were to be the servants or devotees of those saints. Shortly after the introduction of Christianity, we meet many names of men formed by prefixing the word *Giolla* to the names of the celebrated saints of the first age of the Irish Church, as GIOLLA-AILBHE, GIOLLA-PHATRAIG, GIOLLA-CHIASAIN. . . . And it will be found that there were very few saints of celebrity, from whose names those of men were not formed by the prefixing of Giolla. . . . This word was not only prefixed to the names of saints, but also to the name of God, Christ, the Trinity, the Virgin Mary. . . .'* In the Isle of Mann, however, the earlier form is invariably *MacGil* or *MacGille*, so it is probable that most of our Mylchreests are derived from *Macguilley*. The process of change is probably as follows : *Macguilley* becomes *Maccuilley* or *Magguilley;* the *a* of *mac* being unaccented disappears with the consonants, leaving *M'uilley*, which

* Four Mast., Vol. III., pp. 2-3 (note).

then becomes *Mylcy*, pronounced *Mully*. MYLCHREEST, as the name is now generally spelled, is invariably pronounced MULLEYCHREEST or MOLLEYCHREEST by old Manx people. This name, and all those commencing with '*Mylc*' are purely Manx.

'Gillacrist, son of Niall . . . slain,' A.D. 1014.*

MACGILCHREEST [1511], MACGILLEYCHREEST [1540], MAULCHRIST [1663], MACLECHRIST [1683], M^cYILCHRIST [1713], M^cYLCHREEST [1714], MULLE-CHREES [1722], MYLECHREEST [1717], MYL-CHREEST [1739], MOLLECHREEST [1741].

Marown, German (c), elsewhere (u).

MACVORREY, (obsolete) ' Mary's son,' has now universally become MORRISON. The Anglicised forms MORISONE and MORESON are found as early as 1430. The latest date at which MACVORREY occurs is 1624. It appears in the Manorial Roll of 1511.

MORREY and VORREY (obsolete), found in Jurby in 1613, became MURRAY before the end of the century.

MYLVORREY, contracted from *MacGuilleyvorrey*, ' the son of Mary's servant,' is also Anglicised into MORRISON, but the original name still survives, though it is not so common as formerly.† A cross at Kirk Michael was erected to the memory of a lady named MAEL-MURU, which is clearly identical with MYLVORREY. *Mael* prefixed to a woman's name is certainly unusual ; but we find MEL-CORCA, the name of an Irish princess in the Landnámabóc.† The spelling of this name has proved a great puzzle to the keepers of the Parish Registers, as will be seen from the great variety of forms following :

* Four Mast., Vol. II., p. 783.
† See Manx Note Book, No. 9, pp. 5-7.

YLUORRY [1507], MACGILVORRY [1511], MACILVORY [1570], ILLUORREY, MACYLWORREY [1598], ILLE-VORRY [1611], MACYLVORREY [1625], *MALEVORREY [1628], MACYLEVORREY [1644], MACILLVERY [1683], *MOLLYVORREY [1685], MACLEVORY [1695], MYLEVOREY [1713], *MOLLYVERREY [1717], *MOLLEYBOIREY [1721], *MOLLEVORY [1725], MACYLVOIREY [1730], MYLWOIREY [1737], *MOLLE-BORRY [1740], MICKLEWORREY [1742], M^cYLVORREY [1744], MYLEVOIREY [1762], MYLVORREY [1763], MYLVOREY [1782], MYLEVOIRREY [1786].

* These forms are perhaps derived from *Maol-vorrey* (the word *Maol* or *Mael*, meaning 'bald, shorn, or tonsured,' being anciently prefixed to the names of saints to form proper names), and the old pronunciation MOLLEWORREH would seem to point to the same con-clusion, though both they and such forms as MOLLE-CHREESE and MULLECHREEST can be satisfactorily obtained from *MacGuilley*. 'The Irish name MAOL-MAIRE, or MAOLMUIRE, signifies servant of the Virgin Mary.'* (See MYLCHREEST.)

> Jurby (vc), Ballaugh, Maughold, Bride, German (c), else-where (u).

COOBRAGH (obsolete) from *MacGiolla Cobraght* (Cuth-bert), 'The son of Cuthbert's servant.' 'St. Cuthbert, Bishop of Fearna, in England, died,' A.D. 686.† St. Cuthbert of Lindisfarne was a favourite saint among Celts as well as Saxons.

> c.f. Kirkcudbright.

M^cGILCOBRAGHT and GILGOBRAGHT [1511], COOBRAGH [1606], COOBRIGH [1649].

> * Four Mast., Vol. III., p. 6 (note).
> † *Ibid.*, Vol. I., p. 293.

It is only found in the Parish of Jurby, and after 1649 it does not occur.

MACFADEN [1511] (obsolete), from *Mac Paidin*, 'Paidins, or little Patrick's son,' also FADEN [1611].

Compare—(Irish) MAC FADDEN, which was the name taken by the Baretts of Munster.

MᶜGILPEDER and GILPEDER [1511] (obsolete). 'The son of Peter's servant,' and 'Peter's servant.'

ANDREW [1408], MᶜANDRAS [1417], MACGYLANDERE [1429], MAC GILLANDRAS, MᶜGILLANDER [1430], MAC GILANDREW, GILANDREW [1511] (obsolete).

MᶜGILPATRICK and GILPATRICK [1511] (obsolete). Found as late as 1645 in Marown.

'Gilla-Padraig, son of Imhar,' A.D. 981.* Compare—(Irish) FITZ PATRICK.

GILBEALL and MACGILBEALL [1511] (obsolete), perhaps a corruption of *Gill Phail*, 'Paul's servant.'

MC MYCHEL [1511], (obsolete), 'Michael's son.' St. Michael was the Christian Warrior's Patron. 'Donn MAC GILLA-MICHIL, Chief of Clann Conghaile,' A.D. 1310.† We find Ballavitchal in our local nomenclature.

MAC ADDE [1511] (obsolete). A Scotch diminutive of MAC ADAM.

FAYLE, originally *Mac Giolla Phoil*, 'the son of Paul's servant.'

'MAG GILLAPHOIL of the fair seat.'‡

Bishop Philips, in his MS. version of the Manx

---

* Chron. Scot., p. 229.   † Four Mast., Vol. III., p. 497.
‡ O'Huidhrin, p. 133.

Prayer Book, written about 1625, gives the form
PAYL for PAUL.

Compare—(Irish) GILFOYLE, KILFOIL.

MAC FALLE [1408], MAC FAILE [1429], MAC FAILE
[1430], M'FAYLE [1504], FAIL [1511], MAC FAYLL
[1521], FAYLE [1608], FFAYLE [1623], FAILE
[1713].

FELL, not found before 1750, may be either a
corruption of the above, or from the Scandinavian
fjall, which in the British Islands has become *fell*.
It is a common name in Cumberland, whence it
may have been imported into the Isle of Man.
(MAC FELIS, found in 1511, may have some connection with it.)

Braddan, Marown (vc), Santon, Jurby, Lezayre (c), elsewhere (u).

SAYLE is possibly a corruption of FAYLE. It is almost
entirely confined to the north of the island.

MAC SALE [1511], SALL [1601], SAYLE [1624], SAILE
[1701], SAIL [1709].

Andreas (vc), Jurby, Bride, Maughold (c), elsewhere (u).

QUAYLE, contracted from *Mac Phail*, ' Paul's Son.'
PHAIL is anglicised from MAELFABHAILL. ' MAEL-
FABHAILL, son of Muircheartach, slain by the
Norsemen.'*

This is one of the most widely distributed names
in the island.

MAC FAYLE [1511], MAC QUAYLE, QUAYLE [1540],
QUAYLLE, QUALL [1601], QUALE [1602], QUAILE
[1604], QUAIL [1656].

Malew, Onchan (vc), Rushen, Arbory, Santon, German,
Braddan, Ballaugh, Lezayre, Maughold (c), elsewhere (u).

* Four Mast., Vol. I., p. 537.

CALLISTER and COLLISTER,* contracted from *Mac Alister*, ' Alexander's son.' The Greek name *Alexandros* was adopted by the Scotch, as the Latin *Magnus* by the Scandinavians. Several of the Scotch Kings were called Alexander.

' Eisht haink ayn OLLISTER mooar Mac Ree Albey.'†
' Then came great OLLISTER, son of the King of Scotland.'

It is found chiefly on our northern coast, the nearest to Scotland.

MAC ALISANDRE [1417], MAC ALEXANDER [1429], CALLISTER [1606], COLLISTER [1799].

COLLISTER is quite a late form, and is not nearly so common as CALLISTER.

Compare (Gaelic) MAC ALLISTER.

Jurby, Michael (vc), Lezayre, Ballaugh, German, Malew (c), elsewhere (u).

MAC GILACOSSE [1430] (obsolete), possibly from *Mac Guilley Iosa*, ' Jesus' servant's son.'

MAC GILLAWS [1430] (obsolete), possibly a corruption of *Mac Guilley Aedha*, ' Aedh's servant's son.' AEDH was an early Irish saint.

MAC GILCOLUM [1430] (obsolete) is a corruption of *Mac Guilley Columba*, ' Columba's servant's son.' ST. COLUMBA, the famous Irish missionary, has a *keeill* in Arbory dedicated to him. This name is now found in the form ' Malcolm,' in Scotland.

* This name is not, strictly speaking, hagiological, but as a non-Celtic name, introduced through Roman influence, it belongs in substance to the same class.
† Traditionary Ballad ; Train, p. 52.

*Part II.—Surnames derived from Personal Names of
purely Native Origin.*

We now come to the Celtic patronymics formed
from personal names of purely native origin. As many
of these are capable of being translated, being originally
significant of personal qualities, it is often difficult to
distinguish between the regular names and the mere
nicknames, whose derivatives in family nomenclature
are discussed in the following chapter. In making
this distinction our guide must be the old Irish records,
which give us some of these words as regular names,
while others appear only as descriptive epithets
appended to the names. Several of these native
names were borne by persons who attained the
honours of saintship, and thus, like other hagiological
names, give rise to secondary formations with the
prefix *Giolla.*

CROW, or CROWE, is a translation of *Mac Fiachain,*
    ' Fiachan's son,' the personal name FIACHAN
    meaning ' Crow.'

    ' Fiachan, Lord of Conaille . . . died A.D. 787.'*

On the inscribed crosses we find FIAC, UFAAC
or O'FAAC, *i.e.,* probably, *ua feic,* ' the descendants of FIAC and (MA)LFIAAC, possibly *Mal-fiach,*†
' prince raven ' (FIACHAN being the diminutive of
FIAC).

The MAC FIACHAINS were one of the minor families of the English Pale who complied with the
Statute 5 Edward IV., by which it was enacted

---

* Four Mast., Vol. I., p. 395.
† *Mál* is more probable in this context than *Mael.*

'that every Irishman that dwells betwixt or amongst Englishmen . . . . shall take to him an English surname.'　'In obedience to this law,' says Harris (works of Sir James Ware, Vol. II., p. 58), 'the SHANACHS took the name of FOXES; the MAC-AN-GABHANS, of SMITHS; . . . . and many others; the said words being only literal translations from the Irish into the English language.'

CROWE [1582], CROW [1629].

> Maughold, Bride, Lonan, Andreas, Lezayre, Onchan (c), elsewhere (u).

FARGHER, or FARAGHER, contracted from *Mac Fearghoir*, 'Fearghoir's son.'　This name FEARGHOIR, which occurs in the Tale of Diarmid and Grainne, is derived from the root *ferg*, 'brave' or 'violent.'

> 'FEARCHOIR, son of Muireadhach, Abbot of Lannleire . . . died A.D. 848.'*

Compare (Gaelic) FARQUHAR, FARQUHARSON.

FAYRHARE [1343], MAC KARHERE† and MAC KARHARE [1422], JOHN FARKER, Abbot of Rushen [1504], MAC FARGHER, FARGHER [1511], FERGHER [1540], FARGHERE [1570], FARHAR [1626], FARAGHER [1649], PHARAGHER [1735].

> Marown, Malew (vc), Andreas, Arbory, German, Rushen, Lonan (c), elsewhere (u).

MC FERGUS [1422] (extinct), from the same root *ferg*, with *gus*, 'strength.'

KAIGHAN, or KAIGHIN, contracted from *Mac Eachain*, 'Eachan's son.'　The name EACHAN means 'horseman' or 'knight.'　'Don of EACHAN.'

The surname KAIGHAN may possibly be the

---

* Four Mast., Vol. I., p. 479.
† This is in the British Museum copy of the Statutes only.

same name originally as KEIGEEN, as a contraction of *Mac Taidhgin* or *Mac Ædhagain* (see KEIGEEN), or even from *Mac Cahain* (see CAIN). It is remarkable that KAIGHAN is confined to the north of the island, and KEIGEEN to the south, the former being of much earlier occurrence than the latter.

Compare (Gaelic) MAC EACHAN, MC GACHAN.

These are common names on the adjacent coast of Galloway.

MAC HAUGHAN (?) [1417], MAC CAIGHEN [1422], McCAGHEN [1511], KAIGHIN [1611], CAIGHAN [1643], KAIGHAN [1667], CAIGHIN [1745].

Michael, German (vc), Bride (c), Ballaugh (u), elsewhere (w).

KEIG, or KEGG, contracted from *Mac Taidhg*, 'Tadg's son.' TADG (modernised as TEAGUE) should be regarded as a proper name, although its meaning seems to be 'poet.' In Ireland the name is irrationally considered equivalent to Timothy.

'MAC TAIDHG who is lasting in battle front.'*
'Muircheartach MAC TAIDHG slain A.D. 1159.'†

'BALLYHEIGE, in Kerry, has its name from the family of O'TEIGE, its full Irish name being BAILE-UI-THADG.'‡

Compare (Irish) MAC TEIGE, MAC KEAGUE, MAC KAIGE, MAC KEAG, (Gaelic) MAC CAIG.

MAC KYG [1408], MAC KEG, MAC COAG [1511], KEAGE [1623], KEGG [1630], KEIGE [1653], KEIGG [1684], KEIG [1697].

Jurby, Lezayre, Malew, Santon, Rushen (c), elsewhere (u).

KEIGEEN, or KEGEEN, contracted from *Mac Taidhgin.*

* O'Dubhagain, p. 12.   † Four Mast., Vol. II., p. 1134.
‡ Joyce, 4th edition, p. 349.

The name TAIDHGIN, 'little Tadhg's son,' being a diminutive of TADHG.

KEIGEEN may perhaps be contracted from *Mac Egan*, which is itself a contraction of *Mac Ædhagain*. The name ÆDHAGAN, a diminutive of ÆDH, may be rendered 'the little fiery warrior.' (See KAIGHAN.)

The name AþACAN, *i.e.*, ÆDHACAN or ÆDAGAN occurs on a cross at Kirk Michael, the legend on which Dr. Vigfusson translates: 'Mal Bricti the Smith, son of AþACAN (ÆDHAGAN) raised this cross for his own soul.'

'Moelisa Roe MAC EGAN, the most learned man in Ireland, in Law and Judicature, died A.D. 1317.'*

Mageoghan, in his version of the Annals of Clonmacnoise, gives this entry:

'Moeleissa Roe MAC KEIGAN, the best learned in Ireland in the Brehon Lawe.'

The MAC EGANS were hereditary Brehons and professors of the old Irish laws. They compiled the vellum MS. called *Leabhar Breac*, or 'Speckled Book,' the most remarkable repertory of ancient Irish ecclesiastical affairs.

Compare (Irish) KEEGAN.

KEGEEN [1697], KEIGEEN [1715].

Rushen (c), Malew, Patrick (u), elsewhere (w).

The names QUIGGIN, and its later and more uncommon form QUAGGIN, are also probably contractions either of *Mac Taidhgin* or *Mac Ædhagain*, but no intermediate form has been found. MAC QUIG and MAC KEAG, names found in Ireland at the present day, have a common origin.

* Four Mast., Vol. III., p. 517.

QUARRY, contracted from MAC GUAIRE, ' Guaire's son.'
'GUAIRE fled' at 'the battle of Carn Conaill, fought on Whit-
Sunday, A.D. 646.'*

Compare (Gaelic) MAC QUARRIE.

It is a very uncommon name in the Isle of Mann.

MAC QUARRES [1504], MAC WHARRES [1511], QUARRY
[1684].

QUINE, contracted from *Mac Coinn*, or *Mac Cuinn*,
' Conn's son ' (*Conn*, ' counsel '). ' CONN, of the
hundred fights,' was one of Ireland's greatest
legendary heroes.

' MAC CUINN, son of Donnghaile, royal heir of Teathbha,
died A.D. 1027.'†

A.D. 1403, 'The king, to all, to whom, etc.,
greeting, Know that we have conceded of our
especial grace to LUKE MAC QUYN of the Island
of Mann, scholar, certain alms called particles in
the Island aforesaid, and which were given, confirmed, and conceded perpetually to the scholars by
our predecessors, former Kings of England. . . .'‡

Compare (Irish) QUIN, O'QUIN.

MAC QUYN [1403], QUINE [1504], QUYN [1511].

Braddan, Marown, Maughold, German, Lonan (c), elsewhere (u).

QUINNEY, contracted from *Mac ' Connaidh*, Connaidh's
son.' (*Connaidh*, ' crafty,' is the adjectival form of
Conn.)§

Compare (Gaelic) MAC WHINNIE, (Irish)
MC WEENY.

---

* Chron. Scot., p. 91.
† Four Mast., Vol. II., p. 814.
‡ Manx Society, Vol. VII., p. 223.
§ By Manx-speaking people this name is pronounced as if spelt
KUNYAH.

QUINNYE [1429], MAC INAY (?) [1511], MAC QUINYE [1529], QUINEY [1652], QUINNEY [1692].

Santon (vc), Arbory (c), elsewhere (u).

CAIN, or CAINE, contracted from *Mac Cathain*, 'Cathan's son.' This name may be rendered 'warrior' (*cath*, 'a battle').

The O'CATHAINS, now O'KANES, were of the race of Eoghan, who was son of Niall of the Nine Hostages, Monarch of Ireland, who died A.D. 406.

'The race of EOGHAN of valiant arms,
Who have obtained the palm for greatness without fraud,
The acmè of the nobility of Erin.'*
'EOGHAN UA CATHAIN, abbot . . . died A.D. 980.'†

Compare (Irish) KANE and O'KANE.

MC KANE [1408], MAC CANN [1430], MAC CANE [1511], CAIN [1586], CANE [1601], CAINE [1609], CAYNE [1610].

Jurby,'German (vc), Michael, Ballaugh, Braddan, Marown, Lezayre, Malew, Santon (c), elsewhere (u).

CALLIN, contracted from *Mac Cathalain*, 'Cathalans' son' (*cathal*, 'valour'). MAC CATHALAIN is corrupted into CAHALLAN and CALLAN in Ireland, the latter being now the usual form.

'Maelcraeibhe UA CATHALAIN.)‡
Compare (Irish) CALLAN.

In some cases it may possibly be a contraction of MAC ALLEN, 'Allen's son.'

MᶜALEYN [1511], CALLYNE [1601], CALLIN [1623].

German, Maughold, Malew (c), elsewhere (u).

KERMODE and CORMODE, contracted from *Mac Dermot*,

* O'Dubhagain, p. 21.   † Four Mast., Vol. II., p. 713.
‡ Four Mast., Vol. I., p. 565.

a shortened form of *Mac Diarmid*, 'Diarmaid's son.'

'The fifth year of DIARMAID, A.D. 544.'[*]
'CATHAL MAC DERMOT, the son of Teige, Lord of Moylurg, and tower of the glory of Connaught, died A.D. 1215.'[†]

The MAC DIARMIDA or MAC DERMOTS were princes of Moylurg in Co. Roscommon. They split into three families, 'the head of whom was styled the MAC DERMOT, and the other two, who were tributary to him, were called MAC DERMOT *Ruadh*, the Red, and MAC DERMOT *Gall*, or the anglicised.'[‡] It has been supposed that the Scandinavian þormoðr is an accommodation of DIARMAID. It may, however, be a distinct Scandinavian name containing the usual prefix þor, though, as it is not found in the Sagas, probably not. We find in the History of Olave the Black, King of Mann, from the Flateyan MS., under date A.D. 1229, that 'when Ottar Snakholl, Paul Balkaison, and Ungi Paulson heard this, they sailed southwards to Sky, and found in Westerfiord THORKEL THOMODSON, whom they fought and killed, with two of his sons, but his third son THORMOD escaped by leaping into a boat, which floated alongside of a vessel, and fled to Scotland, but was lost on the passage.'[§] It seems probable that, considering the forms which KERMODE has always taken in the Isle of Man, that it came to us through the Scandinavians, though originally of Celtic origin.

Compare (Gaelic and Irish) MAC DERMOT.

KERMODE is much commoner than CORMODE.

---

[*] Four Mast., Vol. I., p. 183.   [†] Four Mast., Vol. III., p. 185.
[‡] O'Donovan, Introduction, p. 20. [§] Manx Society, Vol. IV., p. 144.

MAC KERMOTT [1430], MAC CORMOT, MAC GERMOT, [1511], KERMOD [1586], KYRMOD, CORMOD [1601], CORMODE [1656], KERMOTT [1611], KERMODE [1694].

Andrease (vc), Jurby, German, Ballaugh, Lezayre, Marown, Rushen, Lonan (c), elsewhere (u).

CONNELLY, contracted from *Mac Conghalaigh*, 'Conghalad's son' (*Congal*, 'a conflict').

'Donnchadh, son of Donnchadh Ua CONGHALAIGH, royal heir of Ireland, was slain A.D. 1016.'[*]

It is a very common name in Ireland, but is scarcely found in the Isle of Man now, though formerly common in Jurby.

CANNELL, from *Mac Conaill*, 'Conall's son,' though it may sometimes be a contraction of *Mac Domhnaill*, 'Domhnall's son.' '*Domnhall* is a diminutive of the root *dom = dominus*, "a lord or master." The "d" by aspiration is often omitted in sound, which has given rise to the family name MAC CON-NELL, now common in ULSTER.'[†] The confusion between MAC CONNELL and MAC DONNELL may have been promoted by the fact that Connall was actually the name of an ancestor of the O'Donnell family.

'CONNALL Gulban, son of Niall of the Nine Hostages (from whom are descended the CINEL-CONAILL), was slain.'[‡]

The Scotch clan of MAC DONALD derive their name from DONALD, eldest son of Reginald, second son of the celebrated Somerled of Argyle, and King of the Isles.

* Four Mast, Vol. II., p. 791.
† MS. letter from Dr. Joyce.   ‡ Four Mast., Vol. I., p. 147.

Compare (Irish) CONNELL, (Gaelic) MAC DONALD, MC WHANNEL.

The name CANNELL is peculiar to the Isle of Man.

MAC CONNELL [1511], CANNELL [1606], CANNEL [1615], CONNIL [1623], CANNAL [1655].

> Michael, German (vc), Jurby, Braddan, Ballaugh, Marown, Andreas, Rushen, Lonan (c), elsewhere (u).

CONILT and CONILL (extinct), probably merely forms of CANNELL.

CONYLT, MᶜCONYLT, HONYLT, MᶜHONYLT, and MᶜGIL HONYLT [1511], COWNILT [1649], COONYLT [1652], CONILT [1659], CONILL [1660], QUOONILL [1654], COONILL [1661].

It was formerly common in Maughold, but disappeared early in the eighteenth century.

KENNAUGH, contracted from *Mac Cainncach*, ‘Cainneach’s son’ (*Cainncach*, ‘ devout ’ or ‘ chaste ’).

> ‘CAINNECH, of Achadh Bo, born A.D. 516.’*

He was a saint who died A.D. 598.

This name is peculiar to the Isle of Man.

Compare (Irish) MᶜKENNA.

MAC KENNEAGH, KENEAGH, MAC KENAG (?) and KENAG (?) [1511], KENEAIGH [1636], KENNAUGH [1668], KENNAGH [1676], KENNIAGH [1697], KENAGH [1714].

It is almost confined to the parish of German.

> German (vc), Michael, Santon (u). Scarcely found elsewhere.

KANEEN, contracted from *Mac Cianain*, ‘ Cianan’s son.’

* Chron. Scot., p. 539.

(*Cianan* is a diminutive of *Cian*, which is itself a diminutive of *ci*, ' to weep.')

' CIANAN, Bishop of Doimhliag, died A.D. 488.'*

Compare (Irish) KEENAN, (Gaelic) MAC KINNON. KYNYNE [1422], KENEEN [1666], KENEN [1676], CANEEN [1729], KANEEN [1740], KENAN [1783].

A purely Manx name.

It is almost confined to the parishes of Andreas and Jurby.

Andreas (vc), Jurby (c), elsewhere (u).

KNEEN, probably also a contraction of *Mac Cianain*. In our early documents it seems to be confused with NEVYN or NEVYNE. Andrew John NEVYN is one of the 24 Keys in 1417, while Jenkin M'NYNE in 1429 is called Jenkinc MAC NEVYNE in 1430. If it is a corruption of NEVYN, which is common in Scotland at the present day in the form NIVEN, it will have quite a different origin: from (Gaelic) *Naomh*, ' a saint.'

It is a purely Manx name.

MAC NYNE [1429], KNEENE [1504], KNEEN [1598].

Bride (vc), Ballaugh, Marown, Andreas, Lezayre, German, Santon, Rushen (c), elsewhere⁀(u).

DOUGHERTY, originally *O'Dochartaigh*, ' Dochartach's descendant ' (*Dochartach*, ' stern ').

' Donnall O'DOCHARTAIGH, lord of the territory of Kinel-Enda and Ard Mire, died A.D. 1119.'†

The name is almost confined to the parishes of Andreas and Jurby, and is now very uncommon everywhere in the Isle of Man. In Ireland it is very common.

* Four Mast., Vol. I., p. 153.   † Four Mast., Vol. II., p. 1009.

DAUGHERDY [1630], DOUGHERTY [1666].

> Andreas, Jurby (formerly c).

KNEAL and KNEALE, contracted from *Mac Niall* 'Niall's son.' This is a name of Celtic origin, meaning 'champion,' but it was adopted by the Scandinavians at a very early period, and largely used by them. 'NJÁLL, m. a pr. name (from the Gaelic), Landnámabóc.'*

It has been a famous name in Celtic history from the time of NIALL of the Nine Hostages, who reigned over Ireland from 384 to 411 A.D., to that of Hugh O'NEIL, Earl of Tyrone, in Queen Elizabeth's reign. The Egilla Saga says that one NIAL, or NEIL, was King of Man in A.D. 914. The Flateyan MS. mentions 'Thorkel, the son of NEIL,' in 1229.

Compare (Irish and Gaelic) MᶜNIEL and MᶜNEAL. (Scandinavian) NIELSEN and NILSSON. (English) NELSON (which see).

MᶜNELLE [1408], MAC NEYLL [1430], MAC NELE [1511], MAC NEALLE [1521], KNEAL [1598], KNEALE [1666].

It is much commoner in the north than in the south of the island.

> Andreas, Bride (vc), Jurby, Maughold, Lonan, Patrick, Ballaugh, Lezayre, German, ˛Santon, Michael (c), elsewhere (u).

NELSON is probably, in the Isle of Man, a translation of MAC NIAL. It is found chiefly in the southern parishes, where KNEALE is uncommon.

NEALSON [1430], NELSSON [1511], NELSON [1653].

> Rushen, Malew (c), elsewhere (u).

> * Cleasby and Vigfusson, p. 456.

KELLY, contracted from *Mac Ceallaigh*, 'Ceallach's son' (*ceallach*, 'war, strife').

'Death of CEALLACH, son of Maelcobba in the Brugh, A.D. 654.'[*]

'CEALLACH, Joint Monarch of Ireland, died A.D. 656.'[†]

The name is as common in the Isle of Man as it is in Ireland. Connell Mageoghan, who translated the Annals of Clonmacnoise, in 1627, gives the following account of the O'KELLYS, under A.D. 778: 'Though the O'KELLYS are so common everywhere that it is unknown whether the dispersed parties in Ireland of them be of the families of O'KELLY, of Connaught, or Brey, ... so as scarce there is a few parishes in the Kingdom, but hath some one or other of these Kellys.'[‡]

McHELLY [1417], McKELLY [1429], MAC HELLIE [1430], KELLYE [1601], KELLY [1605], KELLEY [1628].

Braddan, Marown, Michael, German (vc); elsewhere (c), except in Maughold and Lezayre.

KILLEY, originally *Mac Gilla Ceallaigh*, anglicised in Ireland into *Mac Killey Kelly* and *Killy Kelly*. The MAC and the KELLY have been dropped, leaving KILLEY, which is identical in meaning with GILL (see GILL). (Gaelic, *Guilley*; Irish, *Giolla*, 'a servant.') Indeed, in the Isle of Man, formerly, the same person was called GILL and KILLEY indifferently.

'The Clan of MAC GILLA CEALLAIGH, the honourable.'[§]

The name is of late introduction, and is purely Manx.

* Chron. Scot., p. 95.　　† Four Mast., Vol. I., p. 269.
‡ O'Donovan, Notes, pp. 2, 3.　　§ O'Dubhagain, p. 67.

KILLIE [1610], KILLEY [1651], KILLY [1704].

> Maughold, Lonan, Onchan, Malew, German (c), else-
> where (u).

QUILLIN, contracted from *Mac Cuilen*, ' Cuilen's son '
(*Cuileann*, ' a whelp ').

> ' CUILEN, son of Cearbhatt, slain A.D. 884.'*
>
> ' ADHUC MAC GUILLIN was slain A.D. 1355.'†
>
> ' The MAC QUILLANS of the Ronte, Co. Antrim,
> are said to have been originally Welsh or Anglo-
> Normans, quasi, MAC or AP LLEWELLIN,'‡ but
> this does not appear likely.

MAC WILLINE [1429], O'QUYLLAN and QUELEN [1511],
QUILLINE [1654], QUEILIN [1657], QUILLIN [1659],
QUILLEN [1682].

> It was formerly common in the parish of Arbory,
> but is now rare.

MOORE, contracted from *O'Mordha*, ' Mordha's descendant.'   (*Mordha* is derived from *mór*, ' great.')

> ' AIMERGIN UA MORDHA, A.D. 1c26.'§

O'MORDHA is anglicised O'MORE and MORE, which has
now usually become MOORE.   The O'MORES were
a powerful sept in Ireland.

> ' JENKIN MOORE, Deemster, A.D. 1499.'‖

MOORE [1499], MORE [1511].

> MORE is the usual form till the end of the 16th
> century.   It is a common name in Ireland, Scot-
> land, and the North of England, as well as in the
> Isle of Man.

> Braddan, Santon, Malew, Arbory (vc), Ballaugh, Marown,
> Maughold, German, Bride, Rushen, Lonan, Patrick, Onchan
> (c), Michael, Andreas, Jurby (u).

---

* Four Mast., Vol. I., p. 537.   † Four Mast., Vol. III., p. 609.

‡ O'Donovan, p. 23.   § Four Mast., Vol. II., p. 811.

‖ Statue Law Book, p. 6.   This date, though given as 1419, is
probably 1499.

KINLEY, contracted from *Mac Cinfaolaidh*, ' Cinfaoladh's son,' a name which may be translated ' wolfhead' (*cean*, ' head '; *faol*, ' wolf ').

> ' The first year of CEANNFAOLADH, son of Blathmac, in the Sovereignty of Ireland, A.D. 670.'*

Compare (Irish) MᶜKINEELEY,† MᶜKINLEY, MᶜGINLEY, KINEELEY, and KENEALEY; (Gaelic) MᶜKINLAY.

KINLEY [1604].

> Ballaugh, Marown, Andreas, Lezayre, Malew, Santon, Lonan (c), elsewhere (u).

DUGGAN, contracted from *O'Dubhagain* (Dubhagan's descendant '). *Dubhagan* is a derivative of *Dubh*, ' black.' O'DUBHAGAIN was the chief poet of O'Kelly of Ibh Maine, and was the author of the topographical poem called after him. He died in 1372.

DOGAN [1540], DUCKAN [1649], DUCCAN [1675], DUGGAN [1723].

This name is almost confined to the parish of Malew, where, at one time, it was very common. It is scarcely found anywhere now in the Isle of Man, though a common name in Ireland.

DOWAN [1680] (obsolete) is of similar origin to DUGGAN, being from *Dubhan*, a diminutive of *Dubh*, ' black.' ST. DOWAN's Day was celebrated on the 4th of February in Ireland. Compare (Irish) DUANE, DOWNES, DOAN.

This name lingered in Andreas till the middle of the eighteenth century.

CORKAN, contracted from *Mac Corcrain*, a corrupted

---

* Four Mast., Vol. I., p. 281.

† In Four Mast., Vol. I., p. 18, is given a full account of the curious legend of MAC KINEELEY, and his famous cow called *Glasgaivlen*.

form of *Mac Corcurain*, 'Corcuran's son' (*corcur*, 'purple').

> 'The Clan Ruainne, of the flowery roads,
> A sweet, clear, smooth-streamed territory,
> MAC CORCRAIN is of this well peopled cantred
> Of the white-breasted brink of banquets.*
>
> 'Cathasach Ua CORCRAIN,' A.D. 1045.'†

Donagh MAC CORCRANE was one of O'Carroll's freeholders in 1576, when O'Carroll made his submission to Queen Elizabeth.

Compare (Irish) CORCORAN, CORKAN.

CORCAN [1511], CORKINE [1521], CORKAN [1611], CORCHAN [1720].

It was never a very common name in the Isle of Man.

Marown, German, Michael (c), elsewhere (u).

ALLEN, probably from *Alainn*, 'handsome.'

> 'Killing of Dor, son of Aedh ALLAN,'‡ A.D. 624.

The Stuarts were descended from the great Norman family of FITZ ALAN.

ALLAN, according to Train, was Governor of the Isle of Man in A.D. 1274.

> 'ALAN of Wygeton has letters of presentation to the Church of St. Carber in Mann, vacant, and in the King's gift,'§ A.D. 1291.

ALLEN is not a common name in the Isle of Man, being chiefly confined to the parishes of Maughold, Andreas, and Bride. Many of those bearing the name are probably descendants of the five successive vicars of Maughold, the first of whom came from Norfolk.

---

* O'Huidhrin, p. 133. † Four Mast., Vol. II., p. 849.
‡ Chron. Scot., p. 79. § Manx Society, Vol. VII., p. 113.

ALEYN [1511], ALAYNE [1540], ALLEN [1648].

CAVEEN, contracted from *Mac Caemhain*, 'Caemhin's son' (*cacimh*, 'beautiful').

> 'And the privilege of first drinking [at the banquet] was given to O'CAEMHAIN by O'Dowdha, and O'CAEMHAIN was not to drink until he had first presented it [the drink] to the poet, that is, to Mac Firbis.'*

> 'O'KEVAN of Ui-Fiachrach flourished' A.D. 876.†

Compare (Irish) KEEVAN.

It is an uncommon name in the Isle of Man, being confined to the parishes of Malew and Arbory.

CAVEENE [1649], CAVEEN [1662].

COWIN and COWEN, contracted from *Mac Eoghain*, which has been corrupted into *Mac Owen*. The name *Eoghan* is glossed by Cornac as meaning 'well-born,' and suggests the Latin (originally Greek) *Eugenius*.

The celebrated OWEN *More* was King of Munster, in the time of Conn of the hundred battles, whom he obliged to divide the whole of Ireland equally with him.

> 'MAC GILLA COWAN and a few of O'Connor's people were slain' A.D. 1330.‡

It is much commoner in the Isle of Man than in Ireland and Scotland.

McCOWYN [1408], M'OWEN [1422], M'COWEN [1429], McCOWNE [1511], COWIN [1611], COWN [1651], COWEN [1685].

> Bride, Lonan (vc), Braddan, German, Andreas, Malew, Patrick (c), elsewhere (u).

---

* Chron. Scot., Introduction, p. 13, being an extract from Tribes and Customs of Hy. Fiachrach, p. 440.

† Annals of Ulster.

‡ Four Mast., Vol. III., p. 547.

QUIRK, contracted from *Mac Cuirc*, ‘ Corc’s son.’ CORC
was King of Munster early in the fifth century.

> ‘Ceinnedigh O’CUIRC, Lord of Muscraighe, was slain ’
> A.D. 1043.*

It is a common name in the south of Ireland.

M^cQUYRKE, QUYRKE [1511], QUEERKE [1601], QUIRK
[1641].

> Patrick (vc), Ballaugh, Malew, Braddan, Andreas, Maug-
> hold, Arbory, Santon, Rushen, Lonan (c), elsewhere (u).

CORRIN and CORRAN, contracted from *Mac Odhrain*,
(contracted *Oran*), ‘ Odhran’s son,’ (*Odar*, ‘ pale-
faced ’). St. Patrick’s charioteer was called ST.
ODHRAN.

> ‘ODHRAN, his charioteer, without blemish,’ A.D. 447.†

Compare (Gaelic) MAC ORAN.

M’CORRANE [1422], M’CORRIN, CORRIN [1504], M^cCOR-
RYN, M^cCORYN [1511], COREAN [1611], CORRAN
[1627], CORINE [1629].

> Malew, Braddan, German (vc), Santon, Rushen, Arbory
> (c), elsewhere (u).

COROOIN (pronounced CORRUNE), probably contracted
from *O’Ciardubhain*, ‘ Ciardubhan’s son.’ (*Dubhan*
means ‘ little dark (man),’ and as *Ciar* also means
‘ dark-coloured ’—*vide* KARRAN—it had probably
lost its significance before *dubhan* was added.)

> ‘Maenach Ua CIRDUBHAIN, successor of Mochta of
> Lughmadh, died.’‡

The Annals of Ulster in the same year call him
O’CIERUVAN.

CIARDUBHAN has in Ireland been contracted into
KIRWAN.

* Four Mast., Vol. I., p. 139.　　† Four Mast., Vol. I., p. 139.
‡ Four Mast., Vol. II., p. 849.

Corooin may possibly be a contraction of *Mac Carrghamha*. 'This name is anglicised Caron by O'Flaherty, in his *Ogygia*, part iii., c. 85, and Mac Carrhon by Connell Mageoghan, who knew the tribe well. The name is now anglicised Mac Caroon.'*

'Mag Carrghamha is over their battalions of the stout and lordly chiefs.'†

Corrowane [1430], Carowne [1632], Caroone [1644], Carrowne [1646], Coroin [1651], Curuin [1665], Keerowne [1669], Carrooin [1709], Corooin [1740].

Malew, Braddan, Lonan (c), elsewhere (u).

Karran, Carran, Carine, a contraction of *Mac Ciarain*, 'Ciaran's son.' The name Ciaran (*Ciar*, mouse-coloured) was borne by one of the twelve great saints of Ireland, after whom a large number of Irish children were formerly named.

'St. Ciaran, son of the artificer, abbot of Cluain-mic-Nois, died on the ninth day of September, A.D. 548.'‡

'Mac Ciarain, airchinneach of Sord,' A.D. 1136.§

This name may possibly be derived from *Mac Carrghamha*. (See Corooin.)

It is probable that Karran has come to us through the Scandinavians, though, of course, they originally imported it from Ireland. Kjaran and Kvarran are not uncommon in Iceland, and Scandinavians in Ireland took the name Cuaran,—

* Four Mast., Note, Vol. III., p. 55.
† O'Dubhagain, p. 13.
‡ Four Mast., Vol. I., p. 185.
§ *Ibid.*, Vol. II., p. 1053.

hence its different form to MYLCHRAIN and CRAIN, which see.

'"The Book of Leinster" says that Gormlaith was likewise mother of the Norwegian-Irish King Amlaff CUARAN (Olaf KVARAN); whilst the Irish chronicler, Dugald Mac Firbis, mentions this same Olaf KVARAN as married to Sadhbh (Save), a daughter of Brian Boru.'*

Compare (Irish) MᶜCARRON, MᶜCAROON, KERRINS, (Gaelic) MᶜKERRON.

MᶜCARRANE [1430], MᶜCARREN [1504], KERRON [1507], MᶜKERRON [1511], MᶜKARRON [1540], MᶜKERRAN [1540], MᶜKARRAN [1570], KARRAN [1711], CARRAN [1648], CHARRAN [1680], CARRON [1691], CARINE [1729].

This last form is found chiefly in the parishes of Marown, Arbory, and Malew, and is not common.

German, Marown (vc), Jurby, Malew, Arbory, Patrick, Lonan, Maughold (c), elsewhere (u).

MYLCHRAINE and MYLECHARANE (pronounced MOLLECARANE or MULCRANE), contracted from *Mac guilley Ciarain*, 'the son of Ciaran's servant.' (See KARRAN and CRAINE.)

'Maclmuire MAC GILLACHIARAIN,' A.D. 1155.†

MYLECHARAINE, the miser of the Curragh, is the subject of one of the most popular ballads in the Manx language. The name is now less common than formerly, and is still chiefly found in the Curragh district.

MᶜGILCRAYNE [1511], MACYLERAN [1673], MᶜYLREAN [1688], MᶜYLKIARRAINE [1689], MᶜYLCARRANE

* Worsaae—The Danes and Northmen, p. 323.
† Four Mast., Vol. II., p. 1098.

[1696], MYLECHARAINE [1740], MYLCHRAINE [1766], MYLCHARANE [1782].

Jurby, Andreas, Lezayre, Ballaugh (c), elsewhere (u).

CRAIN and CRAINE, contracted from *Mac Ciarain*, ' Ciaran's son.' (See KARRAN and MYLCHRAINE.)

It seems to be a purely Manx name, not being found elsewhere, except in the form CRANE, which has probably quite a different origin.

M^cCROYN [1408], M^cCROYNE [1417], M^cCRAINE [1422], MACCARRANE [1422], M^cCRAYNE [1504], CRAINE [1586], CRAIN [1607], CRAYNE [1638], CRANE [1736].

German (vc), Jurby, Braddan, Andreas, Santon, Ballaugh, Lezayre (c), elsewhere (u).

QUIDDIE, MACQUIDDIE [1511], CUDDIE [1653] (obsolete), probably from *Mac Guilley Cuddy*, a shortened form of *Mac Guilley Mochuda*, ' St. Mochuda's servant's son.'

' ST. MOCHUDA, Bishop of Lismore and Abbot of Raithin, died,' A.D. 636.*

CUDDIE is found as late as 1680.

BRIDSON, contracted from *Bridgetson*, the anglicised form of *Mac Brighde*. The original name was MAC GIOLLA BRIGHDE, ' Bridget's servant's son,' but the *Giolla* dropped out at a comparatively early date. ST. BRIDGET, Abbess of Kildare, born about A.D. 450, was the most highly venerated of the Irish female saints, and, consequently, many were named after her.

' SAINT BRIGHIT, virgin, Abbess of Cill-dara, died' A.D. 525.†

' GIOLLA-BRIGHDE, son of Dubhdara, chief of Muintir Golais, was wounded' A.D. 1146.‡

---

* Four Mast., Vol. I., p. 255. † Four Mast., Vol. I. p. 171.
‡ Four Mast., Vol. II., p. 1081.

Another form of this name, MAELBRIGHDE, is much commoner in Ireland from the ninth to the eleventh century, than MAC GIOLLABRIGHDE, and in the Isle of Man we find it on the Runic Stone in Kirk Michael Churchyard, on the southern side of the gate: MAIL : BRIGDI : Sunr : Athakus : Smith : raisti : crus, etc. 'MAELBRIGD, the son of Athkaus, the smith, raised this cross.' This name has, however, recently been read 'MAL BRICTI,' by Dr. Vigfusson.

'MAELBRIGHDE, son of Spealan, Lord of Conaill,' A.D. 867.*

MAELBRIGHDE, 'Bridget's tonsured servant,'† has become obsolete both in Ireland and the Isle of Man. There is a St. MAELBRIGHDE.

Compare (Irish) KILBRIDE, (Gaelic) MᶜBRIDE.

The name Bridson appears to be peculiar to the Isle of Man.

MᶜGILBRID [1511], BRIDSON [1609], BRIDESON [1628].

Marown, Malew, Santon (vc), Braddan, Maughold, Arbory (c), elsewhere (u).

MOUGHTON and MUGHTIN, possibly derived from a diminutive of *Mochta*, but no authority can be given for this.

ST. MOCHTA was a disciple of St. Patrick.

'MOCHTA, after him his priest.'‡

MOUGHTON [1673], MUGHTIN [1714], MOUGHTIN [1742].

The name is now very uncommon. It is so unintelligible to strangers that some of those bearing it have changed it to MORTON.

Jurby (vc), Ballaugh (c), formerly elsewhere (u).

* Four Mast., Vol. I., p. 511.
† See note on *Maoi* under MYLVORREY.
‡ Four Mast., Vol. I., p. 129.

CURPHEY, contracted from *Mac Murchadha*, 'Murchad's son' (*muir*, 'sea,' *cathaide*, 'warrior'). MURCHAD was formerly anglicised MURCHOE, now MURPHY. 'Domhnall Dall UA MURCHADA, chief sage of Leinster,' A.D. 1127.* (This would now be anglicised 'Blind Daniel MURPHY.')

'Diarmid MAC MURCHADA, King of Leinster,' A.D. 1137.†

MAC MURCHADA is sometimes anglicised MURRAY.

It has been suggested that CURGHEY, the earlier form of the name in the Isle of Man, is a contraction of CURRAGHEY (belonging to the *Curragh*). It is certainly true that the name is much more common in the *Curragh* district than elsewhere, but still this derivation appears more apt than likely. It is a purely Manx name. Some of the Curpheys themselves hold that the name was originally CURRY, that it became CURGHEY in Manx lips, and that it was brought back into English as CURPHEY. There is a FINLO MAC CURRY mentioned in the Statute Law Book, under date 1504. (See MAC CURRY, p. 69.)

MᶜCURGHEY [1422], COURGHEY, CHURGIE [1601], CURGHEY [1609], CURPHEY [1643].

CURGHEY is the usual form till the middle of the eighteenth century.

KINNISH and KENNISH, contracted from *Mac Aenghuis*, 'Aenghus's son' (*aen*, 'one,' *gus*, 'strength').

'Duneath MᶜAONGUIS,' A.D. 620.‡

---

* Four Mast., Vol. II., p. 1027. † Four Mast., Vol. II., p. 1057.
‡ Annals of Ulster.

'Domhnall MacAENGHUSA, Lord of Ui-Ethach,' A.D 957.*

(This would now be anglicised Daniel MAGENNIS, Lord of Iveagh.)

'The river called Banthelasse issuing out of the desert mountaines of Mourne, passeth the country of Eaugh, which belongeth to the family of Mac GYNNIS.'†

Compare (Irish) MᶜGUINESS, (Gaelic) MᶜGINNIS.

MᶜINESH (?) [1511], KYNNISHE [1601], KINNISH [1626], KENISH [1649], KEANISH [1734], KENNISH [1732].

Maughold, Santon (vc), Braddan, Marown, Lonan, Malew (c), elsewhere (u).

CARNAGHAN, contracted from *O'Cernachain*, 'Cernachan's descendant' (*Cethernach*, 'a foot-soldier,' a 'kern ').

> 'Two other chieftains, it is certain to you,
> Are over the victorious Tuath-Bladhach;
> Of them is O'CERNACHAIN of valour.'‡

Compare (Irish) KERNAGHAN.

This name was formerly almost confined to the parish of Maughold, and is now scarcely found anywhere.

CASHIN and CASHEN, contracted from *Mac Caisin*, 'Caisin's son' (*caisin* is a diminutive of *cas*, 'crooked '). The name CAISIN must originally have meant a crooked-eyed, crooked-legged, or metaphorically stupid, person.

CAISIN was the son of Cas, the descendant of Cormac, who was the younger son of Olioll Oluim, King of Munster.

'CAISIN, scribe of Lusca,' A.D. 695.§

CASHEN is found in Ireland.

---

* Four Mast., Vol. II., p. 677.   ‡ Dubhagain, p. 45.

† Camden, Ireland, p. 109.   § Four Mast., Vol. I., p. 299.

M^cCASH, M^cCASHEN [1511], M^cCASHE [1540], CASHEN [1641], CASHIN [1677], CASSIN [1687].

> Braddan, Lezayre (c), elsewhere (u).

CALEY, contracted from *Mac Caolaidhe*, 'Caoladh's son' (*caol*, 'slender').

> 'To O'CAOLAIDHE the territory is fair.'*

Compare (Irish) O'CAYLEY, CAYLEY, KYLY, KYELY, KIELY, (Gaelic) M^cALLEY.

M^cCALEY [1511], M^cCALLE [1521], CALLY [1605], CALLIE [1617], CALEY [1642], CALLEY [1676].

> Lezayre (vc), Michael, Ballaugh (c), elsewhere (u).

CORTEEN, from *Mac Cruitin*, 'Cruitin's son' (*cruit*, a 'hump'). CRUITIN becomes CURTIN by metathesis.

> 'Ceallach MAC CURTIN, historian of Thomond,'
> A.D. 1376.†

CORTIN [1652], CORTEEN [1659], CORTEENE [1686].

> It is almost confined to the parish of Maughold, and is a purely Manx name.

COTTEEN is probably merely a corruption of CORTEEN. It was formerly common in the parish of Malew, but is now scarcely found. Edward COTTEEN was a member of the House of Keys in 1813.

COTTEENE [1653], COTTEEN [1654].

COGEEN contracted from *Mac Cagadhain* (corrupted into *Mac Cogan*), 'Cagadhan's son' (*caghad*, 'just').

> 'MAC CAGADHAIN . . . .
> is over the noble Clann Fearmaighe.'‡

Compare (Irish) COGAN, MAC COGAN.

It is very uncommon in the Isle of Man.

---

* O'Huidhrin, p. 87.   † Four Mast., Vol. IV.
‡ O'Dubhagain, p. 57.

The name CREGEEN, is frequently softened into COGEEN in conversation.

COTGEEN [1737], COJEEN [1771], COGEEN [1785].

CALLOW, contracted from *Mac Calbach*, 'Calbach's son.'

CALBACH is pronounced CALWAGH, which is easily softened into CALLOW. It seems to mean 'bald,' cognate with the Latin *calvus*, a word which was adopted into the Teutonic languages at an early date, so that we have old English *Calugh*, *Calewe*, Anglo-Saxon *Calu*, 'bald.' Milton speaks of 'callow young,' 'callow' here referring to the condition of the young unfledged bird. 'Richard le CALEWE' is in the Parliamentary writs for A.D. 1313. ALLOW and ALOE are met with as Christian names in the Isle of Man till the middle of the seventeenth century, which points to the possibility of another derivation.

CALOWE, CALO [1511], CALLOW, M'ALOE [1586], CALOW [1611].

Maughold, Bride (vc), Jurby, Braddan, Lezayre, Malew, Arbory, Lonan (c), elsewhere (u).

KERMEEN, perhaps contracted from *Mac Heremon*, 'Heremon's son.' HEREMON was the seventh in descent from Milesius, and became Monarch of all Ireland.

Compare (Irish) HARMON, ERWIN, IRWIN, KIRWAN, (English) CURWEN.

MAC ERMYN [1429], MAC ERYMYN, and MAC KERMAYNE [1511], MAC CORMYN [1521], KERMEEN [1630], KERMEN [1642], KIRMEENE [1668].

This name is now uncommon everywhere. Formerly, Maughold (vc), Braddan, German (c), elsewhere (u).

COLVIN and CALVIN (obsolete) may be derived from
Calbhin, a diminutive of *Calb*, 'bald' (see CALLOW).
COLBIN [1610], CALVIN [1650], COLVIN [1668].
COWELL and COWLE contracted from *Mac Cathmaoil*
(corrupted into *Mac Cawell*), 'Cathmaol's son.'
The personal name CATHMAOL has been explained
as meaning 'battle-heap.'　On a cross at Kirk
Bride the name CAᵽMUIL or CAᵽMAOIL is given
to a woman, which is very unusual.

'CIONAIDH UA CATHMHAOIL,' A.D. 967.*

'Conor MAC CAWELL, chief of Kinel Ferady,' A.D. 1252.†

They were the ancient chiefs of Kinel Ferady,
and were famous in Ireland for their learning, and
the numerous dignitaries they supplied to the
Church.

COWELL and COWLE are purely Manx names.
MᶜGILCOWLE, MᶜCOWLE, MᶜCOWELL, COWLE [1511]
COWELL [1690], COWEL [1700], COWILL [1711],
COWL [1728], COWEL [1737], COWIL [1777].

Bride, Andreas (vc), Marown, German, Lezayre, Patrick,
Malew, Santon (c), elsewhere (u).

COOLE and COOIL, contracted from *Mac Cumhail*,
'Cumhall's son' (*comhal*, 'courageous'). Finn
MAC CUMHAIL, or Finn MAC COOLE, the Fingal of
Ossian, was the hero of many beautiful legends.
Compare (Irish) COYLE.
MᶜCOIL, MᶜCOLE [1511], COOLE [1666], COOILE,
MᶜCOILE [1711], COOIL [1731].

Andreas, German, Rushen (c), elsewhere (u).

QUILL, contracted from *Mac Cuill*, 'Coll's son.'　One
of the three first traditionary rulers of the Milesian

colony was called MAC CUILL. According to an ancient Irish poem he was so called because he worshipped the hazel-tree (*coll*).*

'Ceaunfaeladh ua CUILL,' A.D. 1048.†

QUILL is found in Ireland. It is very uncommon in the Isle of Man.

McCUILL [1511], QUILL [1624].

Maughold, Malew, Bride, Lonan (u), elsewhere (w).

KAY, KEY, KIE, KEE, contracted from *Mac Aedha*, 'Aedh's son.'

'Cucail MAC AEDHA,' A.D. 1098.‡

' AEDH (ay, pronounced like the ay in say), genitive AEDHA, is interpreted by Cormac Mac Cullenan, Colgan, and other writers, to mean fire. . . . This name has been in use in Ireland from the most remote antiquity. . . . It was the name of a great many of our ancient kings; and the Irish ecclesiastics named AEDH are almost innumerable. . . . The usual modernised form of *Mac Aedha* is MAGEE, which is correct, or MᶜGEE, not so correct, or MAC KAY, which would be correct if it were accentuated on the last syllable, which it generally is not.'§

The form KEE may possibly be a contraction of *Mac Caoch*, ' the dim-sighted (man's) son.'

Compare (Irish and Gaelic) MᶜKIE, MᶜKEY, MᶜKEE, MAGEE, MᶜGEE, MᶜGHIE, MᶜGHEE, MᶜKAY.

None of these names are common in the Isle of

* Four Mast., Vol. I., pp. 24, 25.
† *Ibid.*, Vol. II., p. 853.
‡ *Ibid.*, Vol. II., p. 961.
§ Joyce—Irish Names of Places, 2nd Series, p. 147.

Man, KAY being almost confined to the parish of Michael, and KIE, KEY, and KEE to Jurby, Andreas, and Patrick.

M^cKEE [1408], M^cKEY [1429], M^cKAY [1430], M^cKYE and M^cKIE [1511], KEE [1610], KEY [1616], KAY [1617], KIE [1618], KEAY [1637].

> Michael, Jurby, Andreas, Patrick (c), elsewhere (u).

QUAY, probably contracted from *Mac Kay*. It is a purely Manx name, and much commoner than KAY, KIE, KEY, or KEE.

MAC QUAY [1429], MAC QUA [1511], QUAY [1628].

> Maughold, Santon, Malew, German, Michael, Patrick (c), elsewhere (u).

KEW, contracted from *Mac Hugh*, the anglicised form of *Mac Aedha*.

In translations from the Irish MSS., AEDH is always made HUGH, which is a Teutonic name with an altogether different meaning.

> ‘Brian MC HUGH Oge, Mac Mahon, and Ever Mac Cowley came in with those their complaints.’*

M^cKEWE [1511], KEW [1649].

It was always an uncommon name, and is now scarcely found.

KEAREY (obsolete), from *O'Ciardha*, usually anglicised CAREY.

> ‘Aedh Ua CIARDHA,’ A.D. 999.†
> Formerly common in Braddan.

KEARIE [1629], KERY [1698], KEAREY [1703].

CROGHAN, contracted from *Mac Ruadhagain* (corrupted into *Mac Rogan*), ‘Ruadhagan's son.’ *Ruadhagan* is a diminutive of *ruad*, ‘red.’

> ‘Murchadh Donn O'RUADHAGAIN,’ A.D. 1103.‡

---

* Camden (Ireland), p. 123.   † Four Mast., Vol. II., p. 743.
‡ Four Mast., Vol. II., p. 973.

CROGHAN may possibly have the same origin as CREGEEN. It is not a common name in the Isle of Man.

CROGHAN [1511], CROUGHAN [1618].

Jurby, German, Lonan (c), elsewhere (u).

CREGEEN, contracted from O'CRIOCAIN, 'Criocan's son.'

A.D. 1022, 'Cathal O'CRIOCAIN.'*

CREGEEN may possibly be contracted from *Mac Riaghain* (corrupted into *Mac Regan*). Riaghan is a diminutive of *riach*, 'gray,' or sometimes 'swarthy.'

Compare (Irish) CREIGHAN, CREGAN.

CRIGENE [1649], CREDGEEN [1654], CREDJEEN [1708], GREGEEN [1722].

Jurby, German, Lonan (c), elsewhere (u).

CREEN (obsolete), contracted from *Mac Bracin*, now *Mac Breen*, 'Breen's son.'

'Diarmaid UA BRAEIN,' A.D. 1170.

Compare (Irish) BREEN and MAC BREEN.

CREENE [1601], CREEN [1719], CRIN [1727].

It is not found after the middle of the eighteenth century.

GILLOWYE, MAC GILLOWYE, LOWEY (obsolete). Perhaps the descendants of LUIGH or LEWEY, a name borne by the son of CORMAC GAILENG. The name LUGHAIDH was anglicised LOWAY in Ireland.

GILLOWYE and MAC GILLOWYE are only found in 1511, but LOWEY survives as late as 1734, and was at one time common in several parishes.

* Four Mast., Vol. II., p. 803.

Lowey [1609], Lowie [1611], Lewie [1629], Loweay [1670], Lowy [1707], Loway [1734].

Formerly Maughold (vc), Jurby, Rushen (c), elsewhere (u).

Mylrea seems to be contracted from *Mac Guilley rea (ray)*. Its meaning presents considerable difficulties, as the ordinary derivation from *ree*, 'king,' is disposed of by the pronunciation *ray*. Both Professors Mackinnon and Rhys, whose opinions have been asked, incline to a connection with the Gaelic Gilray, but will not commit themselves to an explanation of either Mylrea or Gilray.

Compare (Irish and Gaelic) Gilray, Gilivray.
Mac Gilrea [1511], Illerea [1598], Illirea [1599], Maclerea [1601], Maccillrea [1603], Illeray 1618], Molerie* [1631], McYlleriah [1650] McYlrea [1654], Illyreah [1660], Mallereay* [1684], Mollereigh* [1690], Mallereigh* [1691], Mallery* [1693], Mylreey [1754], Mylrea [1750], and many other forms.

Jurby, Ballaugh, Braddan, Malew (c) ; elsewhere (u).

Mylroi and Mylroie, contracted from *Mac Gilroy*, a corrupted form of *Mac Giolla-ruaidh*, 'Giolla-ruadh's son,' or 'the red-haired youth's son.' 'When an adjective, signifying a colour or quality of the mind or body, is postfixed to *Giolla*, then it has its ancient signification—namely, a youth, a boy, or a man in his bloom ; *Giolla-ruadh, i.e.,* the

---

* These forms look as if they might be derived from *Maol*. See note on Mylvorrey. McYlrea is the commonest form during the eighteenth century.

red-haired youth ; *Giolla-riabhach*, the swarthy
youth ; *Giolla-buidhe*, the yellow youth, etc.'*
' Bæthan MAC GILROY,' A.D. 1408.†
Compare (Gaelic) MᶜILROY.

MELROIE [1601], MᶜYLEROIJ [1612], MOLLEROY [1631],
MYLRIOIYE [1718], MYLROIJ [1724], MᶜYLROY [1730],
MYLEROI [1744], MYLROI [1759], MYLREOI [1762],
MYLROIE [1782].

It is almost confined to the parish of Lonan.

Lonan (c) ; Braddan, Ballaugh (u) ; elsewhere (w).

LOONEY, contracted from *O'Luinigh*, 'Luinigh's descendant ' (*luinneach*, 'armed ').

' Gillacrist O'LUINIGH, Lord of Cinel Moen,' A.D. 1090.‡

The O'LOONEYS were chiefs of Muintir Loney,
in Tyrone.

Compare (Irish) O'LOONEY, LOONEY.

M'LAWNEY [1504], LOWNYE [1540], LOWENY [1602],
LOWNIE [1623], LEWNEY [1626], LOONEY [1644],
LONEY [1681].

Jurby (vc), Marown, Lezayre, Malew, Santon, Onchan,
Lonan (c), elsewhere (u).

HOWLAN, from *O'Hualaghain*, or *O'h-Uallachain*,
' Hualagan's descendant.'

' Donnell O'HUALAGHAIN, Archbishop of Munster,' A.D. 1182.

In Ireland this name has been anglicised NOLAN
and HOLLAND.

HOWLAN [1696], HOWLAND [1702].

Found in Bride formerly, now very uncommon.

---

* Four Mast., Vol. III., p. 2 (O'Donovan's note).
† *Ibid.*, Vol. IV.
‡ *Ibid.*, Vol. II., p. 939.

BOYD, probably from *Mac Giolla Buidhe*, 'Giolla-bhuide's son,' or the 'yellow-haired youth's son.' (See note on *Giolla*, under MYLROI).

'Conn MacGILLABHUIDHE, Abbot of Mangairid,' A.D. 1100.*

MAKABOY was Archdeacon and Rector of Andreas, A.D. 1270.

MacGILLA BUIDHE, in Ireland, is corrupted into MacGILLA BOY, and then into McAvoy, McEvoy, MacBoyd, and BOYD, though McAvoy and McEvoy are strictly speaking contractions of MacAEDHA BUIDHE. 'Aedh, the Yellow's son,' where *Buidhe* is a mere nickname. The name BODDAGH (extinct), which is probably the same name originally, as BOYD, had, by the middle of the eighteenth century, been in every case changed into BOYD, which latter name is still pronounced BODDAGH by a few old Manx people. BODDAGH may, however, be derived from *Buadach*, 'victorious,' or from the nickname *Bodach*, meaning 'churl.'

McOBOY, McBOOY, McBOWYE, BEDAGH [1511], BOY [1611], BOID [1617], BODDAUGH [1671], BOIY [1680], BODAUGH [1682], BODDAGH [1701], BOYD [1742].

BOYD is not such a common name now as formerly.

Ballaugh, Michael (vc), German, Lezayre (c), elsewhere (u).

CANNON and CANNAN, contracted from *Mac Cannanain*, 'Cannanan's son' (*Ceann-fhionn*, 'white head').

'CANANNAN, son of Ceallach Tanist of Ui Ceinnsealaigh, A.D. 950.†

'From the family of O'CANNANAIN, of Tirconnell,

---

* Four Mast., Vol. II., p. 965.   † Four Mast., Vol. II., p. 667.

LETTER-KENNY, in Donegal, received its name, which is a shortened form of LETTER-CANNANAN, the O'CANNANAN'S hill-slope.'*

Compare (English) CANNING.

MACCANNON [1511], CANNAN [1638], CANNON [1676].

Jurby, Maughold, German, Marown (c), elsewhere (u).

CONROY, contracted from *O'Mulconry*, 'Mulconry's descendant.'

'Maline Bodhar O'MULCONRY took Cluain Bolcain,' A.D. 1132.†

This name was always uncommon in the Isle of Man, and is now scarcely found.

CONRAI [1605], CONROI [1617], CUNRIE [1618], CONROY [1670].

In Ireland it is frequently anglicised KING.

CUDD, contracted from *McHud*.

McHUD [1675], McHOOD [1711], CUDD [1750].

It is found in the parishes of Patrick and Lezayre, but is very uncommon.

KELLAG, MACKELLAG [1511] (obsolete), possibly connected with *kellagh*, 'a cock' (see KENNAUGH).

MACARTHURE [1511] (obsolete). The MACARTHURS are said to be descended from Cormac Cas.

MACCLAGHELEN [1511] (obsolete), possibly a corruption of *MacLoughlin*. It is found as late as A.D. 1616.

'Conchobar MACLOCHLAINN,' A.D. 1122.‡

[LOUGHLANN, the land of lakes, is the name given by the Irish to Norway.]

---

* Joyce, Vol. I., p. 140.   † Four Mast., Vol. III., p. 265.
‡ Four Mast., Vol. II., p. 1015.

MacCORRY and MacCURRY [1504] (obsolete), contracted from *MacComraidhe*, 'Comrad's son.'

> 'Ui Mac Uais the most festive here
> Have O'COMHRAIDHE at their head.'*

The name O'COMHRAIDHE is still extant, but for many centuries reduced to obscurity and poverty. In the sixteenth century it was anglicised COWRY. It is now more usually CORRY and CURRY.'†

MacNAMEER (obsolete), from *MacNamara*, the anglicised form of *MacConmara*, 'Cumara's son' (*cu-mara*, 'sea-hound').

> 'Royal dynast of fine incursions
> Is MacCONMARA, of Mag Adhair.
> The territories of wealth are his country.' ‡
> 'MacCONMARA was defeated,' A.D. 1311.§

This family derives its name from its ancestor CUMARA, son of Domhnall, who was the 22nd in descent from Cormac Cas.

MacNAMARA [1511], McNAMEER [1610], McNAMEAR [1793], after which date it is not found.

The name MEARE [1607], MEERE [1621], McMEER [1698], is probably a further corruption. It was formerly common in the parish of Jurby. The name MONIER, which was found in the parish of Lezayre in the last century, is also said to have been a corruption of McNAMEER.

MAC NAMEE [1511] (obsolete), a corrupted form of *Mac Conmeadha*.

> 'Amhlaeibe, the son of MacCONMEADHA.'‖

It is found as late as 1698. It was always uncommon.

---

* O'Dubhagain, p. 13. † O'Donovan, p. 43.
‡ O'Donovan, p. 127. § Four Mast., Vol. II., p. 499.
‖ Four Mast., Vol. II., p. 951.

MacRory [1511] (obsolete), anglicised from *Mac Ruaidhri*, 'Ruadhri's son' (*ruadh* 'red'; *righ*, king ').

'. . . . MacRuaidhri, gentle,
Over Teallach Ainbith, the formidable.'*

In Ireland MacRuaidhri is now usually anglicised Rogers.

Innow [1408], Ivenowe [1417], Yvens [1429], Yvene [1430] (obsolete), probably connected with Ywain, Owen, Eoghan.

* O'Dubhagain, p. 55.

CHAPTER II.

THE Celtic surnames of the Isle of Man, which are
derived from the profession or trade of an ancestor, or
from some epithet indicating his personal characteristics or his local origin, are for the most part
patronymic in form, having in their original documentary shape the prefix *Mac*. In the first place we shall
enumerate the surnames which indicate the profession
or rank in life of the ancestor of the family by which
they are borne.

JOUGHIN, from *MacJaghin*, ' Deacon's son.'

> ' The priests sonnes that follow not their studies prove for
> the most part notorious theeves. For they that carry the
> name of MACDECAN, MACPHERSON, and MACOSPAC, that
> is the deane's or deacon's son, the parson's son, and the
> bishop's son, are the strongest theeves that be.'*

JOUGHIN is a purely Manx name. It is almost
confined to the northern parishes.

* Camden : Account of Ireland, p. 145.

McJoychene,* McJoyene* [1422], M'Joughin [1430], MacJoghene [1570], Joughin [1657], Joghin [1673].

> Maughold, Bride, Andreas (c), elsewhere (u).

MacPerson [1430], McPherson [1511] (obsolete), 'The parson's son.' It is a common name in Scotland.

Taggart (sometimes pronounced Taggard), contracted from *Mac-an-t-sagart*, 'The priest's son.'

> In 1511, Otes MacTagart is entered for the Mill of Doway. It was afterwards called Mullen Oates, now Union Mills, in the parish of Braddan.
>
> Compare (Gaelic and Irish) MacTaggart, Mac Entaggart.

MacTaggart [1430], Taghertt [1540], Taggart [1614], Tagert [1660], Taggard [1681].

> Malew (vc), Ballaugh, Braddan, Marown, Onchan, Maughold, Santon (c), elsewhere (u).

Ward, originally *Mac-an-bhaird*, 'The bard's son.'

> 'The sons of Mac-an-Baird.'†

McWard [1511], Ward [1660].

> Very uncommon.

Mac y Chlery, 'The clerk's son,' has, in the Isle of Man, been almost universally written in the English form of Clark, Clarke, or Clerk, but, though rare, the Manx form existed.

> Compare (Irish) Ua Cleirigh, which became O'Clery.
>
> Clerk is derived from the Latin *clericus*, the

---

* These names are in the British Museum copy only.
† Four Mast., Vol. I., p. 609.

name formerly given to those who possessed the accomplishments of reading and writing.

'Conchobar UA CLEIRIGH, lector of Cill-dara,' A.D. 1126.*

John CLERK was ' Judge of Mann,' in 1417.

'Gubon M'Cubon CLEARKE, commissary to Bishop Pulley, Bishop of Sodor,' A.D. 1430.†

CLERK [1417], CLEARKE [1430], M'CLEARY [1521], M᷾CLEARE [1532], CLARKE [1586], MAC Y CHLERY [1617], CLARK [1621].

Jurby, Andreas, Lezayre, Bride, German, Malew, Arbory (c), elsewhere (u).

SKELLY, contracted from *O'Scolaidhe*, the 'story-teller's descendant' (*scculaidhe*). The ' story-teller ' was a regular official at the courts of the old Irish kings.

' O'SCOLAIDHE of sweet stories.'‡

'Gilla-Isa-MAC-AN-SKEALY,' A.D. 1237.§

'After the English Invasion the family of O'SCOLAIDHE or O'SCOLAIGHE, now SCULLY, were driven into the county of Tipperary.'‖

Compare (Irish) SCULLY, SKELLY, SKALLY, and SCALLY.

M᷾SCALY [1408], SKELLIE [1630], SKEALLEY [1631], SKALLY [1640], SKELLY [1677], SKALY [1715].

It was formerly a common name in the parish of Jurby, but is now scarcely found anywhere.

KEWISH (pronounced KEOUSH), contracted from *Mac-Uais*, ' The noble's son.'

Colla UAIS is said to have been the 121st Milesian Monarch of Ireland.

KEWISH [1618], KEVISH [1653], KEWSH [1683].

Jurby (vc), Bride, Ballaugh, Malew (u), elsewhere (w).

---

* Four Mast., Vol. II., p. 996.   † Statute Law Book, p. 24.
‡ O'Dubhagain, p. 12.   § Four Mast., Vol. III., p. 291.
‖ O'Donovan, p. 25.

QUILLEASH, possibly a contraction of *Mac Cuilluais*, 'The noble Coll's son.'*

CUILLEASH [1624], QUILLEISH [1631], COLLEASH[1672], QUILLEASH [1694].

BREW, contracted from *MacVriw*, 'The judge's son.' The '*Briw*,' now the *Deemster*, the Scandinavian term having superseded the Celtic, gave 'Breast laws' to the people. He was identical with the Irish *Brehon*. It is possible that BREW may be contracted from *MacBrugaidh*, 'The farmer's son.'

BREW is a purely Manx name.

Compare (Irish) MACBREHON, now universally translated JUDGE.

M^cBROW [1408], M^cBREWE [1417], BREW [1616], BRIEW [1648], BREW [1660].

Andreas, Lonan, Santon (vc), Ballaugh, Maughold, Lezayre, Malew, Onchan (c), elsewhere (u).

GILL and GELL, contracted from *Giolla*, or *guilley*, a 'young man' (see MYLCHREEST, KILLEY), are almost certainly the same name originally, the former being the earlier form. They are now used indiscriminately.

'Very little doubt can exist of the Irish having had, in early times, the word *Gilla* for a youth, servant-boy, or lackey ; and the name of GILLA or GILDAS, uncompounded, is certainly more ancient than the Danish invasions.'†

After King Magnus Barfod fell in battle in Ulster, in A.D. 1103, 'An Irishman named HARALD GILLE came forward and passed himself off for a son of that Monarch by an Irishwoman ; and, after proving his descent by walking over a red-hot iron, actually became King of Norway.'‡

GILL was Prior of Furness in A.D. 1134.

Compare (Irish) GILL, (Gaelic) MACGILL and MACKILL.

* See QUILL (*ante*).   † O'Donovan, p. 55.   ‡ Worsaae, p. 346.

GILL [1134], MacGYLLE [1430], M^cGELL [1504], M^cGILL, GELL [1511].

> GILL.—Santon, German, Lezayre (c), elsewhere (u).
> GELL.—Rushen (vc), Marown, Malew, Patrick, Santon (c), elsewhere (u).

TEAR and TEARE, contracted from *Mac-an-t-saoir*, 'The carpenter's son.'

> 'Ciaran MAC-AN-TSAIR,' A.D. 990.*
> 'The importance attached by the Act, 5 Ed. IV. (see introductory chapter) to the bearing of an English surname, soon induced many of the less distinguished Irish families, of the English Pale, and its vicinity, to translate or disguise their Irish names, so as to make them appear English ; thus MAC-AN-T-SAOR was altered to CARPENTER.'†

Compare (Gaelic) MacINTYRE, MacTIER, (Irish) MacENTIRE, MACATEER, MATEER, TEER, TIER.

MACTYR [1372],‡ M'TEARE, M'TERRE [1504], MacTERE [1511], TEARE [1599], TEAR [1611], TERE [1688].

The curious name, MacTEREBOY, found in 1511, now obsolete, would seem to be the above name, with *buidhe*, ' yellow,' added.

It is much commoner in the north of the Island than the south.

> Ballaugh, Jurby (vc), Maughold, Andreas, Bride, Lezayre (c), elsewhere (u).

GAWN and GAWNE, contracted from *Mac-an-Gabhain*, 'The smith's son.'

The smith, in olden times, was a very important personage, as being the maker of armour and weapons, and as this trade, like others in that day, descended from father to son, its designation would soon become used as a surname.

MacFirbis states in his book of Genealogies that

---

* Chron. Scot., p. 233.　　† O'Donovan.　Introduction, p. 26.
‡ Manx Society, Vol. XXIII., p. 392.

the Mac-an-Ghobhan were historians to the
O'Kennedys of Ormond.

'Maelbrighde Mac-an-Ghobhann,' A.D. 1061.*

Henry Gawen was 'Atturney' in 1517.

Compare (Irish) McGowan, Gowan, Gavan,
(Gaelic) McGavin, (English) Smithson.

MacGawne† [1422], M'Gawen, M'Gawn [1430],
Gawen [1517], Gawne [1586], Gawn [1599], Gown
[1601].

    Malew, Rushen (vc), Jurby, Ballaugh, Arbory (c), else-
where (u).

MacCray [1511], Cry [1611], Crye [1623], is possibly
from *MacCraith*, 'The weaver's son.' In Ireland
and Scotland this name is now found in the form
Macrae.

Nideragh [1611], Nidraugh and Nedraugh [1623]
(extinct), has possibly some connection with the
Manx word *fidderagh*, 'weaving.'

Clague and Cleg, contracted from *MacLiaigh*, 'The
leech's son' (*Liagh*, 'leech').

    'In the *Tain B'o Cuailnge*, a *Fáth-Laig*, or Prophet-
Leech, heals the wounds of *Cúchulaind*, after his fight with
Ferdiad. It is probable, therefore, that in Pagan times the
Liag (leech) belonged to the order which may be conven-
tionally called Druidic, and that charms and incantations
formed part of the means of cure. The position assigned to
the Leech by the laws in the middle ages was a very high
one. He ranked with the smith and the *Cerd*, or artist in
gold and silver ; and the *Ollamh*, or doctor in leech-craft,
ranked with an *Aire Ard*, *i.e.*, one of the highest grades of
lord. He had also a distinguished place at assemblies, and
at the table of the king. Leech-craft became hereditary in
certain families, some of whose names indicate their profession, as O'Lee, *i.e.*, O'Liaigh.'‡

---

* Four Mast., Vol. II., p. 881.   † In the British Museum copy only.
‡ Ency. Brit. art. on Celtic Literature.

On a stone at the Friary, Arbory, Professor Rhŷs has recently discovered the name MAC LEOG, in the Ogam character. This late form would seem to show that Ogam writing lingered in the Isle of Man till the ninth century.

'MACLIAG, Chief Poet of Erinn,' A.D. 1014.*

'Gilla MACLIAG (Gelasius), the son of Rory, the successor of St. Patrick, and Primate of Armagh and of all Ireland . . . . died A.D. 1173.'†

In 1405, Gilbert CLEG received letters of protection from Henry IV. to come to the Isle of Man.‡ It is possible, but not probable, that the forms CLEG and CLEGG may be derived from (O.N.) *kleggi*, 'a horse-fly.' The word *Cleg* is used in the Isle of Man, as well as in Scotland and the north of England, to designate this insect. CLAGUE is now the commonest form, but did not become so till early in the eighteenth century.

CLEG [1405], MacCLEWAGE, MacCLUAG [1511], CLEVAGE [1521], CLOAGGE, CLOAGE [1601], CLAIGE [1622], CLOGUE [1625], CLEAGE [1644], CLAUGE [1652], CLAGUE [1655], CLOAUGE [1660], CLUAGE [1673], CLOIAGE [1674], CLUAG [1676], CLAIG [1696], CLAIGUE [1702], CLOAG [1719], CLAGE [1775], CLEGG [1790].

Marown, Santon (vc), Malew, Michael, Jurby, Lezayre, Ballaugh, Braddan, Lonan, Maughold, Rushen (c), elsewhere (u).

KERD and MAC KERD [1511] (obsolete), from *Ceard*, 'an artificer, artist-mechanic.'

KINVIG and KINRED seem to have been originally nicknames, which became surnames at a comparatively recent date. The prefix *kin* is the genitive of *kione* 'head,' which would preclude their being simply

* Chron. Scot., p. 257.   † Four Mast., Vol. III., p. 13.
‡ Manx Society, Vol. VII., p. 231.

appellations from a personal peculiarity, as *kione-beg*, 'little head,' and so we must suppose that the Christian names were appended to the original forms, as JUAN-Y-KIN-VIG, 'John of little-head,' STEEN-Y-KIN-RAAD, 'Stephen of road-end,' where these titles refer to *Juan's* and *Steen's* abodes, and that their sons would be MAC KINVIG and MAC KINRAADE, the MAC being soon omitted.

KINVIG [1641], KINRED [1611], KINRADE [1622], KINDRED [1644].

There are only two names denoting nationality: CRETNEY [1611], a contraction of MAC BRETNAGH, 'Welshman's son'; and MAC FINLOE and FYNLO [1511] (obsolete), 'Dane's son,' and 'Dane,' but this latter derivation is very doubtful.

NOTE.—The still existing, though very uncommon, name CREETCH [1698], which was found in the forms CRECH [1621], and CREECH [1641]; and the following obsolete names, all probably of Celtic origin, which are found in our early documents, are very obscure. Possibly some of them are incorrectly transcribed.

MAC DOWYTT, MAC ESSAS (possibly from *Esaias*) [1408], MAC KNALYTT [1417], MAC CROWTON, MAC HOWE [1422], MAC EFFE, MAC KIMBE, MAC QUANTIE [1430], MAC CAURE, MAC CURE, CUNDRE (which survived till quite recently), and MAC CUNDRE, GILHAST and MAC GILHAST, MAC CLENERENT, MAC CRAVE, MAC KYM, MAC LYNEAN, MAC LOLAN (possibly for MACLELLAN), MAC QUARTAG, QUATE and QUOTT [1511], MAC VRIMYN [1532].

CHAPTER III.

MOST of the Scandinavian names in the Isle of Man have had the Celtic 'Mac' prefixed, the contraction of which has very much altered their form. These names are not so common now as they were in the sixteenth century.

ASCOUGH [1511] (obsolete), from *ask-ulfr*, 'ash wolf.'

CASEMENT, contracted from *Mac-ás-Mundr*. The (O. N.) *ás* is equivalent to the Anglo-Saxon *ós*, i.e. *semideus*, which we find in such names as OSWALD and OSWY.

> '*Mundr* was the sum the bridegroom had to pay for his bride as agreed on at the espousals. It is used as the latter part of several proper names.'*

Compare (O.N.) AS-MUNDR found in the *Land-námabóc* and *Flateyjarbóc*.

> MACCASMONDE [1429], MACCASMUND [1511], CASYMOUND CASMYN [1540]. CASMOND [1601], CASEMENT [1612], COSTMINT [1624], CAISMENT [1679].

It is almost confined to the northern parishes. It is not so common now as formerly.

> Maughold, Lezayre (vc) formerly, Jurby, Ballaugh, Andreas (c), elsewhere (u).

---

* Cleasby and Vigfusson—Icelandic Dictionary, p. 437.

CASTELL and CAISTELL, contracted from *Mac-as-Ketill*.* *Ketill* is equivalent to the English 'kettle.' In the Icelandic poets of the tenth century the uncontracted form was used, but in the eleventh it began to be contracted into *Kel*. Its frequent occurrence in nomenclature doubtless arises from the use of the Vé-kell, or ' Holy Kettle,' at sacrifices. Cumming reads 'OSKETIL'† on the fragment of a cross in the Museum at Distington, which was formerly at Kirk Michael, but Dr. Vigfusson makes this name ' ROSCIL ';‡ and Worsaae speaks of ' the well-known Scandinavian name ASKETIL ' being ' found on the remains of a runic inscription in the Museum at Douglas ';§ but this refers to the same stone, as ' Douglas' is an error for ' Distington.'

ASKELL is found in the *Flateyjarbóc;* OSCYTYL was Abbot of Croyland in A.D. 992, and ASKEL, king of Dublin, in A.D. 1159.

> 'Our beloved and faithful Gilbert MACASKEL.' ‖
> 'To Gilbert MAKASKILL, Keeper of the Isle of Man.'¶

Compare (O.N.) ASKETIL, ASKELL, (English) ASKETIL, ASKETEL (found in the Hundred Rolls), KETTLE, CASTLE, (Gaelic) GASKELL.

MACASKEL [1311], MAKASKILL [1312], CASKELL and MACCASKELL [1511], CAISTIL [1699], CAISTELL [1725], CASTIL [1733], CASTELL [1750], CASTLE [1789].

It is now hardly found anywhere, though formerly common in Bride, to which parish it was almost confined.

---

* For *as*, see CASEMENT.
† Cumming. Runic Remains.
‡ Manx Note Book, No. 9, pp. 18-19.
§ Worsaae, The Danes and Northmen, p. 283.
‖ Manx Society, Vol. VII., p. 153.
¶ *Ibid.*, p. 154.

COTTIER and COTTER (pronounced COTCHIER), contracted from *MacOttarr*, 'Ottar's son.' The Norse name, OTTARR, seems to be formed from *Otta*, 'twilight,' and the ending *hari*, which probably means 'sword.' In Anglo-Saxon spelling it is OHTHERE. The voyages of a Norseman so named are related in King Alfred's Anglo-Saxon version of Orosius. At Kirk Braddan there is a cross read by Dr. Vigfusson as follows :—UTR : RISTI : CRUS : ÞONO : AFT : FROCA . . . . 'Odd raised this cross to the memory of Froca . . . .' and he remarks ' *Ut* probably represents the Icelandic *Odd*, though this is not certain.'* Under A.D. 1098, we find in the *Chronicon Manniæ*, that 'A battle was fought between the Manxmen at Santwat, and those of the North obtained the victory. In this engagement were slain the Earl OTHER and Macmaras, leaders of the respective parties.'†

'MACOTTIR, one of the people of Insi Gall (the Hebrides),' A.D. 1142.‡

OTTAR was king of Dublin, A.D. 1147.

OTTARR is common in the *Flateyjarbóc*.

COTTER is the usual form to the middle of the eighteenth century, when it was generally supplanted by COTTIER, which is now almost invariably the form used. Tradition has it that two Huguenot families, called COTTIER, escaped from France at the time of the massacre of St. Bartholomew, 1572, and that their descendants settled in

* Manx Note Book, No. 9, p. 16.
† Chronicon Manniæ, Manx Society, Vol. XXII., p. 58.
‡ Four Mast., Vol. II., p. 169.

the parish of Lezayre. The name COTTIER, however, or rather MACCOTTIER, was found here before
that date, but still it is possible that its origin
may not be the same as that of COTTER.

> OTER, OTHER [1098], MACOTT' (?) [1417], MACCOTTER
> and MAC COTTIER [1504], COTTIER [1616], COTTER
> [1625], COTTAR [1647].

> Lezayre (vc), Ballaugh, Marown, Braddan, Maughold,
> Rushen, Onchan, Malew, Arbory, German, Santon, Bride,
> Michael (c), elsewhere (u).

CORKHILL, contracted from *Mac-þór-Ketill.** þorr, the
God of thunder, the keeper of the hammer, the
destroyer of evil spirits, the son of mother earth,
was the favourite Deity of the North. Cumming
reads þURKETIL on a cross in Kirk Braddan, but
Dr. Vigfusson makes it þURLIBR.†

In the annals of Roger de Hoveden we read
under date A.D. 1044 that 'the noble Matron Gun-
hilda . . . with her two sons, Hemming and
TURKILL, was expelled from England.'‡

Bishop THORGIL took part in Haco's expedition
in A.D. 1263.

Both þORKELL and þORGILS are common in the
Landnámabóc and the *Flateyjarbóc.*

> 'Donald MACCORKYLL was Rector of the Church of St.
> Mary of Balylagh, in 1408,'§ and 'Edward CORKHILL one
> of the Deemsters of Mann,' in 1532.‖

Compare (Gaelic) MACTORQUIL, MACCORQUO-
DALE.

> MACCORKYLL [1408], MACCORKILL [1430], MᶜCROKELL,

CORKELL [1511], CORKHILL [1532], CURKELL [1632],
CORKILL [1650], CORKIL [1652].
Ballaugh, Maughold, German, Lezayre, Michael, Santon,
Andreas (c), elsewhere (u).

CORLETT (sometimes pronounced CURLEOD), is from
the (O.N.) personal name Þorljótr (the initial *c*
representing the Celtic prefix *Mac*). The word
ljótr means 'deformed,' or 'ugly,' but that can
scarcely be its meaning in this compound. Dr.
Vigfusson thinks that *ljót* is the same as the old
Teutonic *lcòd*, 'people.' It is not found by itself
in the *Landnámabóc*, though, in combination with
Þórr it is common there. In the *Flateyjarbóc*,
written two centuries later, this compound name
occurs twice. *Ljótr* is found on the cross in the
old churchyard at Ballaugh in combination with
Liut, as LIUTWOLF.*

'The name *Thor* has always been thought to sound well,
and is much used in proper names. Þorljotr is found in
many runic stones in Denmark. The MACLEODS, in Scotland, have always claimed a Scandinavian origin, and their
name is probably from *Mac ljótr*, the Þor not having been
inserted.'† 'The MACLEODS of Cadboll, and the MAC-
LEODS of Lewis, not only quarter the Manx *trie cassyn* (three
legs), but use the same motto, *quocunque jeceris stabit;* which,
I think, clearly points out that the chiefs of that name are
descendants from the Norwegian sovereigns of Mann and
the Isles, or some other Manx connexion.'‡

In the parishes of Ballaugh and Lezayre nearly
one-fourth part of the population are CORLETTS.
Compare (Welsh) LLOYD.

CORLETT [1504], MACCORLEOT [1511], MACCORLEAT
[1521], CURLEOD [1600], CORLOD [1629], CURLET

* Manx Note Book, No. 9, pp. 11, 12.
† Cleasby and Vigfusson, p. 743.
‡ Oswald, in Manx Society, Vol. V., p. 7.

[1666], CORLEOD [1677], CORLOT [1678], CORLET [1618].

Ballaugh, Lezayre, Bride, Andreas (vc), Jurby, Malew, Rushen, German, Michael, Braddan, Lonan (c), elsewhere (u).

COWLEY, and KEWLEY (pronounced COWLAH and KEOLAH), contracted from *MacAulay*, the shortened form of *MacAmhlaibh*, ' Anlaf's or Olaf's son.'

The Scandinavian name ANLEIFR, ÁLEFER, ÓLÁFR was rendered by ANLÂF in the Saxon Chronicle, and by AMHLABH in the Irish Chroniclers; thus RIGH AMHLAB was King Olave the White in Dublin. We have it in the form AULAFIR* on the cross at Kirk Michael, and on the cross at Ballaugh in the curious form OULAIBR, which Dr. Vigfusson says is unique. OLAF was a royal name in Man, and must at one time have been common. The derivation from OLAF seems most probable; but it so happens that the native Irish name AMHALGHADA was also pronounced AULAY.

Aumond M'OLAVE was Bishop of Man from A.D. 1077-1100, and, in 1102, OLAVE, son of Godred Crovan, commenced his reign.

' Flann MACAULAY killed,' A.D. 1178.†

ÓLÁFR was a favourite proper name in the north, and was common both in the *Landnámabóc* and the *Flateyjarbóc*. Some of our COWLEYS may be of English origin, but KEWLEY is a purely Manx name.

In the parishes where COWLEY is common, KEWLEY is rare, and *vice versâ*.

---

* Manx Note Book, No. 9, pp. 12, 13. † Four Mast.

MacCowley [1504], Cowley [1587], Kewley [1611], Cowlay [1626].
Cowley—Lezayre, Ballaugh, Maughold (c), elsewhere (u).
Kewley—Braddan, Marown, Lonan (c), elsewhere (u).

Crennell, and Crellin (the latter by metathesis from the former) were both probably contracted from *MacRannall* or *MacRaghnaill*, 'Reginald's son.' Raghnall is the Celtic form of the common Scandinavian name Rögnvaldr (*rögn.* a collective name for the Gods, is a frequent commencement of proper names, and *valdr*, 'ruler,' is equally common as an ending). It was not common in Ireland till the thirteenth century.

'Godfrey MacMicRagnaill, king of Dublin,' A.D. 1075.*

Rögnvaldr occurs in the *Flatcyjarbóc.*

Reginald or Ragnvald was the name of several of the Kings of Man.

Andrew Reynesson was one of the Keys who signed the Indenture in 1417.

'Brian, the son of Gilcreest MacRannall.'†

John Crellin was a lieutenant in Peel Castle, in 1610.

Crellin appears to be a purely Manx name, but, as in Cottier, there is a tradition of French origin, which, in this case, is said to be from the noble family of De Crillon. It is remarkable that in the parishes where Crellin is common, Crennell is scarcely found, and *vice versâ.*

MacReynylt [1511], Crenilt [1627], Crynilt [1639], Crenylt [1640], Creniel [1642], Crennil [1646], Crinnell [1651], Crenil [1702], Crennell [1715].

---

* Annals of Ulster.   † Four Mast., Vol. III., p. 547.

CRELLIN [1610], CRILLIN [1702], CRELLING [1730].

CRENNELL—Bride, Andreas (vc), Maughold (c), elsewhere (u).

CRELLIN—German (vc), Michael, Patrick, Arbory (c), elsewhere (u).

CRINGLE, possibly from (O.N.) KRINGLE, which is found as a nickname in the *Landnámabóc* (*Kringla*, 'a circle ').

CRINGLE [1641], CRINGAL [1672], KRINGEL [1774].

It is very uncommon.

GARRET, contracted from (O.N.) *Geirrauðr*. The first element in this name is *geirr*, ' spear.' The ending *rau r* in proper names has been supposed by Professor Bugge to have been derived by several successive corruptions from *frid*, ' peace.'

GEIRÖÐR occurs twice in the *Flateyjarbóc*. It may also be from (O.N.) GEIRVALDR, which corresponds exactly to GERALD, or, in some cases, it might come from the Celtic MACART : cf. BALLYMACARRET, ' MacArt's town.'

Several GERRARDS were governors of the Isle of Man.

' GARRET, Earl of Desmond,'* A.D. 1369.

GARRETT [1586], GERRARD [1592], CARRETT [1609], CARRET [1610], CARRAT [1644], GARRAD [1677], GARRET [1661], CARRAD [1679], KARRET [1648], KARRETT [1698], KARRAD [1701].

It is spelt in the Registers with G, C, and K, indifferently, but the former predominates.

Andreas (vc), Bride, Jurby, Maughold, Michael, Lezayre, German, Ballaugh (c), elsewhere (u).

---

* Four Mast., Vol. II., p. 694.

CHRISTIAN has come to us from Iceland, in the form of KRISTÍN. The Celtic *Mac* was prefixed to it, and then it gradually became anglicised into its present form.

KRISTIN is found in the *Flateyjarbóc*.

James, the seventh Earl of Derby, in one of his letters to his son, said : ' There be many of the CHRISTIANS in this country—that is CHRISTINS [for that is] the true name ; but they have made themselves chief here.'* It is a very common name in the Isle of Man, especially in the parish of Maughold.

Compare (Scandinavian) CHRISTIAN, CHRISTIANSEN.

MacCRYSTYN [1408], CHRISTIANE [1499],† CHRISTIAN,‡ MacCHRISTENE [1504], MacCRISTYN, MacCHRASTENE [1511], MacCRISTIN, MacCRISTEN [1586], CHRISTIN [1610], CHRISTING [1626], CRISTEN [1632].
Maughold, Andreas, Jurby, Bride, Lezayre, Malew, Rushen, Onchan (vc), Braddan, Marown, Arbory, German, Santon, Lonan (c), elsewhere (u).

GOREE and GORRY, corrupted from (O.N.) *Goð-freyðr*. Bugge and others connect *freyðr* with *frid*, ' peace,' but this is very uncertain. *Goðfreyðr* would naturally pass through the various stages of GODFRAITH, GODRED, and GORED to GORË in Scandinavian lips. In Ireland it became GOTHFRAITH, GOFFRY, and finally GORRY.

GOTHFRAITH is found in the *Four Masters*, and

---

the most curtailed form is exhibited in DERRY
GORRY, 'Godfrey's wood,' in Monaghan.

> '*Er-derry haink er huc Ree Goree.*'
> 'Until there came to them King Goree.'

GODRED and ORRY.

> [*This monograph on the connection between* GODRED *and*
> ORRY *was sent to the writer by the late Dr.*
> *Vigfusson.*]

A grammarian named Thorodd, a housewright
and church-builder by trade, living early in the
twelfth century, having listened, while building the
cathedral of Holdar, in the north of Ireland (*circa*
1110), to the teaching of Latin that took place
whilst he sat at work, took a fancy to those studies
and became 'a great master in that art,' and afterwards wrote an essay, in the Norse tongue, on the
Icelandic alphabet. In order to show how short
and long vowels, or single and double consonants
make all the difference, and result in words widely
different in sound and sense, he gives appropriate
sentences, containing one of each, drawn from
mythology, history, old saws, and the like. I could
never make out the origin of one of these till I
came to the Isle of Man, and there I found the
key to it. The sentence runs thus:

> 'Vel líka Goþroeþc góþ roéþe,'

That is,

> 'Godroth loves well good oars.'

Godrod (Godfrod is a still older form) is an
ancient royal name. But where did our grammarian pick up the word and the sentence? Since
the time of Godrod, the famed Northman king,

Charlemagne's antagonist, there had been no famous king in Scandinavia of that name. It cannot have been this Godred, separated by three centuries from the writer's time, never known but dimly in Iceland, and now clean forgotten by the lapse of time. Observe, also, that in Iceland the name never even obtained. Of all countries, Man is the only one where, in the twelfth century, Godred was still a favoured name. And hearing and seeing, during my stay in Man, King Orry everywhere—he being to the Manx a sort of King Alfred, the fountain-head of all that is old and time-honoured—the thought struck me : ' Here is the Godred of the Icelandic grammarian.' A train of sound-changes, easily understood, transforms Goþroeþ to Orry, or King Orry of the present day —Goþroeþ = Go'reth = Goré ; then there must have been a time when the name was only sounded with King : King-go'ré = Kingoré, and dropping ' King,' and parting the word in the wrong place we have Ore, whence Orry; thus the initial *g* was lost. The ' Godrod ' of the grammarian, who loved the oars, or good oarsmen, is, I think, the Godredus of the Rushen Abbey Chronicles, surnamed Crowan, who, after a chequered life, died in 1095. The Manx of that day were a people of sailors— their king, of necessity, a sailor king; his strength, even his life and fortune, lay in his galley. To the ancient clipper-built galleys the oar and the oarsmen were what steam is to modern vessels. No wonder, then, that a Manx king loved good oarsmen. Thorodd's essay is separated from the king by some thirty-five years, but his memory would still be green, and men would still be living who had served on his galleys. At that time there was still trade communication between Iceland and the Orkneys and Shetland. Sodor and Man were more out of the Icelander's way, but would still be known to him. The crews, according to the rules of navigation in those days, would stay in Iceland the winter over, as 'winter sitters.' In turn Icelanders would now and then visit the Western Isles, for the crews were mixed. The story of King Godred, his adventures, his ships and oarsmen, would have been the topic of entertainment many an evening. A century later the Icelanders knew of the Manx king, Reginald, who, like the sea-kings of old, for three consecutive years had never sat ' under a sooty roof '—a true son of the galley. An Icelandic saga on the Earls of Orkney and Shetland has come down to us, where the Isle of Man comes in for a chance notice, but no saga of Manx kings is known, though such may well have been written, or told at any rate. The lives of these sea-kings survived the longest, into the thirteenth century, when the ship, oars, sail, and rudder were dropping out of Norse and Danish hands into those of the Hansa merchants. The inhabitants of Sodor and Man were the last sailors of the old Norse kin.

GOREE [1627], GORRY [1712].

It is almost confined to Peel and was never common.

LACE and LEECE (probably originally the same name) possibly from *Leif*, or *Leifr*, 'an inheritance,' a name very frequently found in the *Land-námabóc.*

In Lincolnshire there is a place called LACEBY, which in the *Domesday Book* is written LEVESBI, and in the *Hundred Rolls*, LEYSEBY.

Compare (Norman) LACY.

LACE [1643], LEECE [1679], LASE [1693], LEESE [1695], M^cYLEESE [1746].

It is not so common as formerly.

Bride, German (vc), Maughold, Santon, Andreas, Lezayre, Patrick (c), elsewhere (u).

MACALCAR [1511] (obsolete), probably from (O.N.) *Alfgeirr.*

SCARFF. Dr. Vigfusson suggests that this name is probably derived from (O.N.) *skarð,* 'a mountain pass.' SKARð is common in local names in Iceland, and we find SCARF-GAP in Cumberland, so that the surname may have been taken from one of the places so called. Other possible derivations are from *skarði,* 'hare-lip,' a nickname which was a frequent Danish proper name on Runic stones, or from *skarf,* 'a cormorant,' which is used as a nickname in the *Landnámabóc.* The cormorant is still called 'the Scarf,' in the Shetlands. SCHARF is found in the *Hundred Rolls.*

The name is now very uncommon.

MACSKERFFE [1408], SKERF [1417], MACSKERFF [1511], SCARFF [1620].

SKILLICORNE, a name peculiar to the Isle of Man, is puzzling. It is most probably derived from a local name now forgotten, beginning with the word *skellig*, 'rock.' We have *Skellig* and *Cornaa* separately among our local names, but not in combination.

CORNI is found as a personal name in the *Land-námabóc*, and SKYLI in the *Flateyjarbóc*.

Sir Philip SKILLICORNE was a vicar in 1521.

SKYLYCORNE [1511], SKILLICORNE [1521], SKYLLESKORN [1540], SKILLICORN [1650], SKILLECORN [1651].

Maughold, Andreas, Lezayre, Malew (c), elsewhere (u).

CHAPTER IV.

EXOTIC SURNAMES.

UNDER this head we include the Surnames which are neither of Celtic nor of Scandinavian formation, but have been introduced by immigration subsequent to the period of Norse domination. Amongst these the first place in order of time belongs to the HIBERNICISED ANGLO-NORMAN NAMES.

'After the murder of the Great Earl of Ulster, William de Burgo, the third Earl of that name, in 1333, and the consequent lessening of the English power in Ireland, many, if not all the distinguished Anglo-Norman families seated in Connaught and Munster became Hibernicised—*Hibernis ipsis Hiberniores*—spoke the Irish language, and assumed surnames like those of the Irish, by prefixing *Mac* to the Christian names of their ancestors. . . . Thus the De Burgos, in Connaught, assumed the name of MACWILLIAM. . . . from these sprang many offsets . . . as the MACGIBBONS, MAC-WALTERS,'* etc.

Members of these families settled in the Isle of Man, particularly in the south-western portion, and contracted their names of MACWALTER and MACWILLIAM into the decidedly harsh QUALTROUGH and QUILLIAM.

* O'Donovan, Introduction, pp. 21, 22.

GARRET may come from the Anglo-Norman GERALD, but is more likely to have come to us from the Scandinavians.*

GALE, also possibly of Anglo-Norman origin; as 'the Burkes of Gallstown and Balmontin, County Kilkenny, who descended from the Red Earl of Ulster, took the name of *Gall*, or foreigner,' † and the Stapletons, of Westmeath, took that of *Mac an Ghaill*, is more probably a name given by the natives to strangers who settled in the Isle of Man.

KERRUISH (pronounced KERREUSH), contracted from *MacFeorais*, 'Pierce's son,' and CORRIS, from *MacOrish*, another form of *MacFeorais*. The powerful Anglo-Norman family of Bermingham, Barons of Athenry, took the name of MACFEORAIS or MACORISH from an ancestor PIERCE, PIERAS, or FEORAS, the son of Meyler Bermingham.‡

'Andrew MACFEORAIS,' A.D. 1321.§

It is remarkable that in the parishes where KERRUISH is found, CORRIS is not. The former is almost confined to the parish of Maughold, while the latter is very common in the parish of German. The distich

> 'CHRISTIAN, CALLOW, and KERRUISH,
> All the rest are refuse !'

is still to be heard in Maughold, and is not so sweeping a condemnation as might be supposed,

---

* See p. 86.
† O'Donovan, Introduction to Poems, pp 22-24.
‡ O'Donovan, p. 22.
§ Four Mast., Vol. III., p. 370.

as 'all the rest' are not numerous. It is perhaps worth relating the popular etymology of this name. A ship was wrecked off Maughold Head. The people on shore, observing that four of the ship-wrecked mariners had stripped and were swimming to shore, exclaimed *kiare rooisht*, 'four naked!' The swimmers settled in the parish. Hence the name and its frequency there.

Compare (Irish) CORRISH, CORUS, CHORUS, (Gaelic) MACJORIS.

MCCORRIS [1511], CORRAS [1601], KERUSH [1610], CORES [1628], KERRUISH [1643], CORRIS [1647], KERROUSH, KERRISH [1666], CORRISH [1674], KERRUSE [1701], KERISH [1704], KERRISH [1708].

KERRUISH, though it appears in 1643, is not the usual form till the eighteenth century; till then KERRISH is more common.

KERRUISH—Maughold (vc), hardly found elsewhere.
CORRIS—German (vc), Malew, Patrick (c), elsewhere (u).

CORKISH is probably merely CORRIS with 'k' interpolated. Note the Irish form CORRISH, and observe that CORKISH is not found before 1660; also, that it does not occur in any of the parishes where CORRIS does.

CORKISH [1660].
Arbory, Bride, Rushen (c), elsewhere (u).

QUALTROUGH, contracted from *MacWalter*, 'Walter's son,' (see WATTERSON).

'Thomas MACWALTER, constable of Bunfinn,'* A.D. 1308.

The FITZWALTERS were the ancestors of the princely line of Hamilton, in Scotland.

In the parishes of Rushen and Arbory half the

---

* Four Mast., Vol. III., p. 489.

population is called either QUALTROUGH or WAT-
TERSON, and in the parish of Malew one-fourth.
> MacQUALTROUGH [1429], QUALTROUGH [1430], MAC-
> WALTER, MacWHALTRAGH, WATER [1511], McQUAL-
> THROUGH [1521], QUALTRAGH [1654], QUALTERAGH
> [1698].
> Rushen, Arbory, Malew (vc) elsewhere (u).

WATTERSON, or WATERSON, a corruption of WALTER-
SON,* is a translation of *MacWalter*. It seems
probable that the English-speaking MacWALTERS
would adopt this name, whilst the Celtic would
consent to have their name contracted into QUAL-
TROUGH. We find WATER as a corruption of
Walter in England. Thus in the Churchwardens
books at Ludlow we have 'The account of
WATTARE Taylor and Wyllyam Partynge, beynge
churchwardens, in the xxxii yere of the rayne of
Kyng Henry the eighth A.D. 1541.'† This is also
shown in the account of Suffolk's death in Shakespeare's Henry VI., where the murderer says:

> ' My name is WALTER Whitmore.
> How now ! Why start'st thou ? What doth death affright !
> *Suffolk*—Thy name affrights me, in whose sound is death.
> A cunning man did calculate my birth,
> And told me that by *Water* I should die.'

Some think that WATTERSON is a translation of
Mac-yn-ushtey, ' Water-son,' but this is very doubtful. The only entry in the Registers of such a
name is at Malew in 1669, when it states distinctly
that ' William MACYNUSTEY ' was ' an Irishman.'‡

---

* It should, however, be stated that WALTERSON is not found in
the Manx Registers before 1547, and that it only occurs once.
† Bardsley Surnames, p. 215.
‡ Manx Note Book, No. 8, p. 186.

KODERE was formerly used as a synonym for WATTERSON, members of the same family being called indifferently by one name or the other. KODERE, however, was evidently used merely as a nickname, as it is not found in the Parish Registers. Professor Rhŷs ingeniously conjectures that KODERE may be a contraction of *MacOtter*, and that WATTERSON is OTTERSON.

WATTERSON is as common in the southern parishes as Qualtrough.

WATERSONE * [1422], WATTERSON [1504], WATER, WATERSON [1511], WALTERSON [1547].
Rushen, Arbory, Malew (vc), German, Patrick (c), elsewhere (u).

QUILLIAM, contracted from *MacUilliam*, 'William's son.' The name ' MACWILLIAM † (A.D. 1213,) in Ireland was taken by the De Burgos, whose descendants were numerous in the counties of Galway and Mayo. In 1225 King Henry III. granted the province of Connaught to Richard de Burgo. Another Richard de Burgo was Governor of the Isle of Man A.D. 1292.

Compare (Irish and Gaelic) McWILLIAM, (English) WILLIAMSON, WILLIAMS.
Marown, Malew, German, Patrick (c), elsewhere (u).

CREBBIN, contracted from *MacRoibin*, ' Robin's son.' A minor branch of the Barrets, of Tirawley, in Connaught, took the surname of MACROBERT.

Compare (Irish) CRIBBIN, GRIBBIN, GRIBBON,

* In the British Museum Copy only.
† Four Mast., Vol. III., p. 180.

(Scotch) ROBSON, ROBERTSON, (Welsh) PROBERT, (English) ROBERTS, ROBINSON.

> MACROBYN [1511], CREBBIN [1640], CRIBBIN [1666], CREBIN [1668].
>
> Jurby, Andreas, Rushen (vc), Braddan, German, Arbory (u), hardly found elsewhere.

CUBBON contracted from *MacGibbon*, 'Gilbert's son.'

> 'The descendants of Gilbert Fitzgerald, a younger son of John Fitzgerald, ancestor of the houses of Kildare and Desmond, assumed the appellation of MACGIBBON.'*

Compare (Irish) GIBBON, GIBBONS, MACGIBBON, McKIBBIN, (Gaelic) MACCUBBIN, (English) GIBSON, GILBERTSON, GIBBS, GUBBINS.

> GYBONE [1429], M'CUBBON [1430], MACGIBBON [1511], CUBBON [1605], CUBBIN [1645], CUBON [1649], GUBBON, CHUBBON [1679].

KINRY, contracted from *MacHenry*, 'Henry's son.'

> 'MACHENRY,' A.D. 1248.†

Dr. Joyce, however, says that the MACHENRY in Ireland is derived from *Innerighe*, 'early riser,' and that many MACHENRYS now call themselves EARLY and YARDLY. We find 'MACINNERIGH'‡ in O'Huidhrin's poem, and in 1511 we have MACENERE as well as MACHENRY, so it looks as if some, at any rate, of the KINRYS derived their names from this source. In the Isle of Man KINRY has been invariably translated into HARRISON, which has now, except in the parishes of Andreas and Bride, almost entirely superseded it.

> MACENERE, MACHENRY [1511], KYNRY [1669], KINRY [1693].
>
> Andreas, Bride (c), Lezayre (u), hardly found elsewhere.

---

* O'Donovan, p. 23. † Four Mast., Vol. III., p. 200.
‡ O'Huidhrin, p. 119.

CRIGGARD and KRICKART (obsolete), contracted from *MacRichard*, 'Richard's son.'

'MACRICHARD,' A.D. 1462.*

The MACRICKARDS or MACRICHARDS were descendants of the MACWILLIAMS.

CRICKART [1649], KRICKART [1657], CRIGART [1664], CRIGGARD [1771].

The name was formerly common in the parish of Jurby.

MACSHARRY and MACSHERRY [1511] (obsolete), is a corruption of *MacGeoffrey*, 'Geoffrey's son.'

'The Hodnets of the Strand, a Shropshire family, took the surname of MACSHERRY,'† when they settled in Ireland.

We have KNOCKSHARRY, possibly so called from a proprietor of this name, though the derivation usually given is from *Sharragh*, a 'foal.'

'Magrath MACSHERRY, Bishop of Conmaicne,' A.D. 1230.‡

Since the Isle of Man became subject to English rule a considerable number of English, Scotch, and other family names have been imported. Some of these have undergone some corruption in insular use, while a few have even been translated into Manx, often, of course, with very grotesque misapprehensions of their meaning. We mention here those which are known to have been in use for, at least, several generations, omitting such as are of merely incidental occurrence :

---

* Four Mast., Vol. IV.   † O'Donovan, p. 24.
‡ Four Mast., Vol. III., p. 250.

OATES and OATS. This surname is not uncommon in England, and is probably a derivative of the Norman Christian name OTE or OTES. 'Sir Ote' was one of the brothers of Gamelyn (see the 'Tale of Gamelyn,' erroneously ascribed to Chaucer). It is not so common in the Isle of Man now as formerly. It was occasionally found as a Christian name also.

> Braddan, Santon (vc), Marown, German, Onchan (c), elsewhere (u).

CORJEAG is an attempt at translating the English CAVENDISH (imagined to mean 'giving dish'!)

> 'CURJEIG, s.f. an alms dish. . . . This word is used for the surname of Cavendish (in Manks), but more probably giving dish.'*

At the end of the sixteenth century a family called CAVENDISH settled in the parish of Michael, where they held property in 1583 (*vide Liber Vastarum*), and from 1611 (when the register commences) to 1650 their births, marriages, and deaths are duly entered under that name, but after that time, though the family is known not to have died out, the name disappears, and CORJEAG entirely supplants it, the two names having co-existed since 1611. CORJEAG† is still almost confined to Michael, occurring rarely in the adjacent parishes and not at all elsewhere.

> CORJEAGE [1611], CORJAIGE [1617], CORJEAG [1626], COR-JAGE [1658], CORJAGUE [1736], CORJEGGE [1796].
> Michael (c), Ballaugh, German (u).

---

* Cregeen, Manx Dictionary, p. 51.

† Several people of this name, who have moved into Douglas, have changed their name into CAVENDISH again.

GUMMERY, a corruption of MONTGOMERY. A MONT-
GOMERY settled in Kirk Michael, and married
in 1668, when he is styled MUNTGUMMERY;
at the baptism of his first child MOUNTGOMERY;
two years later MCGUMMERY; in 1688 GUMERY,
in 1693 GUMMERY, and in 1705 MCGUMMERY.

> GUMMERY is now the accepted form.
> This name is confined to Kirk Michael.

CARALAGH (obsolete) is a correct translation of
'*Careful.*' An English family of this name settled
in the parish of Braddan at the end of the sixteenth century, and their name was soon trans·
lated.

> CARALAGH [1623], CARALAUGH [1656].
> Braddan (c) formerly, Santon (u), not found elsewhere.

COTTINGHAM (obsolete), possibly from one of the
villages so named in England, was formerly a
common name in Maughold and Braddan. It
is not found after the middle of the eighteenth
century. It took a variety of forms in Manx
lips.

> COTTINGHAM [1604], COTTIHAM [1628], COTTIGAM [1644],
> COTTIAM [1647], COTTEMAN [1732].

RADCLIFFE and RATCLIFF, *i.e.*, *Red-cliff*, has been
a common name in the north of the Island
from an early period. It is a place-name in
Lancashire, where this family was at one time of
some importance.

> RADCLIFFE [1497], RATCLIFFE [1540], RATCLIFF [1674],
> RATCLIFT [1676], RATTLIFFE [1693].
> Andreas (vc), Maughold, German, Bride (c), elsewhere (u).

BANKES, formerly BANCKS [1637], (now extinct in the Isle of Man). This family held property in the parish of Onchan for many years. BANKS'S HOWE was named from them.

BACON. The first member of this family settled in the Isle of Man in 1724.

CÆSAR [1643] (obsolete). The principal family of this name held property in Santon, and at Ballahick, in Malew.

CALCOTT, or CALCOT, contracted from *Caledcott* (cold-cot), the name of their estate in Cheshire. They were a powerful family in the Isle of Man in the sixteenth and seventeenth centuries, but their name is now very uncommon.

'The Prioress of Douglas and Robert CALCOTE for the freshwater fishing of Douglas this year as in the preceding year 4/2.' (*Lib. Assed.*, 1511.)

'Robt CALCOATS, receiver of the Castle of Man,' 1532.*

CALCOTE [1511], CALCOATS [1532], CALCOTTS [1586], CALCOTT [1629], CALCOT [1689].

CRYSTAL and CRISTALSON are corruptions of CHRISTOPHER and CHRISTOPHERSON respectively, which have come to us from Scotland. They both occur in 1511, but are very uncommon now.

CHRISTORY is also a corruption of CHRISTOPHER. It was formerly common in the parish of Jurby, but is now uncommon everywhere.

CRYSTORY [1624], CHRISTRY [1640], CHRISTERY [1714], CHRYSTRY [1738], CHRISTORY [1750].

---

* Statute Law Book, p. 29.

CRAIG, formerly usually CORRAIGE (*Caraig*, a 'rock,') is a translation of the French *Delaroche*. A French family of this name settled in Scotland at an early date, and had their name transformed in this way. The name is uncommon. It may, perhaps, in some cases, be derived from the (O.N.) *Kráka* (Danish *Krage*), 'a crow,' which is found in the *Landnámabóc* as a nickname. BALLACORAIGE is the name of a farm in Ballough.

CORRAIGE [1599], CORRAIG [1700], CRAIG [1776].

FARRANT, from *far, fare*, signifying 'travel,' and *and* signifying 'life,' 'spirit.'
Compare (old German and English) FERRAND.
It may, perhaps, be contracted from FERDINAND.
FARAUND [1511], FARRANT [1653].

ELLISON [1670], contracted from ELIASON, is found chiefly in the northern part of the Island.
Compare (Danish) ELISSEN, ELIASSEN.

FLETCHER [1621]. Edward FLETCHER was Deputy-Governor in 1621, and Governor in 1622. This family, a branch of a well-known family in Lancashire, held considerable property here in the seventeenth and eighteenth centuries. The estate of BALLAFLETCHER in Braddan, which was their property, formerly contained five quarterlands.

FAIRBROTHER [1682], a translation of the French *beaufrère*, probably came to us from Scotland. It was formerly common in Peel, but is not found in the Island now.

FREER, from (French) *frère*, 'brother,' was formerly common in Jurby.

> FFREER [1607], FREER [1690].

CREER, probably from *MacFreer*.

> CRERE [1611], CREER [1622], CREERE [1652].

NELSON (see Chap. I., Part II.) ought to come under this section when it is of independent origin, but, as we have already said, it is usually a translation of KNEAL in the Isle of Man.

GREAVES [1740], GRAVES [1779]. Found in Peel.

GICK [1663], GICKE [1666].

> Malew, Santon (c), elsewhere (u).

HARRISON [1504] is, in many cases, merely a translation of KINRY (which see), but, doubtless, many immigrants bore this name when they arrived, as it is constantly found at an early date, and is, moreover, common in the Isle of Man.

HEYWOOD [1643], from EWOOD, the name of their property in Lancashire. Peter HEYWOOD, on his English estates being confiscated in 1643, came to reside in the Isle of Man. His son became Governor, and the family attained considerable power and influence in the Island. The name is not found here now.

CLEATOR is probably a name of English extraction, though McCLETTER being found in 1511 would seem to point to a Celtic origin.

> Cf. CLEATOR-MOOR in Cumberland.

> McCLETTER [1511], CLEATER [1670], CLEADER [1696], CLATOR [1700], CLAYTOR [1713], CLEATOR [1715], CLAITOR [1751].

> Bride (vc), Jurby, Andreas, Lezayre (c), elsewhere (u).

HUTCHIN, HUTCHEN, HUDGEON, from the root *hig*, *hog*, *hug*, 'thought,' 'study.'

Compare (Scotch) HUTCHEON, McHUTCHIN.

(English) HUTCHINSON.

HUCHON [1511], HUTCHEON [1540], HUTCHIN [1570], HUTCHEN [1586], HUDGEON [1785], MacHUTCHIN [1801].

It is now very uncommon.

Formerly (c) in Marown, German, Rushen, and (u) in Maughold, Malew, Lonan, Arbory, Patrick.

HAMPTON [1689], from a common English place-name.

Braddan, Michael (c) formerly.

MADDRELL. A Lancashire place-name, chiefly found in the south of the Island.

MATHERELL [1499],* MADDRELL [1643].
Malew, Rushen, Arbory (c), elsewhere (u).

NORRIS, formerly NORRES.† This family followed the Stanleys from Lancashire to the Isle of Man, where they held several important official positions.

'Gubon John NORRES'‡ [1422], 'Sir Huan NORRES'‡ [1499], NORRIS [1586].

PARR, formerly PARRE,† is first found in the Isle of Man in 1504.

Richard PARR was Bishop in 1637. Various Rectors and Vicars, also Deemster PARR, the

---

* This date is given in the Statute Law Book as 1419, but 1499 is probably correct.

† These names are not found in the Island now.

‡ Statute Law Book.

learned author of ' Parr's Abstract,' were members of the same family.

It was a well-known Lancashire family.

SANSBURY, generally SAMSBURY formerly. Possibly derived from the village of SAMLESBURY in Lancashire. The SAMSBURYS were owners of Ronaldsway before the Christians.

SAUNESBURY [1511], SANSBERIE [1521], SAMSBURY [1586], SANSBURE [1654], SANSBURY [1657].

The name is much less common than formerly.

Malew, German (c) formerly, elsewhere (u).

STANLEY [1408].* A younger branch of the Derby family settled in the Isle of Man for two or three generations, and held property chiefly in Arbory.

STOWELL and STOLE.

This name is placed amongst the exotic surnames because no Celtic or Scandinavian etymology appears to be adducible for it. Its early occurrence with the prefix *Mac*, however, is an argument in favour of its being of native origin.

McSTOLE, McSTOILE [1511], McSTOYLL [1540], STOLE [1649], STOIL [1654], STOWELL [1772].

Stowell has now gradually superseded the older forms.

Malew, Arbory, Santon, Lonan (c), elsewhere (u).

STANDISH [1511].* A Lancashire place-name. It was never common in the Isle of Man.

WILLIAM STANDISH was proprietor of Pulrose in Braddan in 1511.

* These names are not found in the Island now.

TAUBMAN, a name of German extraction. It is not uncommon in Germany. In modern German it would mean 'deaf man,' but its real signification is, doubtless, something very different.

TUBMAN [1601], TAUBMAN [1610], TUMMAN [1651], TUNMAN [1652].

Malew, German, Arbory (c), elsewhere (u).

THOMPSON, first found in 1598, has never been a common name in the Isle of Man.

TYLDESLEY,* a Lancashire place-name.

Thurstan de TYLDESLEY was one of the Commissioners for Sir John Stanley in 1417. Thurstan TYLDESLEY was Receiver-General in 1532, and Thomas TYLDESLEY, Water Bailiff in the same year, and Deputy Governor in 1540. They lived at the Friary (Bemeccan) in the parish of Arbory. They were powerful and devoted adherents of the Stanleys.

VONDY is not so common as formerly.

MACWANTY? [1417], GAUNTY? [1429], MACGUANTIE, [1430], VANTIE [1602], VONDY [1606], VANDY [1608].

Jurby, Bride, Malew (c), elsewhere (u).

SKINNER. Now scarcely found.

McSKYNNER [1511], SKINNER [1623].

Formerly Andreas (vc), Jurby (c) elsewhere (u).

VINCH is the same name as FINCH.

FINCH was a proprietor in Douglas, whence FINCH Road. During the eighteenth century the name was much commoner than it is now.

VINCH [1685], FFINCH [1727], FINCH [1750].

---

* This name is not found in the Island now.

WATTLEWORTH.   A curious name, formerly much commoner than it is now.

WATERFORTH? [1422], WATTLEWORTH [1652], WATELE-FORT [1673].

German (vc), Malew (c), elsewhere (u).

WOODS [1586].

Maughold, Lezayre, Santon, Rushen (c), elsewhere (u).

SHERLOCK.

SHURLOGE [1650], SHURLOG [1652], SHERLOCK [1663].

There is a BALLA-SHURLOGE in Arbory.   The name is now scarcely found.

Formerly Malew, Arbory (c), elsewhere (u).

CHAPTER V.

THE oldest names recorded in the Isle of Man are those in the ogam character, which was in use about the fifth and sixth centuries. In the curious old Irish 'Tale of the Children of Lir,' who are said to have lived in the Isle of Man, we are told that 'their ogam names were written and their lamentation rites were performed, and heaven was obtained for their souls through the prayers of Mochaomhog,' who may possibly be identified with Coemanus or Germanus, one of the earliest Manx bishops. However this may have been, we find, as might have been expected from the constant early connection of the Isle of Man with Ireland, that the names on these inscriptions are mainly of purely Irish origin. The earliest discovery of an ogam inscription, that at Balla-queeny, near Port St. Mary, was by the Rev. F. B. Grant, only fourteen years ago. This inscription has been deciphered by Professor Rhŷs: BIVAICUNAS MAQUI MUCOI CUNAVA, and by Mr. Kneale: BIFAIDONAS MAQI MUCOI QUNAFA, which he renders '[The Stone] of Bifaidon, the son of Mucoi Conaf.' On further consideration Professor Rhŷs thought it possible that

BIVICUNAS should be read BIVAIDDONAS. According to him the nominative of this should be BIVAIDDU, which he compares with BEOAEDH, a name which occurs in the 'Martyrology of Donegal.' He thinks that the termination *aedh* is related to the Irish *aed*, now translated 'Hugh,' and that this *aed*, and its longer form *aidan*, has driven the related form *aidu*, which we have in the above compound, out of use. Mr. Kneale remarks that BIFODON occurs in an Irish ogam. MACQUI or MACQI is the ancient form of MAC, 'son.'

MUCOI is a word which occurs frequently in ogam inscriptions; it has probably some connection with the Irish *mucaidh*, a swineherd or owner.

CUNAVA or QUNAFA is the first part of a longer word.

On another stone close by are the words DOVAIDONA MAQUI. DOVAIDONA(S) is the genitive of DOVAIDU, which may be connected with *aed*, as BIVAIDDU.

A fragmentary inscription, at Bemeccan in the parish of Arbory, has recently been read by Professor Rhŷs as follows: CUNAMAGLI MA[QI, etc. CUNAMAGLI is a genitive. There was a Breton saint called CONOMAGLI. A later form CONMÆGYL is given in the Saxon Chronicle as the name of one of the Welsh kings vanquished by Ceawlin at the battle of Deorham in A.D. 577. Its corresponding Irish forms are CONMAL and CONMHAL, where MÁL probably means a prince or hero.* Professor Rhŷs has also recently discovered, on the back of the *Mael-Lomchon* cross at Kirk Michael, an inscription which bears a strong resemblance to the so-called 'scratch' ogams found in Scotland and Orkney. These ogams are of later date

* For full discussion of these ogams see Manx Note Book, Nos. 8, 10, and 12.

than the ordinary ogams, which have been chiefly found in the South of Ireland and in South Wales. This inscription has been read by the Earl of Southesk as follows: MUNCOMALL AFI UA MULLGUC, ' Mucomael, son of O'Maelguc.'*

MUCO is equivalent to MUCOI (see pp. 109, 110).

MAEL as a suffix is probably connected with *Mál,* ' a prince,' rather than with *Mael,* ' a servitor,' which is almost invariably a prefix.

MAELGUC. Here *Mael* probably means servitor, while *guc* may be connected with *Cueg* or *Cuic,* which has become the surnames QUIG or KEAG in Ireland, and QUIG(GIN) and KEIG in the Isle of Man.

Next in order of time come the names on our numerous crosses inscribed with the Scandinavian letters called runes; these crosses were for the most part erected between the middle of the eleventh and the end of the thirteenth century. The pure Norse names are given first: AÞISL, which is probably equivalent to EADGILS, is found on the *Mael-Lomchon* cross at Kirk Michael. A very interesting monograph on this name, which was sent to the writer by the late Dr. Vigfusson, is appended.

' It is not his life, now but a dream and shadow, but his name we want to discuss. In the whole range of Northern nomenclature, old and modern, outside this Manx Cross, it is only once that we meet with this name, viz., the old King Aþisl of Upsala, supposed to have lived in the fourth or fifth century. His name would be a riddle to us, but for the old English Epos, " Beolwulf," where the story of this very king is told, and his name is given as EÁDGISL, answering to Norse

* See *Academy,* November 26, 1887.

Auð-gisl, which last name therefore must somehow have been ground and worn into Aþisl. But how is the question? How came this ancient Upsala king by his name in this worn, ground-down form, quite unknown in Sweden or elsewhere in Scandinavia? The full name Auð-GISL occurs some five or six times in the Icelandic Sagas, hence the name was known in its old form; once it must needs have sounded so in the old lay *Ynglingatal* (the generations of the Ynlings, or ancient kings of Upsala). How is it, then, that that very poem as it was taken down by the Icelandic chroniclers gives Aþisl, especially as there is no full analogy for the change? Auþ could never in a Norse mouth change into Aþ. The Kirk Michael Runic Cross gives, we think, the clue. Here in fact we meet for the first time with a flesh and blood Aþisl, a man married to a lady of a Gaelic name. We infer from this that Aþisl is a Manx form of the old Norse and Swedish AuþGISL; the name in fact passed through Norse-Celtic mouths and Aþ is due to some analogy—in this case a false analogy—with other Manx names, such as Aþacan. But now about the old Upsala king: how has this Manx form got hold of him, and crept into the text of the Norse poem *Ynglingatal*, and hence into the *Skioldunga Saga*, and the old generation of kings (*Langfedgatal*)? There is, so far as I can see, only one way to explain this, viz., that the poem, before being transplanted to Iceland, had passed through Manx or Sodor mouths and memories, and that the Icelanders learnt it there, or from Manx or Sodor tradition, either in Iceland from "winter sitters" there, or abroad in the Isles themselves. This cannot have taken place at a very early date, for

it would take time to grind Auðgisl down into Aþisl ;
the poem, therefore, must for generations have lived in
the mouths of the men of the Isles.   The Aþisl of the
Kirk Michael Cross would have lived about the end of
the twelfth or early thirteenth century ; but there is no
reason to think that he was the first of that name.   Yet
when that cross was carved Auþisl was in the Manx
changed into Aþisl, but how long since ?   Are, the
Icelandic historian, wrote in the beginning of the
twelfth century ; in his days it was Aþisl, and there was
no trace of an older form.   There is no evidence that
the poem was known in Iceland before his days ; it is
even possible that either he, or a contemporary of his,
unearthed this poem and more of that kind in the Isles
of the West from a bard or minstrel there.   Hence the
Manx form of King Auðgisl's name has obtained in all
Scandinavian histories down to this day.

BJARNAR, the genitive of *Björn*, ‘ bear,’ occurs on the
    Ufaac-Gaut Cross at Andreas, which was wrought
    by ‘ GAUT the son of BJÖRN.’   There are forty-two
    Biorns in the *Landnámabóc*.   It is the name which
    now appears in the forms BARNES and BARNEY.

GAUT or GOUT and GAUTR are different forms of the
    same name, which seems to mean ‘ father.’   *Gautr*
    is a poetical name of Odin.

GRIMS, the genitive of *Grima*, ‘ a hood ’ or ‘ a cowl,’ may
    reasonably be conjectured to be the whole name of
    which the letters R.I.M.S. occur on a cross at Kirk
    Michael.

    Grimr was an epithet applied to Odin from his
    travelling in disguise.   It is a common masculine
    proper name in Iceland.

LIÙT-ULBS is the genitive of LIUT-WOLF (*liot-ulfr* *), 'people wolf.'

ROSCIL is a rare form of the commoner HROSS-KETILL, usually contracted into HROSS-KELL,† 'Horse-Kettle.' ROSKELL is a modern English surname.

RUMUND, or HROMUND, from *Hroðr*, 'fame, reputation,' and *Mundr*,‡ is, according to Dr. Vigfusson, the name indicated by the letters R.U.M.U. found on a cross at Kirk Michael.

SONTULF, or SANDULF, from *Sont* or *Sond*, i.e., *Santh*, 'sooth, true,' and *Ulf*, 'wolf.' ULB or ULF, 'wolf,' is found singly on the Olaf cross, at Ballaugh.

There are also the following compounds with Þórr, viz., ÞÙRBIAURN, 'Thor's bear'; ÞÙR-LIBR, or ÞORLEIFR, 'Thor's patrimony or inheritance'; ÞÙR-ULFS, 'Thor's wolf'; and ÞÙR-VALDR, 'Thor's might.' These names are all common in the *Landnámabóc*.

There are also five Scandinavian female names on the crosses :

ARIN-BIAURG, probably meaning 'hearth-help,' is found on a cross at Kirk Andreas, which describes her as the wife of 'Sandulf the Black.' This name is found in Iceland in its contracted form of ARN-BIORG.

ASRIÞI, or ASRITH, found on a cross in St. Germains, is a contraction of AS-FRIÐR. *Friðr* means 'fair ;' *as*, '*semi-deus*.'

FRIÞU, or *Fritha*, also from *Friðr*. According to the inscription on the cross at Kirk Michael, where her name occurs, she was the mother of 'Olaf the son of Thorwolf the Red.'

---

* See CORLETT, *ante*.   † See CASTELL, *ante*.
‡ See CASEMENT, *ante*.

Os-ruþr, or As-thruth. Thruth was the name of a goddess, who was a daughter of Thor and Sif. This, according to Dr. Vigfusson, is a true Norse name, though he has never met with it except on the fragment of a cross at St. John's Chapel.

þariþ, or Thorrid, a feminine derivative from þórr, is found on a cross at Onchan.

The following names of Celtic origin are also found on the crosses :

Dufgal, from *dubh-gall*, 'black stranger,' still common in Scotland in the form MacDougall. Dougal, or Dugal, is also used as a Christian name.

Mal-Lumcun, or Mael-Lomchon, 'Lomchu's servant.' There is a Cill Lomchon in Ulster, dedicated to St. Lomchu, whose name appears in the Martyrology of Donegal, on the 9th of January. The meaning of the name is not known.

Ucifat is something like Ugfadan, a name given by the Four Masters in A.D. 904.

Mur-ciolu, a female name, is the same as Myrgiol, or Muirgheal, an Irish king's daughter, recorded in the *Landnámabóc*.

The remaining names are difficult to identify :

Crinaas, the genitive of Crinaa, and Eabs cannot be identified.

Onon may possibly be connected with the Norse Onundr.

Druian, or Truian, seems the same name as Droian, found in an ogam inscription in the Shetlands. It

is remarkable that close by this cross, in the parish
of Bride, there is a place called GLEN TRUAN,
where there never has been a *strooan*, ‘ stream.’
The name FROCA occurs once in an Icelandic place-
name, FRACKA-NESS, and once in the *Gold Thoris*
Saga.   Dr. Vigfusson says that it is certainly not
a Norse name.

APPENDIX A.

Obsolete Christian Names.—(a) Men.

APEKE (?).

DERMOT, from *Diarmaid*, ‘ Free man ’ (see KERMODE).

GERMEDE is probably a corruption of the same.

DILNOW and GILNOW are probably from *Giolla-Noo*,
‘ Saint’s servant.’

DONCAN, DONKANE, either from *Donnachu*, ‘ Dun chief,’
or *Donngal*, ‘ Dun stranger.’   DUNCAN is still a
common Christian name in Scotland.

DONALD and DONOLD, from *Domhnall*, ‘ Proud chieftain.’   (See CANNELL.)

FINLO, FINLOW, FYNLO, or PHINLO, is said to mean
‘ Dane,’ but on uncertain authority.

The following have the prefix *giolla*, ‘ servant ’: GIL-
CRIST, ‘ Christ’s servant ’ (see MYLCHREEST); GIL-
PEDER, ‘ Peter’s servant ’; GILREA (see MYLREA);
GILROY, ‘ Red servant ’ (see MYLROI); GILPATRICK,
‘ Patrick’s servant.’

GIBBON or GYBBON is an Irish corruption of *Gilbert*
(see CUBBON).

JANKYN and JENKIN are diminutives of *John*; the latter
is common in Wales at the present day.

JOHNAIGUE, ‘ Young John.’

MOLD, possibly from *Maol*, 'tonsured.'

MOLDONNY, possibly from *Maol-duine*, 'tonsured man.'

RANOLD and RENOLD are corruptions of REGINALD (see CRENNELL and CRELLIN).

SILVESTER (Latin), 'Living in a wood.'

SYMOND and SYMYN are connected with the Hebrew SIMEON.

(b) *Women.*

In the early registers AVERICKE is common, and there are also the forms AURICK and ARICK. The name probably became popular from having been that of AUFRICA, or AFFRICA, daughter of Olave the Black, and heiress of the kingdom of Man, who, in 1305, conveyed her right and interest in the Isle of Man to her husband, Sir Simon de Montacute.

BAHEE, BAHIE, and BAHY, which sometimes degenerate into BAGGY, are obscure. Miss Yonge translates BAHEE, 'life,' but gives no authority.*

There are a number of names with the prefix *cally*, a corruption of *cailleach*, 'a nun, or handmaid,' which is equivalent to *Giolla*, prefixed to a man's name, thus: CALLYCRIST, 'Christ's handmaid'; CALLYBRID, 'Bridget's handmaid'; CALLYPHARICK and CALLYPHERICK, 'Patrick's handmaid'; CALLYBORRY, CALLYVORREY, and CALLAUGHWORRY, 'Mary's handmaid'; CALLYCHROWNEY, probably 'Rooney's handmaid.' ROONEY, Latinised into RUNIUS, is the patron saint of Marown parish church.

COONIE and COONEY?

INY, INE, INNEE, and INNY, usually mean 'daughter,' being corruptions of INNEEN. Thus we find in

* Christian Names, Charlotte M. Yonge.

the registers such entries as ' 1598 AN INE ILL-
WORREY,' *i.e.*, 'An Illworrey's daughter '; ' 1609
CALLY PHARICK INE GAWNE,' *i.e.*, 'Cally Pharick
Gawne's daughter.' Here INE clearly means
daughter, as second Christian names were un-
heard of at the dates given. INE and INNY, however, also appear as Christian names, as in INNY
KEIG. In this case they may correspond with the
Irish female name EITHNE, which has been corrupted into AINE and HANNAH. AINE was one of
the grand-daughters of the Irish king Lear. The
name means ' joy,' ' praise,' and also ' fasting,'
according to Miss Yonge.

JONY is probably a corruption of JOHANNA.

MALLY is a corruption of MARY. Miss Yonge gives
MOISSEY as a Manx corruption of Mary, but the
name does not occur in the parochial registers.

MARRIOD and MARRIOTT are also corruptions of Mary.

APPENDIX B.

Nicknames used in the Isle of Man.

IN other than Celtic countries surnames have most frequently originated from nicknames descriptive of the
personal peculiarities of some early ancestor. Thus in
England we find families bearing such names as
WHITE, BLACK, SHORT, LONG, etc.; and amongst
the Romans, the cognomina CRASSUS, ' fat '; VARUS,
' bow-legged '; CINCINNATUS, ' curly,' and many
others, continued to be borne by the descendants
of the men to whom they were originally applicable.
That this mode of forming surnames is less common
among the peoples of Celtic speech is a fact which

is probably due to the organisation of the clan
having been more fully developed, and preserved to a
later date amongst these peoples than elsewhere.
It is certainly not the fact that descriptive nicknames
were uncommon amongst the Celts. On the contrary,
the quick fancy of this race has always displayed itself
in the readiness with which sobriquets of this kind were
invented. Many such distinctive epithets amongst the
Welsh and Irish have become famous in history, as
HYWEL DA, 'Howel the Good'; DONALD GORM,
'Blue Donald'; MALCOLM CANMORE, 'Malcolm Great-
head'; CON BACACH, 'Con the Lame'; O'CONOR
DON, 'Brown O'Conor,' etc.

Sir Henry Piers, writing in the year 1682 to Anthony,
Lord Bishop of Meath, gave the following account of
Irish sobriquets :* 'They take much liberty, and seem
to do it with delight, in giving of nicknames; and if a
man have any imperfection or evil habit, he shall be
sure to hear of it in the nickname. Thus if he be blind,
lame, squint-eyed, gray-eyed, be a stammerer in speech,
be left-handed, to be sure he shall have one of these
added to his name; so also from his color of hair, as
black, red, yellow, brown, etc.; and from his age, as
young, old; or from what he addicts himself to, or
much delights in, as in draining, building, fencing, or
the like; so that no man whatever can escape a *nickname,* who lives among them—so libidinous are they in
this kind of raillery, they will give nicknames *per antiphrasim,* or contrariety of speech,' etc. Dr. Joyce
writes :† 'In early life I knew a village where more
than half the people were familiarly known by *nick-*

* O'Donovan, p. 19.
† Joyce, Irish Names of Places, 2nd series, p. 156.

names, which were always used, the proper names being hardly ever mentioned. One man, on account of his endurance in faction fights, was called GADDERAGH, which literally means a tough fellow like a *gad,* or withe ; another was never called by any name but CLOOSEDARRAG, ‘ Red ears ’; a third was PHIL-Á-GADDY, or ‘ Phil the thief ’; a fourth SHAUN-NA-BOINTRE, ‘ John the (son of the) widow ’ ; and one man, who was a notorious schemer, was universally called, by way of derision, or *per antiphrasim,* THOMAS - Á - SAGART, “ Tom the priest.” ’

In the Isle of Man, as in all small stationary communities, nicknames were much used. Indeed, in certain parishes where there were many bearing the same name, as CORLETT, in Ballaugh, and QUALTROUGH, in Rushen, they were an absolute necessity for the sake of distinction. It has been thought advisable, by way of illustration of what has been said on this subject in Chapter II., to furnish some specimens of the nicknames which were formerly recorded in the Parish Registers, as well as of those which are still in use. They will be discussed under the following heads : Nicknames derived from (1) Character or appearance ; (2) Place of abode or origin ; (3) Parents’ Christian names ; (4) Trade or occupation.

The earliest nicknames from *character or appearance* are on the inscribed crosses, where we find ‘ THORWOLF the *Red,*’ (*raupa*) ; ‘ GRIM the *Black* ’; and ‘ SANDULF the *Black* ’ (*suarti*), of Scandinavian origin ; and THORLAF NEACI, where NEACI is probably Celtic (*vide* UA NIOC, Four Mast., 1032 and 1128).

‘ YE NATURAL,’ referring to idiocy, is unfortunately a somewhat common entry in the Registers.

'TOMMY SCATTY,' 'puny,' or 'lean' Tommy.

'CANNELL-EAR;' perhaps from the size of those appendages.

'JOHN COWLEY, STOOP,' and 'KATHREN THE CRIPPLE,' signify bodily infirmities.

In 1660 'Ann Watterson (BEN VANE'S sister)' was buried in Malew. BEN VANE perhaps means 'White Benjamin.'

In the Maughold Register we find 'OLD CARRAD BANE Buryed ye 14 November, 1683.' Old CARRAD, or GARRET, had probably white hair.

'ILIAM DHONE,' 'Brown-haired William,' is the well-known WILLIAM CHRISTIAN, Receiver-General and Governor of the Island, who was 'shott to death,' at Hango Hill, on the 2nd January, 1662.

'KELLY THE RED,' and 'JIMMY THE RED,' doubt-less refer to the colour of the hair. 'JANE GAWN, MANN,' perhaps betokens masculine qualities. 'WM. KELLY, CROSS CAP'; 'THOS. CORLETT, SOLOMON'; 'JOHN CRIDEEN, SMILE'; 'JOHN KNEAL, GRUMBLE'; 'WM. PRESTON, JOY'; 'THOS. FARGHER, CROKE'; are vividly descriptive of the temperaments of their owners. 'JIM-Y-LORD,' 'PRINCE,' and 'PRINCE-BEG,' may have designated a haughty demeanour. 'TURK' was a common synonym for an unruly child. 'JINKS' was doubtless up to many little games.

Such nicknames as 'MY LOVE,' 'VEEN' *i.e.* 'DEAR,' and 'BRAVEBOY,' were perhaps given *per antiphrasim*, as Sir Henry Piers hath it.

The burials of 'THOS. MᶜYLCARANE, A BATCHELOR,' and 'ROBT. SKEALLEY, A MARRIED MAN,' are recorded just as if there were something unusual in either con-dition.

'JOHN CORLETT, MUNLAA,' was well known many years ago in the parish of Ballaugh. He was called 'MUNLAA,' or 'Mid-day,' from his skill at being able to discern the exact dinner-hour, at all seasons, without the aid of a watch, and, as watches were uncommon in those days, it was a valuable qualification.

'SPEED,' and 'CUT-THE-WIND,' denote fleetness of foot. The latter appertained to a woman who lived in Ramsey early in the present century. She disappeared mysteriously, and is supposed to have been drowned.

'CANNELL THE TIMBER' may have had a wooden leg. 'PHILLY THE TWEET' is probably a euphonistic form of Philip the *Toot*, or stupid. 'JOHN CURGHEY, STRIKE,' died long before strikes were fashionable. The nicknames of WILLIAM CHRISTIAN, and EDWARD CHRISTIAN, his son, *i.e.*, 'NO' and 'NO BEG,' would seem to be of an entirely negative character, if it were not that 'NO' is corrupted from *yn-oe*, 'the grand-father.' 'CHRISTIAN NO' belonged to Lezayre, and had property in the parish of Maughold. He was ex-communicated by Bishop Murray (*circa* 1825), and died a miserable death from starvation in consequence. (This was the last case of excommunication in the Isle of Man.) At one time he held the 'staff' land, in Maughold, which, it is said, entitled him to keep his hat on in Court.

'JOHN COTTIER, WIN,' 'JOHN GARRETT, CUP,' 'SIL-VESTER QUIGGIN, QUARTER,' and 'JOHN WATTERSON, SON TO JO, CALLED 2D,' are curious and mysterious epithets.

2. Nicknames from *place of abode or origin* are numerous and very convenient, and it is from nick-names of this kind that the two surnames, KINRIG and

KINRED, have probably arisen (see pp. 77, 78). Landed proprietors, till quite a recent period, were almost universally known by the names of their properties. Many of these appellations, which at first sight appear to be nicknames, are really meant to denote places of abode : *e.g.*, *salley* for Ballasalla, *vane* for Ballavarvane ; *trollag*, *nank*, and *croke* for the farms of the same names. The following verse from a clever squib, written in 1837, when there was considerable agitation against the House of Keys and their mode of election, gives a good specimen of their form of nomenclature :

> ' " They'll have BALLAVARVANE," says JACK MEARY VOOAR.
> " Back to KARANE," says JUAN JEM MOORE.
> " Why not BALJEAN ?" says DAVY ST. ANN.
> " He's too cross in the grain," says the UNION MILL MAN.'

The name of the proprietor was, however, usually attached to the farm as ' BRIDSON BALLAVARVANE,' ' MOORE BALJEAN.' Sometimes the titles were more familiar as ' BILLY BALLURE.'

In the registers we find such entries as ' ELIN TAYLOR, FILIA OULD THO. BELOWN,' *i.e.*, daughter of old Thomas of Belown ; DAN CURGHEY, CALLED DAN BALDROMA.' The sobriquets of ' MOUNTANIER,' ' HIGH-LAND,' ' JOHN KELLY OF YE MOUNTAINS,' ' JOHN STOLEY VULLEE,' *i.e.*, of the *mullagh*, or top of the mountain, all show that their bearers lived in lofty localities. ' VILLY VAROOLE ' is an alliterative rendering of WILLY of BARRULE (the mountain), ' ED. CROW (VULGO) GAREE ' (sour land), ' CLADDY ' and ' CLADDAGHBOY ' (*claddagh*, river meadow), ' KAIGHAN Y PHURT ' (of the port), all refer to their various abodes. ' KAIGHAN Y PHURT ' is a well-known family in Kirk Michael. ' WM. GELL, BATCHELOR FROM CASTLETOWN,' ' THO. STEVEN, SON OF WILL OF THE GATE,' ' THO. MCYLLERIAH, SON TO H M

AT BALLAQUAILE,' were all, doubtless, satisfactory defini-tions at the time. In the older register books, when a stranger was buried, we generally find a reference to it. Thus 'ROBERT HOWARD FROM RAMSEY (SAXONAGH),' *i.e.*, Englishman. 'WM. COWLEY, VULGO DICT ERINAGH,' *i.e.*, commonly called Irishman. 'JANE, DAUGHTER OF JOHN WRIGHT and MARGARET GREY, FOREIGNERS,' 'MARGARET, DAUGHTER OF A FRENCHMAN.' This latter is decidedly vague, so is 'AN ENGLISHMAN BURIED.' 'EL-LINOR BRISCOE, A PASSENGER.' 'CORLETT, POLAND,' is somewhat incomprehensible. He may have been in the country referred to, but it is not very likely. Under Malew Baptisms, 1656, we find 'MARY TUNMAN, DAUGHTER TO JO. ATT GREEN.' The Green is doubtless the Bowling Green Estate, of which the Taubmans are still the proprietors. In England such designations have frequently become surnames, *e.g.*, GREEN, ATTWOOD.

3. Nicknames from *fathers'* or *mothers' Christian names* are very common. Many of these are nurse or pet-names. Thus Kennish in his poem 'The Curraghs of Lezayre':

> 'Now, I'll be bail his name is Quaile—
>   I see it in his face.'
> 'As sure as life,' exclaimed the wife,
>   'He's something to that race.'
>
> 'Yes, you are right, good dame,' said I,
>   'That is my father's name,
> Though not the one that I go by,
>   Nor like unto the same ;
> I'm called by all, both great and small,
> BILL-HOMMY-BEG-TOM-MOAR,'

i.e., Bill, the son of little Tommy, the son of big Tom, 'TOM-MOAR' being the grandfather. And again—

> 'And he who won the race I think,
>   If I do not mistake,
> Was JOHNNY-ROB of Ballacrink.'

A small selection of such sobriquets will suffice: 'JOHN KNEAL, ROBIN;' 'EWAN CHRISTIAN, HUGHEE;' 'WM. GARRETT, JACK;' 'JOHN COWLY, SAUL;' 'JOHN CALEY, HOMMY;' 'ROBERT CROW, PAUL;' 'JOHN BRIDSON, GILES;' are specimens of a large number found in the registers, and are probably all fathers' names. 'JOHN CLARKE, BAHEE;' 'JOHN KILLIP, NELLY;' 'WILLIAM CUBBON, ANNIE;' 'J. CORLETT, VESS,' *i.e.*, Bess; 'DICK QUAYLE, VESSIE,' *i.e.*, Bessie; 'JOHN CORLETT, INNY-KEIG;' 'TOM CUBBON, VARY,' *i.e.*, Mary; are probably their mothers' names. 'GILBERT TEARE, TOM NAN,' had probably both his father's and mother's name. WILLIAM CORLETT was known by the totally different name of 'BILLY GARRETT;' and we find the burial of 'JANIE BRIDSON, wife to JOHN BRIDSON,' called 'JO LAURANCE' Females seem rarely to have borne this form of nickname, but we find 'MARY LOONEY, ALS GUAGGIN ALS MARY THOM DOO,' *i.e.*, Mary Black Tom. Such extraordinary compounds as 'JEM-JEMMY-JEM-JEM-JEM,' 'OCKY-DICKBEG-DICKBOB,' 'TOM-BILLY-SAM-HARRY-PHAUL' were not unknown. 'THOMY-HOM-HOMY' Thomas the son of THOMAS, the son of Thomas. 'JUAN-JACK-NED,' *i.e.*, John the son of John, the son of Edward, was a well-known character. He is said to have rolled an eighteen gallon cask of ale all the way up the long hill from Laxey towards Douglas, and when he arrived at the top to have taken it up in his hands and drunk out of the bung-hole! Such titles as 'BILLY ILLIAM,' 'ILLIAM JOE,' 'NANCY JOE,' 'DICKY DAN,' are not uncommon.

4. Nicknames from *trades* and *occupations*, 'DAN TEARE, PHYSICK,' and 'JOHN KEWN YE, DOCTOR,' remind

us of the country practitioners once so numerous. They dealt largely in charms, but nevertheless some of them were excellent bone-setters. Many of the present generation will remember 'Chucas the Strang.' It is well known that Bishop Wilson prescribed for the body as well as the soul ; and even a hundred and thirty years ago there does not seem to have been a regular medical man on the island. 'Corlett, Coblerbeg ;' 'John Moore, Tucker as fuller;' 'Robert Clague, fidler;' 'John Craine, weaver at ye Carlaane ;' 'John Kewn, soldier and slater,' a curious combination ; 'John Norris, hatmaker ;' 'John Bridson, glazier;' 'Thomas the Breekman,' *i.e.*, brickmaker; 'John Creer, thatcher;' 'John Cannel, walker,' *i.e.*, fuller; 'John Coole, plumber;' 'Thomas Bridson, celpman,' *i.e.*, kelp burner; 'John Maddrell, milner ;' 'John Crellin, glover ;' and 'Evan Cannell, coobragh,' *i.e.*, cooper; are quoted from the registers to show the usual trades engaged in. They perhaps hardly come under the head of nicknames. 'John Corlett, pinder,' and 'Dan Cowle, pinner,' were persons whose duty it was to put strayed cattle into the parish pound. 'Thomas Quiggin, runner,' was the Governor's messenger. 'Thomas Jones, officier,' was a Customs official. We find the following entries in the registers : 'Alice Evons, daughter to Robert (called the Cow-boy) and Megory Shurloge ;' 'William Carlett, son of William, vulgarly called Willy Curry Quemb,' and 'William Mylrea vulgò Willy Churry.' These two latter had probably to do with horses. 'Mary Clarke, daughter to the blind fiddler ;' 'Margt, daughter to Taleyr y Killey,' *i.e.*, Killey the tailor ;

'WILLIAM CURLETT, VULGÒ PLEW.' This title appears in the same family for generations. It was probably originally given to a ploughman. 'THOS. TEARE, SHECTER,' *i.e.*, executor. This name has continued in the same family for one hundred and fifty years. 'WILLIAM CAIN, FLUTE,' was doubtless a performer on that instrument. 'WM. QUACKYN, JOCKEY,' who died in 1740, may have been a rider in the 'Isle of Man Derby,' which is said to have been originated by the Earls of Derby on Langness long before the Epsom Derby was thought of! 'EDWARD TEARE, VULGÒ NED Y GHAUE,' *i.e.*, Ned the smith.

'STOWELL THE GOBBAG,' probably a fisherman. *Gobbag* is the dog-fish. 'THOMAS KNEAL, PESSON,' *i.e.*, parson, probably an itinerant preacher.

The following extract from a paper in *Blackwood's Magazine* for March, 1842, which depicts the fancy nomenclature of a Scotch fishing village in a most graphic and amusing manner, will show how the Scotch nicknames compare with the Manx:

' The fishers are generally in want of surnames. . . . There are seldom more than two or three surnames in a fish town. There are twenty-five George Cowies in Buckie (Cowie is the name of an ancient fishing village). The grocers in 'booking' their fisher customers invariably insert the nickname or tee-name, and in the case of married men write down the wife's along with the husband's name. The married debtors have the names of their parents inserted with their own. In the town register of Peterhead these signatures occur: Elizabeth Taylor, spouse to John Thomson, Gouples; Agnes Farquahar, spouse to W. Findlater, Stouttie. . . . It is amusing enough to turn over the leaves of a grocer's ledger and see the tee-names as they come up. Buckie, Beauty, Bam, Biggelugs, Collop, Helldom, the King, the Provost, Rochie, Stoattie, Sillerton, the Smack, Snipe, Snuffers, Toothie, Tod Cowie. Ladies are occasionally found who are gallantly and exquisitely called the Cutter, the Bear, etc. Amongst the twenty-five George Cowies in Buckie there are George Cowie, doodle; George Cowie, carrot; and George Cowie, neef. A stranger had occasion to call on a fisherman in one of the Buchan fishing villages of the name of Alexander White. Meeting a girl he asked: "Could you tell me fa'r Sammy White lives?" "Filk Sammy Fite?" "Muckle Sammy Fite." "Filk Muckle Sammy Fite?" "Muckle lang Sammy Fite." "Filk Muckle lang Sammy Fite?" "Muckle lang gleyed Sammy Fite" (squint-eyed) shouted the stranger. "Oh! its Goup-the-Lift ye're seeking," cried the girl, "and fat the deevil for dinna ye speer for the man by his richt name at ance?"'

MANX PLACE-NAMES.

(*OF CELTIC ORIGIN.*)

CHAPTER I.

GENERIC TERMS FOR TOPOGRAPHICAL FEATURES.

CELTIC place-names may be divided into two classes: simple and compound, the latter being much more numerous. The simple names usually consist of substantives in the nominative, which constitute generic terms denoting the general class of the topographical features, while the compound names have also a second element, almost invariably an affix, which particularizes the place, or distinguishes it from others. These affixes may be either adjectives expressing colour, shape, size, situation, and other qualities, or substantives commemorating the names of persons, animals, vegetables, etc., or they may be the genitive cases of generic topographical terms. A list will be given first of the *generic terms for topographical features*, whether simple or compound, and having thus put in the backbone, as it were, the affixes, which form much the larger class, will follow, and receive a fuller discussion. The commonest generic terms for topographical features are :

Cronk, which occurs as a prefix seventy-six times, *Glione* fifty times, *Gob* thirty-nine times, *Creg* thirty-six times, *Keeill* thirty-four times, *Close* twenty-three times, *Chibber*, *Knock*, and *Purt* twenty-one times, and *Slieau* twenty times.   Of the non-topographical prefixes *Balla*, occurring four hundred times, is far in excess of any other.

It will be convenient to group the names which come under this heading, whether simple or compound, according to their connection with : (*a*) Hills, Highlands, and Rocks ; (*b*) Sea-coast ; (*c*) Glens, Lowlands, Rivers, and Bogs ; (*d*) Position ; (*e*) Human Habitations, including Buildings and Divisions of Land ; and (*f*) The Animal and Vegetable Kingdom.

It will be noticed that most of the simple names have the definite article, either in English or Manx, prefixed.

Part I.

SIMPLE NAMES.*

The most interesting of the simple names is that of the Island itself; for it must be remembered that ISLE OF MAN, or its Manx original, ELLAN VANNIN, is comparatively a late form, and that the early designation was a single word.   Cæsar called it MONA, Orosius MEVANIA, Pliny MONAPIA, Ptolemy MONAOIDA or MON-

---

* Some of the names under this heading may be parts of compound names, of which the other portion has been lost ; but whenever this is known to have been the case, they have been placed under 'imperfect names.'

ARINA, and Gildas EUBONIA or EUMONIA.   In the Welsh records it was called MANAW (the Irish genitive being MANANN), and in the Icelandic Sagas MÖN, which form is correctly transliterated MAUN on the *Malbricti-Gaut* Cross at Kirk Michael.   Controversy has raged about the meaning of these names, or rather name, as they are all variants of the same word; but of the various derivations given, the only one, in the writer's opinion, likely to be correct is that recently advanced by Professor Rhŷs* as follows: ' The Irish MANANNAN is fabled to have been the name of the first king of the ISLE OF MAN, whence that appellation has sometimes been assumed to be derived.   But this is an error, and it inverts the whole relation of the names; for the matter is not as simple as it looks.   It comes briefly to this: MANANNAN gave his original name, in a form corresponding to MANU and its congeners, to the island, making it MANAVIA INSULA . . . for which we have in Welsh and Irish respectively MANAU and MANANN.   Then from these names of the Island the god derives his, in its attested forms of MANAWYÐAN and MANANNÁN, which would seem to mark an epoch when he had become famous in connection with the Isle of Man.'

Thus we gather that the mythical MANANNAN, God of the Sea, merchant and pilot, gave his name in its earliest form to the Isle of Man, and then, in his turn, derived his own extant name of MANANNAN from that of the Island.   Professor Rhŷs conjectures that the earliest form of MANU should be MANAVJU, or MANA-VJONOS.   From this form MONA, MONAPIA (or MANAVIA,

* Hibbert Lectures, 1886.

as Stokes, 'Celtic Declension,' p. 18, doubtfully reads it), and the later more contracted forms naturally follow.

It is not necessary to go into the disputed question of whether the correct spelling is MAN or MANN. Both forms are used in the Records between the fifteenth and seventeenth centuries, but at the earlier dates MAN is rather more common than MANN. Dr. Haviland, in a recent paper read before the Isle of Man Natural History and Antiquarian Society, has made a strong point in favour of MAN, by showing that it was necessary that the title of the King of Man and the Isles should be *Rex Manniæ et Insularum*, not *Rex Maniæ et Insularum*, 'King of Madness and the Isles.'

(a) *Hills, Highlands, Rocks.*

Cronk (M), 'a hill.' A word not found in the earlier records, though it is now more common than *cnoc*, of which it is a corruption (see p. 142), in THE CRONKS, 'The Hills.' In the north of Ireland *cnoc* is universally corrupted into *croc*. In Manx the change has gone further still.

Broogh (F), 'a brow, hill, hillock, bank.' Usually, but incorrectly, applied in Manx local names to the steep slope of a hill, or of a bank by a river, in THE BROOGH,* 'The Brow.' This is the name of an old earthwork.

Liargagh, lhargagh (M), 'the slope of a hill.' Usually of a more gentle slope than *Broogh*, in THE LHERGY, 'the slope,' and LARGY, 'slope.' [(I) LARGY, (G) LARGIES.]

---

* It is seldom used in this sense, but is so translated to distinguish it from *liargagh*.

Aeree, eary (F), 'a moor.' In NARY and NEAREY (*yn-acry* and *yn-eary*), 'The moor.' In Scotland *airidh* (*airie*) means a hill pasture, a shieling. It has not survived in modern Irish place-names, though there are several instances of it in the *Martyrology of Donegal*, as ARIDH-LOCHA-CON. *Aeree* is always applied to highlands. [(G) AIRIE.]

Rinn (K), 'the long ridge of a mountain,' and *Rheynn* (M), 'a division.' They are, almost certainly, originally the same word. The words *rinn*, in Irish, and *roinn*, in Gaelic, mean a promontory, point, headland, peninsula, and also a share or division—especially of land. This latter meaning would arise from the fact that divisions are very commonly made by mountain ridges. Thus THE RHEYN, or THE RHINE, 'The Ridge,' is a ridge of land dividing the parishes of Braddan and Marown. [(I) RINE, (G) THE RINNS, in Islay.]

Dreem, Dreeym (M), 'a back.' Used in local names of the back of a hill, as in THE DRUM, 'The hill-back.' [(I) DRUM.]

Reeast (M), 'a desert, a waste, a rough uncultivated piece of ground.' Invariably applied to uplands, as in THE REEAST MOOAR, 'The Big Waste.' On the place so called, in the parish of Michael, there are several circular enclosures, about twenty feet in diameter, surrounded by white quartz. In one of these was discovered a grave, twelve feet long by four feet broad, having a tall, upright stone at one end of it. About twelve inches below the ground there was a layer of white quartz closely packed over the entire length of the grave, and beneath this an urn of coarse clay, covering charred bones. It measured three feet two inches round the top, and five and a half inches across the base, and was fourteen inches high. It was unfortunately broken when being carried away.

In Ireland and Scotland *riasg* means a marsh, or marshy land, while in the Isle of Man the corresponding word *reeast* is applied to rough land, whether wet or dry. This word is not now used in colloquial Manx. [(I) REASK.]

Carrick, carrig (F), 'a rock or crag.' In CARRICK, 'Rock,' the name of a treen in Lezayre, and in THE CARRICK, 'The Rock,' a detached rock in the sea. This name is rarely found inland. [(I and G) CARRICK.]

Creg and *craig* (F). Contractions of the above, in THE CRAIG, 'The Rock.' [(I and G) CREG.]

(b) *Sea-coast.*

Gob (M), 'neb, beak, bill.' Used in local names of pointed promontories, as in THE GOB, 'The Point.'

Mooiragh (K), 'a void place cast up by the sea'; 'a flat piece of land extending along the sea' (Joyce). In THE MOORAGH, the best rendering of which is 'The Sandbank.' 'In the *Book of Rights* it is spelled *Murmhagh*, which points to the etymology: *muir*, the sea; and *magh*, a plain.'* [(I) MURROW of Wicklow.]

Carn (M), literally 'a heap of stones.' In THE CARN

---

* Joyce, Irish Names of Places, 4th edition, p. 466.

—the fanciful name of a detached rock in the sea.

(c) Glens, Lowlands, Rivers, Bogs.

Cooil (F), 'a nook' (K); 'a hiding-place' (C). In THE COOIL, 'The Nook.' [(I) COOLE.]

Glack (F), 'the hollow of the hand.' Used in local names of a hollow, as THE GLAICK, 'The Hollow.' [(I) GLACK, (G) GLAIK.]

Lag, Laggey (M), 'a hollow.' In THE LAG, and the latter and more uncommon form, probably, in THE LAGAGH, 'The Hollow,' a swampy place.

Claddagh (M), 'a lake, a shore, a low, uncultivated land that lies upon a river' (K); 'the bank of a river' (C). In Manx local names it is applied to meadow-land by a river, as in THE CLADDAGH, 'The River Meadow.' In Ireland and Scotland it is usually applied to a stony or shingly beach, and also, in Ireland, to miry places inland. [(I) CLADDAGH, Islay, CLADICH.]

Garee (F), (C), 'a sour piece of land.' In Galloway it is a common term for a rough hillside, or stony place. In the Isle of Man it has much the same meaning, but it is also used of boggy or sour lands, and is usually low land, though sometimes used of highlands. Thus THE GAREY, 'the stony,' or 'boggy place.' Being generally spelled *Garey* in local names, it is, unless the locality is known, impossible to distinguish it from *garey*, 'a garden.' [(G) GAIRY.]

Alt (F), 'a brook, a stream, particularly in the mountains' (K); 'a high place' (C). This latter signification is the primitive one, it being cognate with the Latin *altus*. In Galloway it is applied to a height, a glen, and even the stream in the glen. In Ireland it is generally understood to mean a cliff or the side of a glen. In the only name in which it occurs in the Isle of Man—ALT, a branch of Sulby Glen—it is uncertain whether it refers to the glen side or the stream. [(I) ALTS, (G) THE ALLT.]

Slogh (K), 'a pit.' Is always pronounced *sloc*, just as in Irish, by Manxmen. O'Reilly gives '*sloc*, S.M., a pit, hollow, hole, cavity, pitfall, mine.' The *slogh* given by Kelly seems to be an anglicised form of the Celtic *sloc*. We have it in THE SLOC, of which the most suitable rendering is 'The Gully.' It is on the south-east slope of CRONK-NA-ARREY-LHAA, and is well known as being the place where there are several ancient hut-dwellings ; also in Y SLOGH, 'The Pit'—on the shore close by—the name of a little stream. Jamieson's description of *sloch*, 'an opening in the higher part of a hill where it becomes less steep, and forms a sort of pass,' applies exactly to THE SLOC in the Isle of Man. There is a cognate Icelandic word, *slakr*. There is a SLOCK in Galloway, where it is also common as a compound.

Curragh, 'a bog, fen, marsh.' In THE CURRAGH, 'The Bog,' the name given to the large extent of boggy land in the north of the Island, where remains of the Irish elk have been found. It formerly contained large ponds, or small lakes, which, as late as 1690, were called 'meres.' It is now drained by THE LHEN, or THE LANE ditch, but the lower parts are still boggy. [(I) THE CURRAGH.]

Moainee, moanee (F), 'a turbary.' A derivative of
  moain, 'peat, turf.' In THE MOANEY, 'The
  Turbary.'
Ellan (F), 'an island.' In NELLAN (*Yn-ellan*), 'The
  Island.' It is here used of a piece of higher land
  surrounded by marshes. Such *ellans* are common
  in the Curragh.

(e) *Human Habitations, whether Buildings or Divisions
  of Land.*

Peeley (F), (C), 'a fortress, tower'—as in PEEL. This
  was the name no doubt originally given to the ancient round tower, which is of the same type as the
  round towers in Ireland, in the centre of the little
  island off PEEL-*town*. It was afterwards applied
  to the Island itself and to the later and more ex-
  tensive fortifications, which were probably erected
  there by the Stanleys. These were repaired by Fer-
  dinando, Earl of Derby, and an old engraving, dated
  1593, represents them as being at that time in perfect condition, but since then they have fallen into
  ruins. At a comparatively late period (1595) this
  name was first applied to the town on the mainland,
  which was then called PEEL-*town*. Its oldest name
  was probably the Celtic PURT-NY-HINSHEY, 'Port of
  the Island.' The Norsemen called it HOLM-TUN,
  which became HOLME-TOWN, and even HALLAND-
  TOWNE. The forts on the border between England
  and Scotland were called PEELS. Jamieson gives
  '*pele, peyll, peel, paile*—a place of strength, a fortification, properly of earth.' [(G) PEAL HILL,
  (in England) PILLTOWN, PIEL-A-FOUDRY.]

Rath (I and G), 'a fort.' In THE RHAA, 'The Fort.' This word is not found in our dictionaries, and is not known colloquially, but certainly exists in local names. [(I) RAIGH and RAY, (G) RHA.]

Carn (M), 'a heap of stones.' In THE CAIRN, 'The heap of stones,' or 'The Cairn.'* These cairns are common upon the mountains, and are popularly supposed to have been raised either in memory of the dead, or of some remarkable event. There are also the more modern cairns set up to mark the tops of mountains by the Ordnance Survey. [(I) CARN, (G) THE CAIRN.]

Faaigh, faaie (F), 'a green, flat, grass plot, paddock' (K); 'a field near or under a mansion-house, better manured than the other fields' (C). Almost every farm has THE FAAIE, 'The Flat,' in the situation described by Cregeen.

Croitt (F), 'a croft, a small close adjoining the house.' *Croft*, 'a piece of ground adjoining to a house' (Jamieson). The word 'croft' is common in English.

> 'Tending my flocks hard by in the hilly crofts
> That brow this northern glade.'—MILTON.

THE CROFT is found upon most farms, and is generally used of a small field.

Bwoailtyn, 'folds' (see *Bwooaillee*). Probably in BOTCHIN and BOSHEN, also possibly in BOLTANE and BAL-THANE, found in the computus of Abbey Tenants, in 1540, as BYULTHAN.

Doon (M), 'a close.' In THE DHOON, 'The Close.' The Irish and Gaelic *dun*, and Welsh *din*, mean 'a

* This word has been adopted into English.

fort,' or 'a fortified hill,' but, in Manx, *doon* seems
to have retained the original meaning of a fence or
enclosure, and hence the space enclosed. It is
represented in English by the word *town*. [(I and
G) Doon.]

(*f*) *The Animal and Vegetable Kingdom.*

The two following names have probably been given
from fancied resemblances.

Boa (F), 'a cow.' In The Boe, 'The Cow,' the name
of a large rock in Castletown Bay. There is a
large black rock in mid-channel of the Luce, in
Galloway, called The Bo Stane.

Goayr (F), ' a goat.' In The Goayr, ' The Goat,' the
name of a small rock off the coast.

Guilc, Guilcagh (K), ' Broom.' In The Guilcagh, 'The
Broom.' This is the name of a farm, which was
probably so called from the quantity of the broom
plant growing there. [(I) Guilcagh.]

Doubtful.

The following simple names are of uncertain derivation, and are therefore classed as *doubtful*.

Braid (K), ' the upper part.' In Manx local names it
is usually applied to uplands, as in The Braid,
'The Upland,' though in the case of The Braids
in the parish of Maughold, which are gullies cut
on the mountain-side by heavy rains, and the
compound name Braid-ny-Glionney, it seems to
be used in much the same sense as the Irish word
braid (*braghad*)—*i.e.*, a deeply-cut glen or gorge.

Cnapan (I), 'a little hillock.' Possibly in THE NAPPIN, 'The Little Hillock.' This farm, in the parish of Jurby, is popularly derived from *Yn abban*, 'The Abbey,' but this is very doubtful, as it is not even Abbey land. There are also farms called the *East* NAPPIN and the *West* NAPPIN. There is a *kecill* on the *West* NAPPIN, which is evidently of later date than such buildings usually are. It is surrounded by a large grave-yard, fenced with an earthen bank. Inside the chapel there is a piscina. [(I) NAPPAN.]

Boircand (I), 'a large rock; a stony, rocky district.' The latter meaning appropriately describes the rough, upland district, in the parish of Patrick, called BOIRREAN. This word is not found in our dictionaries and is not known colloquially.

There is a small stream at the north of the Island, called THE DHOOR, which name is also given to the district through which it flows. It is just possible that it may be from the Irish and Gaelic *dobhar*, 'water,' of which the Manx *dubbyr* is probably a corruption. THE DHOOR may then be translated 'The Water.' [(I) DOWER, DORE, (G) DOVERAN.]

The name BEAREY, applied to a mountain, probably has some connection with *Eary*, 'a moor.'

Meayl, Meyll (K), 'a cape, bare headland, top of a hill.' In THE MEAYLL, 'The Cape.' This name has been placed under the heading 'doubtful,' simply because, in this special case, the name is only of recent introduction into our maps—the old name of the hilly district so called being THE MULL, which is of Scandinavian origin. It is invariably pronounced *Mull*. There is, however, no doubt that the word *meal*, meaning primarily a lump, mass, or heap of anything, is used in Ireland and Scotland of mountains, hills, hillocks and promontories. In Galloway there are four mountains, of over 1,400 feet high, called MEAULL. [(I) MOYLE, (G) MEAULL.]

Quing (F), ' a yoke.' This word would seem to be found in THE WHING, ' The Yoke,' the name of a place in the parish of Andreas.

Cregeen translates *S'cregganagh*, ' how full of small rocks.' In YN SCREGGANAGH it is probably used substantively, with the meaning of ' The Rocky Place,' which exactly describes the shore under Clay Head, where the name is found.

Aash (M), ' ease, rest.' Possibly in NAISH (*Yn aash*), ' The Rest.'

Colloo (F), the Manx name for the Calf Island, would appear to be a corruption of the O.N. *kalv*, as *garroo* of the earlier *garw*. Cregeen and Kelly were evidently much puzzled about its derivation. The former says : ' Conjectures in such cases are endless—some persons will have it to be from *cooyl-halloo* (behind the land), others that it is from *coayl* (loss), and others that it is so called on account of it being formerly frequented by puffins, this word COLLOO being their principal note ' ! Kelly gives ' *Calloo* or *Calv*, the Calf of Man,' but wisely does not attempt any explanation.

Sniaul, the Celtic name of the highest mountain in the Island, would likewise seem to be a corruption of the O.N. SNÆFELL. Our lexicographers are also ingenious in their surmises about this name. According to Cregeen it is from *sniaghty*, ' snow,' while Gill takes refuge in *niful* or *niul*, ' a mist, or bog,' and the Gaelic *Neul*, ' a cloud,' as possible derivations.

Part II.

COMPOUND NAMES.

(a) *Mountains, Hills, Rocks.*

Slieau (M), ' mountain, hill.' The usual name in the Isle of Man for a mountain, as in SLIEAU-REE, ' King's Hill.' [(I) SLIEVEBLOOM, (G) SLEWCREEN.]

Baare (M), ' top, point, extremity.' Generally of the top of a hill, as in BAREDOO, ' Black-top.' [(I) BARROE, (G) BARNESS.]

Mullagh (M), ' top, summit.' Has much the same meaning as *baare*, as in MULLAGHOUYR, ' Dun-top.' [(I) MULLAGHBANE, (G) TULLOCHARD.]

Cnoc (K), ' hill,' is used of a lower elevation than SLIEAU, being even occasionally applied to tumuli, as in KNOCK-E-DOOINEY, ' Man's Hill.' It is a very common prefix. [(I) KNOCKAGAPPLE, (G) KNOCKBRECK.]

Ard (M), ' a hill, a highland, a rising ground.' As in ARDWHALLAN (*Whuallian*), ' Whelp's Hill.' [(I) ARMAGH, (G) ARDNAMURCHAN.]

Eanin, eaynin (F), ' a precipice.' In ENYM-MOOAR, formerly ENIN-MOOAR, ' Big Precipice.' This farm is close by the almost precipitous western side of CRONK-NY-ARREY-LHAA. *Eanin* is used colloquially in Manx, though it is not found in Irish or Gaelic.

Ughtagh (F), 'an acclivity.' Only in UGHTAGH-BREESH-MY-CHREE, 'Break-my-heart Hill.' This word is not now known colloquially. It is used by Bishop Wilson, in Matthew vii. 32, for the 'steep place' down which the swine ran, but *caynee* is substituted for it in the modern version. [(I) UGHTYNEILL.]

Geaylin (F), 'a shoulder.' Is used of the shoulder of a hill; it occurs in one local name only: GEAYLIN-NY-CREGGYN, 'Shoulder of the Rocks.' [(I) SHA-NAGOLDEN.]

Clagh (F), 'a stone.' As in CLAGHBANE, 'White Stone.' [(I) CLOGHLEA, (G) CLAWBELLY.]

The following are also found as simple terms:

Cronk. As in CRONK-NY-MONA (*Moainee*), 'Hill of the Turbary.' This is one of the commonest prefixes in the language. [(I) CROCKANURE.]

Broogh. As in BROOGH-JIARG-MOOAR, 'Big Red Brow.' [(I) BROUGHDERG, (G) BROUGHJIARG.]

Liargagh, largagh. As in LARGYRHENNY (*rennee*), 'Fern's Slope.' [(I) LARGYNAGREANA, (G) LHARGIE Point.]

Aeree, eary. As in EARY-KELLAGH, 'Cock Moor.' [(G) ARIENGOUR.]

Reeast. As in REEAST-MOOAR, 'Big Waste.' [(I) RIASKMORE, (G) RISKMORE.]

Rinn, rheynn. As in RHENSHENT (*shecant*), 'Holy Ridge.' [(I) RINVILLE, (G) RINGREER.]

Dreem, Dreeym. As in DREEMRUY, 'Red Hill-back.' [(I) DRUMROE, (G) DRUMNAKILL.]

Creg, craig. As in CREGLEA (*lhecah*), 'Grey Crag.' [(I) CREGBOY, (G) CRAIGDHU.]

(b) Sea-coast.

Gob. As in Gob breac, ' Speckled Point.' [(I) Gub-bacrock.]

Kione (M), ' a head.' As in Kione Doolish, ' Douglas Head.' In local names *kione* means either ' head,' in the sense of headland, point, promontory, an instance of which has been given already, or ' end,' as in Kentraugh (*kione-traih*), ' Shore-end.' [(I) Kenmare, (G) Cantire, (W) Penmaenmawr.]

Carrig, carrick (see p. 134). As in Carrick *Rock* in Ramsey Bay. The addition of the word ' rock ' would tend to show that the meaning of *carrick* must have been generally forgotten when it was made.

Carrick is seldom found inland in the Isle of Man, while its contraction, *creg*, occurs both inland and on the coast.

[(I) Carrickfergus, (G) Carrick *Point.*]

Stroin (F), literally ' a nose,' is used in local names of a promontory or headland, as in Stroin-Vuigh, ' Yellow Headland.' [(I) Sroankeeragh, (G) Stronhavie.]

Baie, baih (F), ' a bay.' Possibly a word of English origin, as in Bay-ny-carrickey, ' Bay of the Rocks.'

Traie, traih (F), ' shore, strand.' As in Traiebane, ' White Shore.' [(I) Tralee.]

Purt (F), ' a port, harbour, landing-place.' As in Purt-Mooar, ' Big Port.' [(I) Portrush, (G) Port-Patrick.]

Or, or *ooirr* (K), ' a border, coast, limit,' only in Or

VOOAR, 'Big Coast.' *Ooirr-ny-Marrey* is 'The margin of the sea.'

Ellan. As in ELLAN VANNIN, 'Mannan's Isle,' the Manx name of the Isle of Man. *Ellan* is, however, more frequently used of a piece of land surrounded by marshes, as in ELLAN-Y-VODDEE, 'Isle of the Dogs.' [(I) ELLANFAD, (G) ELLAN-NA-ROAN.]

Innis (K), 'an island.' Occurs only as a prefix in the ancient poetical name of the Isle of Man : INNIS-SHEEANT, 'Holy Isle.' In a rescript from Pope Pius II., dated 1459, to Thomas Stanley, we find that the island, having been honoured by the relics of certain saints, 'has been commonly called down to the present day the Holy Island ' (*Insula Sancta*).

Boa. In BOE *Norris*, 'Norris's Cow,' an islet in Castletown Bay.

(c) Glens, Lowlands, Rivers, Bogs.

Glione and *Glion* (F), ' a glen.' As in GLIONE-FEEAGH, ' Raven's Glen.' It is, however, more usual in its English form, as in GLEN-DARRAGH, 'Oak Glen.' [(I) GLENDUFF, (G) GLENCOE.]

Coan, Couan (M), ' a valley.' As in COANRENNEE, 'Ferns' Valley,' or 'Ferny Valley.' This word is used colloquially in Manx, though there is nothing in Irish or Gaelic to correspond with it.

Lag, Laggey. As in LAGBANE, ' White Hollow.' *Lag* is also the technical term for a turf cutting, so it is sometimes found high up in the mountains. [(I and G) LAGMORE.]

Lheeance (F), 'a meadow.' As in LEEANEE-VOOAR 'Big Meadow.' [(I) LENAMORE.]

Cooil. As in COOIL-CAM, 'Winding Nook.' [(I) COOL-BANE, (G) CULROSS.]

Barney (F), 'a gap.' In BARNA-ELLAN-RENNY (*rennee*), ' Ferns' Island Gap,' or ' Ferny Island Gap.' [(I) BARNAGEEHY, (G) BARNEY-*water*.]

Claare (M), 'a dish.' In CLAARE-OUR (*ouyr*), ' Dun Dish.' CLAARE-OUYR is an old circular earth-work near St. Marks, exactly the shape of a dish. The Irish word *clar* means ' a level place.' [(I) CLARE, (G) CLAREHILL.]

Loob (M), literally, ' a loop.' Usually applied in Manx local names to winding mountain gulleys, as in LHOOB-Y-REEAST, ' Gulley of the Waste.' Clarke, in the English-Manx portion of the Manx Society's Dictionary, translates slope by *loob ;* but this usage is now obsolete colloquially, though it may be applicable to some of the *loobs* in local names. [(I) LOOBAGH, (G) LOOPMABINNIE.]

Doarlish (F), ' a gap.' As in DOARLISH-CASHEN, ' Cashen's Gap.'

Garee. As in GAREE-MEEN, ' Soft Stony-place.'

Slogh, ' a pit.' In SLOC-NA-CABBYL-SCREEVAGH, ' Pit of the Scabby Horse.'

Awin, ' a river.' As in AWIN-RUY, ' Red River.' [(I and G) AVONMORE.]

Eas (K), ' a cascade, a waterfall.' In NASCOIN (*yn-eas-coon*), ' The Narrow Waterfall.' [(I) ASSAROE.]

Spooyt, ' a spout.' Used in SPOOYT VANE, ' White Spout,' the only name in which it appears in the Isle of Man, to describe a small, narrow waterfall. Jamieson describes *spout* as meaning a boggy spring. [(G) SPOUT BURN.]

Logh (F), 'a lake, pool.' As in LOUGHDOO, 'Black Lake.' It is used only of inland waters in the Isle of Man, and these have now been for the most part drained. [(I) LOUGHREA, (G) LOUGHNESS.]

Pooyl (F), 'a pool, pond.' As in POOYLBREINN, 'Stagnant Pool.' In the case of POOYL-VAISH, 'Death Pool,' *pooyl* would seem to mean 'bay.' [(I) POLLANASS, (G) POLBÆ.]

Dubbyr (K), 'a pond.' Generally used of a deep pool in a river; but also of pools of rain-water formed in hollow places in wet weather, as in DUBBYR VOOAR, 'Big Pool.' *Dubbyr* is used of a smaller piece of water than *Pooyl*. Jamieson explains *Dub*, 'a small pool of rain-water;' while O'Reilly gives '*Dob*, river, stream.' It is connected with the word *dobbar*, 'water.' [(I) DOWER, (G) DUB OF HASS.]

Curragh. As in CURRAGH GLASS, 'Green Curragh.' [(I) CURRAGH GLASS.]

Moainee, Moance. As in MOAINEE MOLLAGH, 'Rough Turbary.' These turbaries were valuable properties when coals were scarce and dear. [(I) MOAN VANE, (G) MONYBINE.]

Beinn (M), 'a peak, summit, point.' It occurs only once, certainly, as a prefix, in the name of the mountain BEINN-Y-*phot*, or, as commonly spelt, PENNY-*Pot*, 'Point of the Pot,' where *pot* seems to be merely the English word. How this somewhat absurd appellation came to be given to the mountain, the fourth highest in the island, is not known. There is a treen called Ben-Doyle, in the parish of Santon, but, though it is rather high land, it cannot be certainly connected with *beinn*. The plural *binn* is found in Binn-buie, ' Yellow Tops.' This is high land near the coast, the higher parts of which are covered with gorse. [(I and G) Benmore.]

Mullagh. As in Mullaugh-y-Sniaul, 'Top of Sniaul,' commonly called Snæfell.

Beeal (M), 'a mouth.' As in Beal-y-phurt, ' Mouth of the Port.' [(I) Belclare, (G) Bellew.]

Kione. As in Kione-droghad, ' Bridge-end.' [(I and G) Kinloch.]

Gob. As in Gob-ny-strona (*Strooan*), ' Point of the Current.' [(I) Gubbacrock, (G) Gobawhilkin.]

Cass (F), 'a foot.' As in Cass-ny-hawin, ' Foot of the River.' [(I) Coslea.]

(*d*) *Position.*

Lhiattee (F), 'a side.' As in Lhiattee-ny-Beinnee, ' Side of the Summits.' This word would appear to be connected with *lieh*, ' half;' but there is an Irish word *lacka*, a derivative from *leac*, meaning a hill-side, as in Lackabane, of which it may be a corruption.

Bun (M), ' the bottom or end of anything.' Found only in Bunghey (?). [(I) Bunlaghey.]

Corneil (F), ' a corner, an angle.' Probably a word of English origin ; found only in Corneil-y-Killagh, ' Corner of the Church.' By an act of Tynwald, in 1834, the Parish Church of Michael was ordered to be built on the vicar's ancient glebe, and a parcel of land, called CORNEIL-Y-KILLAGH, to be given to the vicar instead.

(e) Human Habitation.

1.—TOPOGRAPHICAL DIVISIONS OF LAND.

Magher (M), 'a field.' As in MAGHER-Y-CHIARN, 'Field of the Lord.' *Machair* in Irish and Gaelic generally means a plain, and seldom a field, which is its invariable meaning in Manx. [(I) MAGHERA-BOY, (G) MACHERBRAKE.]

Faaigh, Faaie. As in FAAIE-NY-CABBAL, 'Flat of the Chapel.' [(I) FAHYKEEN.]

Close (K), 'a close.' As in CLOSE-AN-ELLAN, 'Close of the Island.' This is probably a word of English origin. Jamieson describes it as 'an area before a house, a courtyard beside a farmhouse, in which cattle are fed, and where straw, etc., are deposited, or an enclosure, a place fenced in.' In Manx it simply means a small field. [(G) CLOSE *Hill*.]

Croitt. As in CROT-E-CALEY, 'Caley's Croft.' [(G) CROTFOY.]

Thalloo (M), 'land earth.' In Manx local names, usually of a small plot of ground, as in THALLOO-VELL, 'Bell's Land.' [(I) TALLOWROE, (G) TALLOWGUHAIRN.]

Pairk (M), 'a park.' Used in Manx local names of a large enclosure of grass-land, generally in the mountains, as in PAIRK-NY-EARKAN, 'Park of the Lapwing.' [(I) PARKATLEVA, (G) PARKMACLURG.]

Garey (M), 'a garden.' As in GAREY FEEYNEY, 'Vine

Garden.' It is often confused in local names with *garee* (see p. 135). [(I) GARRYOWEN, (G) GARRIE-FAD.]

Mwannal (M), 'a neck.' Used in local names of a narrow part of a field, as in MWANNAL-Y-GUIY, ' Neck of the Goose.'

Stugg, Stuggey (M), 'a lump, a large portion ' (K), ' A part or piece of a thing.' (C) In Manx local names it is used of a piece of a field fenced off, so as to render the large piece more regular in shape, as in STUCKEYDOO, formerly STUGGADOO, ' Black Piece.' A stout, short man or woman in called colloquially a *sthugga*. In Fifeshire a stout woman is called a *stug*.

Bwoaillee (F) (pl. *bwoailtyn*), ' a fold.' As in BWOAILLEE LOSHT, ' Burnt Fold,' and BUILTCHYN RHENNY (*rennee*), ' Ferny Fold,' or 'Ferns' Fold.' It is a very common word in local nomenclature, especially in field-names, which are not to be found in maps. It was an old custom to fence off a portion of a field and then to turn sheep and cattle into it. When it was thoroughly manured they were transferred to another similar space. These were called *bwoailtyn*, or *builtchyn*. Spenser, in his ' View of the State of Ireland,' describes a different usage there : ' There is one use amongst them, to keepe their cattle, and to live themselves in *boolies*, pasturing upon the mountain and waste wild places, and removing still to fresh land, as they have depastured the former.' Here *booley* refers to the mountain-hut where they lived. It was also applied in Ireland to any place where cattle were fed or milked. In the Isle of Man it means simply a fold or pen, and is quite as common on the low as on the high lands. [(I) BOOLDARRAGH.]

Croa (K), 'a pen,' generally of a sheep-fold. As in CROCREEN, 'Ripe or Withered (?) Pen.' There is an Icelandic word, *kro,* with the same meaning, but it is probably taken from the Celtic. In Ireland it also means a hut or hovel. [(I) KRO-KEVIN.]

Uhllin (C), 'a stackyard or hay-yard.' In MAGHER-YN-ULLIN, 'Field of the Stackyard.' This word would seem to be a corruption of the Irish *ith-lann,* 'corn-house.'

Cleigh, Cleiy (M), 'a hedge, a bank.' As in CLYBANE, 'White Hedge.' [(I) CLYDUFF, (G) CLAYGRANE.]

Scrah (K), *Scraig* (C), (F), 'a turf, a sod.' Probably in SCRAVORLEY (*voalley*), ' Sod Fence. [(I) SCRALEA.]

2.—BUILDINGS, WELLS, ROADS, ETC.

Keeill (F), 'a cell, a church.' As in KEEILL VREESHEY, ' Bridget's Cell.' These tiny churches were probably erected for the most part by the Culdees, between the fifth and eighth centuries. The Culdees were religious recluses who spent their lives in solitary prayer and bodily mortification. The Isle of Man must have been a favourite resort of theirs, as the sites of nearly one hundred of these *keeills* are still to be found ; of which about thirty possess names. They were evidently not intended for congregations, as their internal measurement does not exceed twenty feet by twelve feet, and they are, moreover, distributed so promiscuously that the theory started by the *Traditionary Ballad,** and eagerly accepted by most of those who have written on the subject, that there was one for every *treen,*† cannot be substantiated by the facts. [(I) KILBREEDY, (G) KILMORIE.]

Cabbal (F), 'a chapel.' As in CABBAL-YN-OURAL LOSHT, 'Chapel of the Burnt Sacrifice.' *Cabbal* is quite a modern word, and seems to be merely a corruption of 'chapel.' Cumming draws an elaborate distinction between the *cabbal* of the fifth century and the *keeill* of the sixth, which, apart from the fact that the word *cabbal* was unknown at that date, seems a very doubtful one.‡

Rhullick (C), *Ruillic* (Cl), *Relic* (Gi), 'a graveyard.' As in RULLICK-NY-QUAKERYN, 'Graveyard of the Quakers.' [(I) REILICK-MURRY.]

Oaie (F), 'a grave, a tomb.' In OAIE-NY-FOAWR, 'Grave of the Giant.' Nothing corresponding to this word is found in either Irish or Gaelic.

Lhiaght (M), 'a tombstone, a pile of stones in memory of the dead.' Found only in LHIAGHT-E-KINRY, 'Kinry's Tombstone.' This was erected in memory of a person of this name, who was rash enough to wager that he would run naked from Douglas to Bishop's Court and back on a snowy day, and who perished in the attempt.§

Cashtal (K), 'a castle.' As in CASHTAL REE GOREE, 'King Orree's Castle.' [(I) CASTLEDARGAN, (G) CASTLEDOUGLAS.]

* Train, History of the Isle of Man, p. 52.
† For *treen*, see *post.*
‡ Manx Soc., Vol. XV.
§ Feltham's Tour, Manx Soc., Vol. VI.

Rath. Probably occurs in *The* RAA MOOAR, ' The Big Fort,' now a heap of stones in a commanding position by the shore in the parish of Maughold. The supposition that this may be the remains of an ancient fort is strengthened by the fact that the rocky point below is called GOB-YN-CASHTAL. [(I) RAHARD.]

Thie (M), ' a house.'   As in THIE JUAN NED, ' John Ned's House.' [(I) TYFARNHAM, (G) TYDEAVERYS.]

Soalt (F), ' a barn.'   As in THOLT-E-WILL, ' Will's Barn.' [(I) SAUL.]

Droghad (F), ' a bridge.'   As in DROGHAD FAYLE, ' Fayle's Bridge.' [(I) DROGHEDA, (G) DROCH *Head.*]

Mwyllin (C), *Mwillin* (K) (pl. *Mwiljin*), ' a mill.'   As in MULLEN-E-CORRAN, ' Corran's Mill.'   Early in the sixteenth century water-mills were established in large numbers by the Lord of the Isle, who ordered the old *querns*, or hand-mills, to be broken up, so that the farmers were compelled to send their corn to be ground at his mills. It would appear that, in spite of these regulations, some of the *querns* survived, as many fines for not bringing corn to be ground are recorded in the manorial books.   We learn from the Statute Book that ' all the mulcture, toll and soken of all corn and graine within the Island '* belonged to the Lord, who no doubt derived a considerable revenue in this way. [(I) MULLENMORE.]

Chibber (F), ' a well.'   As in CHIBBER VOIRREY, ' Mary's Well.'   The numerous well-names in the

* Statute Law Book, Vol. I., p. 85 (A.D. 1636).

Isle of Man are usually found near old ecclesiastical sites, as the holy recluses would naturally build their *keeills* near springs, where they would construct wells both for their own personal convenience as well as for baptizing their disciples. Some of these wells were formerly much venerated, as their waters were supposed to possess sanative qualities, and to be of special virtue as charms against witchcraft and fairies. They were generally visited on Ascension Day and on the first Sunday in August, called *yn chied doonaght yn ourr*, ' the first Sunday of the harvest,' when the devotees would drop a small coin into the well, drink of the water, repeat a prayer, in which they mentioned their ailments, and then decorate the well, or the tree overhanging it, with flowers and other votive offerings, usually rags. They believed that when the flowers withered or the rags rotted their ailments would be cured. These rites have been observed in the Isle of Man within the memory of those now living. There is a well on GOB-Y-VOLLEE, called CHIBBER LANSH (where the meaning of *lansh* is uncertain), consisting of three pools, which was formerly much resorted to for the cure of sore eyes. The cure could only be effective if the patient came on Sunday and walked three times round each pool, saying in Manx, *Ayns enym yn Ayr, as y Vac, as y Spyrryd Nu*, ' In the name of the Father, and of the Son, and of the Holy Ghost,' and then applied the water to his or her eye. [(I) TOBERA-KEENA, (G) TOBERMORY.]

Crosh (F), ' a cross.' As in CROSH-MOOAR, ' Big Cross,'

and CROSH *Sulby*, ' Sulby Cross,' both of which have
disappeared. [(I) CROSSGAR, (G) CROSSMAGLEN.]

Carn. As in CARN GERJOIL, ' Joyful Cairn.' [(I)
CARNACALLY, (G) CAIRNGORM.]

Raad (M), ' a road.' As in RAAD-JIARG, ' Red Road.'
The rainbow was called RAAD REE GORREE,
' King Orry's Road.'

Bayr (M), ' a road ' (K), ' a way, avenue ' (C). As in
BAREGARROW, ' Rough Road.' [(I) BOHERKILL.]

Cassan (M), ' a path.' As in CASSAN KEIL, ' Narrow
Path.' [(I) CASSANKERRY, (G) CASSENCARIE.]

Cronk and *Knock* are used in local names for artificial
structures, such as tumuli and barrows, as well as
hills. Thus CRONK-E-DOOINEY, ' Man's Hill,' and
KNOCK-E-DOOINEY with the same meaning.

Clagh is also used for stone pillars erected as memorials.
As in CLAGH ARD, ' High Stone.'

Doubtful.

The following generic terms can only be classed as
doubtful.

Lann (I, G, and W), ' an enclosure, a house, a church,'
is not found in our dictionaries, and is not known
colloquially, though we have the word *ullin* (*eith-
lann*, ' corn-house,' see p. 151). Dr. Joyce remarks that when it means ' house ' it is a purely
Irish word; but that in its ecclesiastical signification it was borrowed from the Welsh. It would
seem, however, that its earliest meaning was simply
an enclosure, and it is in this sense that it is probably found in the only name in which it occurs
as a prefix in the Isle of Man—LANJAGHIN,

'Deacon's Enclosure,' or 'Joughin's Enclosure.'
[(I) LANDMORE, (G) LANDIS.]

Braid. In BRAID-NY-BOSHEN (*bwoailtyn*), 'Upland of
the Folds,' and BRAID-NY-SKARRAG, 'Upland of
the Skate.' The mountain-ridge so called is supposed to be the shape of a skate; also in BRAID-
NY-GLIONNEY, 'Gorge of the Glen.'

There is in Ireland a word *cor*, commonly used as a
topographical term in the meanings of round hill,
a round pit, or cup-like hollow, a turn or bend in a
road. In the Isle of Man it seems to occur in two
names only, viz.: CORMONAGH (*moanagh*), 'Round
Turfy Hollow,' and CORLEA (*lhccah*), 'Round Gray
Hill.'

The other *cors* are either from the (O. N.) personal
name *Cori*, or from the adjective *coar*, 'pleasant,' or
at least either *cori* or *coar* would be more appropriate topographically than *cor*, except in the two
names above. There are also CORRONY, which is
a corruption of (O. N.) CORNA, and CORRADY, which
is obscure. There is a CORRODY in Ireland, which
name is said to be connected with a peculiar legal
tenure.

Cor is not found in Manx dictionaries, and it is
not known colloquially. [(I) CORDEAGH.]

Boireand. As in BORRANE-CREG-LIEH (*lhccah*) 'Rocky
District of the Gray Crag,' as its translation would
seem to be; but it is a name actually applied to an
old earthen fortification near the Niarbyl, on the
seashore. There are four forts marked in the
Ordnance Survey along the sea-line in this district.
Just above it there is an earthwork called

Borrane Balebly, about thirty yards long by twenty-two broad.

The name of the Lhane* Mooar, or the Lhen Mooar, which drains the Curragh, is etymologically obscure, though it probably means 'The Great Ditch.' Sir Herbert Maxwell, in explaining Lane Burn in Galloway, quotes Jamieson. '*Lane.* 1. A brook, of which the motion is so slow as to be scarcely perceptible; the hollow course of a large rivulet in a meadow ground. 2. Applied to those parts of a river or rivulet which are so smooth as to answer to this description.' There is no word corresponding to *lhane* or *lhen* in our dictionaries, except the adjective *lane*, 'full,' and it is only known colloquially as applied with the meaning of trench or ditch to the great Curragh drain. Certainly the current of the water in the Lhane Mooar is quite slow enough to answer Jamieson's description, though it can hardly be accepted as a satisfactory derivation.

Part III.

DIMINUTIVES (SIMPLE AND COMPOUND).

There are certainly two terminations that denote smallness in Manx: *an* (I and G, *an*) and *aeg* (I and G, *og*), and possibly there are two others, *een* (I, *in*) and *en* (I, *en*); but these are not so easily identified. Of these, *an* is the most common; but in many of the words ending in it the original meaning of smallness has been quite lost. Thus:

---

* Not connected with *lann*, 'an enclosure.'

Strooan (F), 'A stream, rivulet.' As in STROAN-NY-CRAUE, 'Stream of the Bone.' There is nothing in Manx to correspond to the Irish and Gaelic *sruth*. [(I) SRUTHANMORE.]

Carnane (diminutive of *carn*). As in *The* CARNANE, 'The pile of stones or cairn,' and CARNANE-BRECK, 'Speckled Cairn.' [(I) CARNANE BANE.]

Creggan, originally a diminutive of *creg*, is explained by Kelly as meaning 'a hillock, a rocky place, a barrow, a heap of stones,' and by Cregeen as 'a place or piece of ground left uncultivated in consequence of being rocky or containing stones; generally overgrown with gorse or underwood.' The most suitable translation would appear to be 'rocky hillock.' As in *The* CREGGANS, CREGGAN MOAR, 'Big Rocky Hillock,' NY-CREGGANYN, 'The Rocky Hillocks,' and probably CROGGANE, 'Rocky Hillock.' [(I) CREGGANE, (G) CRAIGENBUY.]

In the following the diminutive signification has been retained :

Knockan, 'hillock.' As in KNOCKAN and KNOCKAN-AALIN, 'Beautiful Hillock.' [(I and G) KNOCKAN-DOO.]

Cronkan. As in CRONKAN-RENNY (*rennee*), 'Ferns' Hillock,' or 'Ferny Hillock,' and in the corrupt form *cronnan*, as in CRONNAN-MOOAR, 'Big Hillock.'

Laggan, 'a little hollow.' As in LAGGANDOO, 'Black Little Hollow.' [(I) LAGANEANY, (G) LAGGAN-HARNIE.]

Loghan, 'a pond.' As in LOUGHAN-Y-GUIY, 'Pond of the Goose.' [(I) LOUGHANASKIN, (G) LOCHINBRECK.]

(See *cnapan* under Simple Names.)

Aeg, literally 'young,' is not recognised either in our

dictionaries or colloquially as a diminutive, though it has undoubtedly the same signification as the Irish *og*, anglicised *og, oge, ogue*, which is very common both in personal and local names. It occurs in the following:

Lheeanag (F), 'a little meadow.' As in *The* LEENAG.

Cronnag. A corruption of CRONK-AEG, 'Little Hill,' and the plural NY CRONNAGYN, 'The Little Hills.'

Crossag (*crosh-aeg*). In *The* CROSSAG BRIDGE, 'The Little Cross Bridge,' near Rushen Abbey. This is probably the oldest bridge in the island, dating from the thirteenth century. Its breadth in the centre is only three feet three inches.

Crammag. The farm so called is popularly derived from *crammag*, 'a snail,' and the explanation given is that this farm is so steep that either nothing but a snail could get up it, or that you must ascend the hill at a snail's pace. It is quite true that the farmhouse is situated on so steep a slope that it is very difficult to get a cart up to it; but perhaps the following explanation is a more satisfactory one: Joyce, in treating of *crom*, 'bent, inclined, crooked,' refers to two diminutives of it: *Cromane* and *Cromage*, which, he says, signify 'anything sloping or bending, and give names to many places.'* Sir Herbert Maxwell mentions a place called CRAMMAG, in Galloway, as being the name of a sea-cliff. The best translation of CRAMMAG would seem, therefore, to be 'The Little Cliff.'

(The termination *aeg* is also found as a diminutive in the following affixes: *sceabag, cuilleig, kill-eig, beishteig*.)

* Series 2, p. 399.

The diminutive *een* perhaps occurs in CLYEEN, which may be a corruption of *Cleiy-een*, 'Little Hedge,' the name of a farm adjoining the Northern Tynwald at CRONK URLEY. Possibly this name may have some connection with the ancient fence round the court. *Cleiy* means a mound, dyke, or rampart of any kind, as well as a hedge.

The diminutive *en* is perhaps found in the doubtful RUSHEN (*ros-een*), 'Little Wood' (see *post*).

CHAPTER II.

THERE are divisions of land for administrative purposes, the names of which appear on our maps, but are not apparent as topographical features. The largest of these, the *Sheading*, is undoubtedly of Scandinavian origin (see *post*).

The name of the next division in point of size, *skeerey*, 'a parish,' when regarded merely as a civil division—and the civil divisions are certainly older than the ecclesiastical—is also probably of Scandinavian origin ; but, when regarded as an ecclesiastical division, its name, *skeeylley*, may possibly be a corruption of the Scandinavian *skeerey*, and the Manx *keeilley* (gen. of *keeill*), as in SKEEYLEY* CHARMANE, ' German's Church Division ' (or Parish), though in this case also a purely Scandinavian derivation appears more probable (see *post*). *Skeeley* forms the prefix to fifteen out of the seventeen parish churches in the island.

About the next division, the *treen*, there has been

----

* Kelly writes this SKEEYL-Y-CHANNANE, which cannot be correct. SKEEYLEY is pronounced as one word by Manx people.

considerable controversy, which, however, has not been successful in elucidating its meaning. Kelly does not mention it in the Triglott Dictionary. Gill has: ' Treein, " an ecclesiastical division of the country . . . being a third part." ' Cregeen : ' Treen (F), "a township that divides tithe into three."' If it ever was a third part, the division of which it was a third has disappeared. Dr. Joyce remarks that '*Trian (treen)* denotes the third part of anything; it was formerly a territorial designation in frequent use . . . it generally takes the forms of *trean* and *trien*, which constitute or begin the names of about seventy townlands in the four provinces.'* There are, on an average, ten *treens* in a parish in the Isle of Man, and as in all the *sheadings* except one there are three parishes, the *sheadings* contains about thirty *treens*. Now in Ireland the *baile*, Manx *balla* (see below), was the thirtieth part of a barony, and, assuming that the Irish barony and the Manx *sheading* are equivalent divisions, it may be conjectured that the *treen* and the *balla* were originally identical. From the Ballaugh Register, A.D. 1600, we learn that the owners of the *treens* were obliged to keep their portion of the churchyard and its fence in order, which portions were ' marked out as followeth in order by the most ancient men of the parish ;'† and there is a further note in the register to the effect that there were twenty yards allotted to each *treen*, there being eight and a half *treens*, so that the circumference of the churchyard was one hundred and seventy yards. The *treen* owners had also to keep the parish pinfolds in

* Joyce, 4th Ed., p. 242.
† Manx Note Book, No. 2, p. 57.

order. The *treens* include both cultivated and uncultivated land, *i.e.*, quarterlands and intacks.

Balley, *Balla* (M), 'a town, an estate, a farm, a village.' As in BALLAGLASS, 'Green Farm.' *Balla* is the modern form, *balley* or *bally* being almost universal before the seventeenth century. It receives the gloss *locus* in Cormac's glossary and the Book of Armagh. Cormac also gives *baile* as the equivalent of *rath*, and it is frequently found in this sense in the Irish annals. Its primary meaning seems to have been an enclosure, a place fenced round, where it is identical with the Irish and Gaelic *balla*, and the Manx *boayl*. All these words are possibly derived from the late Latin *ballivum*. When St. Mochna founded his monastery, in the seventh century, he is said to have enclosed it with a *balla*. The following relating to the *balla* is from a tract printed in the appendix to 'The Tribes and Customs of the *Hy Fiach-raich*': 'These countries were sub-divided into townlands, which were called *ballys* . . . and each townland was divided into quarters . . . and now the lands are generally set and let, not by the measure of acres, but by the name of quarters . . . a quarter being the fourth part of a townland. . . . I have been sometimes perplexed to know how many acres a quarter contains, but I have learned it is an uncertain measure, and anciently proportioned only by guess, or according to the bigness of the townlands whereof it was a parcel.'* *Balla* has quite lost its meaning of a definite division corresponding with

* Miscellany of Celtic Society, p. 49.

the *treen*, and is now prefixed to the name of nearly every farm in the island, without regard to its size. It is therefore by far the commonest local term in the Isle of Man, as it is in Ireland. It should be mentioned that in three *treen* names in the parish of Braddan it seems to have entered into composition with the (O. N.) *dalr*, as BALDALL BREW (*Balla Dalr Vriew* or *Brew*), 'Judge's Dale Farm,' or 'Brew's Dale Farm,' and BALDALL CHRISTE, in 1511, BALDAL CHRISTORY, 'Christory's Dale Farm.' In the same district there is a farm called BALDALREGNYLT, 'Reginald's Dale Farm,' in 1511, but now BALLAREGNILT, 'Reginald's Farm.' [(I) BALLYBANE, (G) BALLY-MELLAN.]

Boayl (M), 'a place.' As in BOAL-NA-MUCK, 'Place of the Pig.' This word is cognate with *balla* (see above).

Lieh (M), 'a half.' As in LEAKERROO, 'Half Quarter.' In the Isle of Man it is only found as a prefix in connection with *kerroo*. [(I) LAHARRAN.]

Kerroo (M), 'a quarter.' As in KERROO-GARROO, 'Rough Quarter.' In land measurement in the Isle of Man the *kerroo* is invariably used for the fourth part of a *balla* or *treen*, and includes the cultivated land only within it. Thus the Manx speak of a *kerroo-valley*, or, in English, a *quarter-land*, which is a further proof of the identity of the *treen* and *balla*; but, when an epithet is affixed to *kerroo*, *valley* is dropped. The size of the *kerroo* of course varies with that of the *treen*, though *quarter-lands* in the same *treen* are also of different sizes;

being, as a rule, from sixty to eighty acres, except in the parish of Lonan, where they are somewhat larger. The original size of the *kerroo-valley* was probably from fifty to sixty acres, which is about the extent of land which one plough could turn up in the course of a year. The *treens* or *ballas* therefore vary from 240 to 320 acres, though there are some exceptional ones either much larger or much smaller. There are in the Island $639\frac{1}{2}$ *quarterlands* of Lord's lands and 169 *treens*, making rather less than four *quarterlands* to a *treen*. There are also $99\frac{1}{2}$ *quarterlands* which belonged to the dissolved Monastery at Rushen, called *Thalloo-ab*, or 'Abbey-land,' and $32\frac{3}{4}$ *quarterlands* belonging to the various baronies. The abbey and barons' lands were not divided into *treens*. [(I) CARROW-KEEL, (G) CARRUCHAN.]

CHAPTER III.

DISTINCTIVE AFFIXES.

Part I.—Substantives.

THE following words are found as AFFIXES, as well as PREFIXES and SIMPLE NAMES:

Baare, in CREG-Y-VAARE, 'Crag of the Summit.'

Beinn, in LHIATTEE-NY-BEINNEE, 'Side of the Summits,' and GOB-NY-VEINNY, 'Point of the Summits.'

Slieau, in KIONESLIEAU, 'Mountain End;' COOIL-SLIEAU, 'Mountain Nook;' FOLIEU (*Fo-yn-hlieau*), 'Under the Mountain;' GOB-NY-DAA-SLIEAU, 'Point of the Two Mountains;' BALLA-KILLEY-CLIEU, 'Farm of the Church Hill,' where there is a *treen* chapel.

Aeree or *eary*, in BALLIREY, formerly BALLEARY, 'Moor Farm;' CRONKAIREY, 'Moor Hill;' BLOCKEARY (?), BALLANEARY (*yn-eary*), 'Farm of the Moor.'

Ard, in BALLANARD (*yn-ard*), and BALLANAHARD, 'Farm of the Height;' KERROO-NA-ARD, 'Quarter of the Height.' CASHTAL-YN-ARD, 'Castle of the Height;' and CASHTAL-YN-ARD is the remains of a stone circle and stone cists, with avenues,

standing on the top of a rounded hill called ' *The*
ARD,' which is about 500 feet above the sea ; the
length of the remains is, from east to west, 105
feet, breadth at west end 50 feet, at east end 40
feet. This place is also called CASHTAL REE
GOREE, but this is quite a modern name.

Rhen, in MULLEN-RENEASH, 'Waterfall Ridge Mill,' and
GOB-Y-RHEYNN, ' Point of the Ridge or Division.'

Cronk, in KERROO-NY-GRONK, ' Quarter of the Hill ;'
KEEILL CRONK, ' Church Hill ;' CREG-NY-CROCK,
' Crag of the Hill,' and probably in BALLACROAK,
' Hill Farm.' This farm is on a hill where there
are two fine specimens of chambered barrows.

Cruink, the plural, is found in BALLACRUINK and
BALLACRINK, ' Hills' Farm,' and probably in GLEN-
DRINK and GLENTRUNK, ' Hills' Glen.' On BALLA-
CRINK, in Onchan, there are the remains of a stone
circle and of a tumulus.

Craig and Creg, in BALNYCRAIG (*balla-ny*), ' Farm of the
Crag ;' ' GEAYLLIN-NY-CREGGYN, ' Shoulder of the
Crags ;' GOB-NY-CREG, ' Point of the Crag,' and
BOIRANE-CREG-LIEH (*lheeah*), ' Rocky Ground
of the Grey Crag.'

Creggyn, the plural, in ALT-NY-CREGGAN (*creggyn*),
' Mountain Stream of the Crags.' Boulders abound
in and about the course of the stream.

Creggan, in BALLACREGGAN, ' Rocky Hillock Farm.'
On the farm of this name in the parish of Rushen
are the ' Giants' quoiting stones,' probably the
remains of a megalithic monument.

Liargagh, in BALLERGHY, or BALLARGHEY, 'Slope
Farm.' This is a very common name. In CRONK-

NY-LHERGHY, 'Hill of the Slope;' DREEM-NY-LHERGHY, 'Back of the Slope;' BALNALHERGY (*balla-ny*), 'Farm of the Slope.'

Broogh, in MAGHER-Y-BROOGH, 'Field of the Brow.'

Eanin, in KIONE-NY-HENIN, 'End of the Precipice.' There are the remains of a stone circle, and also of hut dwellings, near this cliff.

Ughtagh, probably in BALLANAHOUGHTY, 'Farm of the Acclivity.'

Dreeym, in LAGGAN-Y-DROMMA, 'Little hollow of the (Hill-)back;' BALDROMMA, '(Hill-)back Farm;' BALDROMMA HEOSE, 'Upper (Hill-)back Farm;' BALDROMMA HEIS, 'Lower (Hill-)back Farm;' KEILL-PHERIC-A-DRUMMA (*y Dromney*), 'Patrick's Church of the (Hill-)back.'

Kione, in EARY-NY-KIONE, 'Moor of the End (of the Hill);' GOB-NY-KIONE, 'Point of the Head,' where *kione* is a promontory.

King, the plural, in PORT-NY-DING, 'Port of the Heads.'

Cromoge (I), in GLIONE CRAMMAG, 'Little Cliff Glen.'

Reeast, in AWIN-NY-REEAST, 'River of the Waste;' LHOOB-Y-REEAST, 'Gulley of the Waste.'

Garee, in BALLAGAREE, 'Stony Land Farm;' KIONE-NY-GAREE, 'End of the Stony Land;' CLOSE-NY-GAREY, 'Close of the Stony Land.'

Garey, in BALLAGAREY, 'Garden Farm.'

Clagh, in SLIEU-NY-CLOGH, 'Hill of the Stone,' near St. Mark's, where there is a huge granite boulder; in KERROO-NY-CLOUGH, 'Quarter of the Stone;' CLY-CLOUGH, 'Stone Fence;' LHERGY-CLAGH-WILLY, 'Willy's Stone Slope.'

Rheyn, in GOB-Y-RHEYNN, 'Point of the Division.'

Glionc, in BALLAGLIONNEY, BALLALONNEY and BALLA-
LONNA, 'Glen Farm;' and BRAID-NY-GLIONNEY,
'Gorge of the Glen.'

Lheeanee, in BALLALHEANEY, 'Meadow Farm;' CLOSE-
NY-LHEANEY, 'Close of the Meadow.'

Lheeanag, in CRONK-Y-LEANNAG, 'Hill of the Little
Meadow.'

Lag, in BALLALAG, 'Hollow Farm;' RHULLICK-Y-LAGG-
SHLIGGAGH, 'Graveyard of the Shelly Hollow;'—
this is the Manx name of the large stone circle
on the Mull.

Lig, the plural, in BALLALIG and BALLIG, 'Hollows'
Farm.' On BALLALIG, in the parish of Braddan,
there is a tumulus, where urns have been found.

Barney, in BALLABERNA and BALLABENNA, 'Gap Farm;'
and possibly in CHIBBYR-Y-VAINNAGH, 'Well of the
Gap.'

Coan, in BALLAGAWNE, formerly BALLACOAN, 'Valley
Farm;' BELEGAWN (*Beal-y-coan*), 'Mouth of the
Valley;' PURT-NY-COAN, 'Port of the Valley;' and
possibly in BALLACOINE and BALLACOYNE, 'Valley
Farm.'

Cooil, in BALLACOOILEY, 'Nook Farm;' CROT-NY-
COOILLEY, 'Croft of the Nook.'

Awin, in CASSNAHOWIN (*ny-awin*), 'Foot of the River;'
BALNAHOWIN, 'Farm of the River;' BALLAHOWIN,
'River Farm;' MULLENLAWNE (in 1602 MULLIN-
NY-HAWIN), 'Mill of the River;' LAG-NY-AWIN,
'Hollow of the River;' BILLOWNE, formerly BE-
LOWNE, (*Beeal*), 'River Mouth,' and LIARGEY-NY-
HOUNE, 'Slope of the River.' There is a stone
circle at BILLOWNE.

Strooan, 'Stream or Current,' in BALLASTROOAN, 'Stream Farm;' CASS-NY-STROOAN, ' Foot of the Stream;' CASS-STROAN,'Stream Foot;' BULTROAN (*Bwoaillee*), 'Stream Fold,' where the stream flows past a cattle-fold; GOB-NY-STRONA, 'Point of the Current,' at the end of Maughold Head, where the tides meet.

Eas, in RHENEAS or RHENAS, 'Waterfall Ridge;' MULLEN RHENEASH, 'Waterfall Ridge Mill.'

Alt, plural *altyn*, in GLIONE AULDYN and GLEN ALTYN, 'Mountain Streams' Glen.'

A a, a, ah, in MULLEN DOWAY (obs.) (*doo-a*), ' Black Ford Mill,' now UNION MILLS, on the river Doo.

Logh, in CASHTAL-LOGH, ' Lake Castle;' BALLALOUGH, 'Lake Farm ; DOLLOUGH MOAR (*doo*), 'Big Black Lake,' and DOLLOUGH BEG, ' Little Black Lake;' GLENLOUGH, 'Lake Glen.' All these *Loghs* are either drained or have become very diminutive.

Loughan, in KNOCK-A-LOUGHAN (y), ' Hill of the Pond.'

Currach, in GLENCORRAGH, ' Bog Glen.'

Moainee, in BALLAMONA, 'Turbary Farm ;' CROIT-NY-MONA, 'Croft of the Turbary;' CLY-NA-MONA, ' Hedge of the Turbary ;' GULLET CREEAGH MOAINEE, ' Turbary Stack Gullet ;' CRONK-NE-MONA, ' Hill of the Turbary.'

Ros (see *Doubtful Names*), in PULROSE, formerly POOYL-ROISH, 'Wood Pool.'

Carrick, in BAIE-NY-CARRICKEY, ' Bay of the Rocks.'

Boe, in SANDWICK BOE, ' Sandcreek Cow,' where *Boe* is a large rock.

Beeal, in OOIG-NY-VEEAL, ' Cave of the Entrance.'

Ellan, in CLOSE-AN-ELLAN, ' Close of the Island ;' BALLELLIN, formerly BALLELLAN, ' Island Farm ;'

BARNA-ELLAN-RENNY, ' Ferns' Island Gap,' or
' Ferny Island Gap.'

Ellan in these names does not refer to an island
in the sea, but to patches of cultivated land which
were formerly surrounded by swamps, but are now
for the most part drained.

Innis, in PURT-NY-HINSHEY, ' Port of the Island,' as
PEEL was sometimes called formerly.

Purt, in BALLAFURT, 'Port Farm;' CROT-Y-FURT-CALLOW,
' Callow's Port Croft;' GOB-NY-PORT-MOAR, ' Point
of the Big Port.'

Traie, in KENTRAUGH, formerly KENTRAIE (*kione-traie*),
' Shore End.' This property abuts on the shore.
In LAG-NY-TRAIE, ' Hollow of the shore ;' MAGHER-
Y-TRAIE, ' Field of the Shore.'

Bun, or *Bunt*, in BALLABUNT, formerly BALNYBUNT,
' Farm of the End,' or ' End Farm.' This farm is
on the boundary between the parishes of Braddan
and Marown. *Bunt* is used in colloquial Scotch
for the tail or end of anything.

Balla, in SHENVALLA, ' Old Farm,' and CORVALLEY,
' Pleasant Farm.'

Kerroo, in BALLAKERROO, ' Quarter Farm.'

Lieh, in BALLIE, ' Half Farm.'

Magher, in BALLAVAGHER, ' Field Farm.'

Bwoaillee, in ARDUAILEY, ' High Fold ;' and its plural,

Bwoailtyn, in BRAID-NY-BOSHEN, ' Upland of the
Folds;' and LAG-Y-VOTCHIN, ' Hollow of the Folds.'

Faaie, in DREEMFAAIE, ' Shoulder of the Flat.'

Carlane (see *Doubtful Names*), in STROAN-NY-CARLANE,
' Stream of the Sheep-fold.'

Lane, in KIAN-NY-LANE, ' End of the Trench.'

Dhoon, in BALDOON, 'Close Farm.'

Close, in *Bastin's* CLOSE, *Island* CLOSE.

Cleiy or *Cleigh*, in MWYILLIN-NY-CLEIY, 'Mill of the Hedge.' This is one of the little mills which were formerly used for crushing gorse. In BALNYCLYBANE, 'Farm of the White Hedge ;' BALLACLYBANE, 'White Hedge Farm.'

Croa, in BALLAGROA, 'Pen (or Fold) Farm.'

Injeig, in BALLINJAGUE, 'Paddock Farm.'

Croit, in COOIL CROFT, 'Croft Nook.'

Keeill, in numerous farms called BALLAKILLY, 'Church Farm,' or 'Cell Farm.' These are invariably found near the sites of ancient *keeills*, or modern churches, which were usually built on old sacred sites. In BALLAKILLEYCLIEU, 'Church Hill Farm;' BALLACURNKEIL, formerly BALLACARN-Y-KEIL, 'Cairn of the Church Farm;' GLION-Y-KILLEY, 'Glen of the Church;' LAG-NY-KEILLEY, 'Hollow of the Church,' also probably in BALLAGILLEY. An old burial-ground was discovered on this property some years ago. At LAG-NY-KEILLEY, at the foot of the precipitous west side of CRONK-NY-ARREY-LHAA, there are the remains of an old chapel, ST. LUKE'S (see *post*), surrounded by a wall about two feet high. Within this enclosure, according to tradition, are the graves of the early Manx kings. LAG-NY-KEEILLEY is the name of the little glen close by, which divides the parishes of Patrick and Rushen.

Cabbal, in CREGACABLE (*y-Cabbal*), 'Crag of the Chapel ;' and MAGHER CABBAL, 'Chapel Field,' near KILLABRAGGA.

Ruillic, in MAGHER-Y-RUILLIC, 'Field of the Graveyard,' where there are the remains of a *Keeill,* of
a well, and near the well a large flat block of
granite, having in its centre a cavity, which may
have formed the socket of a cross. In CABBAL
RULLICKY, 'Graveyard Chapel;' and SHEN ROL-
LICK, 'Old Graveyard.'

Oaie, in CRONK-NY-HEY, 'Hill of the Grave.'

Rhaa, in LHERGY RHAA, 'Rhaa Slope,' where *raa,*
'fort,' is the name of the farm.

Cashtal, in BALLEY-CASHTAL, which is now translated
into English, and called 'Castletown.' It was so
called from its famous castle, RUSHEN. In GOB-
YN-CASHTAL, 'Point of the Castle,' and in the
curious combination *Fort* CAISHTAL. This is an
ancient fortified earthwork near the Cloven Stones.
All the Manx *cashtals,* with the exception of those
of RUSHEN and PEEL, are ancient earthworks.

Soalt, in KNOCK-E-THOLT (y), 'Hill of the Barn.'

Mwyllin is very common in BALLAWYLLIN, in one
case corrupted into BALLAWOOLIN, 'Mill Farm.'
It is found also in RHENWILLEN, 'Mill Ridge;'
where there is a windmill. Windmills are now
very uncommon in the Isle of Man. They were
never, however, nearly as numerous as watermills.
In CRONK-NY-MWYLLIN, 'Hill of the Mill;' PORT-Y-
VULLEN, and PUIRT-NY-MWYLLIN, 'Port of the
Mill;' BOLEE WILLIN (*bwoaillee*), 'Mill Fold.'

Droghad, in KIONEDROGHAD, 'Bridge End.'

Lane (see *Doubtful Names*), in BALLALHANE, 'Lhen-
trench Farm;' and KIAN-NY-LHANE, 'End of the
Lhen-trench.'

Crosh, in BALLACROSHA and BALLACROSS, 'Cross Farm.'
BALLACROSHA is the name of the farm upon which
the village of BALLAUGH stands, where, till recently,
there was a cross inscribed with runes.

Carn, in BALLACURNEKIEL, formerly BALLACARN-Y-KEIL
(*keilley*), 'Cairn of the Cell (or Church) Farm ;' and
in the adjoining farms BALLACURNEKIEL-MOAR,
'Big Cairn of the Cell Farm; and BALLACURNEKIEL-
BEG, 'Little Cairn of the Cell Farm.' There was
formerly a *keeill* on BALLACURNEKIEL, but now all
that is left of it is a cairn of stones. The name
of the mountain on which these farms lie is spelled
SLIEAU CURN or SLIEAU CAIRN, formerly SLIEAU
CARN, 'Cairn Mountain.'

Carnane, originally a diminutive of *carn*, is now used
with precisely the same meaning. It is found in
BALLACARNANE, 'Cairn Farm,' and BALLACARNANE,
BEG, 'Little Cairn Farm.' There are the remains of
a *keeill*, with its burying ground, on this farm.

Bayr, in BALLAVARVANE, BALLAVARANE and BALLA-
VARRAN, 'White Road Farm ;' also in CASHTALL-Y-
VARE-VANE, 'Castle of the White Road,' where there
are the remains of an earthwork. All these are
corruptions of *bayr-vane ;* in BALLAVARE, BAL-
LAVAIR and BALLAVEAR, 'Road Farm ;' BEALE-
VAYR (y), 'Entrance of the Road ;' CROT-Y-VEAR,
'Croft of the Road ;' and probably in GOB-NY-
GARVANE, 'Point of the White Road.'

Traie, possibly in CONTRARY *Head*, *contrary* being supposed to be a corruption of *kione-traie*, 'Shore End.'

Lann, ' an enclosure,' in STROAN-NY-CARLANE, 'Stream
of the Sheep-fold ;' and *The* CARLANE, or *The*

KIRLANE (*keyrr*), 'The Sheep-fold.' This place is near the mouth of the *Lhen* ditch, and the *Stroan* is a small stream, which flows into the ditch; so it is possible that the termination *lane* has something to do with this ditch; but, if so, the explanation of the prefix becomes more difficult.

Chibber, in LAG-NY-CHIBBYR, 'Hollow of the Well;' and in GARA-NA-CHIBBERAUGH, 'Garden of the Wells;' *Chibberaugh* being possibly intended for *Chibberaghyn*, the plural of *Chibber*.

The following are found as affixes only:

Glaise, glais or *glas* (I), 'a small stream, a brook,' is not found in our dictionaries, and is not known colloquially, but it almost certainly is the affix in the name of the largest town in the Island, DOUGLAS, or, as it is called by Manx-speaking people, DOOLISH. Joyce writes: 'Douglas is very common, both as a river and townland designation all over the country, and it is also well known in Scotland; its Irish form is *Dubhghlaise*, black stream.'[*] We may therefore translate Douglas, 'black stream;' the name was probably originally BALLADOUGLAS; but no trace of this can be found. Douglas Head is called KIONE DOOLISH by the Manx, who would soften *glaish* into *lish*, as they do *glass* into *lesh* (see *post*). The popular interpretation of the name is that it is a compound of the names of the two rivers, DOO and GLASS, which unite above the town, but, apart from other difficulties, 'black gray' is not a probable name.

Lhing (G), *Lhingey* (C) (F), 'a pool;' in BALLALING,

* Joyce, 4th Ed., p. 456.

'Pool Farm ;' and AAH-NY-LINGEY, 'Ford of the Pool.' [(I) DUBLIN.]

Creagh (F), 'a stack ;' in *Gullet*-CHREAGH-MOAINEE, 'Turbary Stack Gullet ;' and LOUGH-NY-GREEAGH, 'Lake of the Stack ;' the stack being of peat turves.

Cassan (M), 'a path ;' in GOB-NY-CASSAN, 'Point of the Path.' [(I) ARDNAGASSAN.]

Laagh (F), 'mire, mud, slush ;' as in BAL-NY-LAGHEY, now BALLAUGH, 'Town of the Mire;' as the village is called which has transferred its name to the parish. Vicar-General Wilks, Rector of Ballaugh from 1771-77, explained this name, in answer to a query of Mr. Pennant's, as being ' from ye Manx: BAL-NY-LAGHEY, which *laghey* signifies *mire* or *mud*, where wth this Parish formerly abounded from ye number of quags or mires in ye E. side thereof.' In 1595, it is found written BALLALOUGH, 'Lake-town ;' but the Rector's derivation is probably the correct one. The greater part of the Parish was formerly occupied, by the then undrained *Curragh ;* and, even since the *Lhen* trench has been made, there is a good deal of marshy land at the eastern end of the parish. [(I) GORTNALAHAGH.]

Farrane, 'a spring, a fountain ;' in BALLANARRAN, 'Spring farm' (there is a spring by the farm), and in SLIEAU-NY-FREOGHANE, a map maker's error for SLIEAU-NY-FARRANE, 'Hill of the Spring.' There is a spring which gushes out on the side of this hill, and, as its name is always pronounced *Farrane*, not *Freoghane*, 'bilberry,' by the Manx people, there can be little doubt but that the derivation given is the proper one. It seems probable that the name CREGG-YN-ARRAN or CREG-Y-ARRAN, may mean the 'Rock of the Spring,' as the initial *f* is frequently elided in Manx; and moreover the only other possible interpretation, 'Rock of the bread,' is not in any way appropriate.

Cuilleig (F), 'a nook;' a diminutive of *cooil* originally, in CHLEIG-NY-CUILLEIG, 'Hedge of the nook.'

Boalley (M), a wall; probably in SCRAHVORLEY, 'Sod wall or fence.'

Spuir (K), 'a spur;' in BALLASPUR, 'Spur farm;' possibly from some pointed rock on the farm. Joyce thinks it probable that the corresponding word, *spor*, in Irish was borrowed from English. [(I) KNOCKASPUR.]

Keilleig (C) (F), 'an enclosure belonging to a church or chapel;' probably originally a diminutive of *keeill*, in CRONK-Y-KEILLEIG, 'Hill of the church enclosure.' There are the remains of a *keeill*, and its little graveyard at this spot.

Cott, coit, 'a cott or cottage built on a croitt' (K). It would seem, however, to be more probably simply a corruption of the English word. It is found only in BALLAHOTT, formerly BALLACOTT, 'Cottage farm.'

Keim (Gi), 'a stile;' in MAGHER-Y-KEIM, 'Field of the stile.'

Relating to the Sea.

Roayrt (F), 'spring tide;' in CARRICK ROAYRT, 'Spring-tide Rock.' This rock is only covered completely at spring tides.

Kesh (C) (F), *Kiesh* (K), ' froth, foam ; ' in *Balla Kesh,*
' Foam Farm.' This farm is by the sea, and in gales
the foam is blown up upon it. *Kesh*, though not
found in Irish or Gaelic, is used in colloquial Manx.

Ushtey (M), ' water ; ' in Gob-yn-Ushtey, ' Point
of the Water.' This is a headland in the sea.
[(I) Ballinisha, (G) Benaskie.]

Sloat (M), ' a small pool, or low water,' always by the
sea ; in Gob-ny-Sloat, ' Point of the Low Water ; '
and Traie-ny-Sloat, ' Strand of the Little Pool.'
The Irish *slod* means ' a little standing water.'

From Various Circumstances.

There are a number of affixes which may be grouped as
relating, (*a*) to battles or other events ; (*b*) to memorials
of the dead ; (*c*) to supposed resemblances ; and (*d*) to
customs, legends, and superstitions.

Considering that the Isle of Man has been the scene
of numerous battles and skirmishes, the names which
record their occurrence are singularly few.

Caggey (M), ' a war, a battle, a fight ; ' in Magher-y-
Caggey, ' Field of the Battle.' Forty years ago
this field at Ballanard in the parish of Onchan contained a complete semi-circular entrenchment, but
it has since then been almost entirely levelled.

Troddan. This word is not given by Kelly in the
Triglot, or by Cregeen. The Rev. W. Gill, in the
Manx Society's Dictionary, states that it means
' the haunt of cattle, a place of pasture.' The
Rev. W. FitzSimmons, who revised this portion of
the dictionary, rightly looks with suspicion on this
statement, and adds : ' I am very doubtful as to

this article. *Troddan* is a quarrel—a contest.'
O'Reilly gives *trodan*, 'a quarrel.' Joyce says:
'*Trodan* signifies "a quarrel;" and from this word
we have the names of two places in Armagh.'*
We may, therefore, translate KNOCK-Y-TRODDAN,
'Hill of the Contest.' This fortification, now
known as CASTLE WARD, is partly natural and
partly artificial, and, though popularly called ' The
Danish Camp,' it is almost certainly of neolithic
origin. It is just opposite MAGHER-Y-CAGGEY,
mentioned above, being about 500 yards from it,
and on the other side of the river GLASS.
[(I) CARRICKTRODDAN, (G) DRUMTRODDAN.]

Fuill (F), ' blood ;' in TRAIE-NY-FUILLEY, ' Strand of
the Blood ;' and MAGHER-A-FUILL, ' Field of the
Blood.' This possibly commemorates some bloody
fight of days long past.

Cragh (F), ' carnage, slaughter, destruction, spoil, prey ;'
in KEEILL CRAGH, ' Slaughter Cell.' This place
may possibly have been the scene of some combat.

Cliwe (F), ' a sword ;' in CRONK-Y-CLIWE, ' Hill of the
Sword.' This is a tumulus close by the site of
the battle of Santwat, which was an internecine
struggle between the Manx of the North and of
the South in 1098, and the name probably commemorates the finding of a sword, which was
buried with some warrior, who had fought on that
occasion.

Armyn (plural of *arm*), ' arms ;' in CRONK ARMYN,
' Arms' Hill,' a tumulus close by CRONK-Y-CLIWE,
would seem to commemorate a similar discovery.

* Joyce, Irish Names of Places, 2nd ed., p. 431.

Craue (F), 'a bone;' in STROAN-NY-CRAUE, 'The Stream of the Bone.' This stream flows through the site of the battle of SCACCAFELL or SKYEHILL, which was fought in 1077, between Godred Crovan and the Manx; also in BALLAGRAUE, 'Bone Farm,' and LHERGY GRAUE, 'Bone Slope.' On LHERGY GRAUE is St. Patrick's Well, where, according to the legend, the Saint's horse fell.

Marroo, the past participle of *dy marroo*, ' to kill,' is used substantively in CRONK-Y-MARROO, 'Hill of the Dead (Man),' in the parish of LONAN, and CRONK-NY-MERRIU, 'Hill of the Dead (Men),' in the parish of Santon. CRONK-NY-MERRIU is forty yards long, twenty yards broad, and twelve yards high. The bodies of those who were killed in battle were interred in huge tumuli, close to where they fought. CRONK-Y-MARROO and CRONK-NY-MERRIU are two of the most important of these.

Dooiney (M), 'a man;' in CRONK-E-DOOINEY, 'Man's Hill,' and KNOCK-E-DOOINEY, with the same meaning. Both these hillocks are tumuli, where human remains have doubtless been discovered.

Asnee (K), *asncy* (C) (F), ' a rib ;' probably in BALLAHASNEY, ' Rib Farm ;' this name may also denote a similar discovery to that in CRONK and KNOCK-E-DOOINEY.

Koir (F), ' a box, or chest ;' in CRONK KOIR, 'Chest Hill.' This tumulus has now disappeared, having been cut through by a road. It would seem probable from the name that, when this road was made, a sepulchral urn, which the Manx people call a *Koir*, was found in the tumulus.

Undin, 'a foundation;' in CHIBBER UNDIN, 'Foundation Well;' in the parish of Malew, which is close to an ancient *keeill*. There are only the foundations of this *keeill* left, which show it to have been twenty-one feet long by twelve feet broad. The water of this well is supposed to have curative properties. The patients who came to it, took a mouthful of water, retaining it in their mouths till they had twice walked round the well. They then took a piece of cloth from a garment which they had worn, wetted it with the water from the well, and hung it on the hawthorn-tree which grew there. When the cloth had rotted away, the cure was supposed to be effected.

Real or fancied resemblance to various parts of the human body, or to well-known animate or artificial objects, has originated various topographical names.

Eddin (F), 'face, front;' in BALLANEDDIN, 'Face Farm,' the name of a farm on the slope of SLIEAU VOLLY in Ballaugh, the contour of which is supposed to be like a human face.

Mollee (F), 'eyebrow;' in BALLAVOLLY, 'Eyebrow Farm,' which is on a higher part of SLIEAU VOLLEY, 'Eyebrow Hill,' than BALLANEDDIN. The point of the same hill is called GOB-Y-VOLLEY, 'Point of the Eyebrow.' There is also an ARD-VOLLEY, 'Eyebrow Height,' in the parish of Malew.

Barnagh (F), ' a limpet, a common kind of shell-fish, which adheres to rock; it is also called *flitter* in English, in this Island' (C); *Baarnagh*, 'a limpet or flitter' (K). The natives of the parish of Michael will tell you that the farm called BARNAGH

JIARG, formerly BALLA BARNAGH JIARG, 'Red Limpet Farm,' was so-called from the fact that its fields are spotted over with tumuli, which lie on the surface like flitters on a rock. This is such an apt description of the actual appearance of the farm, that it is most probably the correct derivation. It cannot be derived from *Barney*, 'a gap,' as there are no gaps on the farm.

Goggan (F), 'a noggin;' in KIONE-Y-GHOGGAN, 'Head of the Noggin,' probably from a fancied resemblance to the small wooden vessel so-called.

Chreel (Gi), 'a dorser of straw, a basket,' used of the deep basket carried by fisherwomen; in CREG-Y-CHREEL, 'Rock of the Creel,' probably also so-called from a resemblance.

Cruit (I), 'a harp;' possibly in LOUGHCROUTE, 'Harp Lake.' It is just possible that this pond, which was once much larger, may have had formerly a harp-like contour. Philips in his Prayer-book, written about 1628, has the word *kruit* for harp, but it is not found in later Manx.

There are also a few names which originate from customs. The most important of these is that of keeping 'Watch and Ward,' which from the time of the earliest recorded Statute in 1417 was constantly enjoined on the inhabitants under severe penalties in the event of failure. In the military orders in 1594 we find that 'Whereas the safe keeping of this Isle consisteth in the dutifull carefull observance of Watch and Ward . . . therefore be it ordained that all Watch and Ward be kept according to the Strict order of the Law, and that none be sent thither but such as are of

Discretion, and able to deserve to be carefull; and that the night watch shall come at Sun-setting, and shall not depart before the Sun-rising, and that the Day Watch shall come at the Sun-rising, and not depart before the Sun-setting.'* There was a warden in each parish, who was responsible for the proper keeping both of the day and night watch. His commission, which was given by the Governor of the Island, ran as follows: 'I do hereby nominate, constitute, and appoint . . . to be yᵉ warden of yᵉ night and day watches within yᵉ parish of. . . . Willing and hereby requiring all persons whom it may concern to take notice hereof and to yield their obedience there unto upon pain of sore punishment as by the Lawes of this Isle and as they will answer the contrary.' That these duties were strictly enforced is clear from the numerous fines for their non-observance which are to be found in the records. 'Watch and Ward' was not finally discontinued till after 1815.

From the lofty and precipitous CRONK-NY-ARREY-LHAA, 'Hill of the Day Watch,' in the south-west, to the little CRONK-NY-ARREY, 'Hill of the Watch,' in the north-east, there is a constant series of watch hills, all of which are in sight of each other. When an enemy approached, beacons were at once lit on these hills, a practice which is probably commemorated in the fanciful name ARCHALLAGAN (*ard-chiollagh-an*), 'High little hearth;' *chiollagh* meaning 'the hearth, the fireside.' ARCHALLAGAN is the name of a hill in the parish of Patrick, which is known to have been a

* Statutes, Vol. I. p. 65.

watch hill. (See also ELBY, WARDFELL in Scandinavian section.)

Sthowyr (M), 'a staff, pole;' in CRONK-Y-STHOWYR, 'Hill of the Staff.' This is a modern name, there being a flagstaff on the top of this hill.

Quackeryn is simply Quakers, with a Manx plural. It is found in RHULLICK-NY-QUAKERYN, 'Graveyard of the Quakers.' The Quakers were much persecuted in the Isle of Man during the sixteenth and seventeenth centuries. They were not even permitted to bury in the parish churchyards.

Slaynt (F), 'health;' in CHIBBER-Y-SLAINT, 'Well of the Health.' This is one of the few wells whose waters, from a slight impregnation of iron, really had some medicinal qualities, though many others, as stated under *Chibber*, were frequented on account of their supposed sanative qualities.

It was customary in the case of disputed boundaries to have a jury, who decided the question on the spot.

Bing (F), 'a jury;' in CRONK-NY-BING, 'Hill of the the Jury,' probably commemorates one of these occasions.

Leigh (F), 'a law,' in BALLALEIGH, 'Law Farm,' close by, was a name probably bestowed for the same reason.

Jaghee (F), 'tithe;' in CREG-Y-JAGHEE, 'Rock of the Tithe,' records one of the places where the clergy's tithe of fish was paid.

Oural (M), 'a sacrifice;' in CABBAL-YN-OURAL-LOSHT, 'Chapel of the Burnt Sacrifice.' This name records a circumstance which took place in the nineteenth century, but which, it is to be hoped, was never customary in the Isle of Man. A farmer, who had lost a number of his sheep and cattle by murrain, burned a calf as a propitiatory offering to the Deity on this spot, where a chapel was afterwards built. Hence the name.

Bashtey (M), 'baptism;' in CHIBBER-Y-VASTEE, 'Well of the Baptism.' This well, which is close by KEEILL-VAEL, in Maughold, was probably once made use of by the religious recluse who lived there to baptize those who were converted by him, as well as for his domestic purposes.

Boght (M), 'a poor person;' in CROIT-NY-MOGHT, 'Croft of the Poor,' and MOANAMOGHT (*Moainee*), 'The Poor's Turbary.' It was a custom in each parish to reserve a small portion of arable land, and in parishes where there was bog a small portion of peat-land, the rent of which was divided among the poor.

Ping (F), 'a penny;' in CROIT PINGEY, 'Penny Croft,' probably so named from the lord's rent of it being one penny.

The copious legendary lore of the Isle of Man is scarcely represented in its local nomenclature.

Stoyl (M), 'a stool, a seat;' in STOYL-NY-MANANNAN, or correctly, STOYL-E-MANANNAN, 'Manannan's Seat;' this 'seat,' now usually called 'Manannan's Chair,' was a cromlech. It has now disappeared. (For *Manannan*, see p. 131.)

Foawr (M), 'a giant;' in MEIR-NY-FOAWR, 'Fingers of the Giant,' and LIAGHT-NY-FOAWR, 'Grave of the Giant.' The first of these names refers to the pillars of the stone avenue near KEW, and the

latter to the cromlech in the same place, which
has now disappeared. The avenue doubtless led
up to the cromlech. There is also OAIE-NY-
FOAWR, 'Grave of the Giant,' which is a fine
tumulus about forty-eight feet in diameter and
four feet high, where bones have been discovered.

Grian (M), ' the sun ;' in CARN-Y-GREINEY and CARNY-
GREIE, formerly CARN-Y-GREINEY, 'Cairn of the
Sun.' It seems possible that the names of these
cairns, which are both on mountain tops, may be
connected with ancient sun-worship. A memory
of this cult would seem to have been perpetuated
to comparatively modern times by the custom of
going up to the mountain tops on the first Sunday
in August. In 1732 certain of the parishioners of
the parish of Lonan were presented and punished
for indulging in this 'superstitious and wicked
custom.' [COULNAGREINEY (Islay).]

The solitary affix denoting position, which is to be
found in Manx place-names, is *jerrey* (M), ' the end,' in
YIARN JERREY, 'Iron End,' at Bradda, close to the Mine.

The following names all commemorate death by
drowning, a death unfortunately too common on the
dangerous Manx coasts :

Baase (M), ' death ;' in TRAAIE VAAISH, ' Death Strand ;'
POOYL VAAISH, ' Death Pool ;' and BALLA VAAISH,
' Death Farm.' These are all close together, and
probably record the same occurrence. POOYL
VAAISH is well known on account of its dull black
marble. The steps of St. Paul's Cathedral, in
London, which were presented by Bishop Wilson,
were made of it.

Callin (K), 'a body;' in GOB-NY-CALLIN, 'Point of the
    Body.'

Ineen (F), 'a girl, a daughter;' in CREG-NY-INEEN,
    'Rock of the Girl.'

Thalhear (M), 'a tailor;' in CREG-NY-INNEEN-THALHEAR,
    'Rock of the Tailor's Daughter.' Girls were
    drowned at both these places.

Geay, 'wind,' and *taarnagh*, 'thunder,' are the only
    atmospheric conditions recorded in Manx local
    names.

Geay (F) is found in BALL-NY-GEAY, 'Farm of the
    Wind;' CREG-NY-GEAY, 'Rock of the Wind;'
    GOB-NY-GEE, 'Point of the Wind;' CARNAGEAY,
    'Cairn of the Wind;' BEEAL-FEAYN-Y-GEAY,
    'Wide Entrance of the Wind;' and CHIBBER-Y-
    GEAY, 'Well of the Wind.' [(I) BALLYNAGEE, (G)
    BARNAGEE.]

Taarnagh (M), occurs only in COOIL TAARNAGH,
    'Thunder Nook.'

The two following appear to be simply poetical:

Shee (F), 'peace;' in PORT-E-CHEE, or correctly,
    PURT-NY-SHEE, 'Harbour of the Peace.' The
    last Duke of Athol, who was king of the Island,
    lived at PORT-E-CHEE while Castle Mona was
    being built for his reception. There is also
    CRONK-NY-SHEE, 'Hill of the Peace.' It is just
    possible that this latter may record some treaty
    of peace, but PORT-E-CHEE is comparatively a
    modern name.

Cree (F), 'a heart;' in CHIBBER-NY-CREE-BANEY, 'Well
    of the White Heart;' CRONK-Y-CREE, 'Hill of the
    Heart;' and BALLACREE, 'Heart Farm,' close by.

None of these have any pretensions to be shaped like a heart, so that the poetical application of the name seems the more probable. UGHTAGH-BREESH-MY-CHREE, 'Break my Heart Hill,' is a fanciful name given to a long steep hill in the parish of German.

Relating to Offices and Trades.

There are not many local names under these headings.

Ree (M), 'a king;' probably in SLIEAU REE, 'King's Hill;' BOL REIY, 'King's Fold;' CLOSE REI and CLOSE REIGH, 'King's Close;' and CASHTAL REE GOREE, 'King Orree's Castle.' This last, however, is merely a modern and fanciful name for the ruins on The Ard, in the parish of Maughold. [(I) MONAREE, (G) ARDREE.]

Chiarn (M), 'a lord,' signifying the lord of the island; in SLIEAU CHIARN, 'Lord's Hill;' KEEILL-YN-CHIARN, 'Cell of the Lord;' CLOSE-Y-CHIARN, 'Close of the Lord;' CHIBBER-Y-CHIARN, 'Well of the Lord;' and MAGHER-Y-CHIARN, 'Field of the Lord,' in the parish of Marown, on which is found the so-called 'St. Patrick's Chair,' in which the saint is said to have sat when he gave his blessing to the Manx. It is really the remains of a cromlech. The lower portion is a platform of stones and sods, seven feet six inches long by three feet six inches deep. On this platform stand two upright slabs of blue slate, on the west faces of which are crosses. There appears to have been another slab formerly.

Aspick (M), 'a bishop;' in BALLASPICK, and a corrupt BALLASPET, 'Bishop's Farm;' and in CURRAGH-AN-ASPICK (*yn*), 'Curragh of the Bishop.' This was the bishop's turbary in the Curragh at Ballaugh, and was the largest in the island. [(I) MONASPICK, (G) ERNESPIE.]

Abb (M), 'an abbot;' in RENAB, 'Abbot's Ridge.' The abbot of Rushen was formerly a spiritual baron, and had great influence in the island. [(I) BALLANAB, (G) BALNAB.]

Saggyrt (M), 'a priest;' in BALLATAGGART, 'Priest's Farm.' This name may possibly be derived immediately from the personal name TAGGART, which, however, is itself derived from *sagyrt* (see p. 72). [(I) DERRYNASAGART.]

Pesson (M), 'a parson;' appears to be simply a corruption of the English word. We have it in BALLAPHESSON, 'Parson's Farm;' and CROIT-E-PHESSON, 'Parson's Croft.' These are both glebes. [(I) BALLYFAESOON.]

Managh (M), 'a monk;' in CLOSE MANAGH, 'Monk's Close,' which, according to the *Liber Vastarum* of 1606, was 'a piece of ground of one daymath of hay;' BALLAMANAGH, 'Monk's Farm.' There are several BALLAMANAGHS, which are liable to be confounded with the more numerous BALLAMEENAGHS, 'Middle Farms.' The following note concerning one of these abbey farms from the records is interesting as showing the peculiar customary rents:

In 1692 the abbey tenants of BALLAMANAUGH, in Sulby, petitioned William, Earl of Derby, for a reduction of rent, 'setting forth the great loss they had sustained by having the greatest part of their tenement washed away by the violence of Sulby river.' On inquiry 'it was found that a fourth part of the s^d tenem^t of BALLAMANAUGH was taken away and wasted by the said river.' Therefore a fourth part of the customs was abated, which a later report tells us resulted in 'great inconvenience in making allowance of the fourth part of a goose or hen.' [(I) ARDNAMANACH.]

A reference to index (3) will show that all these ecclesiastical names are of Latin origin.

Druaight (M), (K), 'sorcery,' (C) 'a druid ;' in CABBAL DRUIAGHT, 'Druid's Chapel.' This chapel, with a burial-ground, is close to Ballahutchin in the parish of Marown. It is on a slightly elevated circular mound, about forty-eight feet in diameter. The chapel itself is fifteen feet by twelve feet. Just enough remains of the walls to show its form. This name, however, is due to modern inventiveness. If old it would certainly have been corrupted into some such form as the Irish *Drui*, (gen.) *druad*, in LOUGHNADROOA, or GOBNADRUY.

Briw (M), 'a judge ;' in KNOCK-E-VRIEW, 'Judge's Hill ;' and BALLAVRIEW, 'Judge's Farm.' This latter is close to the site of the ancient southern Tynwald in Baldwin.

Meoir, 'a moar,' the official appointed to collect the Lord's rents and fines ; in BALLAVOAR, 'Moar's Farm.'

Crutire (I), 'a harper ;' probably in GLENCRUTCHERY, formerly GLENCRUTTERY, 'Harper's Glen.' This word is not found in our dictionaries, which give *claascyder* for a harper, and *claasagh* for a harp. Bishop Philips, however, whose Manx Prayer-book was written about 1628, gives the word *kruit* for a harp.

Gaauc (M), 'a smith;' in BALLAGAUE, 'Smith's Farm;' and perhaps in BALLAGAWNE with the same meaning, which, however, is more probably directly from the personal name GAWNE. [(I) BALLYGOWAN, (G) BALNAGOWAN.]

Seyir (M), 'a carpenter;' in BALLASEYR, 'Carpenter's Farm,' and OOIG-NY-SEYR, 'Cave of the Carpenter.' [(I) RATHNASEER.]

Fidder (M), 'a weaver;' in THIE-NY-FIDDER, 'House of the Weaver.' Weaving, more especially of flannel, is still carried on in the country.

Beaynee (K), 'a reaper;' in CLOSE-NY-VEAYNEE, 'Close of the Reaper.'

The two following, which scarcely come under the above headings, may be placed here.

Joaree (M), 'a stranger, an alien, a foreigner;' in EAIRY JORA, formerly EAIRY JOAREY, 'Stranger's Moor,' and BALLAJORA, 'Stranger's Farm.' In the Isle of Man formerly all who were not natives were called strangers or foreigners.

Maarliagh (M), 'a thief;' in GLIONE MAARLIAGH, 'Thief Glen.' It is not known how this name was acquired.

The following names arise from industrial occupations having been carried on at the places they indicate.

Fasney (M), 'a winnowing;' in STROOAN FARSEE,

'Winnowing Stream,' so called from the mill which it drives.

Garmin (M), 'a weaver's beam;' in BALLAGARMAN, 'Weaver's Beam Farm.' The cottage industries have one by one disappeared during the present century.

Tuar (I), 'a bleach-green;' in BALLATHOAR, formerly BALLNETHOAR, 'Bleach-green Farm,' and GLIONE-THOAR, 'Bleach-green Glen.' There were formerly Bleach-greens in both these localities. This word is not found in the Manx Dictionaries. [(I) BALLI-TORE.]

The following name has clearly been given because the creek so called could not admit a vessel larger than a boat:

PORT-E-VADA (*y*), 'The Boat Port.' [(I) RINAWADE, (G) PORTAVADDIE.]

Brott, 'broth' (K), in CHIBBERDROTT, 'Broth Well,' would seem to be a fanciful name.

From the Animal Kingdom.

Tarroo (M), 'a bull;' in POOYL THERRIU, 'Bulls' Pool.' [(I) KNOCKATARRIV.]

Boa (F), (gen. pl. *ny baa*), 'a cow;' in CREG-NY-BAA, 'Rock of the Cows.' (This is found as a prefix, but only when used fancifully of a rock in the sea. See pp. 139, 145.) [(I) AGHABOE.]

Maase (M), 'cattle;' in BALLAVAASE, 'Cattle Farm.' This farm in German is where the cattle were formerly kept which were slaughtered for the use of the garrison of Peel Castle; and, probably, in LOUGHAN-NY-MASKEY, or MAIDJEY, 'Pond of the

Cattle.' It has now disappeared. No word corresponding to *maase* is to be found in Irish or Gaelic.

Muc (F), ' a pig ;' in BOAL-NA-MUCK, ' Place of the Pig ' (pigsty). [(I) SLIEVENAMUCK.]

Muc-aill (F), ' a sow ;' in CRONK-NY-MUCAILLYN, ' Hill of the Sows.' By an Act passed in 1629, which was not repealed till 1832, it was made felony to steal a pig. There was formerly a curious breed of wild pigs, called *purrs*, which is now extinct.

Collagh (M), ' a stallion ;' of the male of most animals, but usually of a horse; in CRONK-COLLACH, ' Stallion Hill.'

Mohlt (M), (pl. *muihlt*), ' a wether ;' in GLEN-Y-MULT, ' Glen of the Wethers,' and CREG-NY-MOLT, ' Crag of the Wether.' [(I) ANNAMULT.]

Lheiy (M), ' a calf ;' in BALLALHEIY, ' Calf Farm.' [(I) CLONLEIGH.]

Colbagh (F), ' a heifer ;' in CLOSE-NY-CHOLBAGH, ' Close of the Heifer.' [(I) KILNACOLPAGH.]

Keyrr or *keyrrey* (F), (pl. *kirree*), ' a sheep ;' in GIAU-NY-KIRREE, ' Creek of the Sheep,' where sheep were swum ashore ; and BALLAKEERAGH, ' Sheep Farm.' In Bishop Phillip's Prayer-book sheep is *geragh*. [(I) MEENKEERAGH.]

Eayn (M), ' a lamb ;' in KNOCK-Y-NEAN (*yn-ean*), ' Hill of the Lamb.' [(I) GORTANOON.]

Feeaih, ' a deer ;' in CARRICK-A-FEEAIH, ' Rock of the Deer,' in the parish of Lonan ; in LHEIM FEEAIH, ' Deer's Leap,' at a bend of the narrow stream, just above the chapel at the head of Sulby Glen ; and in CURRAGH FEEHEH, ' Deer's Curragh,' in the parish of German. It is said that the skeleton of an elk has been discovered there.

Eagh, 'a horse;' in BALLANEAGH (*yn-eagh*), 'Farm of the Horse.' [(I) KINEAGH.]

Cabbyl, 'a horse;' in GIAU-NY-CABBYL, 'Cove of the Horse' (this was the cove whence horses were swum across to the Calf Island); and in SLOC-NA-CABBYL-SCREEVAGH, 'Pit of the Scabby Horse.' This word has also been adopted from the late Latin *caballus* by the Norsemen (see *post*). [(I) GORTNAGAPPUL.]

Sharragh (M), 'a foal;' in KNOCKSHARRY, 'Foals' Hill;' CHIBBYR HARREE, 'Foals' Well;' GOB-NY-SHARREY, 'Point of the Foals;' and BALLACHARRE, 'Foals' Farm.' The well-known CAIRN SHARRAGH VANE, 'White Foal Cairn,' is a huge block of white quartz, in the mountains near Druidale. It is now usually called 'THE SHARRAGH VEDN.' [(G) BARSHERRY.]

Moddey (M), (pl. *voddee*), 'a dog;' in COOIL VODDY, 'Dog Nook;' CRONK-Y-VODDEY, 'Hill of the Dog, or Dogs;' ELLAN-Y-VODDEY, 'Isle of the Dog, or Dogs,' in Ballaugh Curragh; CARRICK-Y-VODDEY, 'Rock of the Dog, or Dogs;' and in various BALLAMODDAS and BALLAMODDEYS, 'Dog Farm.' On the farm of this name, in the parish of Malew, there is a granite font, which probably belonged to an adjoining *keeill*. [(I) KNOCKAVADDY, (G) BLAIRMODDIE.]

Quallian (M), 'a whelp, cub,' is in local names applied to a low hill when near a higher one, as in SLIEAU WHUALLIAN, 'Whelp's Hill,' near the loftier South Barrule. Down the steep northern side

of this mountain the witches who survived the
ordeal of being ducked in the Curragh-glass are
said to have been formerly rolled in barrels with
spikes inside. This process would certainly kill
them. There is also CREG-Y-WHUALLIAN, 'Crag
of the Whelp;' LHERGY - AWHALLAN (*Aah-
Whuallin*), 'Whelp's Ford Slope;' and AWHAL-
LAN, 'Whelp's Ford.'

Goayr (F), 'a goat;' in GLIONE-NY-GOAYR, 'Glen of
the Goat;' and CLOSE-Y-GAUR, 'Close of the
Goat.' [(I) GLEUAGOWER, (G) ARDGOWER.]

Shynnagh (M), 'a fox;' in CRONK SHYNNAGH and
CRONK SHANNAGH, 'Fox Hill.' Foxes are now
extinct in the island, but the records tell us that
they formerly existed. [(I) COOLNASHINNAGH, (G)
AUCHENSHINNAGH.]

Conning (F), 'a rabbit;' in CLOSE CONNING, 'Rabbit
Close;' CROFT-NY-GONNING, 'Croft of the Rabbit;'
and CROIT GONNING, 'Rabbit Croft.' [(I)
KYLENAGONEEN.]

Kayt (M), 'a cat;' in CRONK-Y-CATT, 'Hill of the
Cat.' It is tempting to derive the name of this
place from the Irish *cath*, 'a battle,' especially as
there is a tumulus on it ; but, if it were so, it could
scarcely have acquired its present hard sound.
[(I) CARNAGAT.]

Raun (F), 'a seal;' in CARRIGRAUN, 'Seal Rock;' and
GOB-NA-ROINNA, 'Point of the Seal.' Seals were
formerly common off the Manx coast, but they
are now rarely seen. [(I) CAIRICKROAN.]

Maggle (M), 'a testicle;' in SLIEAU MAGGLE, 'Testicle
Hill.' It was probably so-called because the

shepherds brought the mountain lambs together there to be cut.

Ushag, 'a bird;' in CHIBBER-NY-USHAG, 'Well of the Bird.' This word is common in colloquial use, and is found in the Manx Bible. There is nothing corresponding to it in Irish or Gaelic.

Urley (M), 'an eagle;' in CRONK URLEY, 'Eagle Hill,' where a Tynwald Court was held in 1422. It is called RENEURLING in the Statute Law Book, which would seem to be a corruption of REN-URLEY, 'Eagle Ridge,' an appropriate name, as it is a long low hill. Eagles and falcons were formerly common in the Isle of Man, which the Stanleys had received from the English Crown for the nominal obligation of presenting a cast of falcons at each coronation. [(I) CRAIGANULLER, (G) BENYELLARY.]

Feeagh (M), 'a raven;' in GLIONE FEEAGH, 'Raven's Glen;' in EDD FEEAGH VOOAR, 'Big Raven's Nest;' and CROT-Y-DAA FIAG, 'Croft of the Two Ravens.' (The dual in Manx is not plural.) [(I) CARRICKANEAGH, (G) BEANAVEOCH.]

Eairkan (K), *earkan* (C), (F), 'a lapwing;' in TRAIE-NY-EARKAN, 'Strand of the Lapwing;' and PARK-NY-EARKAN, 'Park of the Lapwing.' This word is not now used in colloquial Manx, but it is found in the Manx Bible.

Fannag (F), 'a crow;' in CRONK-NY-FANNAG, 'The Hill of the Crow;' and CREGGAN-Y-ANNAG, 'Rocky Hillock of the Crow.' Urns have been found in the tumulus on CRONK-NY-FANNAG. [(I) MULLANAVANNAG.]

Foillan (F), 'a seagull;' in GOB-NY-VOILLAN, 'Point of the Seagull;' TRAIE-NY-FOILLAN, 'Shore of the Seagull;' and ELLAN-NY-FOILLAN, 'Island of the Seagull.' This was a field, probably once surrounded by water, as it is on the borders of the *curragh*, in the estate of Loughan-y-Eiy. It was in this field that a crannoge or lake dwelling was found some years ago. [(I) CARROWNAWEELAUN.]

Guiy (M), 'a goose;' in LOUGHAN-Y-EIY, 'Pond of the Goose;' CRONK-NY-GUIY, 'Hill of the Goose;' GULLET-NY-GUIY, 'Gullet of the Goose;' and MWANNAL-Y-GUIY, 'Neck of the Goose.' In these last two names it is used metaphorically of the narrowest part, in the one case of a little creek, and in the other of a field. [(I) MONAGAY.]

Thunnag (F), 'a duck;' in BALLATHUNNAG, 'Duck Farm;' and CLOSE TUNNAG, 'Duck Close.'

Kellagh (M), 'a cock' (pl. *kellee*); in AIREY KELLAG, 'Cock Moor;' BALLA-KELLAG, 'Cock Farm;' and EAIRY KELLEE, 'Cocks' Moor.' (This latter may, however, mean Kelly's Moor, being sometimes spelled EAIRY KELLY.) [(I) KNOCKAKILLY.]

Kiark (F), 'a hen;' in GLIONE KIARK, 'Hen Glen;' CLOSE GIARK, 'Hen Close;' BALLACARKEY and BALLAKARKA, 'Hens' Farm.' [(I) SLIEVENAGARK.]

Fedjag (F), 'a feather;' in CRONK-NY-FEDJAG, 'Hill of the Feather.'

Edd (M), 'a nest;' in CRONK NED (*yn edd*), 'Hill of the Nest.' *Edd* is also found as a prefix in EDD FEEAGH VOOAR, 'Big Raven's Nest.' This name is applied to a crag at the south end of Greeba Mountain. [(I) DERRYNANED.]

Beishteig (F), 'a reptile' (C), *peishteig*, 'a little worm'
(K), a diminutive of *Beisht*, 'a beast, brute.' The
old Irish word *beist*, from the Latin *bestia*, was
used in the lives of the Irish saints to denote
a dragon, serpent, or monster. THALLOO-A-
PEISHTEIG, 'Land of the Little Worm,' is probably so-called from worm-earths, without having
any legendary signification. [(I) LOCH-NA-PEISTE.]

Skeddan (M), 'a herring;' in GOB-Y-SKEDDAN, 'Point
of the Herring.' According to an old Manx
legend the fish elected the herring as their king.
The Deemsters swore to execute the laws of the
isle 'as indifferently as the herring's backbone
doth lie in the middle of the fish.' [(I) COOL-
SCADDAN, (G) CULSCADDAN.]

Brack (M), 'a trout,' a name derived from its speckled
skin (*breck*); in GLIONE-NY-BRACK, 'Glen of the
Trout.' [(I) BEALANNABRACK, (G) ALTIBRICK.]

Bollan (F), 'the rock fish,' a red fish resembling a
carp, and frequenting rocky coasts (Gi); in CREG-
VOLLAN, 'Carp Rock;' and TRAIE-NY-VOLLAN,
'Shore of the Carp.'

Shlig (F), 'a shell;' in BALLASHLIG, 'Shell Farm.'
There are several farms of this name on sandy
soil inland, where shells have been found.

Shellan (F), 'a bee;' in GLENSHELLAN, 'Bee Glen.'

Caashey (M), 'cheese;' in GOB-NY-CAASHEY, 'Point of
the Cheese.' Possibly a vessel laden with cheese
was wrecked here.

From the Vegetable Kingdom.

Keyll (F), 'a wood;' in BALLAKEYLL, 'Wood Farm;' and BOOLDOHOLLY (*Bwoaillee doo Keylley*), 'Black Fold of the Wood.' *Keyll* is usually corrupted *killey*, but as this is also the corruption of *keeill*, 'a church' (see p. 151), it is difficult to distinguish between the two. It may, however, be safely assumed that most of the BALLAKILLEYS may be translated 'Church Farm,' as they are generally found in close proximity to sacred sites, which are very numerous, whilst we know from our records that woods have been, and are, conspicuous by their absence.　[(I) BALNAKILLIE.]

Billey (pl. *biljyn*) (M), 'a tree;' in BALLAVILLEY, 'Tree Farm,' now Seafield, in the parish of Santon; in POOLHILLY, POOLVILL, POOLVILLA, and POOL-YILLEY, 'Tree Pool;' and BALLAMILJIN, 'Trees' Farm,' also possibly in BALLAMILLAGHYN.　[(I) AGHAVILLEY.]

Tramman (F), 'the elder-tree;' in GLIONE TRAMMAN, 'Elder-tree Glen;' and BOOIL TRAMMAN, 'Elder-tree Fold.' *Tramman* would seem to have been originally a diminutive of an obsolete *tromm*.

Dar (gen. *darragh*) (M), 'an oak;' in GLIONE DARRAGH and GLEN DARRAGH, 'Oak Glen;' in CRONK DARRAGH, 'Oak Hill;' and possibly in CRONK DERREE, 'Oaks' Hill;' in COOIL DARRY, 'Oaks' Nook;' and AWIN-NY-DARRAGH, 'River of the Oak.' At the upper end of GLEN DARRAGH, in the parish of Marown, there are the remains of a fine stone circle.　[(I) CLONDARRAGH, (G) GLENDARROCH.]

Euar (K), 'the yew;' in BALLURE, 'Yew Farm.' The old chapel in the *treen* of this name has been kept in repair, and is still used. [(I) GLENURE.]

Unjin, 'the ash;' in CHIBBER UNJIN, 'Ash Well;' and CRONK UNJIN, 'Ash Hill.' At CHIBBER UNJIN there was formerly a sacred ash-tree, where votive offerings were hung. The ash was formerly considered a sacred tree, possibly from a recollection of Scandinavian legends with regard to it.

Cullion (K), 'the holly;' in RENCULLEN, 'Holly Ridge;' GLEN COOILIEEN, 'Holly Glen.' [(I) DRIMCULLEN, (G) BARHULLION.]

Drine (M), 'a thorn, or thorn-tree;' in BALDRINE, 'Thorn-tree Farm;' THALLOO DRINE, 'Thorn-tree Land, or Plot;' and THALLOO DRINE BEG, 'Little Thorn-tree Land, or Plot.' *Drine* is the general word for thorn, or thorn-tree, though usually applied more especially to the blackthorn. [(I) AGHADREAN, (G) BEEALCHANDREAN.]

Drughaig (F), 'the hipthorn, or dog-rose' (*drine drughaig* being the correct term); in LOUGH DRUGHAIG, 'Dog-rose Lake.'

Skeaig (K), *Skeag* (C), 'the hawthorn' (for *drine skeag*); in BALLASKAIG, BALLASKEIGE, and possibly BALLASAIG, 'Hawthorn Farm;' and DREEM-Y-JEE-SKAIG, '(Hill-)back of the Two Hawthorns.' Large hawthorn-trees were supposed to be frequented by fairies, and therefore regarded with considerable respect. They were also placed by wells. [(G) KNOCKSKAIG.]

Aittin (K), 'gorse;' in CRONKAITTIN, 'Gorse Hill;' CREGGAN-ASHEN, formerly CREGGAN-ATTEN, 'Gorse

Rocky Hillock;' and GAREY-ASHEN, 'Gorse Stony Land.' This word is not now used colloquially. [(I) COOLATTIN.]

Conney (Gi), 'gorse;' in BALLACONNA-MOOR (*Mooar*), 'Big Gorse Farm;' and perhaps in BALLACUNNEY, 'Gorse Farm.' This latter, however, is more probably 'QUINNEY's Farm.' Gill, on whose authority only the word is given, remarks: 'It is a complete term for the whole genus of furze, distinguished into the following species: *aittin*, " gorse, whins ;" *frangagh*, " great furze, or gorse ;" *fruaighe*, "heath, ling." *Conney* is the general colloquial term for gorse.'

Freoagh (M), 'heath, heather;' in KNOCK-FREIY and KNOCKFROY, 'Heather Hill;' DREEMFROY, 'Heather (Hill-)back;' and BOOILLEY-FREOIE, 'Heather Fold.' [(I) INISHFREE, (G) INNISFRAOCH.]

Guilc and *guilcagh* (K), 'the broom plant;' in BALLAJUCKLEY, 'Broom Plant Farm;' and CRONKJUCKLEY, 'Broom Plant Hill.' [(I) KNOCKGILSIE.]

Shuglaig (F), 'sorrel;' in BALLASHUGLAIG, 'Sorrel Farm;' BALLA-SHUGLAIG-E-QUIGGIN, 'Quiggin's Sorrel Farm;' and BALLY-SHUGLAIG-E-CAIN, 'Cain's Sorrel Farm.' *Shuglaig* is occasionally corrupted into *Shalghaige*, as in BALLASHALGHAIGE.

Cabbag (F), 'sour-dock;' in TRAIE CABBAGE, 'Sour-dock Shore;' and CLOSE CHABBACH, 'Sour-dock Close.' [(I) GLENCOPPOG.]

Sheillagh or *Shellagh* (F), 'the sallow or willow;' in CON-SHELLAGH (*coan*), 'Willow Valley;' and possibly in BALLASALLA, 'Willow Farm;' but

this is more probably from *sallagh* (see *post*).
[(G) BARNSALLIE.]

Jean (K), ' darnel weed ;' in BALJEAN (*Balla*), ' Darnel-
weed Farm.' This word is not now used colloquially, the ordinary word for ' darnel weed '
being *jurlan*.

Sumrac and *sumark* (F), ' a primrose.' This word is
probably a corruption of the Irish *seamrog*, a
diminutive of *seamar*, ' the trefoil, or white clover.'
This has become anglicised into shamrock, in
which form it occurs in BALLASHAMROCK, ' Primrose Farm.'

　　The colloquial Manx for primrose is *sumark-
souree*, ' summer primrose.' These flowers were
formerly gathered on May-eve, and scattered
before the doors of every house as a charm against
witchcraft. [(I) COOLNASHAMROGE, (G) GLEN-
SHIMMEROCK.]

Dullish, *dyllish* (F), ' a sea-weed, which is eaten either
wet or dried, liver worts, dills, from *duill*, a leaf,
and *ush* or *ushtey*, water' (Gi) ; ' a marine eatable
leaf' (C) ; in TRAIE DULLISH, ' Sea-weed Shore.'

Corkey (M), ' oats ;' in BALLACORKEY, ' Oats Farm.'
[(I) FARRANACURKEY.]

Shoggyl (F), ' rye ;' in GLIONE-SHOGGYL, ' Rye Glen ;'
BALLASHUGGAL, ' Rye Farm ;' and BOLE-SHOGGIL
(*Bwoailley*), ' Rye Fold.' Rye is very seldom
grown now. [(I) COOLATAGGLE.]

Coonlagh (F), ' straw ;' in CLOSE CONLEY, ' Straw
Close ;' BALLACONLEY, formerly BALLACOONLAGH,
' Straw Farm ;' and KEEILL-COONLAGH, ' Straw
Church.' The primitive *keeill* was probably thatched.

Sceabag (K), 'a small sheaf;' in BALLASKEBBAG and BALLASKEBBEG, 'Sheaf Farm.' This word is not now used colloquially, the ordinary word for a sheaf being *bunney.*

Traagh (F), 'hay;' in GLENTRAGH, 'Hay Glen.' This word, though not found in Irish or Gaelic, is used colloquially in Manx.

Soo (M), 'juice, a berry;' in BROOGH-NY-SOO, 'Brow of the Berry.'

Feeyn (M), 'wine, or a vine;' in CHLEIG-NY-FHEEINEY,. 'Hedge of the Wine;' GAREY FEENEY, 'Wine Garden;' and TRAIE-NY-FEANEY, 'Strand of the Wine.' These names must either refer to smuggling, or are else purely fanciful, as grapes would not ripen out of doors in the Manx climate.

TRAIE-NY-FEENEY would be a very convenient place for smuggling, but CHLEIG-NY-FHEEINEY is high ground inland, at the head of Glen Rushen.

From the Mineral Kingdom.

The Isle of Man shows but little trace of its mineral wealth in its local names.

Leoaie, 'lead,' though worked from an early period, does not bestow a name on any place.

Yiarn (M), 'iron;' in EAIRN YERREY, 'Iron End,' on Bradda Head; GIAU YIARN, 'Iron Creek;' and possibly in PORT ERIN, formerly PHURT YIARN, 'Iron Port.' It may have been so called from being the landing-place of the ore from the neigh- bouring Bradda mine, but the Scandinavian derivation (see *post*) seems more probable. [(I) CURRY-NIERIN.]

Leac, lhiack (F), 'a slate;' in GOBLHIACK, 'Slate Point.' The slate rock at this point is in large slabs. [(G) ARIELICK.]

Argid (M), 'silver, money;' in CLOSE-YN-ARGYT, 'Close of the Silver or Money.' Perhaps so called from a discovery of hidden money. This word is cognate with the Latin *argentum*. [(I) CLOONARGID.]

Geinnagh (F), 'sand;' in CRAIG-Y-GHENNY, 'Rock of the Sand;' and KERROO-NY-GENNY, 'Quarter of the Sand.' [(I) CLONGANNY, (G) GLENGAIN-NOCH.]

Sooie (K), *sooee* (C), (F), 'soot;' in EARY-NY-SOOIE, 'Moor of the Soot.' So called from the smoke of a chimney connected with a mine which ascends to it.

Personal Names.

Probably the oldest application of personal nomenclature to local names in the Isle of Man occurs in the dedications of the parish churches, which were usually built on the site of older edifices, whose name they took, and of the *keills*, or so-called *treen* chapels, to Celtic saints. The names of these saints would lead us to suppose that Manxmen were, for the most part, Christianized by Irish missionaries; and, indeed, it would have been strange if the proselytizing Irish monks, who wandered all over Europe, had avoided an

---

* So many of the names under this heading must be considered doubtful, that all, whether doubtful or not, are given here.

island so near to them. Of the names of our seventeen parish churches, seven are certainly, two—MAUGHOLD and ONCHAN—almost certainly, and four probably, of Irish origin, the remaining four being of comparatively recent dedication. *St. Patrick's** own name was given to two churches, one called *Kirk* PATRICK, in Manx SKEELEY PHARICK, 'Patrick's Parish Church,' and the other *Kirk* PATRICK OF *Jurby*, the parishes being called PATRICK and *Jurby* (in 1511 *Jourby*). Jurby Point, on which the latter church is situated, is said to have once been an island—the INNIS PATRICK, where the saint is supposed to have landed. Peel Island, however, where there is also a church of very early date dedicated to him, has stronger claims to the name.

The saint now called *Maughold*, who is said to have been one of St. Patrick's earliest disciples, probably gave his name to the parish church called *Kirk* MAUG-HOLD, in Manx SKEELEY MAGHAL, 'Maughold's Parish Church.' It has, however, been suggested that this parish and church has really derived its name from *Macutus*, Bishop of Aleth in Brittany, whose bishopric was afterwards transferred to the town now called St. Malo, which is said to have been named after him. It may, therefore, be desirable to see what evidence

---

* Whether St. Patrick visited the Isle of Man or not is not certainly known, as the ancient records are silent on this point, and the inference from the accounts in the 'Book of Armagh' and 'Tripartite Life' would be that he had not (see under *Maughold*). It was reserved for Jocelyn, a monk of Furness, writing early in the 12th century, who may, however, have had access to information not attainable now, to tell us that he did so ; and his narrative is expanded and embellished by the 'Supposed True Chronicle of Man' and the 'Traditionary Ballad,' both probably of not earlier date than the sixteenth century.

there is in support of both views. The earliest
authority, the 'Book of Armagh,' speaks of a certain
Maccuil, whom it describes as a very bad character,
who was converted by St. Patrick, and sent off to an
island called *Evonia,* or *Eubonia,* an old name of the
Isle of Man. There he found two holy men, *Conindrus*
and *Rumilus,* who had already taught the Word of God
there. After their death he became bishop. The 'Tripartite Life of St. Patrick' contains a similar account,
stating that *Macc Cuill* 'went . . . to sea . . . till he
reached Mann.' There is now no available evidence on
this subject till the thirteenth century, when, in a bull of
Pope Gregory IX., dated 1231, recently published by the
writer in the *English Historical Review,* we find this parish
recorded as that of *Sancti Maughaldi.* In the *Chronicon
Manniæ,* the greater part of which was written in the
fourteenth century, he is on every occasion but one,
when *Maccaldus* is found, called *Macutus.* In the 'Traditionary Ballad,' probably written early in the sixteenth
century, he is called *Maughold,* and in the manorial roll
of 1511, *Maghald.* It is, of course, not possible to
certainly connect the *Maughald* of the thirteenth
century with the *Maccuil* mentioned by the 'Book of
Armagh,' and the phonetic change involved is im-
probable, though not impossible, as *Maccuil* would
be called *Mac Coole* by Manx people, and the final 'd,'
which is not sounded by them, would seem to have
been added with the Latin termination.

The evidence in favour of *Macutus* seems much
weaker. It is simply that his name is mentioned
in the *Chronicon Manniæ,* and that he was a friend of
St. Brendan's, who was supposed to be the originator

of the name of the parish of Braddan. What is more likely than that the monks of Rushen, who, through Furness, were connected with the monastery of Savigny, in France, should transfer the name of a Breton saint of some celebrity in their day to the name of a parish which had been called after an Irish saint, who, when the influence of Ireland and that of the Irish Church had completely passed away, would have been forgotten, and whose name bore a faint resemblance to his. On the whole, then, there seems to be a reasonable presumption that the parish of MAUGHOLD and its church were named after the Irish *Maccuil*.

Lonan, St. Patrick's nephew, has given his name to *Kirk* LONAN, or LONNAN; in Manx SKEEYLLEY LONNAN, 'Lonnan's Parish Church,' the parish being called LONNAN.

Connaghyn, as he is called in the 'Traditionary Ballad,' has bestowed his name on *Kirk* ONCHAN, in Manx SKEEYLLEY CONNAGHYN, 'Connaghan's Parish Church.' The name of the parish is written CONAGHAN, or CONCHAN, in the earliest records, and is to this day pronounced CONAGHAN by the Manx-speaking people. In formal documents the name of the parish is still written CONCHAN, but by the younger people, who do not speak Manx, it is usually spoken of as ONCHAN; this form having arisen in the same way as ORRY from GORRY, *i.e.*, KIRK CONCHAN to KIRK ONCHAN, as KING GORRY to KING ORRY. It is difficult to connect *Conaghan* with any Irish saint mentioned in the martyrologies; but he is probably identical with *St. Con-*

nigen, whose name occurs in the Calendar of Oengus. The popular idea that Conchan was named after *St. Concha* (Lat. *Concessa*), St. Patrick's mother, cannot be accepted philologically.

The parish church of Marown, *Kirk* Marown, in Manx Skeeylley Marooney, 'Marooney's Parish Church,' is dedicated to a saint called *Maronog* in the Irish Calendars, *Marooney* in the 'Traditionary Ballad,' and *St. Runi* (gen. case) in the manorial roll of 1511. In a bull of Pope Gregory IX., dated 1231, the church of this parish is called Kyrke Marona. The prefix *mo,* 'my,' and the affix *og,* 'young,' in *Maronog* or *Moronog,* are both expressive of endearment, and are frequently attached to the names of Celtic saints. The old church of Marown is situated on the hill above Ellerslie. Tradition says that three bishops were buried there, viz. : *Rooney, Lonnan,* and *Connaghan.* In the parish now called Arbory there are two *keeills,* Keeill Cairbre and Keeill Columb, the latter being the famous Irish missionary to the Scots, *St. Columba.* Formerly the parish was sometimes called after one, and sometimes after the other. In 1153 we find *terram Sancti Carebrie;* in 1231 *terram Sti. Columbæ, herbery vocatam;* in 1291 there was a presentation *ad ecclesiam Sancti Carber,* and in the manorial rolls of 1511 we find *Parochia Sti. Columbæ.* In fact these records have the same title for this parish, though it is now generally called Arbory, at the present day. In Durham's map, published in 1595, it is written *Kirk* Kerbery, the Manx form of the name being

SKEEYLLEY CAIRBRE, which is still pronounced by old Manx people as SKEELEY KARBERY. Its usual modern name, ARBORY, has arisen from KARBERY, in the same way as ONCHAN from CON-CHAN. This name ARBORY seems to have come into use at least two centuries ago, for, at the end of the sixteenth century, we find Sacheverell, one of our historians, explaining that it was so called from the number of trees (arbours) there formerly. The church of the parish of SANTAN, or SANTON, in Manx SKEEYLLEY STONDANE,* 'Sanctan's Parish Church,' now *Kirk* SANTAN, called in 1511 ST. SANCTAN, is named after *St. Sanctan*, also an Irish saint, not from *St. Ann*, as the modern map-makers have it. Joyce, in an interesting passage which we quote below, tells us that exactly the same process with regard to this name has taken place in Ireland. 'Three miles above the village of Tallaght in Dublin . . . there is a picturesque little graveyard and ruin called Kill St. Ann, or "Saint Ann's Church;" near it is "Saint Ann's Well;" and an adjacent residence has borrowed from the church the name of "Ann Mount." The whole place has been, in fact, quietly given over to St. Ann, who has not the least claim to it; and an old Irish saint has been dispossessed of his rightful inheritance by a slight change of name. Dalton, in his history of Dublin, writes the name Killnasantan, which he absurdly translates, "The Church of Saint Ann." But in the *Repertorium*

* The intrusive '*t*' is characteristic of Manx, vide *strooan* for *sruthan*, etc.

Viride of Archbishop Alan we find it written Kill-mesantan, from which it is obvious that the *na* in Dalton's Killnasantan, which he thought was the Irish article, is really corrupted from the particle *mo*, " my," so commonly prefixed as a mark of respect to the names of Irish saints. The Four Masters give us the original form of the name at A.D. 952 . . *Cill-Easpuig-Sanctain, i.e.,* the church of Bishop Sanctan. So that the founder of this lonely church was one of the early saints —of whom several are commemorated in the calendars—called Sanctan or Santan. . . . The name is a diminutive of the Latin root *sanct* (holy), borrowed into the Irish.'* The parish church of BRIDE, in Manx SKEEYLLEY BRIDEY, ' Brigit's Parish Church,' now *Kirk* BRIDE, called in 1511 ST. BRIGIDE, is dedicated to *St. Brigit,* the most famous of Irish female saints.

We now come to the names of the parish churches and parishes which are of doubtful, but still probably, Irish origin.

With regard to the first of these, that of GERMAN, which has been given to the cathedral of the diocese, ST. GERMAN'S, as well as a parish church, *Kirk* GERMAN, in Manx SKEEYLLEY CHARMANE, ' German's Parish Church,' the parish being called GERMAN, the *Traditionary Ballad* tells us that St. Patrick, before he left the island, 'blessed St. *Germanus,* and left him a bishop in it to strengthen the faith more and more.'† A difficulty, however, arises from the fact that the name of *Germanus*

---

* ' Irish Names of Places,' Joyce, 2nd series, pp. 22, 23.
† Train, ' History of the Isle of Man,' p. 52.

does not occur in the Irish calendars, and we have only the comparatively recent authority of Jocelin for his being St. Patrick's disciple. By way of solving this it may not, perhaps, be unreasonable to conjecture that *Germanus* was substituted for *Coemanus* by later writers, who would remember the famous saint of Auxerre, while forgetting the obscure Irishman. This *Coemanus*, or, as he is called in Irish Martyrologies, *Mochaemog*, is known to have been one of St. Patrick's disciples.

The name of the parish of BRADDAN, and of its church, in Manx SKEEYLLEY VRADDAN, ' Braddan's Parish Church,' now *Kirk* BRADDAN, has been connected with the famous Irish saint and navigator, *Brandinus*, or *Brendinus*, or with the *St. Brandan*, who, though not mentioned by the monks of Rushen Abbey, was, according to Manx historians, bishop from 1098-1113. This theory does not seem consonant with orthodox philology; but, nevertheless, it may be correct. In 1231 a bull of Pope Gregory IX. mentions *terras Sti. Bradani*, and in 1291 Bishop Mark held a synod at *Bradan*.

The name of the parish church of RUSHEN, in Manx SKEEYLLEY-CHREEST-RUSHEN, ' Christ Rushen Parish Church,' now *Kirk* CHRIST RUSHEN, presents considerable difficulties. The earliest mention of it is in 1408, when it is called the parish church, *Sancti Trinitatis inter prata*, ' of the Holy Trinity among the Meadows.' The lowlands about the church are still intack, not quarterland, and were therefore, probably, marshy, and consequently uncultivated formerly—hence the word *prata*.

In the manorial roll of 1511 it is called *Parochia Sct' Trinitatis in* RUSHEN, and in 1540 *Kirk* CRISTE *in*

Sheding. The most probable interpretation, though others are possible (see p. 160), is that RUSHEN has derived its name from *St. Russein* of *Inis-Picht*, mentioned in the Martyrology of Tallaght, whose name was probably forgotten before 1511, when, RUSHEN being regarded as a place-name, *in* may have been substituted for *noo,* 'saint.' RUSHEN is also the name of the sheading, and of the castle in Castletown. With reference to the name of the church in 1540, *Kirk* CRISTE, or, as it is called at the present day, in Manx SKEEYLEY CHREEST, 'Christ's Parish Church,' or *Kirk* CHRIST, it is remarkable that the only two churches in the island which are dedicated to the Holy Trinity, RUSHEN and LEZayre, are both called *Christ's Church.* Why this is so is unknown to the writer, but it is interesting to note that the same applies to Christ's Church Cathedral in Dublin.

The parish of MALEW, and its church, in Manx SKEEYLEY MALEW, ' Malew's Parish Church,' now *Kirk* MALEW, are generally supposed to have derived their names from St. *Lupus,* the pupil of St. German of Auxerre, who was sent to Britain to confound the Pelagians. In confirmation of this theory may be quoted the inscription on an ancient patten, now in Malew church, *Sancte Lupe ora pro nobis,* and the entry in the Roll of 1511, *Parochia Sti. Lupi.* It is equally probable, however, that the name may come from that of an Irish saint, *Moliba* or *Molipa,* the Latinized form of *Moliu* or *Maliu,* whose name is found in the Calendar of Oengus. In a bull of Pope Gregory XI., dated 1377, relating to a presentation to this church, it is called St. *Moliwe.* This may, of course, refer to either saint, as *Lupus*, like *Rooney*, may have had the prefix *mo*, though it more probably refers to the Irishman, the famous *Lupus* being not so likely to have his name changed.

The names of the four remaining parishes and their churches are probably of much later origin. Both the parishes of BALLAUGH and LE*zayre*, the churches of which were called in 1231 *Stæ. Mariæ de Ballylaughe*, 'of St. Mary of Miretown' (see p. 176), and *Sti. Trinitatis in Leayre*, 'of the Holy Trinity in the Ayre,' respectively, were probably mainly occupied by marshes then, and even later. In 1423 the Charter of John de Stanley, which confirms that of Magnus to the Church of Sodor, mentions 'the village of KILLCRAST,' now LE*zayre;* in 1505 it is called *Kirk* CRISTE, and in the manorial roll of 1511 the parish *Sti. Trinitatis* (see RUSHEN). Manx-speaking people called this church SKEEYLLEY - CHREEST - NY - *Heyrey*, ' Christ's Parish Church of the Ayre.' Here *n* has been changed into *l*, as usual, so that *ny Heyrey*, or *ny Ayre* became *ly-ayre*, or *le-ayre*; and, more recently, by a curious corruption, *Lezayre*. Chaloner, writing in the middle of the seventeenth century, tells us that it was then called *Kirk* CRISTE LE *Ayre*, because it is placed 'in a sharp ayre'! The name of the parish of MICHAEL, and its church *Kirk* MICHAEL, or in Manx SKEEYLLEY MAYL, 'Michael's Parish Church,' does not appear till 1299. The name of the parish of Andreas, and its church *Kirk* ANDREAS, or in Manx SKEEYLLEY ANDREAYS, 'Andrew's Parish Church,' probably dates from the period of Scotch rule (1275-1334), as it is named after the patron saint of that country.

Of the ancient *keeills*, referred to above, the remains of more than one hundred are still to be found, the earliest of which probably date from the sixth century, and of their names about thirty survive.

St. Patrick gives his name to six of them, called KEEILL PHARICK, or KEEILL PHERICK, and one called KEEILL-PHERICK-A-DRUMMA (*y drommey*), ' Patrick's Cell of the Hill(-back).' Near the farm of BALLAKIL-PHARIC, ' Patrick's Cell Farm,' in Rushen, are two huge standing stones, which are probably the remains of a megalithic monument.

St. Bridget has seven, under the various forms of BREESHY, VREESHY, and even BRICKEY and BRAGGA. The KEEILL VREESHEY on Ballaharry farm, near Crosby, has walls about four feet high, built of stones without mortar. The treen of KILMARTIN, and the adjoining farm of BALLAKILMARTIN, perhaps derive their names from *St. Martin*, St. Patrick's uncle. KEEILLCOLUM and BALLACOLUM, close by, were probably called after *St. Columba.*

The Gaelic saint *Ronan* has two cells called KEEILL RONAN ; probably this name is identical with *Maronog* when deprived of its affix and prefix.

St. Lingan, an Irish saint, has two chapels : KEEIL-LINGAN, on the hill above the estate of BALLA-KIL-LINGAN, and CABBAL LINGAN, on the farm of BAL-LINGAN. CABBAL LINGAN is one of the best specimens of *keeills* left. The walls are still about four feet high, and three feet thick, and there is a font in the north-east corner. The enclosure surrounding the chapel is one hundred and eight feet long by sixty-three broad, being oval in form.

ST. TRINIAN'S, the ruins of a church of the thirteenth

century, probably on an older site, was dedicated to *Ringan* or *Ninnian*, of which *Trinnian* is a corruption. This church formerly belonged to the priory of ST. NINNIAN, at Whithorne in Galloway, whose priors were barons of the Isle. It dates probably from the thirteenth century. The legend of its never having had a roof through the mischievous intervention of a *Buggane*, or evil spirit, may be read in any guide-book to the island. There is a CHIBBER DINGAN in the parish of Kirkmaiden in Galloway, and at KILLAN-TRINGAN, near Portpatrick. The name of ST. CRORE, an Irish saint, is given to KEEILL CRORE, near Kirk Patrick. To the Virgin Mary there are dedicated several *keeills*, called KEEILL MOIRREY, and KEEILL VOIRREY; to St. John, *Ean* or *Eoin* in Manx, are dedicated KILANE, and the Manx name of the chapel at Tynwald Hill, KEEILLOWN, 'John's Cell,' and of the hill itself CRONK-KEEILLOWN. St. Michael has several, called KEEILL VAEL, and KEEILL VAIL. The ST. MICHAELIS mentioned in the Papal Bull to Bishop Simon, dated 1231, is the KEEILL VAEL on the Barony in the parish of Maughold, the ruins of which are still to be seen. The KEEILL VAEL, on Langness, is pro-bably a church of the eleventh or twelfth century. According to the engraving of it given by Chaloner, it was roofless more than two centuries ago. It is thirty-one feet long by fourteen feet broad, the height of the side walls being about ten feet. There is an ancient graveyard round it. St. Bartholomew has a *keeill* called KEEILL PHARLANE; St. Matthew one, KEEILL VIAN, and there is a *keeill* called KEEILL-YN-CHIARN, 'Cell of the Lord.'

Closely connected with the *keeills* dedicated to these

saints or recluses are the wells, which were used by them
both for drinking and baptizing their converts (see pp.
153, 154). Of these the names of the following remain:
CHIBBER PHERICK, ' Patrick's Well,' where according to
tradition the saint stopped to drink as his horse stumbled
there; CHIBBER MAGHAL, ' Maughold's Well,' on the
promontory of the same name, is one of the most famous
wells in the island. A drink of its water, taken after
resting in the saint's chair close by, is supposed to be
an unfailing cure for barrenness in women. CHIBBER
VOIRREY, ' Mary's Well;' there are three wells of
this name. One of these, in Ballaugh, may still be
seen bubbling up when the tide is low, about 150 yards
seaward from BALLAKOIG farm, and is thus a witness
of the rapidity with which the land has been eaten
away by the sea at this point; CHIBBER NIGLAS,
' Nicholas's Well,' is close to the ancient alignement
at Braddan; CHIBBER VREESHEY, ' Bridget's Well;'
CHIBBER VAILL (*Vayl*), ' Michael's Well;' CHIBBER
KATREENEY, ' Catherine's Well;' CHIBBER ONEY, a
corruption of CHIBBER RONEY, in the parish of MARONY
(*Marown*), being ' Roney's Well.' *Patrick* again appears
in GIAU-NY-PHARICK (*E*), ' Patrick's Cove;' *Maughold*,
in MAUGHOLD *Head* and ELLAN-NY-MAUGHOL (*E*),
' Maughold's Isle,' the name of a small rock in the sea;
Michael, in RHULLICK KEEILL VAEL, ' Michael's Cell
Churchyard;' and *Moirrey* (*Mary*), in BALLAWORREY,
' Mary's Farm;' and in PURT-NOO-MOIRREY, ' Port
Saint Mary,' or, as it is usually pronounced, PORT-LE-
MORROUGH, by Manx people, the *l* according to Manx
habit being substituted for *n*, in the same way as
Langlish for *Langness*, and LEayre for NY-*ayre*. We

have also GLIONE KEEILL CRORE, ‘Crore’s Cell Glen ;’ STRUAN KEEILL CRORE, ‘ Crore’s Cell Stream ;’ and CRONK-Y-CROGHE, formerly CRONK-Y-CRORE (*E*), ‘Crore’s Hill,’ a large tumulus, which, when it was opened in 1880, contained an urn and some calcined bones. *St. Donan*, or *Donnan*, an Irish disciple of St. Columba’s, who was put to death with fifty companions in the Isle of Eig by a band of pirates in A.D. 617, is probably commemorated in the tumulus called ARDONAN, ‘ Donan’s Height.’ There are several places in the Western Isles and Scotland called KILDONAN. TARRA*stack*, the name of a detached rock in the sea, is possibly a corruption of TARANS *Stack*. There was a St. *Torannan*, Abbot of Bangor (cf. TARANSAY, Hebrides).

The meaning of the name of the two mountains of North and South BAROOLE or BARRULE has given rise to considerable discussion. Possibly it is from *Rule* or *Regulus*, the Abbot, who went to bring the relics of the Apostle St. Andrew to Scotland, and was consequently famous, and may therefore mean ‘ Rule’s Top ’ (*baare*). Among the early legendary bishops of the island there is one *Romulus*, the fifth on the list, whose name may perhaps have been given to these mountains. In the ‘ Tripartite Life of St. Patrick ’ he is called *Romuil*, and is stated to have been one of two holy men who had preached God's Word in Man. Colgan calls him *Romailum*, and Professor Rhŷs conjectures that in Manx this should become something like *Rowell* or *Rowill;* so *Rowell* may have become contracted into *Roole*, as *Cowell* into *Cowle*, and so BAARE-ROOLE into BARROOLE. Of these two mountains the southern, though lower, is the more famous. It was from its summit that the legendary *Manannan* (p. 131) performed his incantations by which he covered the island with a fog, and made one man appear like an hundred ; and it was here that he received the yearly rent from each landholder of a bundle of coarse meadow grass. In 1316 the Manx were routed on its slopes by a band of Irish freebooters. Round its summit is a large enclosure made by a dry wall of about 150 yards in diameter. It was no doubt intended for a refuge by the people, to which they would retire with their cattle on the sudden landing of an enemy. From his Castle of Rushen to South BARRULE was evidently a favourite walk of James, the seventh Earl of Derby, who, in his diary, writes as follows : ' When I go to the mount you call BAROULL, and, but turning me round, can see England, Scotland, Ireland, and Wales, . . . which no place, I think in any nation that we know under heaven, can afford such a prospect.' There is also a KNOCKRULE, ' Rowell's or Rule's Hill,' now usually called *Mount* RULE, and a GIAU ROOLE, ' Rowell's or Rule's Cove.'

We now come to the affixes from the personal names of ordinary men without saintly renown. They were for the most part, doubtless, the first recorded owners of the properties which bear their names.

The name of GLENTRUAN in the parish of Bride is possibly derived from the extinct personal name *Druian* or *Truian* found on an inscribed cross in the parish churchyard close by. It cannot be derived from *strooan*, ' a stream,' because it is not likely that there was ever a stream in the glen.

Surnames.*

The number of these names which, in connection with *Balla*, form the designations of our farms, is very large. Most of them are perfectly intelligible, and can be found in the Index of Personal Names. In the following list, therefore, only those names which have either become obsolete, or so corrupt as not to be easily interpreted at first sight, will be explained sufficiently to facilitate reference to the Index above referred to.

BALLAWHANNEL and BALLAGONNELL, probably 'Cannel's Farm.'

BALLACONDYR and BALLACUNNER, 'Cundre's Farm;' BALLAKILLOWY, 'Gillowy's Farm.'

BALLACRINE, 'Creen's, or Crine's Farm.'

BALLAVARTIN, BALLAVARTEEN, BALLAVARTON and BALLAVARCHEIN, 'Martin's Farm.'

BALLAMACSKEALLEY, 'MacSkealley's Farm.'

BALLASKEALEY, 'Skealey's Farm.'

BALLACOAREY, a corruption of BALLAQUARRYS, as the name is spelled in 1511, 'Quarrys' or Quarrie's Farm.'

BALLACOTCH, possibly 'Cottier's Farm,' COTTIER being pronounced COTCHER.

BALLACREETCH, 'Creetch's Farm.'

BALLASTOLE, 'Stowell's Farm.'

BALLA*whetstone*, 'Whetstone's Farm.' Anthony Whetstone† was the owner of this property in 1670.

BALLATROLLAG, 'Trollag's Farm.'

* All surnames with *Balla*, whether Celtic or Scandinavian, are given here.

† Not a Manx name.

BALLACAGIN, 'Cagin's or Kaighin's Farm.'

BALLAQUEENEY and BALLAQUINEA, 'Quinney's Farm.'
On BALLAQUEENEY, near Port St. Mary, ogam inscriptions have been discovered. CRONK BALLAQUEENY, on this farm was in the spring of 1874 cut into to obtain gravel for the railway to Port Erin, when a large number of graves were discovered. They had slabs over them, and the interiors were lined with thin flags. From the dry nature of the soil, gravel and sand, many of the remains were found entire ; in some instances two bodies had been interred in the same grave, lying on their sides. The graves were arranged forming tangents to a circle, the chapel being in the centre. The chapel showed remains of foundations chiefly built of stones of large size without mortar. In some of the graves Anglo-Saxon coins were found, viz., Edmund (*ob.* 946), Edred (*ob.* 955), and Edwy (*ob.* 958), also a flint implement and a stone axe. The field has now been levelled, and all traces of the graves are obliterated.

BALLAKINDRY, ' Kinry's Farm.' The name KINRY is now almost universally translated into HARRISON.

BALLACARMICK, 'Carmick's Farm.' This name is CARMYK in 1511.

BALLAKILLOWIE, ' Gillowy's Farm.'

BALLASHERLOGUE, 'Sherlogue's, or Sherlock's Farm ;' BALLAWHANE, ' Quane's Farm.'

BALLA*coyll*, probably ' Coyle's Farm.'*

BALLACUNNEY, possibly ' Guinney's Farm.' The name was formerly pronounced *cunyagh*.

DOWN, formerly BALLADOWAN, ' Dowan's Farm ;'

* Not a Manx name.

BERRAG, formerly BALLABERRAG, ' Berrag's Farm.'
The name DOWAN occurs in Andreas, and BERRAG
is common in Jurby early in the eighteenth century.

BALLAKINNAG and BALLAKENAG, ' Kinnag's or Kenag's
Farm.' These names are possibly forms of the
modern KENNAUGH.

KEW would seem to be the remains of BALLAKEW,
' Kew's Farm;' KEWAIGUE of BALLAKEWAIGUE,
' Young Kew's Farm.'

BALLAGILLEY, ' Killey's Farm.'

BALLAKERBERY, ' Carberry's Farm.'

BALLAKOIGE, possibly ' Keig's Farm.'

BALLACOGEEN, where COGEEN is a corruption of
CREGEEN, ' Cregeen's Farm.'

BALLAFADEN and BALLAFADINE, ' Faden's Farm.'

BALLACORAGE, ' Corage's Farm.' The modern name
CRAIG is a corruption of it.

BALLACUSTAL and BALLACUTCHAL, ' Gilcreest's Farm.'
Cregeen says that CUTCHAL or CUSTAL is a
corruption of Gilchreest. BALLAVITCHAL is
perhaps another corruption of the same, though
it looks like ' Mitchell's Farm.'

BALLACAROON, ' Corooin's Farm.'

BALLAREGNELT, formerly BALLAREGNYLT, ' Reginald's
Farm ' (see CRELLIN and CRENNELL).

BALLAVARGHER, ' Fargher's Farm.'

BALLANICKLE, ' Knickell's Farm.'

BALLAGORRA and BALLAGORRY, ' Gorry's Farm.'

BALLAFREER, ' Freer's Farm.' There is an ancient
keeill called KEEILL PHARIC on this farm in the
parish of Marown. There is an old tradition concerning it to the effect that, when St. Patrick and

St. Germanus passed over this spot, a briar tore St. Patrick's foot, lacerating it considerably, whereupon the saint pronounced the following anathema: ' Let this place be accursed, and let it never produce any kind of grain fit for man, but only briars and thorns, as a warning to keep off this wilderness.' Certainly the site of the chapel, like many others, is surrounded by thorns, but the farm is as fertile as those near it. It is said that the vicar of the parish was formerly wont to read prayer in this *keeill* on Ascension-day. On the south-east of the chapel lies its old stone font, two and a half feet long.

There are also the following surnames compounded with various topographical prefixes :

CLOSE VARK, ' Quark's Close,' and *Bastin's** CLOSE. One hundred and fifty years ago *Bastin*, though not a name of native origin, was very common in the parish of Andreas.

CASTLE *Ward*,* the name of the curious fortification in Braddan, popularly called ' The Danish Camp,' but probably of neolithic origin, was called CASTELL MACWADE, ' MacWade's Castle,' in the Manorial Roll of 1511.

CROIT FREER, ' Freer's Croft ;' CROT-Y-VEDN-BREDJEN, ' Widow Bridson's Croft;' THALLOO QUEEN, ' Quyn's or Quine's Plot ;' KERROO *Cottle*,* ' Cottle's Quarter ;' EARY CUSHLIN, ' Cosnahan's Moor.' The Manx pronounce COSNAHAN as if spelled CUSHLAHAN or CUSHLAN.

GLIONE KERRAD, ' Kerrad's or Garret's Glen;' LHERGY *Colvin*,* ' Colvin's Slope ;' MULLENARAGHER,

* Not Manx names.

'Faragher's Mill;' BOILE *Vell** (*bwoaillee*), 'Bell's Fold;' and THALLOO *Vell*,* 'Bell's Plot;' BOOILLEY CORAGE (*bwoaillee*), 'Corage's or Craig's Fold.'

ARISTINE, in 1511, ARESTEYNE (*aeree* or *eary*), 'Steen's or Stephen's Moor;' and the name of the hill where this moor is, SLIEU EARY STANE, 'Steen's Moor Hill.'

BOUL*daley*,* 'Daley's Fold;' CRONK-E-*berry*,* 'Berry's Hill,' now usually called *Hillberry*; CREGGAN ASHEN seems to be a corruption of CREGGAN CASHEN, 'Cashen's Rocky Ground;' MULLEN-E-CORRAN is 'Corran's Mill.'

CREG CUSTANE, 'Costain's Rock;' CREG HARLOT, a small rock in the sea, may possibly be a corruption of CREG CORLEOT, 'Corlett's Rock;' GOB-NY-*Halsall* (*E*),* 'Halsall's Point;' LHOOB-Y-CHARRAN (*E*), 'Carran's Gulley or Loop.' This curious name is applied to a small headland at Bradda. ARNYCARNIGAN* (*ard*) is probably 'Carnigan's Height;' AWIN VITCHAL, 'Gilcreest's or Mitchell's River;' ARYHORKELL, 'Corkell's Moor;' CRONT-E-CALEY (*cronk*), 'Caley's Hill;' GOB-NY-CALLY (*E*), possibly 'Cally's or Caley's Point;' KNOCKALOE, formerly KNOCKALLY, KNOCK-ALOE-MOAR, and KNOCKALOE-BEG, possibly 'Caley's Hill,' 'Caley's Big Hill,' and 'Caley's Little Hill;' LHIAGHT-Y-KINRY (*E*), 'Kinry's Grave;' COOIL NICKAL, 'Knickell's Nook.'

For ALGAR, 'Alfgeirr,' the name of a farm in Baldwin, see the surname MAC ALCAR.

Christian names are also sometimes found as part of a place-name.

* Not Manx names.

BALLADHA (*Ædh*), 'Hugh's Farm;' CREG ADHA, 'Hugh's Crag.'

CREG MALIN is probably 'Malane or Magdalen's Crag.'

GOB-NY-UAINAIGUE (*E*), 'Young John's Point,' and BALLAYONAIGUE, 'Young John's Farm.' This farm has been for a long time held by people named Christian, and is still in their possession. A reference to the Register of the parish of Bride will show that JOHNAIGUE was for generations the name of the eldest son of this family.

BALLAWILL, 'Will's Farm;' LHERGY-CLAGH-WILLY, 'Willy's Stone Slope;' GOB-NY-SILVAS (*E*), 'Silvester's Point,' where Silvas appears to be a corruption of Silvester.

BALLAVARKYS is possibly 'Mark's Farm,' *Markys* being the Manx for Mark. JOHNEOIES, the name of a farm in Andreas, is nothing more recondite than 'Johnnie's.' BARNELL (*bayr*) is 'Nell's Road,' the name of an old woman who lived in a cottage by the roadside. BULLY'S QUARTER and JONS QUARTER, on the Mull, seem to be simply for 'Billy's Quarter' and 'John's Quarter;' BALLA-YEMMY, 'Jemmy's Farm,' and BALLAYEMMY-BEG, 'Jemmy's Little Farm;' BALLAYACK, 'Jack's Farm;' BALLAFAGEEN, possibly 'Little Patrick's Farm' (*Phaidin*). CHIBBER ROLLIN is a corruption of CHIBBER DOLLIN. Dollin was formerly a common Christian name in the Isle of Man. CLOSE ILIAM, 'William's Close;' BALLAROBIN, 'Robin's or Robert's Farm;' BALLAWILLE, 'Willy's Farm;' LEANY GIBBEY, 'Gibby's Meadow;' CRAIG-BANE-Y-BILL-WILLY, 'Willy Billson's White Crag.'

Occasionally both surname and Christian name are found in a local name, as BALLAJUANVARK, 'John Quark's Farm;' BALLA*willy*KILLY, 'Willy Killy's Farm;' STRUAN KERRY *Nicholas*,* 'Kate Nicholas's Stream;' CREG *Willysill* is probably a corruption of CREG-*Willy-Silvester*,* 'Willy Silvester's Crag,' though it is also supposed to be CREG *Willy*SELL, 'Willy Sayle's Crag;' CROIT HOM *Ralfe*,* 'Tom Ralfe's Croft.'

BALLA*yockey*, in Andreas, may possibly be derived from a nickname *yockey*, which appears in the Andreas Parish Register for generations in connection with the Corletts, who were owners of this property. *Yockey* is probably for *jockey*.

There are several affixes which can only be classed as doubtful for various reasons. Some because, though they are found in the dictionaries, and are used colloquially, are, and always must have been, inapplicable in their present form, as far as can now be ascertained, to the places to which they are applied; and others because, though found in the Manx dictionaries,† they are not used colloquially, and not found in any cognate language.

In the first class we have :

Ooyl (F), 'an apple,' which is popularly supposed to form part of the name of BAROOLE (*Baare ooyl*), 'Apple Top.' There is nothing, however, in the shape of the summits of the two mountains so called to lead to this supposition, and even if it were

---

* Not Manx names.

† Such words are open to the suspicion of having been placed in the Dictionaries solely because they seem to occur in local names.

so, the correct form would probably be *Baare yn ooyl*.
The name of the two farms called BALLADOOLE has
also been connected with *ooyl*, but this is very im-
probable. There is a mountain in Galloway called
DUNOOL, 1,777 feet high. [(I) AGHOWLE.]

Lheeah-rio (F), ‘hoar-frost ;’ in CREG-LHEEAH-RIO,
‘Hoar-frost Crag.’ Possibly the rock may have
the appearance of being covered with hoar-frost
at certain states of the tide, but it would require
a vivid fancy to think so.

Scoltey (M), ‘a split ;’ in CRONK-Y-SCOLTEY, ‘Hill of
the Split.’ There is no trace of any cleft or split
in the hill.

Chiass, ‘heat ;’ in GLENCHASS, ‘Heat Glen.’ This
glen is certainly not hotter than any other glen
in the island.

Spyrryd (M), ‘the spirit, the soul ;’ in GIAU SPYRRYD,
‘Spirit Creek.’ Does this refer to a ghostly
apparition, or to the landing of spirits of another
sort ? It seems probable that this was one of
the creeks which were used for smuggling purposes.

Bretin (M), ‘Wales, Britain ;’ in ELLAN VRETIN,
‘Britain Isle,’ the name of a small detached rock
in the sea.

Mooarid (K), ‘greatness ;’ in GIAU-NY-MOOARID, ‘Cove
of the Greatness.’ This cove is a particularly
small one.

Under the second heading there are :

Chuill (Cr), ‘a quill ;’ in CRONK-Y-CHUILL, ‘Hill of
the Quill ;’ STROAN-NY-QUILL, ‘Stream of the
Quill ;’ CROT-NY-QUILL, ‘Croft of the Quill.’

Any of these names might be derived with equal probability from *cooil*, 'a corner,' or QUILL, a surname.

Fedjeen (F), 'the feather of an arrow, or weaver's quill;' in BALLAFAGEEN, 'Weaver's Quill Farm' (more probably from BALLAPHAIDAIN. See Personal Names).

Skilleig (Cr), 'a narrow stripe;' in PORT SKILLEIG, 'Narrow Stripe Port.' This little creek has a very narrow entrance.

Fers (pl. *Fessyn*), 'a spindle;' in GLEN FESSAN, 'Spindles Glen.'

Doagan, 'a firebrand, a burning brand, a brand,' is given by Gill only, not being mentioned by Kelly in the Triglot, or by Cregeen. No such word is known in Irish or Gaelic; yet it is possible that the point called GOB-Y-DEIGAN, 'Point of the Firebrand,' is connected with this word, for not only is it known colloquially as 'Fire Point,' but there has recently been a discovery there of an ancient canoe, which was made by being burned out with red hot pebbles. Thousands of these pebbles, which show the action of fire, are still to be found at this place.

The word *Crout* (F), 'a trick, craft,' of very doubtful authenticity, would seem to occur in KEEILL CROUT, 'Craft Cell,' but this name is probably a corruption of something quite different.

The word *Scuit* (K), 'a spout, a squirt, syringe,' would seem to be found in GOB NY SCHOOT, or SKEATE (as it is variously spelled), 'Point of the Spout.'

In speaking of this place Gill* writes, '*Gub ny Scuit,* a place in St. Maughold's Parish, where there is a small cascade, or jet of water.' It was long supposed to be the abode of a *Buggane,* or monster, by the superstitious Manx people, on account of the wailing noises that proceeded from it, till it was discovered that these noises were caused by the wind flowing through a narrow cleft in the rock just above the fall. (*Scuit* is, probably, merely a corruption of *spooyt.*)

Ros (I and G), 'a promontory, a peninsula, or a wood,' is not found in our dictionaries, nor used in colloquial Manx. O'Donovan, in commenting on *Ros* in Cormac's 'Glossary,' says: 'In the south of Ireland *ross* or *rass* is still used, particularly in topographical names, to denote a wood: *rassan,* a copse or underwood; in the north *ross* means a point extending into the sea or lake.' *Ros* is probably found in PULROSE, formerly *Pooyl-roish,* 'Wood Pool' (*roish* being the genitive of *ros*).

The meaning of the *Sheading* of RUSHEN, or, in its Manx form, YN *Sheadin* RUSHEN, is very obscure. Its most probable derivation has been given under *Personal Names,* but there remains another possible derivation, *i.e.,* from *roisheen,* ' of the little wood.' What renders it possible that *ros* or *rassan* may be the origin of RUSHEN, is the fact that this *sheading* was formerly the Lord's forest, *i.e.,* not actually covered with trees, but uncultivated land, with copses and underwood where cattle and sheep would be pastured, and game would abound. We

* Manx Society's Dictionary, p. 160.

may, perhaps, therefore translate YN *Sheading*
RUSHEN (*roishcen*), 'The Sheading of the Little
Wood,' and the Parish of RUSHEN, which forms
part of the *sheading*, YN SKEEREY RUSHEN, 'The
Parish of the Little Wood.' There is also CASTLE
RUSHEN in the same sheading, and the oldest
name of CASTLETOWN was also RUSHEN.

Arragh, in CLEIGH-YN-ARRAGH, 'hedge of the arrow,
called in English, 'bow and arrow hedge,' may
possibly be a corruption of the English 'arrow.'
CLEIGH-YN-ARRAGH is a long earth rampart of pre-
historic origin, extending for more than a mile on
the north-west slope of Snæfell.

Kimmyrk, 'refuge' (not found in Irish or Gaelic), or
Sumrac, 'a primrose,' in CRONK SHIMMYRK, 'Refuge
Hill,' or CRONK SUMARK, 'Primrose Hill,' as the
name of the isolated pile of rock near the entrance
to Sulby Glen is variously spelled. The former
derivation is favoured by the fact that on the flat
top of this hill there is an embankment embracing
an area of from eighteen to twenty yards, and on
the south-east side there is a second embankment,
both of which were evidently fortifications, and
the latter by the fact that it is now usually called
'Primrose Hill' in English. Neither name is
found in any old record. These refuges on the
summits of hills are very common in the island
(see BARRULE), and that they were made use of, or
intended to be made use of, at a very recent
period, is clear from a proclamation by Governor
Wood issued in 1801, when, there being fears of
an attack by the French, he ordered the captains

of the various parishes to tell off a portion of the less able-bodied men to accompany the women and cattle into the mountains on the first alarm of a landing of the enemy. The *quarter-land* on which the hill is situated is also called BALLA-SHIMMYRK or BALLASUMARK.

Bainney (M), ‘ milk ;’ possibly in CHIBBYR-Y-VAINNAGH, ‘ Well of the Milk ;’ but this might also be a corruption of CHIBBYR-Y-VAINEY, ‘ Well of the Gap.’ In this case the doubt applies to the application, not to the word *bainney*.

The following, which also appear either as prefixes or simple names, are also doubtful :

Bearey, in DREEMBEARY, ‘ Moor back.’

Braid, in EAIRY BRAID, ‘ Upland Moor.’

Aa, a, ah, possibly in KENNA, formerly KINNA (*kione-a*), ‘ Ford Head.’

Lough, possibly in DRUMRELOAGH (ob.) (*Dreeym-ny-Lough*), ‘ Hill-back of the Lake.’ This is now curiously corrupted into DREEMREAGH.

There are a few names which are probably only portions of the originals to which they belonged. They were for the most part clearly substantival affixes of names in which the generic term, usually *balla*, has disappeared. Thus such names as VAISH and VONEY are probably the remains of BALLAVAISH, ‘ Cattle Farm,’ and BALLAVONEY (*moaney*), ‘ Turbary Farm,’ and MAASE-MOAR, ‘ Big Cattle,’ of BALLAVAASEMOAR, ‘ Big Cattle Farm.’ CLEANAGH or CLANNER, formerly GLANNAGH, a piece of flat land at the mouth of SULBY GLEN, is probably a corruption of *glionney*, the whole name having been BALLAGLIONNEY, ‘ Glen Farm.’ CONNEHBWEE (*conney*), ' Yellow Gorse,' the name of a farm, was probably BALLACONNEYBWEE originally; also ASHENMOOAR (*aittin*), ' Big Gorse,' a farm name, was probably BALLANASHENMOOAR, ' Big Farm of the Gorse.'   KELLA, the name of a farm in the parish of Lezayre, is probably the remains of BALLAKELLAGH, ' Cock Farm,' or possibly of BALLAKEYLLEY, ' Wood Farm ;' and LEWAIGUE, in the parish of Maughold, of BALLALEWAIGUE (*Balla hlieau aeg*), ' Little Hill Farm.'   The missing prefix in GEINNAGHDOO, ' Black Sand,' is probably *traie*, ' shore,' though this name may be complete as it stands.   In LAARE VANE, ' White Floor,' the name of a farm in Andreas, the missing prefix is *mwyllin*, ' mill,' as we know that there were formerly small mills called *mullin laare*, the axletree of which stood upright, and the small stones or *querns* on the top of it.   The waterwheel was at the lower end of the axletree, and turned horizontally under the water.   There was no casing round the stone, and there was a peg in it, which, at every revolution, struck the moveable spout attached to the hopper.   This shook the corn down into it, and the ground meal was swept up off the floor from under the stone.

Part II.

ADJECTIVAL AFFIXES.

IT has been found convenient to classify the adjectival affixes under the heads of Colour, Size and Shape, Relative Situation or Position, Sundry and Doubtful.

(i.) *Colour.*—Among adjectival affixes colour naturally holds a prominent place.   It is sometimes difficult to give the exact English equivalent of our terms for the various colours; thus *glass* may mean 'gray,' as in CLAGH GLASS, 'gray stone,' or 'green,' as in MAGHER GLASS, 'green field,' and CRONK GLASS, 'Green Hill,' while AWIN GLASS means 'pale blue, bright, or gray river.'

Doo, 'black, blackish, or very dark,' is very common. It is used chiefly in connection with boggy lands, as in MOANEYDOO, 'black turbary,' or with heather-clad hills, which look dark at a distance, as in BARE-DOO (*Baare*), 'black top.' There is a KERROO-DOO, 'black quarter(-land),' in almost every parish; such farms are usually on the hillsides, which are, or have been, covered with heather, and are often boggy as well. *Doo* is frequently found compounded with *liargagh*, 'the slope of a hill,' in such forms as LHERGYDOO and LARGEE-DOO; KNOCK-DOO and CRONK-DOO, 'black hill,' are common; RHENDOO (*rinn*), 'black ridge;' COOILDOO, 'black nook;' BALLA-DOO, 'black farm;' GLENDOO, 'Black Glen,' a modern corruption of the same, GLENDUFF, and STUGGADOO (*stuggey*), 'Black Portion,' are also found. BOOLDOHOLLY (*Bwoaillee - doo - Keylley*) is probably 'Black fold of the Wood.' The dark colour of peaty water is recorded in LOUGHDOO, 'Black Lake,' and LHOOBDOO, 'Black Gully (loop),' is a small moor-land heather-clad gully between two mountain sides. AWIN-DOO, 'Black River,' is a dark muddy and sluggish stream, which joins the more rapid and brighter AWIN-GLASS, about a mile above the town of Douglas. MULLEN-DOWAY (*doo-aa*), 'Black ford Mill,' is the old name of the place, now called Union Mills. CREGGAN

Doo, 'Black Rocky Hillock;' CREGGYN DOO, 'Black Rocks;' BAIE DOO, 'Black Bay;' *Ghaw* DOO, 'Black Cove;' *Ooig* DOO, 'Black Cave;' and GOB DOO, 'Black Point,' are found on the coast. [(I) BALLYDOO.]

Banc, 'white,' is even more common than *doo.* The whitish and sparkling quartz, which so plentifully sprinkles our hillsides, has probably given rise to the names CRONKBANE and KNOCKBANE, 'White Hill;' EARYBANE and EARYVANE, 'White Moor;' CLAUGHBANE, CLAGHBANE, and CLAUGHVANE, 'White Stone;' BALLACLAUGHBANE, 'White Stone Farm;' BOOILLEYVANE, 'White Fold;' COOIL-BANE, 'White Nook;' CREGBANE, 'White Rock,' and BALLACLYBANE, 'White Hedge Farm.' CRONK-Y-CLAGH-BANE, 'Hill of the White Stone,' is a tumulus with a white stone on top of it. Near Druidale there is a huge piece of white quartz, called *The* SHARRAGH VANE, 'The White Foal.'

The prevalence of corn or white crops has perhaps originated the names BALLABANE and BALLAVANE, 'White Farm,' and MAGHERVANE, 'White Field.' TRAIE VANE, 'White Shore,' and GEINNAGH VANE, 'White Sand,' are from the sparkling white sand. SPOOYT VANE, 'White Spout,' is the name of a pretty little waterfall. LARIVANE (*laare*) 'White Floor,' is explained under *laare* (see p. 231). BANE also occurs in the curious name CRAIG-BANE-Y-BILL-WILLY, 'Willy Bill Son's White Crag.' *Banc* and *Vane* are, in the north of the island especially, corruptly pronounced and spelled *bedn* and *vedn,* as in CARNANE BEDN,

'White Cairn,' which marks the boundary between
the parishes of Onchan and Braddan in the mountains; in CREGBEDN, 'White Rock,' and EARY
VEDN, 'White Moor.' [(I) LOUGHBANE.]

Ruy, 'red,' is not so common as the preceding.
AWIN RUY, 'Red River;' GOB-NY-TRAIE-RUY,
'Point of the Red Shore;' and GLEN ROY, 'Red
Glen,' appear to have been named from ferrugin-
ous deposits in the water. LHARGEE RUY, 'Red
Slope,' and CRONK RUY, 'Red Hill,' become ap-
propriate in autumn, when the bracken turns red.
[(I) OWENROE, (G) CULROY.]

Jiarg, 'red,' also, but of a deeper red than *ruy*.
BROUGH-JIARG-MOOR, 'Big Red Brow,' is a con-
spicuous raised beach in the parish of Ballaugh.
The soil of BALLAJIARG, 'Red Farm,' has a red
colour and is very rich. [(I) BELDERG, (G) BAR-
JARG.]

Dhoan, 'brown,' has the same signification as the
cognate English *dun*. CARRICK DHOAN, 'Dun
Rock,' has probably been so called from being
covered with seaweed, as it is under water at
high tide; also in LAG-DHOAN, 'Dun Hollow.'
[(I) BARNADOWN.]

Glass, as already stated, has several meanings accord-
ing to its application. Thus BALLAGLASS, 'Green
Farm,' in the parish of Maughold, contains GLIONE
GLASS, 'Green Glen,' one of the most beautiful glens
in the island. There are also in this sense KERROO-
GLASS, 'Green Quarter,' ARY-GLASS (*acree*), 'Green
Moor,' and CURRAGH-GLASS, 'Green Bog.' This
latter is a small pool surrounded by the vivid

green of a quaking bog. It is said that reputed witches were formerly ducked there, and if they floated they were rolled down Slieauwhuallian in spiked barrels. GOB-NY-CREGGYN-GLASSEY, 'The Gray Rocks' Point,' is a correct representation of the locality. The AWIN-GLASS, 'Gray River,' or 'Light-blue River,' is a bright stream flowing rapidly over a gravelly bed, and is as different from its muddy neighbour, the AWIN-DOO, as the Rhone from the Saone. In cloudy weather the water looks gray, in sunshine light-blue. These rivers are usually called colloquially *The* DHOO and *The* GLASS, *awin* being dropped. There is a spring in the Ballaugh Curragh called the CHIBBER GLASS,* 'Bright Spring,' which derives its name from the sparkling nature of the water, which bubbles up from the gravel underlying the peat. [(I) KINGLAS.]

Gorrym, 'blue,' is only found in GOB-GORRYM, 'Blue Point,' the sandy headland north of Jurby Point. It must have been so-called from its appearance at a distance, as it is certainly more yellow than blue, when near it.   [(I) CAIRNGORM.]

Lheeah is a rather different gray to *glass*, a duller gray would perhaps be the best description. It is found in CORLEA, ' Round Gray Hill,' and in CARRICK-LEA and CREGLEA, 'Gray Rock.'   [(I) ROSLEA, (G) CRAIGENLEE.]

Ouyr is a lighter dun than *dhoan*, and is even occasionally equivalent to 'pale gray.' It occurs in the names of two mountains, SLIEAU-OUYR, 'Dun

---

* Pronounced CHIBBER LESH.

Mountain,' and MULLAGH-OUYR, 'Dun Top.' [(I) CORROWER, (G) BENOWR.]

Breac (K), *breck* (C), 'speckled,' or 'spotted,' is an epithet applied to ground sprinkled with quartz rocks, as well as to the appearance presented by the varying colours of vegetation. Thus: LHERGY-VRECK, 'Speckled Slope;' CRONKBRECK, and CRONABACK, formerly CRONKBRECK, 'Speckled Hill;' CARNANEBRECK, 'Speckled Cairn;' GOB-BREAC, 'Speckled Point.' The farm of CRONK-BRECK is said to have been formerly held on the tenure of providing a piper for the lord of the Isle. [(I) KYLEBRACK, (G) BENBRACK.]

Buigh, 'yellow,' is usually applied to places where gorse or furze grows freely, as in REEAST BWEE, 'Yellow Moor;' CLOSE BUIGH, 'Yellow Close;' BING-BUIE (*binn*), 'Yellow Tops;' STROIN VUIGH, 'Yellow Nose,' the name of the point under Cronk-ny-arrey-Lhaa; COAN BWEE, 'Yellow Valley;' BALLA-CONNEH-BWEE (*conney*), 'Yellow Gorse Farm;' BALLABUIY and BALLABOUIGH, 'Yellow Farm;' also *Gullet*BUIGH, 'Yellow Gullet,' on Langness. [(I) OWENWEE, (G) BALLABOOIE.]

Size and *shape* are naturally very common epithets in place nomenclature.

The antithesis of big and little, *mooar* and *beg*, is used to compare unequal divisions of land, and the difference between one natural feature and another in its neighbourhood. Thus there is a BALLA MOAR, 'Big Farm,' and a BALLABEG, 'Little Farm,' in every parish; a CRONK MOAR, 'Big Hill,' will be found in juxtaposition with a CRONKBEG,

'Little Hill;' a MOANEY MOAR, 'Big Turbary,' with a MOANEY BEG, 'Little Turbary;' and a GLEN MOAR,' Big Glen,' with a GLEN BEG, 'Little Glen,' though these names also exist when there is no idea of comparison. There are also AREY MOAR, 'Big Moor,' and AREY BEG, 'Little Moor;' BALLAMONA MOOAR (*Moainee*), 'Big Turbary Farm,' and BALLAMONA BEG, 'Little Turbary Farm;' LHEEANEY VOOAR, 'Big Meadow,' and LHEEANEY VEG, 'Little Meadow;' PURT MOAR, 'Big Port,' and PURT VEG, 'Little Port,' and KIONE VEG, 'Little Head.' There are many others, which will be found in the index. *Beg* is occasionally corrupted into *meg* and *mig*, as in BALLAMEG and BALLAMIG, 'Little Farm.' CLYCHUR is perhaps a corruption of *Cleiy-Mooar*, 'Big Hedge.' It is pronounced CLYHŪR. [(I and G) BALLYMORE, BALLYBEG, (G) BALMEG.]

Foddey, 'long,' is only found in BALLAFADDA, 'Long Farm.' This looks as if the Manx *foddey* was only a recent corruption of the Irish *fadda*, the name of the farm having been given before the change. Most of the old *quarter-land* properties are long and narrow, having an *intack* on the mountain on the one side, and on the seashore on the other. The object of this was that each property might share in the advantages of the common pasturage, and of the seaweed, which was and is used as manure. [(I) KILLFADDY, (G) DRUMFAD.]

Liauyr, 'long;' in CREG LIAUYR, 'Long Rock;' and MAGHER LIAUYR, 'Long Field.'

Giare, 'short;' in BALLAGYR and BALLAGARE, 'Short Farm.'   [(I) GLENGAR.]

Lhean, 'broad;' in SLIEU-LHEAN (*slieau*), 'Broad Hill;' EARY-LHEAN, 'Broad Moor;' BEEAL-FEAYN-NY-GEAY, 'Broad entrance of the Wind.' [(I) GORTLANE.]

Kiel, 'narrow;' in THALLOO KIEL, 'Narrow Plot;' MAGHER KIEL, 'Narrow Field;' and KERROO-KIEL, 'Narrow Quarter(-land).'   [(I) GLENKEEL.]

Coon, 'narrow;' in TRAIE COON, 'Narrow Shore;' and NASCOIN, formerly NASCOAN, a corruption of *yn-eas-coon,* 'The Narrow Fall;' an appropriate description of this pretty little fall in the parish of Ballaugh.

Cam, 'crooked, curved, winding;' in GLENCAM, 'Winding Glen;' COOILCAM, 'Winding Nook;' and GIAUCAM, 'Winding Creek.'   Shakespeare uses the phrase 'cleam kam' for wholly awry.   [(I) GLENCAM, (W) MORECAMBE.]

Jeeragh, 'straight;' in *Ghaw*-JEERAGH, 'Straight Cove;' and perhaps in BALLAJERAI, 'Straight Farm.'

Sceilt or *scoilt,* 'cleft' or 'split' (past participle of *dy scoltey,* 'to split'); in RENSCAULT, formerly RENSKELT, 'Cleft Ridge.'   This farm is at the end of the ridge of high land which divides the east and west Baldwin valleys.   There was also a CRONK-SKEALT, 'Cleft Hill,' a tumulus, in the parish of Ballaugh, which contained several urns thirty years ago.   It has since then been carted away to improve the land for agricultural purposes.   [(I) KNOCK-SGOILT, (G) CLACKSGOILTE.]

Cruinn, 'round;' in KERROO CRUINN, 'Round Quarter-(land);' CREG CRUINN, 'Round Crag.'

Birragh (C), 'pointed;' in BALLABIRRAGH, 'Pointed Farm,' and probably in BALLABERRAG or BALLA-BIRRAG. It should be mentioned that BIRRAG was formerly a common surname in the parish of Jurby, where this latter name occurs, and so it may possibly take its name from that of a former proprietor. Both BALLABIRRAGH and BALLABIRRAG are very long and narrow farms.

The relative *situation* or *position* of one place with respect to that of others, has given rise to several place-names.

The adverbs *heose* and *heese*, 'above' and 'below,' are used adjectivally in local nomenclature with the meaning 'upper' and 'lower,' as in BALDROMMA-HEOSE, 'Upper (Hill)-back Farm;' BALDROMMA-HEIS, 'Lower (Hill)-back Farm;' BARROOSE (*Bayr-heose*), 'Upper Road;' GAREY CHEU HEESE (*garee*), 'Upper Side Stony Place,' and GAREY CHEU HEESE (*garee*), 'Lower Side Stony Place,' and in *Gretch* HEOSE, 'Upper Gretch.' [(G) BARHOISE.]

Eaghtyragh, 'upper;' in BALLYAGHTERAGH, 'Upper Farm,' and possibly in BALLEIGERAGH with the same meaning. [(I) BALLYOUGHTERAGH, (G) AUCHNOTTEROCH.]

Fo (adverb), 'beneath;' in BALLAFO*gige*, in 1621 BALLA-FO-*hague* (*haugr* O.N.), 'Beneath *How* Farm;' and in TOWLFOGGY (*fo-haugr*), 'Beneath How Hole.'

Meanagh, 'middle,' is very. common, being generally

used to denote the middle *quarter-land* of a *treen* or the central farm in a parish, as in BALLA-MEANAGH or BALLAMENAGH, 'Middle Farm.' This word may be sometimes confounded with *managh*, 'a monk' (see p. 189). There are also SLIEAU MEANAGH, 'Middle Mountain;' *Burrow* MEANAGH, 'Middle Burrow,' (?) a pile of rocks on Cronk-ny-arrey-Lhaa; and CREG VENAGH, 'Middle Crag.' [(I) DRUMMENAGH, (G) BAL-MEANACH.]

Tessyn (K), *Tessen* (C), 'across' or 'athwart,' is generally applied to farms part of which lie on one side of a highroad, and part on another, as in BALLATERSON and BALLATERSIN, 'Athwart Farm.' The *r* in the Manx place-names is probably correct, as it agrees with the Irish and Gaelic forms. [(I) KILTRASNA, (G) BALTERSAN.]

Ard, 'high;' in DORLISH ARD (*doarlish*), 'High Gap;' CRONK ARD, 'High Hill.' CLAGH ARD, 'High Stone,' is the name of two standing stones or memorial pillars. [(I) LOCHANARD.]

Dowin, 'deep, low;' in GLENDOWNE, 'Deep Glen;' BWOAILLEE DOWNE, 'Deep Fold.' BALLADOYNE, 'Low Farm,' is low-lying land by the river Neb. Also possibly in BALDOOIN, 'Low Farm,' and BALDWIN, formerly BOAYLDIN (*Boayl dowin*), 'Low Place.' Both East and West BALDWIN are deep valleys.

Injil, 'low;' in COOILINGIL, 'Low Nook,' and CRONK-INJIL, 'Low Hill.' CRONKINJIL is close to CRONK-ARD. *Injil* is probably a corruption of the Irish *iscal* or Gaelic *iosal*, as in (I) AGHEESAL, for the

Manx *s* is often hardened into *j* in pronunciation. Thus *booisal* is pronounced *booijal*.

Sodjey, 'further;' in *Burrow* SODJEY, 'Further Burrow (?), near *Burrow* MEANAGH (see p. 240).

The only cardinal point which is found in local names is *sheear*, 'the west,' (*yn neear* with the article), in NERLOUGH (*yn neear*), 'the west lake.' This place is on the 'White House' property in Michael. There is no lake there now.　[(I) ARDANEER.]

The remaining adjectival epithets are too varied to be placed under any special heading :

Garroo, 'rough, rugged,' is very common; in BALLA-GARROW, 'Rough Farm;' KERROOGARROO, 'Rough Quarter-(land);' BAREGARROO (*Bayr*), 'Rough Road;' CRONKGARROW, 'Rough Hill.' [(I) TOR-GARROW.]

Mollagh, 'rough,' is used in connection with swampy grounds; while *garroo* is usually applied to dry uplands. Thus: MOANEY-MOLLAGH (*Moainec*), 'Rough Turbary.'

Creggagh, 'rocky;' in BALLACREGGA and BALLACRAGGA, 'Rocky Farm;' GOBCREGGAGH, 'Rocky Point;' and in CHIBBYRT-CHROGA, 'Rocky Well.'

Claghagh, 'stony;' in KERROOCLAGHAGH, 'Stony Quarter-(land).'

Cloaie, 'stony;' probably in COLD CLAY, a corruption of COOIL CLOAIE, 'Stony Corner;' and in CLOAIE *Head*, formerly KIONE CLOAIE, 'Stony Head,' in the parish of Rushen.　This word is not now used in colloquial Manx, but it occurs several times in the Manx Bible.

Breinn, 'putrid, stagnant;' in POYLLBREINN, 'Stag-nant Pool.'　One of the pools, so called, is at

Langness, and the other at Poolvash. They are only filled with water by exceptionally high tides, so that in the meantime they stagnate.

Geinnee, 'sandy;' in BALLAGENNY, 'Sandy Farm.' This farm is near the sandy shore of the parish of Bride. [(I) GLENGANNAH.]

Shliggagh (Trig. C. Cl.), 'shelly;' in RHULLICK-Y-LAGG-SLIGGAGH, 'the shelly-hollow graveyard.' This is the Manx name of the Mull Stone Circle.

Aalin, 'beautiful;' in KNOCKANALIN, 'Beautiful Hillock.' [(I) GLASHAWLIN.]

Sallagh, 'dirty, filthy;' probably in BALLASALLA, formerly BALLASALLAGH and BALLASALLEY, 'Dirty Town or Farm.' There is a village of this name in the parish of Malew, and a farm in the parish of Jurby.

Broigh, Broghe, also 'dirty;' in GLENBROIGH, 'Dirty Glen.'

Curree, 'boggy;' in BALLACURRY, BALLACHURRY, and BALLACHURREE, 'Boggy Farm,' a very common name; also in BALICURE, the old name of Bishop's Court. There is an earthwork on BALLACHURRY, in the parish of Andreas, dating probably from the seventeenth century, which is a rectangle fifty yards in length by forty in breadth, with walls six yards thick, having a bastion at each corner.

Grianagh, Grianey, Greinagh, Greiney, 'sunny;' in BALLAGRANEY, 'Sunny Farm;' GLEN GREENAUGH, 'Sunny Glen;' and PORT GREENAUGH, 'Sunny Port.' The older name of PORT GREENAUGH was the (O.N.) GREENWYK. [(I) BALLYGREANY.]

Rennee, 'ferny;' in NELLAN RENNY (*yn-ellan*), 'The

Ferny Isle;' LHERGYRENNY, 'Ferny Slope;' BUL-
RENNY and BOLRENNY (*Bwoaillee*), 'Ferny Fold;'
and BARNA-ELLAN-RENNY, 'Ferny Isle Gap.'
Rennee may also be the plural of *renniagh*, 'fern.'
[(I) DRUMRAINY, (G) BLAWRAINE.]

Fluigh, 'wet, moist;' in GAREY FLUIGH, 'Moist, Stony
Place.'   [(I) KILLY FLUIGH.]

Moanagh, Moaney (C), 'turfy;' *Moainee* (K), 'belonging
to turf;' in BALLAMONA, 'Turfy Farm;' formerly
BALLAMOANEY, which is a very common name
(this is frequently, but incorrectly, translated
'Farm of the Turbary,' which is BALLANAMONA);
also in THALLOOVOANAGH, 'Turfy Plot.'   There
is a GLENMONA, a modern name, which simply
means 'Mona (or Isle of Man) Glen.'   [(I) BAL-
LAMONA.]

Losht, 'burnt;' in SLIEAU LOSHT, 'Burnt Mountain;'
and CRONKLOSHT, 'Burnt Hill' (both these hills
are remarkably dry); in THALLOO LOSHT, 'Burnt
Land or Plot;' and in the modern name, CABBAL-
YN-OURAL-LOSHT, 'Chapel of the Burnt Sacrifice.'
[(I) BALLYHUSK, (G) CRAIGLOSK.]

Creoi, 'hard;' in KERROO-CREOI and KERROOCROIE,
'Hard Quarter-(land).'   This epithet is applied to
lands which are hard to till.   [(I) CARGACROY.]

Creen, 'withered or ripe;' in the curious name CRO-
CREEN, 'withered or ripe fold.'   *Creen* is used
colloquially more generally as 'ripe' than 'withered.'
[(G) SLEWCREEN.]

Brisht, 'broken' (past participle of *dy brishey*, to
break); in TRAIE BRISHT, 'Broken Shore;' probably so called from being covered with rough

stones ; and in BROUGH BRISHT, 'Broken Brow.'
Here *brisht* seems to refer to a landslip.

Rea, 'flat, smooth, even ;' in DRIM-REIY (pronounced
ray), 'Flat (Hill-)back,' the old and appropriate
name of St. Marks. [(I) INCHAFFRAY, (G) AUCH-
RAE.]

Roauyr, 'fat, swollen ;' in KIONE ROAUYR, 'Fat Head.'
This is the somewhat fanciful name of a broad
headland.

Meen, literally 'mild, meek,' has in local names the
signification 'smooth or soft ;' as in GAREEMEEN,
'Soft Sour (or Rocky) Land ;' and BALLAMINE and
BALLAMIN, 'Soft Farm.' 'Soft' here means boggy.
[(I) CLONMEEN.]

Meayl, 'bald,' generally speaking, means anything
bald, bare, or hornless. Thus a hornless cow is
called a *mealey*. In the only local name in which
it is found it means 'bare,' as SLIEAU MEAYL,
'Bare Hill.' [(I) KNOCKMOYLE.]

Chirrym or *tirrym*, 'dry ;' in BALLACHIRRIM, formerly
BALYTYRYM, 'Dry Farm ;' CLOSECHIRRYM, 'Dry
Close ;' and possibly in BALTRIM, 'Dry Farm.' [(I)
TULLYHIRRIM.]

Feayr, 'cold ;' in CHIBBER FEAYR, 'Cold Spring.' [(I)
OWENURE.]

Lajer, 'strong ;' in CASHTAL LAJER, 'Strong Castle.'
This is an ancient earthwork on Cronkould. It
is forty yards in diameter, the outside mound
being about eight feet high, and the raised embankment sixteen or seventeen feet thick. There
are numerous barrow-mounds within the enclosure.

Reagh, 'merry, laughing ;' in STROOAN REAGH,

'Laughing Stream,' in Sulby Glen. This is a trickling mountain stream, which, when its water is glancing in the sunlight, might well deserve the above epithet.

Coar (C), 'pleasant, agreeable;' in BALLACOAR, 'Pleasant Farm;' CRONKCOAR, 'Pleasant Hill;' KERROOCOAR and KERROOCOARE, 'Pleasant Quarter (-land);' and SLIEAUCOAR, 'Pleasant Mountain.' If old Manx people are asked the meaning of the name of this mountain, they will say, ' It is called the kindly mountain, because it gives such good turf.'

Tonnagh (C), 'wavy;' in BALLATHONNA, 'Wavy Farm.' The ground of this farm, in the parish of Andreas, is undulating.

Geayee, 'windy,' is properly the genitive case of *geay*, 'wind,' but is used as an adjective. CRONK GEAYEE, ' Windy Hill.'

Noa, ' new ;' in GAREY NOA, ' New Garden.'

Sheeant, 'holy, blessed ;' in RHENSHENT, 'Holy Ridge,' in the parish of Malew ; perhaps so named from its proximity to a *treen* chapel. There are two large boulders, called ' The Giant's Grave,' on this place, which probably formed part of a stone circle. [(G) CLAYSHANT.]

Casherick, ' holy ;' in KEEILL CASHERICK, ' Holy Cell,' in the parish of Maughold. Its walls are barely traceable, but the grave-yard enclosure still remains.

Kelly gives *ab abban*, A.,* belonging to an abbot or abbey; as *thalloo-ab*, 'abbey-land;' *quaiyl-ab*, 'a court baron ;' *keeill-abban*, 'an abbey church ;' while Cregeen gives ' *abb*, A,* abbey,' only.

* Adjective.

We find it in local names, in KEEILL ABBAN, ' Abbey Church,' and CRONK-KEEILL-ABBAN, ' Abbey Church Hill;' both in Baldwin, near the abbey lands of Braddan. Close by was the site of the ancient Tynwald, where a Court was held in 1429. All traces of it have now disappeared.

Braarey (K), ' belonging to a priory or abbey,' a derivative of *braar*, ' brother;' probably in BALLA VRAAREY, ' Priory Farm.' This is by BIMAKEN FRIARY, and is abbey land.

Screbbagh, ' scabbed, scabby;' in SLOC-NA-CABBYL-SCREEVAGH, ' Pit of the Scabby Horse.' This pit is below the cliffs in the parish of Maughold, over which it was formerly the custom to throw diseased animals.

Marroo, ' dead ' (a past participle); in CLAGH-NY-DOOINEY-MAROO, ' Stone of the Dead Man.' It was said that a man, who had been murdered, was left lying on this slab.

Doubtful.

These may be classed in the same way as the doubtful substantival affixes (see pp. 225-30).

The following are used colloquially, and are found in Irish and Gaelic :

Gortagh, ' hungry;' in GIAU GORTAGH, ' Hungry Creek,' a very absurd name as it stands.

Bouyr, ' deaf;' in CRONKBOUYR, ' Deaf Hill,' a tumulus. It appears that the corresponding Irish word, *bodhar*, corrupted into *bower*, is used in local names in Ireland in the same way. Joyce*

---

* Joyce, ' Irish Names of Places,' second series, pp. 46, 47.

surmises that, as some of the places so called
have an echo, their names arose from your
having to speak loudly to them and get a loud
answer, exactly as happens when you speak to a
deaf person. This is an ingenious explanation,
but its application in the case of CRONKBOUYR
would seem doubtful. [(I) GLENBOWER.]

The following is found in Manx, Irish, and Gaelic,
but is not known colloquially in Manx:

Ceabagh, 'cloddy;' in PUIRT CEABAGH, 'Cloddy
Port.' This curious name would seem to be
derived from the appearance of the small rocks
there.

The following are found in Manx, and are known
colloquially, but are not found in Irish and Gaelic:

Mea, ' fat, luxuriant,' in the sense of fertile ; possibly in
GLENMAY, formerly GLENMEA, GLENMEAY, and
GLENMOIJ, 'Luxuriant Glen.' This is very doubtful, because it is always pronounced by old Manx
people as if spelled GLENMOY, or GLENMY.

Gerjoil, 'joyful;' in CARN GERJOIL, 'Joyful Cairn,'
a name also applied to the mountain on which the
cairn stands. It may commemorate some public
thanksgiving.

Skibbylt, 'active, nimble ;' in CRONK SKIBBYLT, 'Nimble
Hill.' No explanation of this absurd name is
possible. It is probably a corruption of something quite different.

Foalley, 'treacherous,' is found in our dictionaries, but
not in Irish and Gaelic, unless *fealltach*, with the
same meaning, has a remote connection. It occurs

in TRAIE FOALLEY, 'Treacherous Shore,' probably so named from quicksands.

The two following are found in our dictionaries, and are used colloquially, but seem utterly misplaced in the compound names in which they are used. The former does not occur in Irish or Gaelic, but the latter does.

Dooie, 'kind;' in POOILDHOOIE, 'Kind Pool;' and KIONDHOOIE, 'Kind Head.' Colloquially, *dooie* is generally used in the sense of 'patriotic,' as in *Manninagh Dooie*, 'A patriotic Manxman.'

Tustagh, 'sensible, intelligent;' in KEEILL TUSTAG. If we may suppose the name to have been originally KEEILL DOOINEY TUSTAGH, 'Wise Man's Cell,' it could be explained as having originated from the occupancy of the cell by some anchorite of far-famed wisdom. The present occupant of the farm of this name, the old *keeill* having disappeared, is skilled in charms.

Imperfect Names.

The names CROGGA and RENNY are certainly part of BALLACROGGA (*creggah*), 'Rocky Farm;' and BALLA-RENNY, 'Ferny Farm.' In the case of *Crogga*, the adjoining estate, of which it probably once formed part, is called BALLACREGGA.

ADJECTIVAL PREFIXES.

Our grammarians tell us that *drogh*, 'wicked,' and *shen*, 'old,' are the only adjectives which precede their substantives; but in local names we find, besides *shen*, *ard*, 'high,' *coar*, 'pleasant,' and *doo*, 'black.' These, however, are usually affixes, and only exceptionally prefixes, while *shen* is always a prefix.

Shen, in SHENVALLA, 'Old Farm;' SHENTHALLOO, 'Old Ground or Plot;' and SHENMYLLIN, 'Old Mill.' [(I) SHANGORT, (G) SHIN VALLIE.]

Ard, in ARDVALLEY, 'High Farm;' ARCHOLLAGAN (*ard-chiollagh-cen*), 'High Little Hearth;' and ARDERRY (*ard-eary*), 'High Moor.'

Coar, in CORVALLEY, 'Pleasant Farm.'

Doo, in DOUGLAS (*Doo-glaise*), 'Black Stream;' DOLLAUGH MOOAR (*Doo-lough*), 'Big Black Lake,' and DOLLAUGH BEG, 'Little Black Lake.' [(I and G) DOUGLAS.]

The name of the farm CAMLORK, in 1511 CAMLORGE, if *cam* is here the adjective 'crooked,' should be placed under this heading; but it seems more probable that it is of Scandinavian origin (see *post*).

The abverb *fo*, 'beneath,' is found in two names without a preceding substantive: FOCHRONK (probably for *Balla-fo-yn-chronk*), '(Farm) under the Hill;' and FOLIEU (probably for *Balla-fo-yn-hlieau*), '(Farm) under the Mountain.'

The preposition *eddyr* occurs in the name EDREMONY, a corruption of *Eddyr-daa-Moainee*, 'Between Two Turbaries or Marshes,' which exactly described its situation formerly. There are only faint traces of the marshes now. [(I) EDERDACURRAGH.]

CHAPTER IV.

THE Scandinavian place-names in the Isle of Man are always descriptive, and are usually compound words, consisting of a local substantive term with an attributive prefixed.   The attributive is usually a common or proper noun in the genitive case, rarely an adjective. In some few cases a substantive term is used simply or emphatically, and without any adjective, as KNEEBE, MULL, in which case the definite article would be either expressed or understood in English.   The generic terms, being affixes (not, as in Celtic languages, prefixes), have been placed in alphabetical order for convenience in reference, but otherwise it will be seen that the Scandinavian names are treated under the same headings as the Celtic.

Part I.—Simple Names.

The simple names in the Scandinavian, as well as in the Celtic place-names in the Isle of Man, are much fewer in number than the compound.

The following are only found as simple names :

Gnipa (F), 'a peak;' in KNEEBE, formerly GNEBE or KNEBE. This name is found on the western slope of GREEBA Mountain, and is most probably the original name of the whole mountain, as 'n' is frequently corrupted into 'r.' The River NEB, which has its source near KNEBE, may also take its name from it.

Gröf (F), 'a pit, hole;' probably in GRAUFF. This *treen*, at Laxey, is actually in a deep hole between two steep hills. A *quarter-land* in this *treen* is now called GRAWE, a modern corruption of *gröf*. [GRÖF, Iceland; GRAVEN, Shetlands; GRAWINE, Orkneys; GRAFFNOSE, Hebrides.]

Kringla (F), 'a dish, circle;' possibly in CRINGLE, but this name is more probably taken direct from the proper name CRINGLE (see p. 86). [CRINGLE-BECK, Lincolnshire; KRINGLETOFT, Denmark.]

Mön (gen. *Manar*), 'The Isle of Man.' This is the invariable form of the name in the Sagas. On a runic stone at Kirk Michael the word *Maun* is found in the following inscription : '*Gout : cirpi : þano : auc : ala : imaun*,' 'Gout worked this (cross) and all in *Maun*.' This *Maun* exactly corresponds in sound with *Mön*.

Múli (M), literally 'a muzzle, snout,' is used in local names of a headland or jutting crag. In the Isle of Man *The* MULL, 'The Headland,' is applied to the high rocky district at the extreme south. It is now spelled *The* MEAYLL in maps, though still called *The* MULL. [MULL of Galloway, MULL (Island); MULI, Iceland.]

Nabbi (M), 'a knoll;' in *The* NAB, 'The Knoll.' [NAB,

Orkneys; NABWOOD, Lincolnshire; THE KNAB, Shetlands.]

The following are also found as affixes:

Ey, 'an island;' in *The* EYE, a rock off the Calf of Man, which has been completely pierced by the action of the waves. It is popularly supposed to mean literally 'The Eye.'

Eyrr (F), 'a gravelly bank;' in *The* AYRE, the sandy and gravelly expanse extending along the north coast of the island.

The following are also found as prefixes:

Holmr (M), 'a holm, islet;' in HOLM (ob.), the Scandinavian name of the islet off Peel Harbour. In a Papal Bull of 1231 this islet is referred to as 'HOLM, SODOR, vel PILE;' and in the charter confirming the grant of Thomas, Earl of Derby, in 1505, of churches and lands in the Isle of Man to Huan, Bishop of Sodor and Man, it is called 'HOLME, SODOR, vel PELE.' [HOLMAR, Iceland; FLATHOLME, England; STOCKHOLM.]

Klettr (M), 'a rock;' in *The* CLYTTS (*klettar*), 'The Rocks.'

Skarð (N), 'a notch, chink,' used in Icelandic local names of a mountain pass; in SKARD, which is high land. [SKARð, Iceland. *Skarð* is also found as a prefix.]

Skör (gen. *skarar*), 'a rim, edge;' in SCARA, 'Edge.' This is, perhaps, only a portion of the original name. *Scar* or *scaur* is used in Scotland of a cliff, or precipitous bank of earth. SCARA is on the edge of a cliff. *Skör* may possibly also occur in *The* SKÖRYN, 'The Edge.' [SCAR, Ireland; THE SKAUR, Scotland.]

The following are both affixes and prefixes, and are explained under the former: *The* GARTH, 'The Enclosure;' *The* HOW, 'The Mound;' *The* STACK, 'The Detached Rock;' HOLM, 'Islet;' the old name of PEEL, and RIG, 'Ridge.'

Part II.—Compound Names.

A´ (F), 'a river;' as in LAXEY (*Lax-á*), 'Salmon River.' It is sometimes difficult to distinguish between *á* and *ey*, 'an island.' The only guides are the ancient form of the name and the appropriateness of the appellation in each case. [LAXA, Iceland.]

Bær, bær, byr, 'a farm or landed estate;' as in CROSBY (*Krossa-byr*), 'Cross Farm.' In the Isle of Man it is invariably found in the Swedish and Danish form, *by*, though its general meaning is, as in Iceland, a farm, not, as in Scandinavia, a town or village. This word is a certain sign of permanent colonization, and wherever it is found it marks out the limits and extent of Scandinavian immigration. It is the commonest Scandinavian affix in the Island.

Bali (M), 'a soft, grassy bank,' used especially of a bank sloping to the sea-shore; only in BIBALOE, formerly BYBALLO (*vé-balli*), 'Grassy Bank House.'

Brekka (F), 'a slope;' as in CORBRECK (*Kora-brekka*), 'Cori's Slope.' *Brekka* is common in Icelandic local names. It was the name given there to the hill where public meetings were held and laws promulgated. [SANDBREKKA, Iceland.]

Dalr (M), 'a dale;' as in NARRADALE (*Narfa-dalr*), 'Narfi's Dale.' BALDWIN, in the parish of Braddan, was in 1511 called *Bal*DALL, 'The Mill of *Bal*DALL' being mentioned, as well as the farms of BALDALL *Christe,' Ball*DALL *Brew*, and *Bal*DALL REYNYLT. Thus *Bal*DALL seems to be a combination of the Celtic *Balla* and the O.N. *Dalr*. [BREIÐDALR, Iceland; BORROWDALE, English Lakes; LAXDALE, Lewis.]

Ey (gen. and plu. *eyjar*), 'an island;' as in LIGGEA (*Låg-ey*), 'Low Island.' [FLATEY, ORKNEY, CHELSEA, ALDERNEY, CAMBRAY.]

Eyrr (F), 'a gravelly bank; either of the banks of a river or of a tongue of land running into the sea;' as in *The Point of* AYRE, 'The Point of the Gravelly Bank,' the long, low promontory at the north-eastern extremity of the Island. *Eyrr* is also found compounded with Celtic prefixes, in *Ballan*AYRE (*Balla-yn-eyrr*), 'Farm of the Gravelly Bank;' *Bayr-ny*-AYRA, 'Road of the *Ayr*,' the road leading to the Point of AYRE; and in the name of the parish *Lez*AYRE, formerly *Le* AYRE, which is probably a corruption of *ny ayre*, 'of the *eyrr*.' In 1231 the Church *Sanctæ Trinitatis in le*AYRE is mentioned in a Papal Bull, and in the sixteenth century the parish church was called *Kirk Christ le-*AYRE, 'Christ's Church of the Ayre.' The substitution of 'l' for 'n' is not, as we have already seen, uncommon in Manx pronunciation. The greater part of this parish was, till the middle of the sixteenth century, under water, as the *curragh* was then undrained, and the land was consequently of very little importance. It may, therefore, have been regarded merely as an appendage of the AYRE. [AERS OF SELLIVOE, Shetland; POINT OF AYR, Wirrall, Cheshire.]

Fjall (N), 'a fell, mountain;' as in SNÆFELL (*Snæfjall*), 'Snowfell,' the name of the highest mountain in the Island. [DOFRA-FJALL, Norway; GOATFELL, Arran; COPEVAL, Harris; FAIRFIELD, English Lakes.]

Fjördr (M), 'a firth, bay;' possibly in *Balla*FURT. This is the sole instance of the even possible occurrence in the Isle of Man of a word so common in Scandinavia; but it should be remarked that the word *fjördr* is applied to deep inlets, which are not found here, while the small crescent-shaped creeks or *viks* are common. In Celtic, *Balla*FURT would mean 'port farm,' and is probably the correct derivation. It is, however, just possible that *furt* may be a corruption of *fjördr*, which in the Hebrides takes the forms *port, fort, forth, furt.* [ERISPORT, Hebrides.]

Garðr (M), 'a yard, an enclosed space,' as in FISHGARTH (*Fiski-garðr*), 'Fish Enclosure (or Pond);' and possibly in the corrupt FISTARD, with the same meaning. *Garðr* takes this form of *garth* in the Orkneys and Shetlands; but in the Hebrides it usually becomes *garry*, which form is also commoner than *garth* in the Isle of Man, as in AMOGARRY, 'Asmund's Enclosure.' (Compare Anglo-Saxon *geard*, English *yard* and *garden*, and provincial English *garth*.) [GRASS-GARTH, English Lakes; ASHMIGARRY, Hebrides; FISKI-GARÐR, Iceland.]

Gata (F), ' a way, path, road ;' probably in KEPPELL
GATE (*Kapal-gata*), ' Horse-road.'

Gil (N), ' a deep, narrow glen, with a stream at the
bottom ;' as in *Glen*GILL (*glione*), ' Ravine Glen;'
and *Traie-ny*-GILL, ' Strand of the Ravine.' This
word has been adopted into Manx, though, doubtless, originally of Scandinavian origin, and is used
in just the same sense as in Iceland. GHYL and
GILL are common in local names in the North of
England and in Scotland, as well as in Iceland.
[DUNGEON GHYLL.]

Hamarr (M), literally ' a hammer,' is used in Icelandic
local names of a hammer-shaped crag—a crag
standing out like an anvil. In the Isle of Man it
is only found in CORNAMA (ob.) (*Korn-hamarr*),
' Corn Crag.' CORNAMA is mentioned as being
one of the abbey boundaries in the parish of
Malew, in the *Chronicon Manniæ*. The same place
is now called CORDEMAN, a curious corruption.
Hamarr is common in Icelandic local names, but
always as a prefix.

Haugr (M), ' a how, mound,' is properly used of the
artificial earthen mounds which were piled over the
bodies of deceased Scandinavian chieftains, who,
in the phrase so common in the *Landnáma-bóc,*
were ' howed ' (*heygðr*) ; but in the Isle of Man it is
also used of headlands by the sea, where, however,
these chieftains were usually buried; hence probably
how became the usual name for such headlands.
We have it in SWARTHAWE (*svart-haugr*), ' Black
How;' and in the northern headland of Douglas Bay,
Banks's HÓWE, so called from a family of that time

who held property there. It also occurs with Celtic
prefixes, as in *Balla* How, *Balna*HOW, or *Balne-*
HOW, ' How Farm ' or ' Farm of the How ;' in
*Balla*foGIGE, a curious corruption of *Balla-fo-haugr*,
' Below How Farm ;' and in the equally curious cor-
ruption *Towl*FOGGY, ' Below How Hole,' an exact
description of the cave on Perwick beach. *Haugr*
is found in combination with *Cronk*, which has
occasionally much the same meaning, in *Cronk-*
HOWE-*moar*, ' Big How Hill,' commonly called ' Fairy
Hill.' [FOXHOWE, English Lakes ; REDHAUGH,
Northumberland ; ARDNAHOE, Islay ; MUCKLE
HEOG, Shetlands.]

Hóll (M), ' a hill, hillock ;' as in STRANDHALL (*Strandar-
hóll*), ' Strand Hill.' [ARNOL, Hebrides.]

Holt (N), ' a wood, copse-wood ;' as in DALLIOT (*Dalar-
holt*), ' Dales' Wood.' *Holt* was the usual word
for a wood in Middle English. [BRANTARHOLT,
Iceland.]

Hryggr (M), ' a ridge ;' possibly in BRERICK (*Bruar-
hryggr*), ' Bridge ridge.' This, and perhaps *Barrick* (*Berr-hryggr*), ' Bare ridge,' are the only names
in which *hryggr* certainly appears as an affix,
though it would seem to occur in ALDRICK, SPALD-
RICK, SOLDRICK, and RARICK, the names of small
creeks. As, however, there is no connection with
a ridge in these creeks, we can only suppose that
the *rick* is a corruption of *vík*. In Middle English
a ridge was called a *rigge*, and in the north of
England, at the present day, *ridge* or *rigg* is constantly used of a hill.

Kálfr (M), literally ' a calf,' is used in local names of a

17

small island near a large one. We have it in CALF *of Man*, which is a translation of MANAR-KÁLFR, as it is written in the Sagas. [RASTAR-KÁLFR, Hebrides ; ISLE OF CALF, Ireland.]

Kluft (F), 'a cleft;' possibly in SCARLET, formerly SCARCLOWTE (*Scarar-kluft*), ' Cleft Edge.'

Land (N), ' land;' possibly in KITTERLAND, ' Kitter's Land.' [JOTLAND.]

Lundr (M), ' a grove,' only occurs in LITTLE LONDON (*Líttill lundr*), ' Little Grove.' This place consists of two or three houses in a wooded dell in the midst of the mountains. *Lundr* is very common in Danish and Swedish local names, and it is also found in the north of England. [LITTLE LONDON, Lincolnshire ; LA LONDE, Normandy.]

Nes (N), literally ' a nose,' is used in local names both of long, low points and high cliffs, but usually of the former, as in LANGNESS (*Langa-nes*), ' Long Nose.' This name is pronounced *Langlish* by old Manx people, and thus furnishes an instance of the change of ' n ' to ' l.' [LANGANES, Iceland ; DUNGENESS, England ; GRISNEZ, France ; AIGNISH, Hebrides.]

Pollr (M), ' a pool, pond,' is only found in DUPPOLLA, (ob) (*Djup-pollr*), ' Deep pool,' which was one of the abbey-land boundaries in the parish of Lezayre, mentioned in the *Chronicon Manniæ*. *Pollr* is cognate with the Manx *pooyll*, Irish and Gaelic *poll*, Welsh *pwl*, and English *pool*. [LIVERPOOL ; BRAKAPOLLR, Iceland.]

Rani (M), literally ' a hog's snout,' used in local names

of a 'hog-backed' hill, possibly occurs in the name
of the mountain COLDEN, formerly COLDRAN
(*Kuldi-rani*), 'Cold Hill.'

Rípr (M), 'a crag;' only in SKEIRRIP (*Skerja-rípr*),
'Skerries' Crag.' *Rípr* becomes *reef* in Lewis,
South Uist and the Orkneys.

Setr (N), (1) 'a seat, residence,' (2) 'mountain pasture,
dairy lands,' may possibly be found in GRYSETH
(ob), (*Grjóta-setr*), 'Stones pasture.' This place,
which appears in the abbey-land boundaries in the
parish of Lezayre, mentioned in the *Chronicon Manniæ*, is now called KELLA. In the Hebrides this
word takes the form *shader*, as in GRIM-SHADER;
in the Orkneys, *Seater*, as in GRIM-SEATER; and
in the Shetlands, *setter*, as in GREEM-SETTER. In
the Shetlands *setter* is often contracted into *ster*,
as in CRUSTER. In Norway the modern *sæters*
are shepherds' huts on the mountain pastures.

Stadr (M), 'a stead, place, abode,' as in GRETTEST
(*Greta-stadr*), now GRETCH, 'Grettir's Place.' In
the Shetlands, by 1576, *stadr* had usually been
shortened to *sta*, and in the Orkneys, in 1502, it
was represented by *stath*, *staith*, *stayth*, and in
1595 *sta*. In the Isle of Man, early in the sixteenth century, the termination *sta* is sometimes
found, but *est* is more usual. *Stadr* forms the
termination of sixty-one names in the *Landnámabóc*.
It is cognate with *stead* in English, and *statt* in
German. [GRYMESTATH, now GREMISTEN, Shetlands; MEALISTA, Hebrides.]

Skógr (M), 'a shaw, a wood;' in the obsolete MIRESCOGE
(*Myrar-skógr*), 'Wood bog,' the name of a monastery

which was formerly situated on an island in the
Lezayre *Curragh*, at a place now called BALLA-
MONA.   In the *Chronicon Manniæ*, under date 1176,
we find that Godred gave to the Abbot Silvanus
a piece of land at MIRESCOGE, where he soon
built a monastery.   In the account of the limits
of the church lands appended to the Chronicle
'The lake at MYRESHAW' is mentioned.   In
North English and Scotch, a wood is called a
shaw; in Middle English, *schawe, shawe*; and in
Anglo-Saxon, *scaga*.

Skör (F), (gen. *skarar*), 'a rim, edge ;' probably in SKIN-
SCOE, formerly SKINNESKOR, 'Skinni's Edge.'
This aptly describes the place, which is on the
edge of steep cliffs by the sea, in the parish of
Lonan.

Stakkr (M), literally 'a stack of hay,' is used in local
names of columnar-shaped detached rocks in the
sea ; as in *Baie* STAKKR, 'Stack Bay.'

Toft, 'a green tuft or knoll, a green, grassy place ;' as
in TROLLOTOFT (*Trolla-toft*), 'Troll's Knoll,' in the
parish of Malew.   In Norway *tuft* means a clearing,
a piece of ground for a house, or near a house.   In
Middle English *toft* is a knoll.   Thus in Piers Plow-
man we find 'a towne on a toft.'   In Later English
it came to mean a piece of ground, a messuage,
a homestead.

Tún (N), 'a hedge, an enclosure, a house,' whence the
English *town*.   Possibly *town* in HOLM TOWN,
'Islet Town' (ob), the old name of Peel, is merely
the English form, and not derived from *Tún*.

Vágr (M), 'a creek, bay ;' as in RONALDSWAY (*Rogn-*

valds-vagr), 'Reginald's bay.' [STORNOWAY, Hebrides ; SCALLOWAY, Shetlands.]

Vað (N), 'a wading-place, a ford ;' as in SANTWAT
(*Sand-vað*), 'Sandford,' near Jurby Point, the scene
of an internecine struggle between the Manx in
A.D. 1098. It should be noted that in the *Chronicon
Manniæ*, RONALDSWAY (see above) appears in the
forms RAGNALDSWATH, ROGNALWATH and RONALD-
WATH, so that it may possibly be derived from *vað*.
[HOLTA-VAð, Iceland.] Compare English *wade*.

Vík (F), 'a small creek, inlet, bay,' as in GARWICK
(*Geir-vík*), 'Spear Creek,' is very common in the
Isle of Man, which shows how frequent the visits
of the *Víkingr*, or Creekmen, must have been
to its shores. In Islay *vík* is corrupted into *aig*
and *ag*, and *agg* is found in the Shetlands ; so it is
possible that the same corruption may appear in
SHELLAG, 'Shell Creek,' on the east side of the
Point of Ayre.

Völlr (M), 'a field ;' found only in the compound term
TINWALD or TYNWALD (*þing-völlr*), which was explained as follows by the late Dr. Vigfusson :*

'In the Isle of Man, as in any ancient Norse
Moot-place, three things are to be noticed : a *plain*
[voll], whereon there were to be found the *hillock,
brink* or *mound*, and *the court*. The court is *due
west* of the hill. The procession on the 24th of
June [5th July, N.S.] proceeds from the court to
the mound. The king, seated on the hill, had to
turn his '' visage unto the east.'' The Manx TIN-

---

* Manx Note Book. vol. xii., p. 174.

WALD and the Icelandic ALL-MOOT correspond in each particular point:

'The *Tin-walld* answers to the Icelandic *þing-voll-r*; the *Tinwald-hill* to the Icel. *Lög-berg,** or *Lög-brekka*;† the *House of Keys* to the Icel. *Lög-rétta*‡ (court); the *chapel* to the *temple* of heathen days.

'The 24th June *procession* answers to the Icel. *Lögbergis-ganga*,§ or *Dóma-út-færsla*,‖ on the first Saturday of every session, the distance between hill and court being about 140 yards in each case. The *path*, being fenced in like the court and hill, and used for this solemn procession when the judges and officers go to and fro between them, would answer to the Icel. *þingvallar-traðer.*¶

'The Manx Deemsters (*Dóm-stiórar*, deem-steerers) answer to the Icelandic Law-man or Speaker. There were two Deemsters in the Isle of Mann, because its central TINWALD is a union of *two older* separate TINWALDS, each of which kept its Law-speaker when the two were united in one central Moot. The Keys answer to the bench of *godes*, being two benches of twelve godes,

---

* *Lög-berg*, 'the law hill, law rock,' where the Icelandic legislature was held.

† *Lög-brekka*, 'law slope or brink,' the hill where public meetings were held and laws promulgated.

‡ *Lög-rétta*, 'law-mending,' the name of the legislature of the Icelandic Commonwealth.

§ *Lögbergis-ganga*, 'the procession to the law rock.'

‖ *Dóma-út-færsla*, 'the opening of the courts.' The Judges went out in a body in procession, and took their seats.

¶ *þingvallar-traðer*, 'Tinwald enclosure or lane.'

just as in Iceland there were four benches of each twelve *godes*.*

'The Hill and the Temple were the two holy spots, not the Court. The king sat on the hill, not in the court. Even at the present day the Manx look on the TINWALD hill as their hill of liberty, and rightly so. Antiquarians wanting to dig into the mound are warned off as right-minded Englishmen would forbid digging into Shakespeare's grave. In days of old, Hill and Court were, as it were, twins. Discussions, enactments of laws and decisions of law points took place in the Court, but anything partaking of proclamation, declaration, publication, was done from the Hill. It was the people's place.

'The arrangement of the Manx TINWALD and the Icelandic ALL-MOOT is one that no doubt obtained in other Teutonic nations, the *hill* for proclamations standing due west of the *high court*. This Court in early days was no doubt held within the *temenos* of a temple, as the Keys still sit in the southern transept of the Chapel of St. John.'

The two older TINWALDS, mentioned by Dr. Vigfusson, are situate at CRONK URLEY, or RENEURLING, near KIRK MICHAEL, for the northern part of the Island, and at KEEILL ABBAN, near St. Luke's Church in Baldwin, for the southern part of the Island. We learn from the Statute Law Book that there was a TINWALD Court held at the former place in 1422, but since that date the summer

* The *godes* composed the *Lög-rétta*, and were the law-givers of the country.

courts have usually been held at St. John's, while mid-winter courts were held between the gates at Castle Rushen till 1610, after which date the practice has been to promulgate the laws from the central TINWALD at St. John's, and usually once a year only, on Midsummer-day, June 24th, being the feast day of St. John the Baptist, which, since the change in the calendar, has been altered to the 5th of July. Of late years the greater amount of legislation has occasionally necessitated a winter promulgation as well, from the same spot.

This TINWALD at St. John's is held on a little artificial hill in the central valley between Douglas and Peel, about eight miles from the former and two and a half miles from the latter. This hill is said to have been originally composed of earth taken from all the seventeen parishes. It is circular in form and consists of four terraces, the lowest of which is eight feet broad, the next six feet, the third four feet, and the topmost six feet. There are three feet between every terrace. The circumference of the hill, which is covered with grass, is 240 feet. The promulgation of the law was formerly attended with considerable ceremony and state. The king sat upon the summit of the hill with his face to the east (*i.e.*, towards the chapel), his sword being held with the point upward before him. Round him were assembled the barons, deemsters, clergy, knights, esquires, and yeomen; and without the fence, which was formerly a wall about a hundred yards in circumference, the Commons. Then the Deemster, or

Deemsters, with the permission of the king or his lieutenant, chose the worthiest of the freeholders to assist in deciding difficult or doubtful points of law, as judicial questions were then decided as well as legislation passed. These *keise*, or chosen, who afterwards became the legislative body called the House of Keys, only existed in olden times by the lord's will, and were selected as occasion arose. The Court having been thus constituted, the Coroner of Glenfaba *Sheading* 'fenced' the Court, proclaiming that no man should make any disturbance on pain of hanging and drawing. The Court then proceeded with the business before it, but it seems clear that no legislation was valid without the assent of the Commons assembled outside the fence. Thus we find that there existed a true primitive folk-moot in the Isle of Man, the nearest parallel to which is the Landesgemeind of Uri and Unterwalden.

At the present day the Commons legislate only through their representatives, the Keys, and the procedure, too, has been shorn of much of its ancient circumstance and display. The Governor, representing the English sovereign, the Council, and the Keys assemble for Divine service in St. John's Chapel, after which the laws are signed. A procession then starts for the hill in the following order: (1) Four sergeants of Police, (2) the six coroners, (3) captains of the parishes, (4) the clergy in file, (5) the four high bailiffs, (6) members of the House of Keys in file, (7) clerk to the Council, (8) members of the Council, (9) the

Bishop, (10) the sword-bearer, who is the officer in command of the troops, (11) the Lieutenant-Governor, (12) surgeon of the Household, (13) Government chaplains, (14) the chief constable —passing through the ranks of a company of English soldiers, who have their barracks at Castletown. On arriving at the hill, the Southern Deemster calls upon the Coroner of Glenfaba to fence the Court, which he does in the following words: 'I fence this Court in the name of our Sovereign {Lord, the King / Lady, the Queen}. I do charge that no person do quarrel, brawl, or make any disturbance, and that all persons answer to their names when called; I charge this audience to witness that this Court is fenced; I charge this audience to bear witness that this Court is fenced; I charge this whole audience to bear witness that this Court is fenced.' The coroners are then sworn in by the Southern Deemster, who after this proceeds to read the marginal notes of the laws in English, being followed by the Coroner of Glenfaba, who repeats the same in Manx. No law is binding unless thus proclaimed from TINWALD Hill. It then becomes 'an Act of TINWALD.' The procession being re-formed, the Court returns to the chapel, where certain necessary money votes are passed, any subject on which a debate is likely to arise being adjourned. [THINGWALL, Wirral; TINGWALL, Shetlands; DINGWALL, Scotland; ÞING-VOLLR, Iceland.]

Vörr (F), used in Icelandic local names of 'a fenced-in landing-place,' is cognate with the English weir.

The CROSSAG Bridge is called, in one edition of the
Chronicon Manniæ, CROSYVÖR (*Krossa-vörr*), ' Weir
Cross.' This bridge spans the Silverburn stream
close by Rushen Abbey, and it is quite possible
that the monks had both a weir as well as a cross
there. [SKERRYVORE, Ireland.]

Þorþ (N), ' a hamlet, village ;' in NORTHOP (*Norðr-þorþ*),
' The North Village.' [NYTHORP, Denmark;
NORTHORPE, Lincolnshire.]

CHAPTER V.

THE name of the largest division of land in the Isle of
Man, THE SHEADING (*Skeiðar-þing*), 'War-ship District,' is clearly of Scandinavian origin.   The following
account of it was given by the late Dr. Vigfusson :

'What does the division of the Isle of Man into six
SHEDDINGS or SHEADINGS mean, and what is the
origin of the word?

'It cannot be related to the Anglo-Saxon *sceadan*,
whence Modern English to *shed* (to part or divide),
for *skeading* would mean rather the act of dividing than
the thing divided; further, this word of this family is
unknown to the Scandinavian tongues, and how could
such a word have got there among a population purely
Norse and Celtic?

'It is a political word, denoting the secular division
of the Island.   Hence it is to the Norse language and
to Norse institutions we have to look for the explanation thereof.   I take it to be a compound word, the
second component part whereof is *þing, thing* (a moot,
or even shire, district); the first component part would

be a monosyllable, ending in *d* or *th*, beginning in *sk*. The *dd* is due to the association of ð and *th*.

'So much for the grammar. Let us next have a look at the state of things in Scandinavia in olden days.

'Ancient Scandinavia, with her vast coast-line, measuring thousands of miles, indented with countless fjords and bays, and the Baltic estuary, stocked with islands, was from time of yore a land of mariners; the sea was their high-road, and from the sea rather than from the land they drew their sustenance; their first vessels were war-ships—galleys. Hence it comes that, from Lofoden down and along the coast of the Baltic, the land, as far inland "as the salmon runs," was divided into "ship-shires," districts, each of which, for defence or war at home or abroad, had to supply, man, and fit out a certain number of galleys. Every freeman born, between twenty and sixty years of age, was bound to serve. The names differ: in Norway this division is called *skip-reiða* (*skip* and *reiða*, to fit out, pay, discharge) ; in Sweden, *skips-lag* (ship-districts) or *snekkja-lag* (galley-districts). Observe that *sneikja* and *skeið* are synonymous words for the ordinary swift war-galley, and that the average number of oars in these galleys was sixteen or twenty. We have here, I think, got the right word, *skeiða-thing* or *skeiðar-thing*, a division into ship hundreds, each of which had to furnish so many *skeiðs* to the king. This would hold good for the Isle of Man. The Norse kings of Man and Sodor were essentially the lords of the sea, and would have established the same division that, since time out of mind, had obtained in their old home. In old Norse, in the tenth century, *sk* was undoubtedly sounded as in English *skin*, but in the course of time it changed into the present Norwegian sound, resembling English *sh*. The Manx, we take it, followed the Norse pronunciation, at least up to the date of separation in the thirteenth century, at which date the present Norse sound had obtained ; hence the word is *sheading*, not *skeading*, as it would be if no change had taken place.

'Practically the sheadings answer to the *hundreds* or *herdds* of Scandinavia. We know that in Upland (Sweden) every hundred had to fit out four ships. The Manx levy would, on the same scale, have been twenty-four galleys, and, taking the average crew to be forty, the full levy of the Island (*i.e.*, the male population between twenty and sixty) would make about one thousand. This would make the whole population some four or five thousand.'* Though the name is of Scandinavian origin, the amount of land represented by the SHEADING would appear to correspond with the Irish cantred, hundred, or barony, containing 120 quarters of land ; for each SHEADING, except Garff, contains three parishes, each parish, on an average, ten *treens*, and each *treen*, on an average, four quarters, *i.e.*, $3 \times 10 \times 4 = 120$ quarters in the sheading. We are told that in the age of the world 3922, ' Ollamh Fodla, king of Ireland, appointed a chieftain over every cantred and a *brughaid* over every townland.'† Now in the Isle of Man the SHEADING is still a division for judicial purposes, and has its officer, the coroner. Its court

* Manx Note Book, vol. xii., p. 175.
† Four Mast., vol i., pp. 53, 54.

formerly formed part of the Court of Common Law. In it was kept the registry of the names and titles of the lord's tenants, and it had cognizance of actions between tenants and felonies committed by tenants. Its manorial business is now transacted in the Courts Baron, presided over by the Seneschal.

Skeerey, ' a parish,' is probably a name of Scandinavian origin, as it has retained the hard ' *k* ' sound. It appears to be derived from *skera*, ' to cut, divide,' which is akin to the English *shear*, Anglo-Saxon *scire*, and English *shire*. It is only in connection with *keeilley* (see below) that it comes under the heading of a prefix, as in the only word in which it occurs uncompounded, *Dreem* SKEEREY, ' Parish Back,' it is an affix. *Dreem* SKEEREY is the name given to a long hill-ridge in the parish of Maughold. *Skeerey* is in use colloquially, and is found in the Manx dictionaries. It is used of the civil parish; but, when the Manx wish to express the ecclesiastical parish, they use the word *skeeylley*, which is probably a corruption of *Skeerey Keilley*, ' Church Division,' though it may be from the (O.N.) *skilja*, ' to part, separate, divide.'

CHAPTER VI.

DISTINCTIVE PREFIXES.

Part I.

SUBSTANTIVES.

By far the larger portion of distinctive prefixes in
Scandio-Manx names are substantives. The following
are prefixes as well as affixes:

Brekka, 'a slope;' possibly in BRACKA*broom*, formerly
> BRECKA*broom* (?) and BRECK*booilley*, ' Slope of the
> Fold;' but the *breck* in these names may be from
> the Celtic *breck*, 'speckled, spotted,' though, in that
> case, the position of the adjective is unusual (see
> p. 236).

Dalr, 'a dale;' in DALLIOTT (*Dalar-holt*), ' Dales'
> Wood;' and in DALBY (*Dalar-byr*), ' Dales' Farm.'
> *Dalr*, however, is not found in Iceland as a prefix
> in local names; so that these derivations are per-
> haps doubtful. Captain Thomas derives such
> names as DALE*more* and DALE*beg*, in Lewis, from
> *dal*, ' a little dale.'

Eyrr, ' a gravelly bank;' possibly in ORRISDALE, for-
> merly ORESTAL (*Eyri-dalr*), ' Gravelly Bank Dale.'

The objection to this derivation, however, is the 's' in ORRISDALE; and the same objection would apply to the derivation from the Danish *ore*, 'uncultivated land, forest.' ORESTAL, in Kirk Michael, is found in 1511; but ORRISDALE, in Malew, is a modern name, and was probably named after the traditional King ORRY (see p. 88); it is, of course, possible that ORESTAL may have the same origin. In the Hebrides and Islay, *eyrr* becomes *Eora*, *Eori*, *Ear*, *Ire*, or *Jure*; so that it may possibly form the first syllable in *Jurby* (*Jure-byr*), 'Gravelly-bank Farm,' which would be a very suitable derivation. [ERRIBOL, Sutherlandshire; ORBY, OWERSBY, Lincolnshire; OREBY, Denmark.]

Haugr, 'a how, mound;' in HOWSTRAKE (Haugr ?   ). [HAUGSNESS, Iceland; HOUGHAM, Lincolnshire; HORGIBOST, Harris.]

Hryggr, 'a ridge;' in REGABY, formerly REGBY (*hryggjar-byr*), 'Ridge Farm;' and CREGBY, probably a corruption of REGBY. [RIGSBY, Lincolnshire.]

Hólmr, 'a holm, islet;' in HOLM TOWN (*holma-tun*), corrupted into HALLAM TOWN, 'Islet Town,' the Scandinavian name of Peel, so called from the island just at the mouth of its harbour. In 1511 Huan Worthyngton paid 11s. 8d. rent for the mill of HOLMTOWN, as per record. [HÓLM-GARÐR, Russia and Iceland.]

Skarð, in SKARSDALE (*Skarðs-dale*), 'Mountain-pass dale.' [SKARÐS-DALR, Iceland; SCARF-GAP, Cumberland.]

Skógr, 'a shaw, a wood;' in SKYEHILL, a modern corruption of *Skogar-fjall*, 'Woodfell,' which we find written in the *Chronicon Manniæ*, under date A.D.

1077, as SCACAFELL, where Godred Crovan conquered the Manx. [SKÓGAR-STRÖND, Iceland ; SKAGA-FIÆRÐ, *Landnáma-bóc.*]

Stakkr, 'a stack,' used of a columnar rock in the sea, is found as a prefix in STACK *Indigo* (?), and STACK *mooar,* 'Big Stack.' [STACKS of Duncansby, Scotland ; STACKS-EYRE, *Landnáma-bóc.*]

Skör (gen. *skarar*), 'a rim, edge ;' probably in SCARLET, formerly SKARCLOUTE, which is probably a corruption of *Skarar-Kluft,* 'Cleft-edge.' [SCOUR-NA-MADAIDH, Skye.]

Toft, 'a green tuft or knoll ;' in TOSABY or TOTABY, formerly TOTMANBY, a corruption either of *Toftar-asmund-byr,* 'Osmund's Knoll Farm,' or of *Toftar-mana-byr,* 'Mani's Knoll Farm.'

The following are prefixes only :

(a) *Mountains, Hills, Rocks, etc.*

Brún (F), 'eyebrow,' used in local names of the brow of a fell or moor ; possibly in BRUNDAL, 'Dale-brow.'

Egg (F), (gen. *eggjar*), 'an edge,' used in local names of the ridge of a mountain ; in AGNEASH (*eggjar-nes*), 'Ridge Ness.' There are the remains of a *keeill* on this farm. [AIGNISH, Hebrides.]

Enni (N), 'the forehead,' used in local names of a steep crag or precipice ; possibly in ENNAUG (*enna-guag*), 'Cave Crag.' (*Guag* is a corruption of *ooig,* see *ögr,* p. 277.) [ENNACLETE, Hebrides.]

Galtr (M), 'a boar, hog,' used in local names of a hog-backed hill ; in GARTEDALE (ob.), formerly GALTE-DALE, 'Hogback Hill Dale.' This place, in the

parish of German, is now called SANDALL.   [GALT-
NESS, Iceland.]

Kambr (M), 'a comb,' used in local names of a crest, a
ridge of hills ; in CAMMALL (*Kamba fjall*), ' Ridges'
Fell ;' and probably in CAMLORK, formerly CAM-
LORGE (*Kamb* ?).   [KAMBSNES, Iceland ; CAM-
NESS, *Landnáma-bóc*; CAMFELL, English Lakes.]

Kollr (M), ' a top, summit ;' possibly in COLBY (*Kolla-
byr*), ' Summits' Farm,' in Arbory and Lonan.   It
should, however, be mentioned that in both these
parishes COLBY is on the side, not on the summit,
of a hill; so possibly the derivation from the proper
name *Kol* or *Koll* is the true one.   [COLBY, English
Lakes, Pembrokeshire, and Essex ; COLEBY,
Lincolnshire ; COLSETTER, Orkneys ; KULBY,
Denmark ; KOLDBY, Samsöe.]

Slakki (M), ' a slope on a mountain-edge,' exactly describes the position of SLEGABY, formerly SLEKBY
(*Slakka-byr*), 'Slope Farm,' in the parish of Onchan.
There is a SLECKBY, with the same meaning, in the
parish of Jurby.   [SLAKKÁ-GIL, Iceland.]

Stein (M), ' a stone ;' in STAYNARHEA (ob.), a corruption
of *Steina-haugr*, ' Stones' how.'   This name, which
appeared in 1540 in the computus of the Rushen
Abbey tenants in Malew, attached to the *Chronicon
Manniæ*, is not now used, its place being taken
by the Celtic SHENVALLA.   [STEINAR, Iceland ;
STENNIS, Orkneys ; STENNESS, Shetlands.]

þrömr (M), (gen. *þramar*), ' the brim, edge, verge ;'
possibly in TROMODE, formerly TREMOTT (*þramar-
holt*), ' Copsewood-edge.'   There was a mill at TRE-
MOTT in 1511 ; and in TREMMISSARY, formerly

TREMSARE (*þramar-setr*), ' Pasture Edge.' This *treen* comes to the edge of the cliffs by Burnt Mill Hill, near Douglas.

(b) Sea Coast.

Alda (F), (gen. *öldu*), ' a wave;' in ALDRICK (*öldu-vik*), ' Wave Creek.' This name looks as if it should be derived from *öldu-hryggr*, ' Wave Ridge ;' but it is certainly a *vik*, not a *hryggr*.

Bora (F), ' a bore hole;' in BURROW (*boru-ey*) *Head*, ' Bore Island Head.' This headland is opposite to the small island off the south-east end of the Calf Island, called The Eye, through which a hole has been bored by the action of the waves. [BORERAY, Hebrides.]

Gja (gen. *gjar*), ' a chasm, rift.' This word has been adopted into Manx in the forms GHAU and GIAU, but with the meaning ' creek or cove.' In the Orkneys it is found in the forms *geo* and *geow*. We have it with the following Celtic affixes : GHAW *cabbyl*, ' Horse Cove ;' GIAU *cam*, ' Winding Cove;' GIAU *gortagh* (?), ' Hungry Cove ;' GIAU *jeeragh*, ' Straight Cove ;' GIAU *lang*,* ' Long Cove ;' GIAU *ny kirree*, 'Cove of the Sheep ;' GIAU *ny moarid* (?), ' Cove of the Greatness ;' GIAU *ny Pharick* (*e*), ' Patrick's Cove ;' GIAU *Rool*, ' Rool's Cove ;' GIAU *spyrryd*, ' Spirit Cove ;' GIAU *veg*, ' Little Cove;' GIAU *yiarn*, ' Iron Cove.'

Giau is used in the Isle of Man, as in the Shetlands, of a smaller and narrower creek than *vik*.

Klettr (M), ' a rock, cliff' (by the sea) ; in CLET ELBY, ' Fireplace Rock.' A *clet* is usually a rock broken

* Lowland Scotch.

off from the adjoining rocks on the shore ; a small rock in the sea. It is used in this sense in the Orkneys and Shetlands.

Mæri (F), 'a borderland,' usually by the sea ; probably in MARY *voar* and MARY *veg*, formerly MEARY *voar* and MEARY *veg*, 'Big Borderland' and 'Little Borderland.' These farms are on the coast. [MÆRI, Norway.]

Ögr (N), 'an inlet, a small bay or creek,' is almost certainly the original from which the Manx *ooig*, 'a den, cave, cavern,' is derived ; as *ooig* resembles *ögr* much more closely than it does the Irish and Gaelic *uamh*. We find it in OOIG *doo*, 'Black Cave ;' OOIG-NY-*seyr*, 'Cave of the Carpenter ;' OOIG-Y-*vccal*, 'Cave of the Entrance ;' OOIG *veg*, 'Little Cave ;' and OOIGYN *doo*, 'Black Caves.' [UIG, Lewis ; ÖGUR, Iceland.]

Sker (N), 'a skerry, an isolated rock in the sea ;' in SKERRIP (*Sker(s)-ripr*), 'Skerry Crag ;' SKER *vreacy*, 'Speckled Skerry ;' in SKERRISDALE, formerly SKARISTAL (*Skers-dalr* or *Skerja-dalr*), 'Skerry Dale or Skerries Dale ;' and probably in KERISTAL. The word *sker* having been adopted into both the English and Celtic languages, as *Skerry* and *Skerries*, it seems probable that such names as SKERRISDALE are derived from the Anglicised form, not from the Scandinavian original. The name SKERRANES, given to some small detached rocks off Langness, seems to be an attempt to combine the O.N. *sker* with the Celtic diminutive *an*. SKERRANES would be appropriately translated 'Small Skerries.' [The SKERRIES, Ireland ; SKERJAFJÖRDR, Iceland.]

Strönd (F), ' a strand, coast, shore ;' in STRAND-HALL (*Strandar-holl*), ' Strand Hill.' [STROND, Harris and Iceland ; STRAND, Shetland.]

(c) *Glens, Lowlands, Rivers, etc.*

Brunnr (M), ' a spring, well ;' possibly in BRONDAL, formerly BRUNDAL (*Brunna-dalr*), ' Spring Dale.'

Fles (F), ' a green spot among bare fells and mountains,' a most appropriate description of FLESWICK (*Flesvik*), ' Green Spot Creek,' the little creek on the north side of Bradda.

Hvammr (M), ' a grassy slope or vale ;' probably in BEMAHAGUE (*Hvamma - haugr*), ' Slopes' How.' The land of this estate slopes gently towards the sea.　[HVAMMSDALR, Iceland.]

Krókr (M), ' a hook, anything crooked,' used in local names of a nook ; probably in CREGNEISH, formerly CROKNES (*Króks-ness*), ' Nook Ness.'　CREGNEISH is the name of a headland and village near the Calf.　It is one of the most primitive and secluded places in the Island.

Myrr (F), (gen. *myrar*), ' a moor, bog, swamp ;' in MIRESCOGE (ob.) (*Myrar-skogr*), ' Wood Bog ;' and possibly in MOREST (*Myrar-staðr*), ' Moor Stead.' MIRESCOGE was formerly a wooded island, surrounded by a lake, which must have been of considerable size, as the fishing of it was let.　When the Lhen trench was made the lake was drained, but its bed was still boggy, and the island became simply a piece of higher and drier ground.　It is now called BALLAMONA.　All this district was called ' The Mires.' [MÝRAR, Flatey.　Compare English *mire*.]

Ra, 'a corner, nook;' in RABY (*Rár-byr*), 'Nook Farm;'
in RARICK (*Rár-vik*), 'Nook Creek;' and possibly
in RAGGATT (*Rár-gata*), 'Nook Path.' These are
the remains of an ancient *Keeill* on RABY Farm.
[VRAABY, Denmark; WRAMILNA, Lincolnshire.]

Saurr (M), 'mud,' used in local names of sourland, or
swampy tracts of moorland; in SURBY, formerly
SAUREBY (*Saura-byr*), 'Sourlands' Farm;' in SAND-
BRICK, formerly SAUREBRECK (*Saura-brekka*), 'Sour-
lands' Slope.' A fine bronze axe-head was found
on SURBY, and there are a curious monolith and
the remains of an ancient *keeill* on the same farm.
[SAURBÆR, Iceland; SOWERBY, Yorkshire and
Westmoreland; SCARBY, Lincolnshire; SÖRBY
Denmark; SORBIE, Dumfries.]

Skaunn (M), poetically 'a shield,' used in local names
of fertile meadow-land, is possibly found in SHO-
NEST (*Skauns-staðr*), 'Meadow-land Stead.' The
small *treen* of this name is now all highland, but
it may at one time have extended into the valley
(see also derivation from proper name, p. 297).

Strengr (M), 'a string, a cord,' used in local names of
a narrow channel of water; possibly occurs in
STRENEBY (*Strengjar-byr*), 'Narrow Channel Farm.'
A small stream flows by this farm.

(d) Artificial.

Braut (F), 'a road;' possibly in BRAUST, formerly
BRAUSTA (*Brautar-staðr*), 'Roadstead.' There is
a farm called BALLYBRUSTE in 1231, and BALLY-
BRUSHE in 1505, which may be identical with
BRAUST.

Brú (gen. *brúar*), 'a bridge;' probably in BRERICK, formerly BRERYK (*Brúar-hryggr*), 'Ridge of the Bridge' or 'Bridge-ridge.' This farm is on the north side of Ramsey, close by the Sulby river, over which there was probably a bridge then, as now.   [BRUGARTH, Shetlands; BROGAR, Orkneys.]

Gata (F), 'a way, road, path;' possibly in GAT-E-WHING (*Götu-whing*), 'Yoke Path,' though it is a curious compound.   In the east of England *gat* is still frequently used for a road or path, as in GATE BURTON (Lincolnshire).   *Gata* has been adopted into Manx in the form *giatt*.

Kirkja (F), 'a kirk, church;' in KIRBY (*Kirkju-byr*), 'Church Farm.'   In a Papal Bull of 1231 the *terras de Sti. Bradani et de* KYRKBYE were mentioned. In 1405 this place, which adjoins the churchyard of Braddan, was called *Villa de* KERBY.   One of its *quarter-lands* is subject to the entertainment of the Bishop, whenever he leaves or comes to the island.   At present the tenants pay a yearly commutation of 10s. in lieu of this service, and they are let off cheaply.   Our parish churches, with two exceptions, have the prefix *kirk*, as in KIRK *Braddan* (see Index).   The word *kirk* is found in every place where the Norsemen settled and became Christians.   [KIRKJUBÆR, Iceland; KIRKWALL, Orkneys;   KIRKERUP, Denmark; KIRKBY and KIRBY, North of England; QUERQUE-VILLE, Normandy.]

Kross (M), 'a cross;' in CROSBY (*Krossa-byr*), 'Cross Farm;' and in CROSSAG, found in one copy of the *Chronicon Manniæ* as CROSYVÖR (*Krossa-vorr*), 'Weir

Cross ;' and in another, CROS-IVAR, ' Ivar's Cross.' The occurrence of *Cross* in local names is also a sign of the settlement and subsequent conversion of the Northmen, but it is not so widely distributed as *Kirk*. [KROSSDALE, Iceland ; CROSBY, Lincolnshire ; CROSSBOST, Lewis ; CROSEBISTER, Shetland ; CROSSPOLL, Islay.]

Kró (F), 'a small pen or fence ;' in CROcreen, ' Withered Fence.' The word *kró*, however, seems to have been originally Celtic ; but it was adopted by the Northmen. [CROIGARRY, Hebrides.]

Skáli (M), ' a hut, shed,' used of temporary shepherds' huts erected in the mountain pastures ; in SCOLABY, formerly SCALEBY (*Skála-byr*), ' Shed Farm.' There is a word *sheal* or *shieling* in Scotland, used of a hut for those who have the care of cattle or sheep. [SKÁLAHOLT, Iceland ; SCALLOWAY, Shetlands ; SCALLOW, Lincolnshire.]

Skip (N), 'a ship ;' possibly in SKIBRICK (*Skipa-hryggr*), 'Ships' Ridge.' [SKEBA, Islay.]

Vé (N), 'a mansion, house ;' in BIBALOE, formerly BYBALLO (*Vé-balli*), ' Grassy Bank House ;' in BEGOAD, formerly BEGOD (*Vé-Godi*), ' Godi's House, or Priest's House ;' and perhaps in BEMACCAN, BYMACCAN, BIMAKEN, BRYMAKEN, or BOWMAKEN (*Ve-Maccan*), ' Maccan's House,' *Maccan* being a possible corruption of *Magnus*. A monastery was founded here in 1373. It would appear that in 1368 Bishop Russell received an intimation from Pope Urban V. to the effect that William Montagu, Earl of Salisbury, the then Lord of the Isle, proposed to assign a site for an oratory of

Franciscan Friars Minor in the village of St. Columba (Arbory), and that, if the site was a suitable one, he had granted the Provisional Prior and brethren of the Province of Ireland permission to erect buildings there, which they did, as above stated. In 1553 it, together with Rushen, was confiscated by the English Crown. In 1606 it was leased to Sir Thomas Leigh Knightly and Thomas Spencer, and in 1626 its annual rent was granted to Queen Henrietta Maria for life. It was then called 'The Lesser Brotherhood, commonly known as the Gray Friars of Bimaken, otherwise Brimaken.' It shortly after this passed into the hands of the Tyldesley family by purchase, and still belongs to their descendants in the female line. The old chapel, which is the only portion now remaining, is used as a barn. The large arched window in the east gable, and the positions of doors, windows, and of a piscina, are clearly traceable.

(c) *Animal, Vegetable, and Mineral Kingdom.*

Dyr (N), 'an animal, beast, usually of wild beasts;' possibly in JURBY (*Dyra-byr*), 'Beasts' Farm.' If the tradition stating that in Scandinavian times the Sulby River flowed out at the Lhen is correct, which seems hardly possible, JURBY *Point* might have been a peninsula, and therefore useful as a game preserve. In the Shetlands cattle that are not housed are called *joor.* [DYRA-FIÆRD, *Land-náma-bóc;* DERBY, England. Compare Greek θήρ, Anglo-Saxon *dcor*, English *deer*, German *thier*.]

Hross (M), 'a horse;' in ROZEFELL (ob.), a corruption of *hross-fjall*, 'Horse Fell.' [HROSSEY, Orkneys.]

Kapall (M), 'a nag, hack;' probably in KEPELL GATE (*Kapal-gata*), 'Horse Road.' Both this and the Manx *cabyl* are derived from the Late Latin *caballus*. [KEPPOLLS, Islay.]

Lamb (N), 'a lamb;' in LAMMALL, formerly LAMBFELL, (*Lamba-fjall*), 'Lambs' Fell' (see p. 296). [LAMBEY, Flatholm.]

Smali (M), 'small cattle;' possibly in SMEALE, the name of a farm in the parish of Andreas. This name, which was probably a compound one originally, may have been SMALA-STAÐR, 'Cattle Stead.' [SMAILHOLM, Roxburghshire; SMAULL, Islay.]

Uxi (M), 'an ox;' in OXWATH (ob.) (*Uxa-vað*), 'Ox Ford,' which is mentioned in the *Chronicon Manniæ* as being one of the Rushen Abbey land boundaries. It is now called ORRISDALE. [OXNEY, Iceland.]

Hrafn, often spelled *hramn* (M), 'a raven;' in RAMSEY, which is either (*Hramns-á*), 'Raven's Water,' or (*Hramns-ey*), 'Raven's Isle' (or from a personal name, see p. 294). It is sometimes difficult to distinguish between *á* and *ey* in local names, as before stated. In this case the difficulty is increased by the early spelling being contradictory. The name in one of the editions of the *Chronicon Manniæ* is RAMSA, and it is pronounced by Manx people as if spelled in this way, while in the other edition it is RAMSÖ, and old maps show the town of RAMSEY on an island, cut off from the mainland by two branches of the Sulby River. A raven was the traditional war standard of the Danish and

Norwegian vikings. [HRAFNA-BJÖRG, Iceland ; RAVENSBURG, Yorkshire.]

Kráka, ' a crow ;' possibly in CREGNEISH, formerly CROKNESS (*Kraku-nes*), ' Crow's Ness ' (see *Krokr*, p. 278, and *Kraki*, p. 296). [CRACKPOOL, Lincolnshire ; KRAKGAARD, Denmark ; KRAK-NESE, *Landnáma-bóc*.]

Shag, a word which seems to be connected with the Icelandic verb *skaga*, ' to stand out,' is used colloquially for the crested cormorant. At the beginning of spring there rises on the middle of the head of the bird so-called a tuft of feathers one and a half inches high, capable of erection, hence the name. We have it in *The* SHAG *Rock*, ' The Cormorant Rock.'

Skarfr (M), ' a cormorant ;' possibly in SCARLET, formerly SCARCLOUTE (*Scarfa-kluft*), ' Cormorant Cleft ' (see *Skör*, p. 274). In Scotland a cormorant is called a *skart*, and in the Shetlands a *scarf*. [SKARFA-NESE, *Landnáma-bóc*.]

Fiskr (M), ' a fish ;' in FISHGARTH, formerly FYSGARTH (*Fiski-garðr*), ' Fish Pond ;' possibly in FISTARD, a corruption of FISHGARTH. [FISKIGARðR, Iceland ; FISGARTH, Trent ; FISHGUARD, Pembrokeshire.]

Lax, ' a salmon ;' in LAXEY, formerly LAXÁ (*lax-á*), ' Salmon Water.' [LAXA, Iceland ; LACHSAY, Skye ; LAXAY, Lewis.]

Skel (gen. *skeljar*), ' a shell ;' possibly in SHELLAG (*Skeljar-vik*), ' Shell Creek,' or (*Skelja-vik*) ' Shells' Creek.' The sandy cliffs at this place are composed of a curious, comparatively recent, shell conglomerate. [SHELIBOST, Harris; SKELBUSTER, Orkneys ; SKELJAVÍK, Iceland.]

Gras (N), 'grass, herbage;' in GRESBY (*Gras-byr*), 'Grass Farm.' [GRESMARK, Iceland; GRASSFIELD, Shetlands; GRASBY, Lincolnshire; GREASBY, Wirral.]

Hagi (M), 'a pasture, or an enclosed field;' probably in HEGNES (*Haga-nes*), 'Pasture Ness.' [HAGI, Iceland; HAGANES, *Landnáma-bóc*.]

Hrís (N), 'shrubs, brushwood,' is a possible derivation of the first syllable of RUSHEN; in RUSHEN, the old name of Castletown, and RUSHEN SHEADING, though the derivation from *St. Russein* (see p. 212) is much more probable. A large portion of the sheading of Rushen was at one time the Lord's forest. *Ris*, or *rys*, for brushwood, is found in Chaucer. [RISBY, Lincolnshire and Denmark; HRÍSHOLL, Iceland; RUSHIGARRY, Harris.]

Kjarr (N), 'copsewood, brushwood;' in CARDLE-*voar*, formerly CARDAL (*Kjarr-dalr*), 'Big Copsewood Dale;' and CARDLE-*veg*, 'Little Copsewood Dale.' [CARNISH, Hebrides; CARNESS, Orkneys; KJARR-DALR, Iceland.]

Korn (N), 'corn, grain;' in CORNAY, or CORNA (*Corn-á*), 'Corn-water;' and CORRONY, a corruption of CORNAY. There is a stone circle near CORNAY, the remains of which cover an area of sixty-five feet by sixty-three feet. A stone, with the following inscription, has recently been discovered by Mr. P. M. C. Kermode, at *Cabbal Keeill Woirrey* on CORNA : KI : KRISþ : MALAKI : OK BAþRIK : AþANMAN : UNAL : SAUþAR : IUAN : RISTI : I : KURNAþAL. '(Here lie in) Christ Malachi and Patrick Adanman O'Neil. Sheep's John carved

(this) in Cornadale.'*   Also in CORNAMA (ob.)
(*Korn-hammarr*), 'Corn Crag,' now corrupted into
CORDEMAN. There have been corn-mills on the
CORNAY stream from time immemorial. [KORNSÁ,
Iceland ; CORNABUS, Islay ; CORNQUOY, Orkney ;
CORNAIG, Tyree.]

Esja (F), 'clay ;' in ESCHEDALR (ob.) (*Esju-dalr*), 'Clay
Dale.' Godred II. is said to have given ESCHE-
DALA to the Priory of St. Bees. This name be-
came obsolete at an early date, as in 1511 it is
called CRAWDALL, in 1794 CROWDALE, and now
GROUDLE ; also in ESCHENESS (*Esju-nes*), 'Clay
Ness,' now called CLAY HEAD, which is in the
same district. [ESJUBERG, Iceland.]

Jörfi (M), 'gravel ;' possibly in JURBY, formerly JORABY
(*Jörfa-byr*), 'Gravel Farm.' This long promontory
is a mixture of gravel and sand.

Grjót (N), 'gravel, pebbles ;' in GRYSETH (*Grjóta-setr*),
'Stones' Pasture.' This farm consists of rocky
upland pasture.

Möl (F) (gen. *malar*), 'pebbles ;' in MALAR LOGH (ob.
after 1673), now called LOGH MOLLO, 'Pebbles'
Lake.' This lake, having been drained, is now a
farm in the parish of Lezayre.

Sandr (M), 'sand ;' in SANDALL (*Sand-dalr*), 'Sand
Dale ;' in SANDWICK (*Sand-vík*), ' Sand Creek ;' in
SANDWICK BOE (*Sand-vík-böe*), 'Sand Creek Cow,'
an islet in Castletown Bay (see *Böc*) ; and in
SANTWAT (ob.) (*Sand-vað*), 'Sand Ford,' where an
internecine struggle between the North and South

---

* Reading and translation of inscription by Mr. P. M. C.
Kermode.

Manx took place, 'and those from the north obtained the victory' (*Chron. Manniæ*). In 1693 this place was called STANTWAY, a 't,' as usual in Manx, having been inserted. It is on the sandy shore close to Jurby Point. [SANDVIK, Iceland; SANDWICH, Kent; SANDAY, Orkneys; SAND-FELLE, *Landnáma-bóc*.]

(*f*) *Sundry.*

Prestr (M), 'a priest;' possibly in DRESWICK (*Prests-vik*), 'Priest's Creek.' There is an old chapel close by. [PRESGARTH, Shetlands; PRESTHUS, Iceland.]

Folk (N), 'people, folk;' in FOXDALE, formerly FOLKS-DALE (*Folks-dalr*), 'Folks' Dale.'

The beacons, which were formerly lit to warn the inhabitants that invaders were coming, are commemorated in the names WARDFELL and ELBY.

Varða (F), 'a beacon, a pile of stones or wood.' In Iceland *varða* is the popular name of the stone cairns erected on high points on mountains and waste places, to 'warn' the wayfarer as to the course of the way. WARDFELL (ob.) (*Vörðu-fjall*), 'Beacon Fell,' now South Barrule, was probably used as a place for a beacon, from its commanding position. The *treen* bordering on South Barrule is still called WARFIELD, a corruption of the same word. [VÖRDU-FELL, Iceland.]

Eldr (M), 'fire, a beacon;' in ELBY (*Elda-byr*), 'Fires' Farm;' and ELBY *Point*, 'Fires' Farm Point.' Close to this place there is a curiously sculptured monolith.

Snær (M), 'snow,' usually found in place-names in the
older form *snæ;* in SNÆFELL (*Snæ-fjall*), 'Snow
Fell,' the name of the highest mountain in the
island. The names of the highest mountains in
all countries have usually some connection with
snow. [SNÆFELL, *Landnáma-bóc.*]

Sól (F), 'the sun;' probably in SOLDRICK (*Sólar-vik*),
'Sun Creek.' *Sólar-hryggr,* 'Sun Ridge,' would
seem the more probable derivation if it were not
for the fact that SOLDRICK is a creek. [SÓLAR-
FJALL, *Landnáma-bóc.*]

Scandinavia was pre-eminently a land of strange
and weird superstitions. Among these the fairies and
giants, or elves and trolls, naturally played a prominent
part, and we consequently find that they have left some
mark on our local names, though scarcely any on the
superstitions that have been handed down by tradition,
which are almost entirely of Celtic origin.

Alfr (M), 'an elf, fairy;' possibly in ALCHEST (*Alfa-
stadr*), 'Elves' Stead.'

Troll (N), 'a giant, fiend, demon, trolle;' in TROLLABY
(*Trolla-byr*) (ob.), 'Trolls' Farm;' and TROLLATOFT
(ob.), 'Trolls' Knoll.' [TROLLA-GATA, Iceland; TROL-
LHÆTTAN, Sweden; TROLLHOULLAND, Shetlands.]

Gandr (M), 'magic;' possibly in GANSEY (*Gands-ey*),
'Magic Isle,' though the strip of land so called,
along the shore of Port St. Mary Bay, is not an
island. Perhaps, however, it may be *Gands-á,*
'Magic Water.' The old name of the White Sea
was GAND-VIK, 'Magic Bay,' probably because the
Lapps who lived on its shores were notorious
sorcerers.

þing (M), literally ' a thing,' is found only in the compound word, þing-völlr, ' Parliament field ' (see p. 261).

We find 'the South,' ' the North,' and ' the East ' in our Scandinavian local names, but not ' the West.'

Suðr (N), 'the south ;' in SODERICK (Suðr-vík), ' The South Creek,' now known as Port SODERICK, and in the name of the old Scandinavian diocese of SODOR, which appellation was incorrectly given to Peel Island. The history of this word is an interesting one, and may therefore be examined in detail. The Scandinavian diocese aforesaid, called SODOR (Suðr-eyjar), or The South Isles, in contradistinction to the Norðr-eyjar, or The North Isles, the Orkneys and Shetlands, included the Hebrides, all the smaller Western Isles of Scotland, and Man. Both were under the suzerainty of Norway and the archiepiscopate of Throndjheim. Before 1145, except, perhaps, for a brief period under Magnus, at the end of the eleventh century, the bishoprics of Suðr-eyjar and MAN were distinct; but from that date till 1458, when, by a Bull of Pope Calixtus, Man was placed under the archiepiscopal rule of York, while the Scotch Isles were formed into a distinct diocese, they seem to have been united, though the political connection with Norway was severed in 1266, and with Scotland in 1334. As proof of this it may be mentioned that Pope Urban V., in writing to Bishop William (who is known to have also been Bishop of Man) in 1367, speaks of a *nobilis mulieris Mariæ de Insulis* . . . . *tuæ diœcesis*. The bishops of this diocese were usually styled *Sodorensis*, though *Insularum* and *Manniæ et Insularum* are occasionally found. The title of *Sodor* seems to have been perpetuated in connection with MAN by the fact, which the recent discovery of a modern transcript of a Bull of Pope Gregory IX., dated 1231, by the present Bishop of the diocese, places beyond a doubt that Peel Island was also called *Sodor*—in the words of the Bull, *Holme, Sodor vel Pile vocatum,* ' Holme (Island), called Sodor or Pile.' In a charter of Thomas, Earl of Derby, to the Bishop of SODOR, dated 1505, these words are repeated ; but this, which, previously to the above-mentioned discovery, was the first mention of *Sodor vel Pile* or *Pele*, might have been explained by the argument that, the old diocese having so long ago passed away, the true meaning of *Sodor* had been forgotten, and that, by way of getting an application for the name, it had been given to this little Island of Peel. But this explanation will not now serve, for in 1231 it was a title given in a formal document of the time of Scandinavian rule, and when the Scandinavian language must have been used by at least the ruling class. The true explanation appears to be that Peel Island, being the seat of the cathedral of the diocese of SODOR, took its name from the diocese instead of giving it to it, as is usually the case. For it is not likely that SODOR was the original name of an island to the west, not to the south, of another. Its earliest name seems to have been the Celtic *Peel* or *Pile*, meaning ' fort,' so called, no doubt, from the ancient

round tower on it. Then the Norsemen called it
Holme (O.N. *holmr*), their usual name for an island
at the mouth of a river. Later still, as we have
seen, the ecclesiastical name of SODOR was given to
it, and in all formal secular documents, after 1505,
relating to it these three names are recited. Having
thus accounted for the permanence of the name
SODOR, it will be interesting to trace how MAN became associated with it. The modern name
of the Bishopric of Man, 'Sodor and Man,'
seems to have arisen from a mistake of a
legal draughtsman in the seventeenth century.
It would appear that by the latter part of the
sixteenth century the terms *Sodor* and *Man* had
clearly become interchangeable, for in a document of Queen Elizabeth's, dated 1570, mention is
made of 'the bishopric of the Island of *Sodor* or
Man.' In 1609 a grant of the Isle of Man was
made to William, Earl of Derby; and in the document conveying this grant all the possible titles of
the bishopric are recited with a precision which
leaves no loophole for error: 'The patronage of
the bishopric of the said Isle of Man, and the
patronage of the bishopric of Sodor, and the
patronage of the bishopric of Sodor and Mann.'
The then bishop, Philips, at once took advantage
of this new title, as in the following year he signs
himself 'Sodor et de Man.' In 1635 Bishop Parr
is called 'Bishop of the Isle of Man, of Sodor,
and of Sodor and Man.' No signature of his
can be found, but his successors, up to the time of
Bishop Levinz, who was appointed in 1684, usually

signed themselves 'Sodorensis,' occasionally 'Sodor and Man ;' but since 1684 the signature has been either ' Sodor and Mann ' or ' Sodor and Man.' The full title of the see at the present day is ' Bishop of the Isle of Man, of Sodor, of Sodor and Man, and of Sodor of Man,' which accentuates the application of the name *Sodor* to Peel Island. [SUðREY, Iceland ; SOUTHREY, Lincolnshire ; SUTHERLAND.]

Norðr (N), ' the north ;' in NORTHOP (*Nord-þorþ*), ' The North Village.' [NORðRA, Iceland.]

Austr (M), ' the east ;' in AUST,* the name of a tumulus near Ramsey. An urn has recently been discovered there. [AUSTACRE WOOD, Lincolnshire.]

Geirr (M), ' a spear ;' probably in GARWICK (*Geir-vik*), ' Spear Creek.' GEIRR is also a man's name (see p. 293).

Hangi (M), ' a body hanging on a gallows ;' possibly in HANGO HILL (*Hanga-hóll*), ' Hill of the Hanged,' on the shore opposite King William's College ; and HANGO BROOGH, ' Brow of the Hanged,' a little further along the shore to the north. There are remains of fortifications at both these places, that at the former having been erected in 1642 by James, seventh Earl of Derby, which seems to have been used for executions. We have it recorded that William Christian (*Iliam Dhoan*) was ' shott to death ' on HANGO HILL in 1662. This interesting place, which consists of a mass of boulder clay and drift gravel, is rapidly being washed away by the sea.

---

* This is placed under prefixes instead of simple names, as it is probably only part of the original name.

The following Scandinavian proper names,* though obsolete as such in the Isle of Man, are found as prefixes in local names :

Asmund (the change of which into CASEMENT has been traced at p. 79), probably in AMOGARRY (*Asmundar-garðr*), 'Asmund's Enclosure.' [ASHMIGARRY, Hebrides ; OSHMIGARRY, Skye.]

Aust may possibly be a man's name, as stated under *austr*, 'east' (p. 292) ; and the tumulus so called may commemorate the burial place of a warrior of this name. The Norsemen were called the *Ostmen* or Eastmen in Ireland. The English used the word *Easterling* in the same sense.

Brun, in BRUNDAL (*Bruns-dal*), ' Brown's Dale,' may be from a man's name (see pp. 274, 278). [BRUNSVIK, Flatey.]

Cleppr, a man's name, from *kleppr*, 'a rock ;' possibly in CLEPS, the name of a farm in Onchan parish, which was perhaps originally CLEPPSBY, 'Clepp's Farm.'

Corne, possibly in CORNAA (*Corna-a*), ' Corne's water ' (see *korn*, p. 285).

Galte, possibly in GARTEDALE, (ob.) formerly GALTE-DALE (*Galta-dalr*), 'Galte's-dale' (see p. 274). [GALTADALR, *Landnáma-bóc.*]

Geirr, as a proper name, is perhaps found in GARWICK (*Geira-vik*), ' Geirr's Creek ;' but GARWICK is more probably derived from *geirr*, 'a spear' (see p. 292), as *geirr*, though very common in compound proper names, as SIGGEIR, is rare uncompounded. [GARBOST, Lewis ; GEIRABÓLSTADIR, Iceland ; GEIRA-STÆD, *Landnáma-bóc.*]

* They are all found either in the *Landnáma-bóc, Flateyjarbóc,* or the Sagas, unless it is stated to the contrary.

Grettir, used poetically in the *Eddas* of a dragon, is found in the *Landnáma-bóc* as a surname, and as such it possibly occurs in the Isle of Man in GRETCH, formerly GRETTEST (*Grettis-staðr*), 'Grettir's Stead;' in GRETCH *voar* (big), and GRETCH *veg* (little), in GRETCH *heose* (upper), and GRETCH *heis* (lower), and perhaps in GREST, another contraction of GRETTEST. On GRETCH *veg* is the ancient tomb where an iron sword was found, which is popularly called ' King Orry's grave.' [GRETTISHAF, Iceland.]

Haraldr (M), (*Her-valdr*), ' Host wielder,' was a common Scandinavian name, which became Harold in English. There were several kings in MAN so called. It seems to have been applied to the mill and treen now called HORALETT, but formerly HORALDRE, which is probably part only of the original name.

Hæringr (M), ' a hoary man,' (*hæra*, ' gray-hair, hoariness ') ; in the old name of one of the Rushen Abbey land boundaries, HÆRINGSTADT (ob.) (*Hæring's staðr*), ' Hæring's Stead.' This place is now called KERROO-MOAR.

Högni (M), ' a tom cat ;' possibly in HEGNES or HOANES (*Hægnis-nes*), ' Hogni's Ness ' (see p. 285), the name of a treen in the parish of Lonan. *Hogni* is the name of a hero in the tale of Beolwulf, and is common in Iceland. HONEY HILL in the parish of Onchan, which ingenious philologists might derive from *Högni*, is a modern name.

Hrafn (M), ' a raven,' is a common proper name, and may occur in RAMSA or RAMSÖE (*Hrafns-a* or *Hrafns-ey*), now RAMSEY, ' Hrafn's Water, or

Hrafn's Isle' (see p. 283). [HRAFNS-TOFT, *Land-náma-bóc*.]

Hrólfr (*Hrod-ulfr*), 'brother wolf,' which has become Ralf in English, and Rudolph in German, possibly occurs in RAUFF,* the name of a *treen* in the parish of Lonan. The name of *Roolwer*, who was Bishop of Man from 1050 to 1065, may be a corruption of *Hrólfr*, and if so it is the only instance of the name in the Insular records. [ROWSAY, Orkneys.]

Ingimarr, contracted into *Ingvar* and *Ivar*, possibly occurs in JURBY, sometimes written formerly IVORBY, 'Ivar's Farm.' This derivation is suggested by Worsaae in his 'Danes and Northmen.' The knight *Ivar* was killed in 1275, when the Scotch conquered the Isle of Man. [IRBY, YERBY, Yorkshire; IRBY-IN-MARSH, Lincolnshire.]

Kitter, a name of Teutonic, if not of Scandinavian origin, is found in KITTERLAND, which is a small island midway between the Calf and the mainland. According to Manx tradition this islet derived its name from Kitter, a great Norwegian baron, who resided in the Isle of Man in Olave Godredson's days, and who was wrecked here.

Kolr and *kollr*, the former from *kol*, 'coal,' the latter from *koll*, 'a summit,' may either of them originate the name of the places called COLBY in the parishes of Lonan and Arbory (see p. 275). In fact the derivation from a proper name is more probable, as neither of these places is on a summit, and there is no coal in the Isle of Man.

* Probably only part of the original name.

Kori, or *Core*, as the name is spelled in the *Landnáma-bóc*, where it is stated to be the name of an Irish thrall in Iceland, is probably found in CORBRECK (*Kora-brekka*), ‘Kori’s Slope,’ and in COR STACK (*Kora-stakkr*), ‘Kori’s Stack.’ [CORA-NESE, *Landnáma-bóc*.]

Kraki (M), ‘a pale, stake,’ used as a proper name; possibly in CREGNEISH, formerly CROKNESS (*Kraka-nes*), ‘Kraki’s Ness.’ It was a nickname of the famous mythical Danish King, *Rolf kraki*, from his having been tall and thin (see p. 284). [KRAKA-NESE, *Landnáma-bóc*.]

Kraun, probably in CRANSTALL (*Krauns-dalr*), ‘Kraun’s Dale,’ and in CRANSTALL *Lough*, ‘Kraun’s Dale Lake.’ This lake, which probably never exceeded the dimensions of a pond, has now almost disappeared. [KRAUNS-DAL, *Landnáma-bóc*.]

Lambe, possibly in LAMMALL, formerly LAMBFELL (*Lamba-fjall*), ‘Lamb’s Fell’ (see p. 283). [LAMBA-STÆD, *Landnáma-bóc*.]

Liöt, probably the same as the old Teutonic word *leöd*, ‘people,’ possibly occurs in LEODEST, now LOW-DAS (*Liots-staðr*), ‘Liot’s Stead.’ We have *liöt* compounded in the extinct name LIUTWOLF on the Ballaugh Cross, and in the common name CORLETT.

Narfi, in NARRADALE (*Narfa-dalr*), ‘Narfi’s Dale.’ [NAR-FAEYRR, Iceland; NARFA-SKER, *Landnáma-bóc*.]

Ormr (M), ‘a snake, serpent,’ a common proper name in Iceland, is found in ORM’s *House* (ob.), mentioned as being on the boundary of the church lands near Laxey, in the *Chronicon Manniæ*; and in ORMESHAN (ob.), on the site of Onchan village, which was granted by Reginald to the Priory of St. Bees. [ORMSTÆD, *Landnáma-bóc ;* ORMSDALE, Iceland ; ORMISSARY, Kintyre ; ORMYSDILL, Arran ; ORMSKIRK, Lancashire.]

Petr, the Icelandic form of *Peter*, is probably found in PERWICK (*Petrs-vík*), ' Peter's Creek.'

Rögnvald (see CRELLIN), ' Gods' wielder ;' in RONALDSWAY, formerly either RÖGNVALDSVAGR, ' Reginald's Bay,' or RANALDWATH, ' Roland's or Reginald's Ford ' (see *vágr* and *vað*). From the *Chronicon Manniæ* we learn that ' in the year 1316, on Ascension Day, at sunrise, Richard de Mandeville, with his brothers and many others of note, and a body of malefactors from Ireland, put into the port of Ronaldsway ' (*portum de* RANALDWATH in the original). They then proceeded to defeat the Manx in a combat on the slopes of Wardfell now called South Barrule. The port here mentioned is now called Derbyhaven, while the farm close by retains the name of RONALDSWAY. On it there are two tumuli near the shore, which perhaps contain the remains of those who fell in the various combats which have taken place there. An iron gauntlet was dug out of one of these in 1836. This name was a common one in Scandinavia, and was borne by several of both the Manx kings and bishops. [RAGNVALDSVAAG, RONALDSHAY, Orkneys.]

Skarfr (M), ' a cormorant,' is perhaps found in SCARLET, formerly SCARCLOUTE (*Skarfs-kluft*), ' Scarf's Cleft (see *Scarf*, p. 284).

Skaunn (M), 'a shield,' possibly occurs in Shonest, the name of a *treen* in the parish of Lonan (*Skauns-staðr*), 'Skaun's Stead.'

Skauri, from *skari* (M), 'a young seagull;' possibly in Skerrisdale, formerly Skerristal (*Skauris-dalr*), 'Skauri's Dale;' and in Scarista (*Skauris-staðr*), 'Skauri's Stead' (see *Sker*, p. 277). [Scarista, Harris; Scarrabus, Islay; Scrabster, Caithness; Skarastaðr, Iceland.]

Skinni, 'a skinner,' a nickname in the *Landnáma-bóc;* in Skinscoe, found in the *Chronicon Manniæ* as Skynnescor (*Skinnis-skör*), 'Skinni's Edge.' [Skinnybocke, Lincolnshire.]

Sölvi, possibly meaning 'the swallow;' in Sulby, formerly written Sulaby, Soulby, and Solbee (*Sölva-byr*), 'Solvi's Farm.' This is the name of the largest river in the Island, and of two farms in the parish of Onchan. It is also found in Sulbrick (*Sölva-brekka*), 'Solvi's Slope or Brink.' [Solva-dale, *Landnáma-bóc*.]

Ullr, or *Ulli*, 'akin to Gothic *wulpus*, "glory,"' the name of one of the gods, the stepson of Thor; in Ulist (*Ulls-staðr*), 'Ull's Stead.'

Þorkell (Þorketill, 'Thor's kettle,' see Corkhill, p. 82); in Thorkelstad (ob.) (Þorkell's-staðr), 'Thorkell's Stead,' or *villa* Thorkell, as it is called in the oldest manorial roll, which was the ancient name of the village of Kirk Michael.

The proper name Cringle, which is still in use as a surname, from *kringla* (F), 'a dish, circle, orb,' is found as a farm name without either prefix or affix, and is therefore probably only a portion of the whole name. The name of the farm may, however, be derived immediately from *Kringla*, 'a circle (see p. 86).

Goree, or *orree* (see p. 87), is a proper name still in existence as a surname in the Isle of Man, and, as it was the name of several of the Scandinavian kings of Man, it would seem not unlikely that it has survived in local nomenclature. The farm called ORRISDALE, in the parishes of Michael and Malew, is said to have obtained its name in this way, but the derivation is a very doubtful one. ORRISDALE, in Michael, was spelled ORESTAL in 1511, and at a later period it was for a time called NORRISDALE, having been the property of a vicar of the parish named *Norris*. ORRISDALE in Malew is comparatively a modern name, and may have been named after the traditional King *Orry*.

Nearly all the Scandinavian surnames which are in use at the present day are found in local names as affixes, with the Celtic prefix *Balla;* such local names are for the most part of comparatively recent origin. These names are CASTELL, COTTIER, CORKHILL, CORLETT, CHRISTIAN, GARRETT, GORRY, LACE, and LEECE (see pp. 79-92).

There are also a few obsolete Scandinavian names found as affixes:

Asmund, possibly in TOTABY or TOSABY, formerly TOTMANBY, according to Munch, a contraction of *Toftar-asmunds-byr*, 'Asmund's Knoll Farm.' TOTMANBY, however, may be more simply derived from *Toftar-mána-byr*, 'Mani's Knoll Farm.' *Mani* (M), 'the moon,' is a common proper name in the

Landnáma-bóc. [MANABERG, Iceland ; MANISH, Skye ; MANBY, Lincolnshire.]

Godi, 'a priest,' used as a proper name ; in BEGOAD (*Vé-Godi*), 'Godi's House.'

Olafr, 'Olave,' a very common proper name in Iceland and Scandinavia, which was borne by several of the kings in Man (see COWLEY, KEWLEY), is possibly found in *Knock*OLD, formerly *Knock*OLE, 'Olave's Hill.' This name is found in the form *Oulaib* on the Ballaugh Cross. [BALOLE, 'Olaf's Farm,' Islay.]

Ullr, or *Ulli* (see p. 298), in *Colo*ONEYS, formerly *Cooil*-ULIST (*Ulls-staðr*), 'Ull's Stead Nook.'

In Johnstone's translation of the *Chronicle of Man*, CROSYVOR is called CROSS IVAR, or 'Ivar's Cross' (see p. 281).

There is a farm in BALDWIN called, in 1511, *Baldall* REYNYLT (? *Balla-ðalr*), 'Reginald's Dale Farm.' It is now corrupted into *Balla*REGNILT.

Part II.—Adjectives.

Adjectives in Icelandic or Old Norse, as in English, invariably precede the substantives which they qualify. There are comparatively few adjectives found in Scandio-Manx names :

Berr, 'bare ;' probably in BARRICK (*Berr-hryggr*), 'Bare Ridge.'

Bla (F), 'blue ;' only in the compound *blá-ber*, 'bleaberry or blueberry,' which is found in *Awin* BLABER, 'Bleaberry River.' [BLÁ-SKOGR, *Landnáma-bóc.*]

Brattr, 'steep ;' in BRADDA, formerly BRADHAUGH

(*Bratt-haugr*), ' Steep How ;' in BRETBY (ob.)
(*Bratt-byr*), ' Steep Farm,' now corrupted into
BRETNEY. *Brant* and *brent* are used in the
North of England for steep hillocks. [BRATTA-
HLID, Greenland.]

Djupr, ' deep,' usually of water ; in DUPPOLLA (ob.)
(*Djup-pollr*), ' Deep Pool,' now called NAPPIN, in
the parish of Lezayre. [DEPEDALE, Lincolnshire ; DIEPPEDAL, Normandy.]

Grænn, ' green ;' in GRENABY, formerly GRENBY (*Græn-
byr*), ' Green Farm ;' in GRENEA (*Græn-ey*), ' Green
Isle ;' and in GREENWYK (ob.) (*Græn-vík*), ' Green
Creek,' now called *Port* GREENAUGH, or *Port*
GREENOCK.

Hvítr, ' white ;' in WHITE HOE (*Hvita-haugr*), ' White
How,' near Douglas. [HVITA-DALR, Iceland;
WHITBY, England.]

Kuldi, ' cold ;' possibly in COLDEN, formerly COLDREN
(*Kuldi-rani*), ' Cold Hill.'

Lagr, ' low, low-lying ;' probably in LIGGEA (*Lag-ey*),
' Low Isle.' [LAGEY, Iceland.]

Langr, ' long ;' in LANGNESS (*Langa-nes*), ' Long Nose or
Long Ness,' the name of the long promontory
forming the northern side of Castletown Bay.
[LANGANES, Iceland.]

Lítill, ' little ;' in LITTLE LONDON (*Litill-lundr*), ' Little
Grove ;' and perhaps in LITTLE NESS (*Litill-nés*),
' Little Headland,' though this is probably
modern.

Meðal, ' middle ;' in MIDDLE SHEADING, formerly
called MEDAL. [MEÐAL-FELL, Iceland; MEÐAL-
LAND, *Strelinga Saga ;* MEÐAL-BÆR, *Flatey-jarbóc.*]

Svartr, 'black ;' in Swarthawe (*Svart-haugr*), ' Black How ;' and probably in Sartfell, or Sartell (*Svart-fjall*), ' Black Fell.' These names record the dark colour of the heather. It is notable that the Icelandic word *ling* is commonly used for heather by Manx people at the present day. [Sort Hill, England ; Svarta-haf, Iceland ; Soterup, Denmark.]

CHAPTER VII.

ENGLISH NAMES.

A NUMBER of English or semi-English names have gradually crept into Manx nomenclature during the six centuries of English rule. Of these only the more interesting are given. The semi-English names are for the most part affixes to the Celtic *Balla*, while the others are either translations of original Manx names, or purely English. Under the first heading we have BALLA-*paddag*, a corruption of BALLA-*paddock*, 'Paddock Farm;' BALLA-*strang*, where *Strang* is one of the titles of the Derby and Athol families; BALLA-*fletcher*, 'Fletcher's Farm,' originally applied to a property consisting of five *quarterlands* in the parish of Braddan, owned by the Fletchers, a Lancashire family, who were one of the most influential families in the Island during the seventeenth century; BALLA*vale*, 'Valley Farm,' in the parish of Santon, where there is a Standing Stone; BAL*laughton*, where the affix is doubtful, was, in the eighteenth century, usually spelled *Balliaghtin*. We have also *Castle* MONA, where *Mona* is the early name of the Island, which was the name given by the Duke of Athol to his residence near Douglas, completed by him in 1804. It is now an hotel. *Gullet* BUIGH, 'Yellow Gullet,' a small inlet on Langness, is probably so called from the colour of the seaweed. BAIE-NY-*Breechyn*, ' Bay of the Breeches,' where *breechyn* is simply a corruption of the English word, is so called because it divides into two branches, or, rather, legs. CREG *Mill* is ' Rock Mill,' and CREG-Y-*Leech* is ' The Crag of the Leech, or Doctor.' The meaning of COLLOO-*way*, ' Calf Way ' or ' Calf Bay (?),' is uncertain, as *way* may, perhaps, be a corruption of O.N. *vagr*, and not English. CRONK*bourne* is ' Hill River.' RUSHEN *Abbey*, founded in 1134, of which very little now remains, is notable as having been the last monastery dissolved in the British Isles.* THOUSLA *Rocks* are the small rocks in the Sound of the Calf. It is not known to what language *Thousla* belongs.

Of Scandio-English names there are :

Little NESS, ' Little Nose,' the name of a headland. *Ness* has practically been adopted as an English local name. *Little* NESS may, however, be a translation of the Scandinavian *Lítill Nés*. GIAU-*lang* is ' Long Cove.'

Of translations we have the following, which are known to be so, either because the Manx name for the same place is still in use among old people, or because it is found in the Records :

ST. ANNE'S HEAD, in the parish of Santon, is a translation of KIONE SANCTAIN, ' Sanctan's Head ' (see p. 209). CASTLETOWN, the ancient metropolis, was formerly called BALLEYCASHTAL, from its Castle

---

* A full account of it is given by Cumming in Vol. XV. of the Manx Society's Publications, pp. 36-42.

Rushen. PORT ST. MARY is a translation of PURT-NOO-MOIRREY. It is still called PORT-LE-MURROUGH by Manx people. The name seems to have been taken from an ancient KEEILL MOIRREY, close to the Port. CLAY HEAD was formerly KIONE CLOAIE; and GROUDALE or CROWDALE was called ESCHEDALA (O.N.), 'Clay Dale.' HILLBERY is a translation of CRONK-E-BERRY. HIGHTON was, till recently, BALLANARD. BLUE POINT was GOB GORRYM. MOUNT KARRIN or MOUNT CARRIN was probably SLIEAU KARRIN or SLIEAU CARRIN, 'Karran's or Carine's Mountain,' formerly. A little to the west of its highest point there is a tumulus forty-four feet in diameter, about six feet above the level of the field. It is surrounded by upright schist stones at short intervals. AWIN LAGG is now usually called THE LAGG RIVER.

OATLANDS is a translation of BALLAOATES, 'Oates' Farm.' On this farm, in Santon, there is a stone circle, and on the outer surface of one of the stones composing it there are some eighteen cup markings, methodically arranged in five rows. MOUNT RULE was formerly KNOCK RULE, 'Rule's Hill' (see p. 218).

RUE POINT is a remarkable rendering of GOB RUY, 'Red Point.' BLACK HEAD is a translation of KIONE DOO, and BLACK ROCKS, of CREGGYN DOO. The SILVER BURN, the modern name of the Castletown River, is a translation of AWIN-ARGID. GREENLAND is a translation of THALLOO GLASS. SKY HILL, formerly SKYALL, is a corruption of the Scandinavian SCACCAFELL (*Skogar-fjall*), 'Wood Fell.' WHITE BRIDGE is a translation of DRODHAD BANE, and WHITE STRAND, of TRAIE VANE. THE ISLAND, a field of triangular shape, cut off by three roads, is a translation of NELLAN. ST. JOHN'S, at Tynwald, is the modern name of the chapel formerly called KEEILLOUN, 'John's Church.' Of considerable historical interest are the names of the ancient ecclesiastical Baronies or Manors. They were the BISHOP'S BARONY, the ABBEY BARONY, the BARONY OF BANGOR, and the BARONY OF SABALL, now SAUL, which were usually united; the BARONY OF ST. TRINIAN'S, the BARONY OF ST. BEADE or ST. BEES, and the PRIORY OF DOUGLAS. They were all freeholds, having been grants made by the rulers of Man from time to time. The Bishop was the Chief Baron. He possessed $19\frac{1}{4}$ *quarterlands*, chiefly in the parishes of BALLAUGH and MICHAEL. Much the largest ecclesiastical property in the island was, however, held by the ABBEY OF RUSHEN, called the ABBEY BARONY, which was founded in 1134 by the Cistercian Abbey of Furness, of which it was an appendage. It had altogether $99\frac{1}{2}$ quarterlands, called THALLOO-AB, 'Abbey Land,' 6 mills, and 77 cottages, in the parishes of Malew, German, Lezayre, Lonan, Braddan, and Rushen. BANGOR and SABALL were two monasteries in County Down, Ireland. They had 6 quarterlands in the parish of Patrick. The BARONY OF ST. TRINIAN'S belonged to the monastery of St. Ninnian, at Whithorn in Galloway. It had 5 quarterlands in the parishes of German and Marown. There is a ruined chapel, probably of the thirteenth century, on this Barony, which is called ST. TRINIAN'S. The PRIORY OF DOUGLAS seems, at an early date, to have been converted into or amalgamated with a NUNNERY, containing 5 quarterlands, where there was an ancient foundation, dedicated to

St. Bridget. All the above Baronies had courts of their own (even the Prioress of the Nunnery is said to have held a court), in which they had the privilege of trying all crimes committed in their districts or by their own people, by a jury of their tenants. The Barony of St. Bees, in the parish of Maughold, which belonged to the Priory of that name in Cumberland, consisted only of $1\frac{1}{2}$ quarterlands, and was therefore naturally considered too small to have a court. It is more usually called the Barony of the Hough, The Barony, or Christian's Barony, from its present proprietors. This Priory also possessed lands in the parish of Onchan at an early period, but seems to have lost them even before its dissolution.

In all these Baronies, or Manors, the ecclesiastical proprietors had the same manorial rights as the lord, though they held of him as paramount by homage and fealty, as we learn from the Statute Book, under date 1417, when the Deemsters informed Sir John Stanley that if any of his 'Barrons be out of the Land, they shall have the space of fourty days. After that they are called in to come and show whereby they hould and clayme Lands and Tenements within' (his) 'Land of Man; and to make Faith and Fealtie, if Wind and Weather served them, or to cease their Temporalities into' (his) 'hands.' And in 1422 we find that the Bishop of Man did his faith and fealtie, also the Abbot of Rushen and Prior of Douglas; while 'the Prior of Withorne, in Galloway, the Abbot of Furnace, the Abbot of Bangor, the Abbot of Saball, and the Prior of St. Beade, in Copeland, were called in, and came not; therefore they were deemed by the Deemsters,' that, if they did not come within forty days, they were to 'loose all their Temporalities.' It would seem, however, that they did come within that period, as their temporalities were not confiscated at that time.

When the monasteries were dissolved in King Henry the Eighth's time, all the above lands, except the Bishop's, were taken possession of by him, together with that belonging to THE FRIARY, also called BIMAKEN FRIARY (see BEMACCAN, p. 281), the Prior of which had no baronial rights, and granted to private subjects under leases from the Crown. They still, however, remained distinct baronies, and were not subject to lord's rent. The number of quarterlands in all these Church properties is about 136, there being about 640 *quarterlands* of lord's land in the island; so that the Church formerly held a very considerable proportion of the whole. The Abbey Rents, as they are called, are still collected separately by distinct officers, the Serjeants, although they, as well as the Lord's Rents, are now received by the Crown.

There are two small properties, one in the parish of Patrick and the other in the parish of Maughold, the former of which, first mentioned in a Papal Bull of 1231 as *terram de baculo Sti. Patricii*, ' The land of the Staff of St. Patrick,' has long since disappeared as a separate property; the latter, which is part of the BARONY OF ST. BEES, still survives under the name of THE STAFFLAND.* This place is considered to be freehold, inasmuch as no rent or service is rendered in

---

* The writer is indebted to Sir James Gell, Attorney-General, for information about the Stafflands.

respect of it to the lord.   The service on which these lands were held seems to have been that of the presentation of a staff or crozier, which the proprietors had to produce for the annual processions on the day of the saint to whom the parish church was dedicated. This in the former case would be St. Patrick, in the latter St. Maughold, or possibly St. Bede, as the barony of which it formed a part belonged to the priory dedicated to that saint.*

The service of the Staff of St. Patrick seems to have been commuted for a money-rent at the time of the Reformation, while the Staffland in Maughold fell into the hands of the Christians of Milntown.   How they acquired it no one knows, but there is an old tradition that, prior to the dissolution of the religious houses, the Christians acted as agents for the Priory of St. Bees in Cumberland, and that, when that priory was dissolved,

---

* It will be seen that these tenures are not peculiar to the Isle of Man from the following :

'Grant of lands in Free Alms in the Isle of Lismore, with the custody of the Staff of St. Moloc.

DEED OF CONFIRMATION.

To all and singular, etc.   We, Archibald Campbell, feudatory Lord of the lands of Argyle, Campbell, and Lorn, with the consent and assent of our most dear father and guardian, Archibald, Earl of Argyle . . . have granted, and as well in honour of God omnipotent, of the Blessed Virgin, and of our holy Patron Molec, and have *mortified*, and by this present writing have confirmed to our beloved John McMolmore, and the heirs male of his body lawfully begotten or to be begotten, all and singular our lands . . . in the Isle of Lismore . . . with the Custody of the Great Staff (Baculi) of St. Moloc, as freely as the . . . other predecessors of the s^d John had from our predecessors . . . in pure and free alms.' (Dated 9th April, 1544.)

the barony in Maughold was so small that it escaped the notice of the Crown officials, and so the Christians continued in possession without being disturbed, and their possession became ownership. According to Hooper's Survey, however, the quit-rents or dues of the STAFFLAND were paid to the lessee of the impropriate tithes of Kirk Maughold; but if this were so, it is at least certain that no rent has been paid during the last two centuries.

The following objects of antiquarian interest have English names:

GODRED CROVAN'S STONE, near St. Mark's, once a huge granite boulder, has during the last forty years been broken up. According to tradition, Godred Crovan, when in a passion with his termagant wife, threw this stone at her and killed her. As it weighed between twenty and thirty tons, this can be readily believed! This stone is mentioned by Sir Walter Scott in his novel, 'Peveril of the Peak,' as is the BLACK FORT, an ancient earthwork in the same district, which has disappeared, though its name remains. THE CLOVEN STONES are the only two stones remaining of a small stone circle, which was nearly complete less than a century ago. They were probably so-called from a supposition that they had originally been one.

KING ORRY'S GRAVE, near Laxey, where a large iron sword was discovered some years ago, is a long barrow. The SADDLE ROAD, at Kirby, is so called from a stone shaped like a saddle, which is fixed in the wall close by a stile. It is supposed to have been used by the fairies in their nocturnal equestrian excursions.

FAIRY HILL, in Rushen, otherwise called CRONK MOAR, or CRONK HOWE MOAR, is the largest tumulus on the Island. Its base is 474 feet in circumference, and its height about forty feet. Its form is like that of a cone, truncated at the summit, and there are indications of its having been surrounded by a ditch. It probably contains an interior chamber, so that its excavation would be very interesting to antiquarians. It is somewhat larger that the great tumulus of *Mæshowe* in the Orkneys.

SAINT MAUGHOLD'S CHAIR, a hollow scooped out of the rock, is close by the same saint's well.

GIANTS' FINGERS is the popular name of several large blocks of quartz, near the summit of the hill above Lhergydhoo, in the parish of German.

ST. LUKE'S CHAPEL,* at LAG-NY-KEEILLEY, is supposed by Cumming to be identical with the *St. Leoc* mentioned in the Bull of Pope Eugenius III., dated 1153. It is traditionally known as the church and cemetery of the Manx kings.

There are a few names which owe their origin to the Derby Family, such as DERBYHAVEN, which was their usual landing-place, as being the nearest landing-place to the usual residence of the later earls when on the Island, Castle Rushen. DERBY FORT, on Langness, close by, was built by James, the seventh earl, in 1645. DERBY CASTLE, near Douglas, now a place of popular resort, is a name dating from the present century. MOUNT STRANGE, also called HANGO HILL, on which there was a block-house built by the seventh earl.

* It is fully described in Vol. XV. of Manx Society's Publications, pp. 89, 90.

BALLA STRANG and THE STRANG are also from one of this family's titles, though it is also a title of the Athols.

Their successors, the Athols, have only MOUNT MURRAY, formerly CRONK GLASS; LORD HENRY'S WELL, on Laxey beach; and some street names. BALLADUKE may possibly have belonged to the Duke of Athol.

The following depict natural and artificial features:

THE CHASMS are deep rents in the cliffs, the result of landslips caused by the undermining action of the sea. THE ANVIL and THE CASTLES are detached rocks. GRANITE MOUNTAIN is the name of a hill near SOUTH BARRULE, where a boss of granite crops out. HEAD GULLET is on Langness. THE SUGAR LOAF ROCK is a detached *stack* in the sea shaped like a sugar-loaf. THE SOUND is the narrow channel between the CALF and the mainland, where there are rapid currents. THE CHICKEN'S ROCK is the name given to the small rock off the Calf, where there is now a lighthouse. ST. MARY'S ROCK, or CONNISTER, is the large rock near the entrance to Douglas Harbour. The meaning of CONNISTER is obscure. THE ROUND TABLE is a stretch of level upland between South Barrule and Cronk-ny-Arrey-Lhad.

The following are from events or circumstances connected with their origin:

BURNTMILL HILL speaks for itself. SPANISH HEAD is said to have been so-called from a vessel belonging to the Spanish Armada having been wrecked there. GRAVE GULLET, on Langness, is probably so called from a body which was washed ashore having been buried there, while TOBACCO GULLET smacks of smuggling. GLEN HELEN commemorates the conversion of the lovely glen of RHENAS into a pleasure resort, the name being taken from that of the wife of one of the directors of the company who purchased it! THE SMELT is the name of a hamlet near PORT ST. MARY, where smelting lead was formerly carried on. THE FORESTER'S LODGE, now in ruins, was on the mountains, and belonged to the lord's forester, who paid a small quantity of oats yearly as an acknowledgment. SIR GEORGE'S BRIDGE, in Braddan, was so called from Sir George Drinkwater, a recent proprietor of Kirby, who had a weakness for being the first person to cross a new bridge. It is now very usually called ST. GEORGE'S BRIDGE ; in a short time the process of canonization will be complete, and then a legend will be attached to account for it ! CORRIN'S FOLLY is a conspicuous tower on Peel Hill. Such buildings, for which there is no practical use, are called Follies. BUSHEL'S HOUSE is the name given to the ruins of a small hut on the summit of the Calf Islet, which, according to tradition, was built by a hermit of that name. (For story, see *Brown's Isle of Man Guide*, pp. 283-4.) BUSHEL'S GRAVE, on the same Islet, is really a look-out post.

HORSE LEAP commemorates a hunting feat, and HORSE GULLET and COW HARBOUR are places where cattle can be easily swum ashore.

KING WILLIAM'S COLLEGE, near Castletown, the principal insular public school, was opened in 1830, and named after the reigning sovereign. A much more appropriate name would have been BARROW COLLEGE, from the Bishop of Sodor and Man of that name, who was virtually its founder. ALBERT TOWER commemorates the landing of Prince Albert at Ramsey, who ascended to that spot in 1847. About six miles east of Ramsey there is a sandbank, on which there is a lightship, called THE BAHAMA BANK, called BAHEMA BANK in 1673. It is also called KING WILLIAM'S BANK, from King William III., who was nearly wrecked there on his way to the battle of the Boyne.

MILNER TOWER, a conspicuous object on Brada Head, was erected to the late Mr. Milner, of ' Safe ' renown, in acknowledgment of his charities to the poor of Port Erin, and his efforts for the benefit of the Manx fishermen.

THE TOWER OF REFUGE, on the ST. MARY'S, or CONNISTER Rock, in Douglas Bay, was erected in 1834, at the initiative of Sir William Hillary.

The origin of the name CROMWELL'S WALK, which is near the shore to the south of Scarlet, is unknown. It is certainly fanciful, as the great Protector was never in the Isle of Man. For ST. PATRICK'S CHAIR, in Marown, see MAGHER-Y-CHIARN.

THE NUNS' CHAIRS is the name given to two holes in the rock on Douglas Head, to which, according to tradition, the unfortunate inmates of the nunnery were compelled to climb if they had committed any fault. THE NUNS' WELL is close by.

THE PIGEONS' COVE, also in this neighbourhood, speaks for itself. THE POLLOCK ROCK, from whence whiting pollock may be caught, will be shortly entirely covered by the extension of the Victoria Pier in Douglas. There was formerly a fort on this rock, which was removed in 1818.

From mills we have MILNTOWN, formerly ALTADALE, and UNION MILLS, formerly MULLEN DOWAY.

From various causes are: POORTOWN, a hamlet near St. John's, possibly so called from the poverty of its inhabitants; and NEWTOWN, an ambitious name given 150 years ago to some cottages near Mount Murray.

ST. MICHAEL'S ISLE, at the northern extremity of Langness, where there is an ancient chapel dedicated to St. Michael, seems to have been so called from an early date.

All the town churches and country chapels now in use are comparatively recent dedications.

Purely fanciful and of recent origin are BAILIE GULLET, SPIRE GULLET; DRUIDALE, which is a portion of AIREY KELLY; RICHMOND HILL, formerly BULRENNY HILL, 'Ferns' Fold Hill;' BRITHER CLIP GUT, FARM HILL, ASH HILL, and EYRETON CASTLE.

From surnames* there are: KALLOW POINT (CALLOW); GORDON, the name of a large property in Patrick; SOUTHAMPTON, in Braddan, from the name of the proprietor, *Hampton*, also HAMPTON'S CROFT; and IVY COTTAGE, from a Lieutenant Ivy.

From Christian names: PORT JACK, BULLYS QUARTER, or 'Billy's Quarter;' JONS QUARTER, or 'John's Quarter;' and MARTHA GULLET.

The following names have been given by those who have lived or visited other lands:

* All surnames and Christian names, forming partly Celtic and partly English place-names, have been put under Celtic personal names.

MADEIRA was the name given to a small piece of mountain clearing by a young man who was impressed for the navy at the end of last century, and who spent a large portion of his time at sea off Madeira. On his return he bought this property and improved it.

MINORCA was so called by a sailor who had served in the siege there.

KILKENNY, NASSAU, WIGAN, and VIRGINIA are names that have probably arisen from the connection of the persons who gave the names with those places, but perhaps they are merely fanciful.

OHIO, the name of a field in the parish of Michael, received its name for the curious reason that the man to whom it belonged, and who sold it, emigrated to Ohio.

CALIFORNIA has an even more remarkable origin. It is a piece of land near Ballameanagh, in the abbey-lands of Braddan, which was formerly very marshy. A man undertook the draining of it on a contract, and it was so much more easily done than was expected, and consequently at such a profit, that it was said that he had made a perfect California out of it. This name was given at the time when fortunes were made in mining in California.

ANTIGUA and BOLIVIA are names given by returned travellers.

ANNACUR was probably originally so named by an Irish owner, who perhaps came from ANNAGAR (*Ath-na-Gearr*, ' Ford of the Cars ').

GILGAL, though seemingly Scriptural, is merely a corruption of GUILCAGH, ' broom.'

STAWARD was a name given by the Bacon family to

a farm in Sulby Glen, it being the name of their estate in Northumberland.

The following names, probably of English origin, are obscure :

AMULTY POINT, ATNAUGH, BELLABBEY, BULGUM BAY, CAIGHER POINT, CLABERRY, CLARAM, CULBERRY, POINT, DALENRA, DALEVEITCH, GIBBDALE, LOCH- FIELD NED, MANUSAN ROCKS, MARTLAND, PISCOE, RHEBOEG, SCOTTEAN.

The French name, MONT PELIER, was, for some unknown reason, given to a mountain early in the present century.

KILKENNY, the name of a farm in Braddan, is com- paratively a modern name, and was probably given by a patriotic Irish settler. If old, it might have been derived from *Keeill Caineach*, ' Caineach's or Kenny's Cell.'

Under divisions of land we have the English word *parish*, which has been generally adopted instead of *skeeyley*, as, for instance, THE PARISH OF ANDREAS for SKEELEY ANDREAYS, and so for all the other parishes. Colloquially, however, the parishes are usually called simply BRIDE, ANDREAS, JURBY, LEZAYRE, MAUG- HOLD, LONAN, ONCHAN, BRADDAN, MAROWN, MICHAEL, BALLAUGH, GERMAN, PATRICK, SANTON, MALEW, ARBORY, RUSHEN.

The old Manorial Records, being written in Latin, are responsible for the term *alia*, 'other,' which is given when there are two *treens* of the same name, thus : DALBY, ' Dale Farm,' and ALIA DALBY, ' Other Dale Farm.' It is frequently corrupted into *all*.

Small portions of land which, though not intacks, were, for some unknown reason, not included in the

designation of *Quarterland*, are called *Particles*. In
1403 King Henry IV. gave to ' Luke Macquyn, of the
Island of Man, Scholar, certain alms called *particles*, in
the Island aforesaid, vacant, as said, and in our gift,
and which alms are appropriated to the support of
certain poor scholars of the Island aforesaid, and which
were given, confirmed, and conceded perpetually to the
scholars by our predecessors, former kings of England;
to have and to hold to the said Luke the alms aforesaid, as long as he shall remain a scholar for the benefit
of the Church, and shall not be promoted.'* In 1429
it would appear that, through the fault of the Bishop
Pully, these *Particles* had been ' dealt into other
uses,'† and they are now on the same footing as the
Quarterlands.

Another land division is called an *Intack*, or *Intake.*
These *Intacks* are usually either mountain land or
strips by the shore. Licenses to enclose or take in
were granted by the lord proprietor, or by the governor
acting for him. This license was subject to the approval
of the Great Inquest, or Jury, as to public ways, waters
and turbaries, and the Inquest affixed a rent upon the
intack thus acquired and caused it to be entered on the
Manorial Roll. Many of the old *quarterlands* were
long narrow strips, having one intack abutting on the
common pasture in the mountains, and another intack
abutting on the shore, whence seaweed was obtained
for manure.

* Manx Soc., Vol. VII., pp. 225-6.
† Statute Law Book, p. 24.

INDEX OF CELTIC ROOT WORDS.

Manx.	English.	Irish.	Gaelic.	Welsh.
Aah	a ford	áth	ath	
Aalin	beautiful	alain	aluinn	
Abb	an abbot	abb	abb	(L. abbas, Syr. abba)
Aeree or eary	a moor	airidh (hill pasture)	airidh	
Aile (ainil)*	fire	aibhle	eibhle	
Ain	circle, ring	fainne	fainne	
Aittin	gorse	aiteann	aittin	eithin
Alt	a mountain stream or glen side	alt	alt	allt (L. altus)
Arbyl	a tail	earbull	earbull	
Ard	a height, high	ard	ard	(L. arduus)
Argid	silver, money	airgead	airgiod	
Armyn	arms	arm	armachd	
Arrey	a mill race			
Arrey	a watch	aire	aire	
Asney	a rib	aisne	aisne	
Aspick	a bishop	easpoc	easbuig	(L. episcopus)
Astan	an eel	easgan	easgann	
Awin	a river	abhainn	abhainn	
Baare	top, end	barr	barr	
Baarney	a gap	bearn, bearna	bearn	
Baase (bays)	death	bās	bas	
Baatey	a boat	bad	bad	
Baih	a bay	bad	bagh	(E. bay, L.L. and Basque baia
Bainney	milk	bainne	bainne	

* All words in brackets in the first column are from Bishop Philips' Manx Prayer-book, written about 1628.

Manx.	English.	Irish.	Gaelic.	Welsh.
Balla	a farm, a town	baile	baile	(L.L. balli-vum)
Bane	white	ban	ban	
Barnagh	a limpet, barnacle	bairneach	fairneach	(L.L. berna-cula)
Bashtey	baptism			(Gk. bap-tisma)
Bayr	a road	bothar		
Beaynee	a reaper	buanidhe	buanaiche	
Beeall(bæal)	an entrance, mouth	bel, beul	beul	
Beg	little	beag	beag	bach
Beinn	top, summit	beann	beinn	
Beisht	beast	biasd	beist	(L. bestia)
Billey (bille)	a tree	bile		
Bing	a jury			
Birragh	pointed	biorach	biorach	
Boa	a cow	bo	bo	bu (L. bos)
Boal, boalley	a road			
Boallagh	a road	bealach (a pass)	bealach	
Boayl (ball)	a wall	balla	balla (a wall)	
Boght	a poor person	bochdan	bochd	
	a stony dis-trict	boireann		
Bollan	a carp			
Bouyr	deaf	bodhar	bodhar	byddar
Brack	a trout	breac	breac	brwych
Braid	upland	braid	braigh	
Breac	speckled, spotted	breac	breac	brwych
Brebag	a kiln			
Breinn	stagnant	brean	brean	
Brisht	broken	brisde	briste	
Briw (briu)	a judge	breithem	breitheamh	
Broighe	dirty	brogach	brogach	
Broogh	a brow (of hill) or a bank	bru, bruach	bruach	
Brott	broth	broth	brot	
Buigh	fellow	brudh	brudhe	
Bun	end	bun	bun	
Bwoaillee (buely)	a fold	buaile	buaile	
Caashey	cheese	cāise	caise	caws
Cabbagh	sourdock	copog	copogach	
Cabbal	a chapel			

Manx.	English.	Irish.	Gaelic.	Welsh.
Cabbyl (kabyl)	a horse	cappall		(L.L. caballus)
Caggey (kagy)	a battle, war	cogadh	cogadh	
Callin (kallyn)	a body	colann	colunn	
Cam	crooked	cam	cam	cam
Carn	a cairn, pile of stones	carn	carn, cairn, cuirn	carn
Carrick	a rock	carraig	carraig	
Casherick	holy	coisreactha	coisrigte	
Cashtal	a castle	caiseal, cashel	caisteal	(L. castellum)
Cass (kass)	a foot	coss	coss	
Cassan (kassan)	a path	casan	casan	
Catt	a cat	catt	cat	cath (and Cornish)
Ceabagh	cloddy	caobach	caobach	
Chiarn	a lord	tighearna	tighearna	
Chiass	heat	teas	teas	
Chibbyr (chibbyrt)	a well	tobar	tobar	
Chirrym	dry	tirim	tioram	
Chleigh (kleyi)	a hedge	cladh	cladh	clawdd
Chuill	a quill			
Claare (gláyr)	a dish, plate	clar (a table)	clar	
Claddagh	a water meadow	cladagh	cladach	
Clagh	a stone	clogh	clagh	clog
Claghagh	stony	cloghach	clachagh	
Cliwe (kleîu)	a sword			
Cloaie	stony			
Close	a paddock, close	close		(L. clausus)
Coan	a valley	cūan (a bay)		
Coar	pleasant			
Colbagh	a heifer	colbthach		colbthac
Collagh	a stallion	collach		
Conney	gorse		conusg	
Conning (konin)	a rabbit	coinin	coinean	(L. cuniculus)
Cooil	a corner, nook	cuil, cūl	cuil	
Coon	narrow			
Coonlagh	straw	conlach	conlach	

Manx.	English.	Irish.	Gaelic.	Welsh.
	a round hill, a hollow	cor		
Corkey	oats	coirce	coirce	ceirch
Cornail (kor-náyl)	a corner	cearna	cearn	cornel (L. cornu)
Cosnee (kosny)	profitable			
Cragh	slaughter, plunder	creach	creach	
Crammag (skellit)	a snail			
Crane	a bone	cnaimh	cnaimh	
Creagh	a stack	cruach	cruach	crug (Corn. cruc)
Cree (kri)	a heart	cridhe	cridhe	
Creel	a basket			.
Creen	ripe, withered	crion		crin
Creg (kreg)	a crag, rock	creag	creag	
Creggagh	rocky	craigeach	creagach	cregiog
Creoi	hard			
Croa	a pen	cro	cro	crau
Croit	a croft		croit	(A.S. croft, Dan. kroft)
Cronk	a hill	crock		
Crosh	a cross	crois	crois	croes (Corn. crows)
Crout	trick, craft			
Cruinn	round	cruinn	cruinn	crwn
Cubeyr	a cooper	cubhair	cubhair	
Cullion	holly	cuillion	cuillionn	
Curragh	a bog, fen	cuirreach	curach	
DAR, darragh (genitive)	an oak	dair, darach	darach	dar
Dhoan	dun	donn	donn	
Dhoon	a close, a fort	dun, duin	dun	(Eng. town, O.H.G. zún)
Doarlish (dorlys)	a gap	dorus		(Eng. door, Ice. dyrr)
Dooiney (duyney)	a man	duine	duine	(A.S. dyn)
Dowin	deep, low	domhain	domhain	dwfn
Dreeym	a back	druim	druim	drum
Drine (drein)	a thorn (tree)	draoighean	draoighan	draen (Corn. drain)
Droghad	a bridge	droichead	droichead	
Drughage	dog-rose			

Manx.	English.	Irish.	Gaelic.	Welsh.
Druiaght	sorcery	druidheacht	druideachd	
Dubbyr	a pond	dobhar (water)	dobhar	dwfr
Dullish	sea-weed	duilliasg	duilleasg	dilysg
Eagh	a horse	each	each	
Eairkan	a lapwing			
Eairn	iron	iarran	iarunn	
Eary, or aeree	a moor	airidh (hill pasture)	airidh	
Eas	a waterfall	eas	eas	
Eayn (yen)	a lamb	uan	uan	
Eaynin	a precipice			
Edd (œdd)	a nest	nead	nead	nyth (Corn. neid)
Eddin (œdyn)	a face	eadan	eudan	
Ellan	an island	oilean	eilean	(A.S. ealand)
Euar	a yew tree	iubhar	iubhar	
Faaie	a paddock, a flat	faithche	faiche	
Faarkery (farkey)	the sea	fairge	fairge	
Fannag	a crow	fannoge	fannog	
Farrane	a fountain, spring	uaran	fuaran	
Feayr	cold	fuar	fuar	oer
Fedjag	a feather	iteog	iteag	
Feeagh	a raven	fiach	fitheach	
Feeaih	a deer	fiadh	fiadh	
Feeyn	wine, a vine	fion	fion	
Fess	a spindle			
Fluigh	moist, wet	fliuch	fliuch	
Foalley	treacherous			
Foawr	a giant	famhair	famhair	
Foddey	long	fada	fada	
Foillan	a sea-gull	faeilean	faoileann	gwylan
Freoagh	heath	fraoch	fraoch	
Freoghane	bilberry	fraochan	fraochan	
Fuill	blood	fuil	fuil	
Gaaue	a smith	gobha	gobhainn	gôf (Corn. and Bre. also)
Garee	sour land			
Garey	a garden	garadh	garadh	
Garroo	rough	garbh	garbh	garw

Manx.	English.	Irish.	Gaelic.	Welsh.
Garmin	a weaver's beam	garmain	garman	
Geay (gyæ)	wind	gaeth	gaeth	
Geayllin	a shoulder	gualann	gualainn	
Geinnagh (gennagh)	sand	gaineamh	gaineamh	
Geinnec	sandy	gainneach		
Giare	short	gearr	gearr	
Glaick	a hollow (of the hand)	glac	glac	
	a stream	glaise		
Glass	blue, grey, green	glas	glas	glas
Glione	a glen	gleann	gleann	
Goayr (goer)	a goat	gabhar	gabhar	gafar (Corn. gavar)
Gob, gub	a mouth	gob	gob	
Goggan	a noggin	noigin	gogan	
Gorrym	blue	gorm	gorm	
Gortagh	hungry	gortagh	gortagh	
HEESE	lower	sios	shios	is
Heose	upper	suas	shuas	uwch
INJEIG	an enclosure			
Injil	low	iseal	iosal	isel
Inneen (innin)	a girl, daughter	inghean	inghean	
Innis	an island	innis	innis	ynys
JAGHEE	tithe			
Jaghin	a deacon			(L. diaconus)
Jean	darnel weed			
Jeeragh	straight	direach	direach	
Jerrey (jere)	end	deirid	deireadh	
Jiarg	red	dearg	dearg	
Joaree	a stranger	deoradh	deoradh	
KEEILL	a cell, church	cill	cill	(L. cella)
Keeyll (kæil)	a wood	coill	coill	
Kcim	a stile	cēim	ceum	
Kellag (kelli)	a cock	coileach	coilleach	
Kemmyrk	a refuge			
Kerroo	a quarter	ceathramh	ceathramh	
Kesh	foam			
Keyrr	a sheep	caera	caora	
Kiark	a hen	cearc	cearc	
Kiel	narrow	caol	caol	cul
Kione (kian)	head, end	ceann	ceann	

Manx.	English.	Irish.	Gaelic.	Welsh.
Knock	a hill	cnoc	cnoc	
Koir	a chest			
(Kruit)	a harp	cruit (a harp), cruitire (a harper)	cruiteir	
LAAGH (laygh)	mire	lathach	lathach	
Laare	a floor	lar	lar	llawr
Lag	a ditch, hollow	lag	lag	
Lajer	strong	laidir	laidir	
Leigh (lyei)	a law	lagh	lagh	
Leoaie	lead	luaidhe	lin	
Lhean	broad	leathan	luaidhe	
Lheanee	a meadow	leana	leathan	llydan
Lheeah	gray	liath	liath	llwyd
Lheeah-rio	hoar-frost	liath-reo	liath-reo-dadh	rheu (Corn. reu)
Lheim	a leap	leim	leum	
Lhiack	slate, slate-rock, a stone	leac	leac	lhechen
Lhiaght	a grave	leacht	leac	
Lhiattee	a side			
Lhieh	half	leath	leth	
Lhiey (lyi)	a calf	laegh	laogh	(Corn. leaugh)
Lhing	a pool	linn	linne	
Liargagh	a slope	leargaidh	leargan	
Liauyr	long	leabhar		
Logh	a lake	loch	loch	llwch (Corn. lo, Bre. louch)
Loob	a loop	lub	lub	
Losht	burnt	loisgthe	loisgte	
MAARLIAGH (merliagh)	a robber	meirleach	meirleach	
Maase	cattle			
Maggle	testicle	magairle	magairle	
Magher	a field	machair (a plain)	machair	
Mair	a finger	meur	meur	
Maynagh	a monk	manach	manach	(L. mona-chus)
Mea	fat, luxuriant			
Meanagh	middle	meadhonach	meadhonach	
Meayl	bald	mael	maol	moel

Manx.	English.	Irish.	Gaelic.	Welsh.
Meayll	a bare head-land	meall	meall	moel
Meoir	a *moar**			
Moainee	a turbary	moin	moine	mawnog
Moanagh	boggy			
Moddey (moaddy)	a dog	madadh	madadh	
Mohlt	a wether	molt	mult	mollt (Corn. mols)
Mollee	an eyebrow	mala	mala	
Mooar	big, great	mor	mor	mawr
Mooarid	greatness	moralachd	morachd	
Mooiragh	a waste by the sea	muirbhach		
Muc	a pig	muc	muc	moch (also Corn. and Bre.)
Mucaill	a sow	muc-ainidhe	muc	
Muckley	a hedgehog			
Muir	the sea	muir	muir	mor
Mullagh	a top, sum-mit	mullach	mullach	
Mwannal (muynal)	a neck	muineal	muineal	mwnwgll
Mwyllin	a mill	muillean	muillean	melin (Corn. belin, Bre. melin)
Noa	new	nuadh	nuadh	newydd
Oaie (jei)	a grave			
Ooyl	an apple	ubhall	ubhall	afal
Or, ooirr	a coast, verge, rim	oir	oir	
Oural	a sacrifice	offrail	ofrail	
Ouyr	dun	odhar	odhar	
Pairk	a park	pairc	pairce	park (L.L. parcus)
Peel	a fortress			pill
Pesson	a parson	pearsun	person	
Ping	a penny	pinghin	peighinn	
Pooyl	a pool	poll	poll	pwll (Ice. pollr, A.S. and Dan. poll)
Purt	a port	port	port	(L. portus)

* The officer who collects the 'Lord's Rent.'

Manx.	English.	Irish.	Gaelic.	Welsh.
QUAIYL	a court			
Quallian	a whelp	cuileann	cuilein	colwyn
Quing	a yoke	cuing	cuing	
RAAD	a road	rōd	rathad	(A.S. râd)
	a fort	rāth	rath	rhawd
Raun	a seal	ron	ron	(A.S. hrōn)
Rea	flat	reidh	reidh	
Ree	a king	righ	righ	
Reeast	a waste	riasg (a morass)		
Rennee	ferny	raithneach	rainich	rhedynawg
Renniagh	fern	raithneach	raineach	
Rheynn }	a division	rann		
Rinn }	a ridge		roinn	
Roauyr	fat, thick	reamhar	reamhar	
Roayrt	springtide	robarta		ryferthwg
	a wood	ros		
Ruillick	a graveyard	reilig (relic)	reidhlic	(L. reliquiæ)
Runt	round			
Ruy	red	ruadh	ruadh	rhudd
SAGGART (sagyrt)	a priest	sagart	sagart	(L. sacerdos)
Scoilt	cleft, spilt	sgoilt	sgoilt	
Scrah	a sod	sgraith	sgrath	
Scuit	a spout (? corr. of spooyt)			
Seyir	a carpenter	saor	saor	
Shag	a cormorant			
Shamrag	a shamrock	seamrog	seamrag	
Sharragh	a foal	searrach	searach	
Shee	peace	sith	sith	
Sheear	the west	iar	siar	
Shellagh	a willow	saileach	seileach	helyg (L. salix)
Shellan (shellian)	a bee	seillean	seillein	
Shen	old	sean	sean	
Shlig	a shell	slig	slige	
Shliggagh	shelly	sligach	sligeach	
Shoggyl	rye	seagal	seagal	
Shuglaig	sorrel		seolbhag	
Shynnagh (shinnagh)	a fox	sionnach	sionnagh	
Skarrag	a skate			
Skeaig	hawthorn	sceach	sgitheach	
Skeddan	a herring	sgadān	sgadan	

Manx.	English.	Irish.	Gaelic.	Welsh.
Skeerey	a parish	sgire	sgireachd	(? English shire)
Skeeyley	a parish church			
Skibbylt	active, nimble			
Slaint	health	slāinte	slainte	
Slieau (slæu)	a mountain	sliabh	sliabh	
Sloat	a pool, low water	slod	sloc	
Slogh	a pit	sloc	slochd	
Soalt	a barn	sabhall	sabhall	
Soo	juice, berry	sugh		sūg
Sooie	soot	suthaighe	suithe	
Sooil (suil)	an eye	suil	suil	
Spooyt	a spout, a waterfall	sput	sput	(L. sputare)
Spuir	a spur	spor	spor	
Spyrryd (spyryd)	spirit	spiorad	spiorad	yspryd (L. spiritus, Bre. speret)
Sthowyr	a staff			
Stroin	a nose	sron	sron	ffroen
Strooan (struan)	a stream	sruthan	sruthan	
Stuggey	a piece	stuaic (a little hill)	stuc	
Sumark	a primrose*			
TAARNAGH (tarniagh)	thunder	tarnach	tairneach	
Tarroo	a bull	tarbh	tarbh	(Gk. tauros)
Tessyn	athwart	tarsna	tarsuinn	traws
Thalleyr	a tailor	tailiur	taillear	tailur
Thalloo (talu)	land	talamh (earth)	talamh	
Thie (tei)	a house	teach	tigh	ty (and Corn., L. tectum)
Thunnag	a duck	tunnog	tunnag	
Tonnagh	wavy	tonnach	tonnach	tonnawg
Towl	a hole, cave	toll		twll
Traagh	hay			
Traie	a strand, shore	traigh	traigh	
Tramman	an elder tree	tromn	troman	
Treein	(a division of land)	trian		

* Probably connected with *Shamrag*, which see.

Manx.	*English.*	*Irish.*	*Gaelic.*	*Welsh.*
Troddan	a contest	trodan		
Tushtagh	sensible			
UGHTAGH	an acclivity	uchdach	uchdach	
Uhllin	a stackyard	id-lann (corn-en-closure)		
Undin	a foundation	funn		(L. fundatio)
Unjin	an ash tree	fuinnseann	uinnsinn	
Urley	an eagle	iolar	iolar	
Ushag	a bird	fuiseog (a lark)		
Ushtey	water	uisge	uisge	(E. whisky)
YIARN	iron	iarn	iarunn	heyrn (A.S. iren)

Abbreviations : A.S., Anglo-Saxon ; Bre., Breton : Corn., Cornish ; E., English ; Gk., Greek ; L., Latin ; L.L., Late Latin.

INDEX OF SCANDINAVIAN ROOT WORDS.

Á, a river
Alda, a wave
Alfr, an elf, fairy
Austr, the east

Balli, a grassy bank
Bær, byr, a farm
Berr, bare
Bora, a bore-hole
Brattr, steep
Brautr, a road
Brekka, a slope
Bru, a bridge
Brun, an eyebrow
Brunnr, a spring, well

Dalr, a dale
Djupr, deep
Dyr, an animal, beast

Egg, an edge
Enni, the forehead
Esja, clay
Ey, an island
Eyrr, a gravelly bank

Fiskr, a fish
Fjall, a fell, mountain
Fjörðr, a firth
Fles, a green spot among bare fells
Folk, people, folk

Galtr, a boar, pig
Gandr, magic

Garðr, a yard, an enclosure
Gata, a way, path, road
Gil, a deep, narrow glen
Gja, a chasm, rift
Gnipa, a peak
Godi, a priest
Gras, grass
Grænn, green
Grjót, pebbles
Gröf, a pit

Hagi, pasture
Hamarr, a hammer
Haugr, a how, mound
Höll, a hill, hillock
Holmr, an islet
Holt, a wood, copse
Hrafn, a raven
Hris, shrubs, brushwood
Hross, a horse
Hryggr, a ridge
Hvammr, a grassy slope, a vale
Hvítr, white

Jörfi, gravel

Kambr, a crest, a comb
Kapall, a nag, horse
Kirkja, a church

Klettr, a rock
Kollr, a top, summit
Korn, corn, grain
Kraka, a crow
Kringla, a circle
Krokr, a nook, anything crooked

Lagr, low, low-lying
Langr, long
Lax, a salmon
Lítill, little
Lundr, a grove

Mæri, a border-land
Meðal, middle
Muli, a muzzle, snout
Myrr, a moor, bog, swamp

Nabbi, a knoll
Nes, a nose
Norð, the north

Pollr, a pool, pond
Prestr, a priest

Rá, a corner, nook
Rani, a hog's snout, a hog-shaped hill
Ripr, a crag

Saurr, mud
Setr, a seat, residence

Skali, a hut, shed
Skarð, a notch, chink
Skarfr, a cormorant
Skaunn, a shield
Skeiðr, a war-ship
Skel, a shell
Sker, a skerry, a detached rock
Skip, a ship
Skögr, a shaw, wood
Slakki, a slope
Snær, snow
Sól, the sun

Stakkr, a stack
Steinn, a stone
Strönd, a strand, coast, shore
Suðr, the south
Svartr, black

TOFT, a knoll

UXI, an ox

VAGR, a creek, bay
Varða, a beacon

Vað, a wading-place, a ford
Ve, a mansion, a house
Vík. a creek, bay
Völlr, a field
Vörr, a lip

ÖGR, an inlet

ÞING, a parliament
Þorp, a hamlet, village
Þrömr, a brim, edge

INDEX OF SURNAMES.

ALLEN,* 50
Andrew, 32
Arinbiaurg, (S) 114
Ascough, (S) 79
Asrith, (S) 114
Asthruth, (S) 115
Athisl, (S) 111

BACON,* 102
Bankes, 102
Bastin,§ 222
Bell, 223
Berrag,§ 221, 229
Berry,§ 223
Birrag,§ 221
Bivaicunas, 109, 110
Bivaiddonas, 110
Bivaidonas, 109
Bjarn, 113
Boddaugh, 67
Boyd,* 67
Brew, 74
Bridson, 55

CÆSAR,* 102
Cain, 41
Caine, 41
Calcot, 102
Calcott, 102
Caley, 59
Callin, 41
Callister, 35
Callow, 60

Calvin, 61
Cammaish, 26
Cannan, 67
Cannel, 43
Cannell, 43
Cannon,* 67
Caralagh, 101
Carberry.§ 221
Carine, 53
Carmick,§ 220
Carnaghan, 58
Carran, 53
Casement, (S) 79
Cashen, 58
Cashin, 58
Castell, 80
Caistell, 80
Caveen, 51
Christian, (S) 87
Christory, 102
Clague, 76
Clark, 72
Clarke, 72
Cleator, 104
Cleg, 76
Clegg, 76
Clucas, 23
Cogeen, 59
Collister, 35
Colvin, 61
Comish, 26
*Conill,** 44
Conill, 44
Connelly,* 43

Conroy,* 68
Coobragh, 31
Cooil, 61
Coole, 61
Corjeag, 100
Corkan,* 49
Corkhill, (S) 82
Corkish, 95
Corlett, (S) 83
Cormode, 41
Corooin, 52
Corran, 52
Corrin, 52
Corris, 94
Corteen, 59
Cosnahan,†
Costain, 28
Costeen, 28
Cotteen,* 59
Cotter, 81
Cottier, 81
Cottingham,* 101
Cottle,§ 222
Cowell, 61
Cowen, 51
Cowin, 51
Cowle, 61
Cowley,* 84
Coyle, § 220
Craig, 103
Crain, 55
Craine, 55
Crebbin, 97
*Creen.** 64

Creer, 97
Creetch, 78
Cregeen,* 64
Crellin, (S) 85
Crennell, (S) 85
Cretney, 78
Criggal,*†
Criggard,* 99
Crinaas, 115
Cringle, (S) 86
Cristalson, 102
Croghan, 63
Crow, 36
Crowe,* 36
Cry, 76
Crye, 76
Crystal, 102
Cubbon, 98
Cudd,* 68
Cunamagli,* 110
Cunava,* 109, 110
Cundre, 78
Curphey, 57
Custal,§ 221
Cutchal,§ 221

Daley,§ 223
Dougherty,* 45
Dovaidona,* 110
Dowan, 49
Druian, 115
Dufgal,* 115
Duggan, 49

Ellison, 103

Faden, 33
Fairbrother,* 103
Faragher, 37
Fargher, 37
Farrant, 103
Fayle, 33
Fell, 34
Fiac,* 36
Fletcher, 103
Freer, 104
Fritha,* 114
Froca,* 116
Fynlo,* 78

Gale, 94
Garret, (S) 86, 94
Gaut,* 113
Gautr,* 133
Gawn, 75
Gawne, 75
Gell, 74
Gelling, 25
Gick, 104
Gilbeall,* 32
Gilcobraght,* 31
Gilhast,* 78
Gill, 74
Gillowye, 64
Gilpatrick,* 32
Gilpeder,* 32
Godred,* (S) 88
Gorree, 87
Gorry, 87
Gout,* 113
Graves,* 104
Grim,* 113
Gummery,* 101

Halsall,§ 223
Hampton, 105
Harrison, 104
Heywood,* 104
Howlan, 66
Howland,* 66
Hromund,* 114
Hudgeon, 105
Hutchen, 105
Hutchin, 105

Innow,* 70
Ivenowe,* 70

Joughin, 71

Kaighan, 37
Kaighin, 37
Kaneen, 44
Karran, 53
Kay, 62
Kearey,* 63
Kee, 62
Kegeen, 38

Kegg, 38
Keig, 38
Keigeen, 38
Kellag, 68
Kelly, 47
Kenag, 44
Kennaugh, 44
Kennish, 57
Kerd,* 77
Kermeen, 60
Kermode, 41
Kerruish, 94
Kew, 63
Kewin, 24
Kewish, 73
Kewley,* 84
Key, 62
Kie, 62
Killey, 47
Killip, 26
Kinley, 49
Kinnish, 57
Kinred, 77
Kinry, 98
Kinvig, 77
Kissack, 23
Kneal, 46
Kneale, 46
Kneen, 45
Knickell, 28
Krickart, 99

Lace, (S) 90
Leece, (S) 90
Lewin, 25
Liutwolf,* 114
Looney,* 66
Lowey, 64
Lucas,* 23

Mac Adde,* 32
Mac Alcar,* (S) 91
Mac Arthure,* 68
Mac Caure,* 78
Mac Claghelen, 68
Mac Clenerent,* 78
Mac Corry,* 68
Mac Craue,* 78
Mac Cray,* 76
Mac Crowton,* 78

*Mac Cundre,** 78
*Mac Cure,** 78
*Mac Curry,** 69
*Mac Dowytt,** 78
*Mac Effe,** 78
*Mac Essas,** 78
*Mac Faden,** 32
*Mac Fergus.** 37
*Mac Finloe,** 78
*Mac Gilacosse,** 35
*Mac Gilbeall,** 32
*Mac Gilcobraght,** 31
*Mac Gilcolum,** 35
*Mac Gilhast,** 78
*Mac Gillaws,** 35
*Mac Gillowye,** 64
*Mac Gilpatrick,** 32
*Mac Gilpeder,** 32
*Mac Hawe,** 78
*Mac Kellag.** 68
*Mac Kerd,** 77
*Mac Kimbe,** 78
*Mac Knalytt,** 78
*Mac Kym,** 78
*Mac Lolan,** 78
*Mac Lynean,** 78
*Mac Mychell,** 32
*Mac Namee,** 69
*Mac Nameer,** 69
*Mac Person,** 72
*Mac Pherson,** 72
*Mac Quantic,** 78
*Mac Quartag,** 78
*Mac Quiddie,** 55
*Mac Rory,** 70
*Mac Sharry,** 99
*Mac Sherry,** 99
Mac Skealey, 73
*Mac Tereboy.** 75
*Mac Vorrey,** 30
*Mac Vrimyn,** 78
*Mac y Chlery,** 72
Maddrell, 105
*Mael-Lomchon,** 115
Malachy†
*Mal-Lumcun,** 115
Martin, 27
*Mitchell,** 223
Moore, 48
Morrey. 30

Morrison, 30
Morton,* 56
Moughtin,* 56
*Mucoi,** 109, 110
*Mucomael,** 111
Mughtin, 56
*Murciolu,** 115
Murray, 30, 57
Mylchraine.* 54
Mylchreest,* 29
Mylecharane.* 54
Mylechreest,* 29
Mylrea, 65
Mylroi, 65
Mylroie, 65
Mylvorrey, 30

Nelson, 46, 104
Nicholas,§ 225
Nideragh, 76
Norris, 105

Oates, 100
Oats, 100
*O'Maelguc,** 111
*Onon.** 115
*Orry,** (S) 88

*Parr,** 105

Quaggin, 39
Qualtrough, 95
Quane, 25
Quark, 26
Quarry, 40
*Quate,** 78
Quay, 63
Quayle, 34
*Quiddie,** 55
Quiggin, 39
Quill, 61
Quilleash, 74
Quilliam, 97
Quillin, 48
Quine, 40
Quinney, 40
Quirk, 52
*Quott,** 78

Radcliffe, 101
Ralfe,§ 225
Ratcliff, 101
*Roscil,** (S) 114
*Rumund,** (S) 114

*Sandulf,** (S) 114
Sansbury, 106
Sauthar†
Sayle, 34
Scarff, (S) 91
Sherlock, 108
Shimmin, 26
Silvester,§ 225
Skelly, 73
Skillicorn,* 91
Skillicorne,* 91
Skinner,* 107
*Sontulf,** 114
*Standish,** 106
Stanley, 106
Stephen, 28
Stephenson, 28
Stevenson, 28
Stole, 106
Stowell, 106

Taggart, 72
Taubman, 107
Tear, 75
Teare, 75
Thompson,* 107
*Thorbiaurn,** (S) 114
*Thorleifr,** (S) 114
*Thorrid.** (S) 115
*Thurlibr,** (S) 114
*Thurulfs,** (S) 114
*Thurvaldr,** (S), 114
Trollag, 219
Truian, 115
*Tyldesley,** 107

Ucifat, 115

Vinch, 107
Vondy,* 107
Vorrey, 30

WARD, 72	Wattleworth, 108	*YVENE*,* 70
Waterson, 96	*Whetstones*,§ 219	*Yvens*,* 70
Watterson, 96	Woods, 108	

All names now obsolete in the Isle of Man as surnames are in italics.

(S) = Scandinavian.

* Not found compounded with *balla*, or other local prefix or affix.

† See Addenda.

§ Rarely found except in connection with place-names.

INDEX OF PLACE-NAMES.

In addition to the names given in the index only, of which either no explanation has been attempted or none is required, there are names marked *, which are also not in the text as such, though their component parts will be found there from the references given.

All the more important Celtic prefixes are given in small capitals, while all affixes which are not correctly spelled in the names to which they belong are given in italics, bracketed. When a name is partly Celtic and partly English or Scandinavian, the English and Scandinavian portions are in italics, and when a name is partly English and partly Scandinavian, the English portion is in italics. Scandinavian names are marked S, Scandio-Celtic names S C or C S, and Scandio-English names S E or E S.

Purely Celtic and purely English names have no distinguishing mark.

Obsolete names are marked ob.

When a name is given more than once, the modern form is placed first.

AAH, 'a ford' (see addenda).
Aah-ny-lingey, ford of the pool, 176
Awhallan (*whuallian*), whelp ford, 195
Abbey barony, 306
,,　lands of Malew
,,　　,,　Onchan
Agneash, S (*egjar-nes*), ridge ness, 274
AEREE, 'a moor,' 133, 143
Airey kellag, Kellag's moor, or (*kellagh*) cock moor, 68, 197
Arernan, ⎰
Arirody, ⎱ ?
Aristine, Steen's moor, 223
Aristonick, aeree, ?
Arybeg, little moor, 237
,, *horkell*, S, Corkell's moor, 223
,, glass, green moor, 234
,, kelly,* Kelly's moor, 197
,, moar, big moor, 237
Albert tower, 313
Alchest, Alkest, S (*alfa-staðr*), elves' stead, 288
Aldrick, S ⎰ (*öldu - hryggr*), wave ridge, 257
⎱ (*öldu-vik*), wave bay, 276

Algar (*Alfgars ? staðr*), Alfgar's (stead), 223
ALIA, Latin, 'other,' 317
Alia begoad, S (? *ve-godi*), other Godi's, or priest's house, 300, 317
,, colby, S (*kolls,* or *kolla-byr*), other Coll's, or summit farm, 275, 295, 317
,, dalby, S (*dalar-byr*), other Dales' farm, 272, 317
,, gnebe, S (*gnipa*), other peak, 251, 317
,, gresby, S (*gras-byr*), other grass farm, 285, 317
,, leodest, S (*liots-staðr*), other Liot's stead, 296, 317
,, raby, S (*rár-byr*), other nook farm, 279, 317
,, sulby, S (*solva-byr*), other Solvi's farm, 298, 317
Alt (see Olt), glenside or mountain stream, 136
Altadale (ob.), S (*alptar-dalr*), swan's dale, 314
Alt-ny-creggan (*creggyn*), mountain stream of the crags, 167

Amogarry, Asmogarry, S (*Asmunds-garðr*), Osmund's enclosure, 255, 293

Amulty Point ?, 316

Andreas, Parish of, Skeeylley Andreas, Andrew's parish church, 208, 213

Annacur ? (modern), 317

Antigua, 316

Anvil, The (a detached rock), 312

Arbory, Parish of, Skeeylley Cairbre, Cairbre's parish church

ARD, 'a height,' or high,' 142, 240

Archollagan (? *chiollagh-een*), little hearth height, or high little hearth, 182, 249

Arderry (*eary*), high moor, 249

,, ole, C S (? *olaf*), Olave's height

,, onan, ? Donan's height, 217

,, rank ?

Ard, *The*, the height, 166

Arduailey (*bwoaillee*), fold height, or high fold, 171, 249

,, valley, high farm, 249

,, volley (*vollee*), eyebrow height, 181

,, whallan (*whuallian*), whelp height, 142

Arnicarnigan, Carnigan's height, 223

Arrogan beg, ? ard,

,,   mooar, ? ard,

Arrysey, Arracey* (*arrey*), watch?, 183

Ashenmooar (? *Balla - yn - aittin*), (farm of the) big gorse, 231

Ash hill, 315

Aust, S (*austr*), east, 292, 293

Atnaugh, ? 316

AWIN, 'a river,' 146

Awin *blaber*, C S, bleaberry river, 300

,, doo, black river, 232, 235

,, glass, gray, blue, or bright river, 232, 235

,, kylley* (*keylley*), wood river, 146, 199

,, lagg*, turf-hollow river, 169

,, ny-darragh, river of the oak, 199

,, ny-reeast, river of the waste, 168

,, ruy, red river, 146, 234

,, vitchal, ? Gilchreest's river, 223

Ayre, *The*, S (*eyrr*), the gravelly bank, 252

,, *The Point of*, S, the point of the gravelly bank, 254

,, sheading, S (*skeiðar-þing*), Ayre ship-district, 268-271

BAARE, ' top, end,' 142

Baredoo, black top, 142, 232

,, mooar,* big top, 142, 236

Baroole, Barroole, or Barrule, *North and South* Roole's top, 217, 218, 225 (see Preface)

Barrule beg*, little Roole's top, 217, 218, 236

Bahama Bank, 'Bahema bank, 314

BAIH, 'a bay,' 144

Baie doo, black bay, 233

,, ny-breechyn, bay of the breeches, 304

,, ,, -carrickey, bay of the rocks, 144, 170

,, ,, -ooig, C S, bay of the cave, 144, 277

,, *stacka*, C S, bay of the stack, 260

Bay Fine ?

,, yn-*ow*, C S*, bay of the how, 144, 257

Baillie Gullet, 315

Bal*dall*, C S (ob.), dale farm, 254

,, mill of dale farm, C S (ob.), 254

Bal*dall*-Brew, C S, Brew's, or Judge's dale farm, 164, 254

Bal*dall* Criste, Bal*dal*-Christory, CS, Christory's dale farm, 164, 254

Baldwin ⎱ Boayldin (*boayl-dowin*),
Baldooin ⎰ low-place, 240, 254

Balicure (ob.), now Bishop's Court, boggy farm, 242

BALLA, 163, 164

Ballabane, white farm, 233

,, beg, little farm, 236

,, barna ⎱
,, benna ⎰ (*barney*), gap farm, 169
,, berna

,, berrag ⎱ Berrag's farm, or
,, birrag ⎰ (*birragh*) pointed farm, 221, 239

,, booie ⎱
,, bouigh ⎰ (*buigh*), yellow farm, 236
,, buiy

Ballabrebbag? (*brebag*), kiln farm (see addenda)

„ brooie (*brooee*), river banks' farm (see addenda)

„ bunt, Balnybunt, end farm, or farm of the end, 171

„ carkey ⎫ (*kiarkey*), hens' farm,
„ karka ⎭ 197

„ carnane, cairn farm, 174

„ „ beg, little cairn farm, 174

„ charree (*sharree*), foals' farm, 194

„ chirrym, Balytyrym, dry farm, 244

„ churree ⎫ boggy farm, 242
„ churry ⎭

„ claughbane (*clagh*), white stone farm, 233

„ clybane (*cleigh*), hedge farm, 172, 233

„ choan ⎫
„ coan ⎪ (*coan*), valley farm,
„ coine? ⎬ 169
„ coyne? ⎭

„ coar, pleasant farm, 245

„ colum, Columba's farm, 214

„ conley, Ballacoonlagh (*coonlagh*), straw farm, 202

„ conna-moor (*conney mooar*), big gorse farm, 201

„ connch-bwee (*conney*), yellow gorse farm, 236

„ cooiley ⎫ (*cooiley*), nook farm,
„ cooley ⎭ 169

„ corkey, oats farm, 202

„ cosney (? *cosnee*) profitable farm (see addenda)

„ cragga ⎫
„ cregga ⎬ (*creggagh*), rocky farm, 241
„ creggagh ⎭

„ creggan, rocky-hillock farm, 167

„ cree, heart farm, 187

„ croak (? *cronk*), hill farm, 167

„ crosha ⎫ (*crosh*), cross farm,
„ cross ⎭ 174

„ crink ⎫ (*cruink*), hills' farm,
„ cruink ⎭ 167

„ crynane beg *⎫ corruption of
„ „ moar*⎭ Carnane, see p. 174

„ cunney ⎧ ? cunney, gorse farm, 201
         ⎩ ? quinney, Quinney's farm, 201

Ballacurn, carn* (*carn*), cairn farm, 174

„ „ kiel, carn-y-keil (*keeilley*), cairn of the cell farm, 172, 174

„ „ kiel-beg, carn-y-keil-beg, little cairn of the cell farm, 174

„ „ kiel-mooar, carn-y-kiel-mooar, big cairn of the cell farm, 174

„ curry (*curree*), boggy farm, 242

„ doo, black farm, 232

„ doole, ? 226

„ doyne (*dowin*), low farm, 240

„ *duke*, duke's farm, 312

„ fadda (*foddey*), long farm, 237

„ fageen? (*fedjeen*), weaver's-quill farm, 227

„ fesson (*pesson*), parson's farm, 189

„ fogige, Ballafohague, (*fohaugr*). C S, under how farm, 239, 257

„ furt ⎧ ? (*furt*), port farm, 171
      ⎩ ? (*fjordr*), C S, firth farm, 255

„ gaie ⎫ (*gaaue*), smith's farm,
„ gaue ⎭ 191

„ gawn, Ballacoan, valley farm, 169, 191

„ gawne, Gawne's farm,

„ *ghaw* (*ghaw*), C S, cove farm,

„ garaghyn (? *garroo*),

„ gare ⎫
„ gyr ⎬ (*giare*), short farm, 238
„ jirr, ⎭

„ garee, stony-land farm, 168

„ garey, garden farm, 168

„ garman (*garmin*), weaver's-beam farm, 192

„ garroo ⎫ (*garroo*), rough farm,
„ garrow ⎭ 241

„ *gilley*, Balygill,* C S, glen farm, 256

„ gilley, ? Killey's farm (or *keeilley*), church farm, 172

„ genny, sandy farm, 242

„ glanny ⎫
„ glionney ⎪
„ gloney ⎬ (*glionney*), glen farm, 169
„ lonna ⎪
„ lonney ⎭

„ glass, green farm, 163, 234

„ glashan,* ? (*glais-een*), little stream farm, 160, 175

Ballagraney
,, graingey ⎫ (*grianey*), sunny
,, grangee ⎬ farm, 242
,, greney   ⎭
,, graue (*craue*), bone farm, 180
,, groa ⎫ (*croa*), pen farm, 172
,, grow ⎭
,, harra ⎫ *? (*sharree*), foals' farm,
,, harry ⎭ 194
,, hasney ? (*asney*), rib farm, 180
,, hawin ⎫
,, howin ⎬ (*awin*), river farm, 169
,, hown   ⎭
,, hot, cott (*cot*), cottage farm, 177
,, *how*, C S, (*haugr*), how farm.
     257
,, huggal* (*shoggyl*), rye farm,
     202
,, jerai ⎫ (*jeeragh*), straight farm.
,, jirey ⎭ 238
,, jiarge ⎫ (*jiarg*), red farm, 234
,, jiarg ⎭
,, jora (*joaree*), stranger's farm,
     191
,, juckley (*guilcagh*), broom-plant
     farm, 201
,, keeragh (*keyrrey*), sheep farm,
     193
,, kellag, Kellag's farm, or (*kel-
     lagh*), cock farm, 68, 197
,, kerroo, quarter farm, 171
,, kesh, foam farm, 178
,, keyll, wood farm, 199
,, kiel* (*keil*), narrow farm, 238
,, kiark,* hen farm. 197
         ⎧ (*keeilley*,) church farm,
,, killey ⎨ 172
         ⎩ (*keylley*), wood farm, 199
,, ,, clieu, (*slieau*), church hill
         farm, 166, 172
,, Killingan (*Keeill-Lingan*),
     Lingans'-cell farm, 214
,, kilmane (*mian*), Matthew's cell
     farm. 215
,, ,, martin, Martin's cell farm,
     214
,, ,, moirrey ⎫
,, ,, murray ⎬ (*moirrey*), Mary's
,, ,, vorrey ⎬ cell farm, 215
,, ,, worrey ⎭
,, ,, patrick ⎫ Patrick's cell
,, ,, pharic ⎭ farm, 214
,, koig, ? 216
,, lag, hollow, ditch, or turf-lag
     farm, 169

Ballalhane ⎫ trench farm, 173
,, lhen   ⎭
,, leigh, law farm, 184
,, lheiy (*lhiey*), calf farm, 193
,, lig, hollows', ditches', or turf-
     lags' farm, 169
.,, ling, pool farm, 175
,, lough, lake farm, 170
,, leney   ⎫ (*lheeanee*), meadow
,, lheaney ⎭ farm, 169
,, managh, Ballamanaugh,
     monk's farm. 189, 190
,, meanagh ⎫ (*meanagh*), middle
,, menagh ⎭ farm, 189, 240
,, meanagh beg,* little middle
     farm, 236, 240
,, ,, moar,* big middle
         farm, 236, 240
,, meg ⎫ (*beg*), little farm, 237
,, mig ⎭
,, megagh ?
,, milaghyn ? ⎫ (*milchyn*), trees'
,, miljyn   ⎭ farm, 199
,, min   ⎫ (*meen*), soft farm, 244
,, mine ⎭
,, moar (*mooar*), big farm, 236
,, modda   ⎫
,, moddey ⎬ dog or dogs farm, 194
,, modha   ⎭
,, ,, beg,* little dog or dogs
         farm, 194, 236
,, ,, moar*, big dog or dogs
         farm, 194, 236
,, mona, Ballamoaney (*moanagh*),
     turfy farm, 170, 243,
     260
,, ,, beg,* little turfy farm,
         170, 237
,, ,, moar,* big turfy farm,
         170, 237
,, myllin ⎫ (*mwyllin*), mill farm,
,, wyllin ⎭ 173
,, naa* ⎫ (*yn-aa*), farm of the ford,
,, nea* ⎭ 170
,, na-hard ⎫ farm of the height,
,, nard   ⎭ 166
,, nahoughty (*ny-ughtagh*), farm
     of the acclivity, 168
,, nank ?
,, narran (*yn-farrane*), farm of
     the spring, 176
,, nass* (*yn-ass*), farm of the
     waterfall, 170
,, *nayre* (*yn-ayre*), C S, farm of the
     gravelly bank, 254

22—2

Ballaneagh (*yn-eagh*), farm of the horse, 192

,, nearey (*yn-eary*), farm of the moor, 166

,, neddin (*yn-eddin*), farm of the face,

,, nimade, Balynemade ?

,, *paddag*, C E, paddock farm, 303

,, phesson, parson's farm, 189

,, rhenny (*rennee*), ferns' or ferny farm, 243

,, saig (? *skeaig*), hawthorn farm, 200

,, salla { Ballasallagh (*sallagh*), dirty farm, 242 / Ballasalley (*shellagh*), willow farm, 201

,, seyr (*seyir*), carpenter's farm, 191

,, shalghaige (*shuglaig*), sorrel farm, 201

,, shamrock (*shamrag*), shamrock farm, 202

,, sharragh, foal farm, 194

,, shellag, C S (*skeljar-vik*),? shell creek farm, 189

,, shimmyrk (*kimmyrk*), ? refuge farm, 230

,, shlig, shell farm, 198

,, shuggal (*shoggyl*), rye farm, 202

,, shuglaig (*shuglaig*), sorrel farm, 201

,, ,, e-Cain, Cain's sorrel farm, 201

,, ,, ,,-Quiggin, Quiggin's sorrel farm, 201

,, skeaig } (*skeaig*), hawthorn
,, skeige } farm, 200

,, skebbag } (*sccabag*), sheaf farm,
,, skebbeg } 203

,, skerroo } ?
,, skirroo }

,, spur (*spuir*), spur farm, 177

,, steer, ?

,, *strang*, C E, Strange farm, 303

,, stroan } (*strooan*), stream farm,
,, strooan } 170

,, stroke, ?

,, sumark, primrose farm, 230

,, taggart (*saggyrt*), priest's farm, or Taggart's farm, 189

Ballatersin } (*tessyn*), athwart farm,
,, terson } 240
,, tesson }

,, thoar, Ballne-toar (*tuar*) { bleach green farm, or farm of the bleach green, 192

,, thonna (*tonnagh*), wavy farm, 245

,, thunnag, duck farm, 197

,, vaaish, death farm, 186

,, vaase, cattle farm, 192

,, ,, mooar, big cattle farm, 192

,, vagher, field farm, 171

,, *vale* (mod.), C F, valley farm, 303

,, vane, white farm, 233

,, varanagh, Balyvarynagh ?

,, vair }
,, vare } (*bayr*), road farm, 174
,, vear }

,, varane }
,, varran } (*bayr-vane*), white road farm, 174
,, varvane }

,, varrey, ?

,, villey, tree farm, 199

,, voar (? *meoir*), Moar's farm, 190

,, voddan, ?

,, volly (? *mollee*), eyebrow farm, 181

,, vraarey } (*braarey*), priory farm,
,, vrara } 246

,, vriew (*briw*), judge's farm, 190

,, yaghteragh (eaghteragh), upper farm, 239

,, yeaman, ?

,, yelse, ?

,, yolgane, ?

,, willin } mill farm, 173
,, woolin }

BALLA[1] (with obsolete, uncommon or corrupt surnames).

Ballacagin, Caigin's or Kaighin's farm, 219, 220

,, camain, Kermeen's farm, 60

,, carmick, carmyk, Carmick's farm, 220

,, caroon, Corooin's farm, 221

,, chleerce, Clark's farm, 72

,, coarey, quarrys, Quarry's farm, 219

---

[1] For other surnames with *Balla* see SURNAMES. It is compounded with almost every surname in the island.

Ballacogeen, Cregeen's farm, 59
  ,, condyr } Cundre's farm, 219
  ,, cunner }
  ,, corage, Corraige's farm, 221
  ,, cotch, Cottier's farm, 219
  ,, coyle, Coyle's farm, 220
  ,, creetch, Creetch's farm, 219
  ,, crine, Creen's or Crine's farm, 219
  ,, cricyrt, Krickart's farm, 99
  ,, custal }
  ,, cutchal } Gilchreest's farm, 231
  ,, vitchal }
  ,, cuberagh, coobragh, Coobragh's farm, 32
  ,, cunney, Quinney's farm, 220
  ,, douraghan, ? Duggan's farm,

  ,, Faden { Faden's farm, 221
  ,, Fadin { (see also p. 224)
  ,, Fletcher, Fletcher's farm, 303
  ,, Freer, Freer's farm, 221
  ,, gennish, Kennish's farm, 57
  ,, gilley, Killey's farm, 221
  ,, gonnell } Connell's or Can-
  ,, whannell } nell's farm, 219
  ,, gorra, gorry, Gorry's farm, 221
  ,, hegg, Balyhigg, Higg's farm, 105
  ,, hestine, steen, Steen's farm, 29
  ,, himmin, Shimmin's farm, 27
  ,, kenag } Kinnag's farm, 221
  ,, kinnag }
  ,, kerbery, Carberry's farm, 221
  ,, kewaigue* (? aeg), Young Kew's farm, 224
  ,, killowie } Gillowy's farm, 219,
  ,, killowy } 220
  ,, kindry } Kinry's farm, 220
  ,, kinry }
  ,, koige, Keig's farm, 221
  ,, Mac Skealley, Mac Skealey's farm, 219
  ,, nickle, Knickle's farm, 221
  ,, queeney } Quinney's farm, 220
  ,, quincy }
  ,, *Regnelt, Regnylt,* Bal*dall Rey-nylt (Kögnvaldr),* C S, Reginald's farm, Reginald's dale farm, 221, 300
  ,, sherlogue, Sherlock's farm, 220

Ballaskelly, skealey, Skelly's farm, 219
  ,, stole, Stole's or Stowell's farm, 219
  ,, trollag, Trollag's farm, 219
  ,, varchein }
  ,, varteen }
  ,, vartin } Martin's farm, 219
  ,, varton }
  ,, vargher, Fargher's farm, 221
  ,, vastin, Bastin's farm, 222
  ,, vell, Bell's farm, 223

  ,, wanton (modern), ? Wanton's farm
  ,, whane, Quane's farm, 220
  ,, whetstone, Whetstone's farm, 219
BALLA (with Christian names)
Balladha (*adha*), Hugh's farm, 224
  ,, faden } (? *phaideen*), little Pat-
  ,, sageen } rick's farm, 224
  ,, juanvark, John Quark's farm, 225
  ,, robin, Robin's farm, 224
  ,, varkish, varkys (? *Markys*), Mark's farm, 224
  ,, will, Will's farm, 224
  ,, wille, Willy's farm, 224
  ,, willy killey, Willy Killey's farm, 225
  ,, worrey, Mary's farm, 216
  ,, yack, Jack's farm, 224
  ,, yemmy, Jemmy's farm, 224
  ,, ,, beg, little Jemmy's farm, 224
  ,, yockey (nickname), ? Jockey's farm, 225
  ,, yonaigue (*aeg*), Young John's farm, 224
BAL for BALLA.
Baldoon, close farm, 172
  ,, drine, thorn-tree farm, 200
  ,, dromma (*drommey*), (hill) back farm, 168
  ,, ,, heis, lower (hill) back farm, 168, 239
  ,, ,, heose, upper (hill) back farm, 168, 239
  ,, jean, darnel-weed farm, 202
  ,, larghey, slope farm, 167
  ,, laugh, Bal-ne-laaghey, Balla-lough (*laaghey*), mire farm or town, or (*logh*), lake farm, or town, 174, 176

Ballaugh, Parish of, 213
„ laughton, 303
„ lister, Balyster, ?
„ lie (*lieh*), half farm, 171
„ lig, hollows' farm, 169
„ na-hard* (*ny-ard*), farm of the height, 166
„ „ -hawin* (*ny-awin*), farm of the river, 169
„ „ -how, Balnehow, C S (*haugr*), farm of the how, 257
„ ny-laghey* (*laaghey*), farm of the mire, 176
„ „ -lerghy ⎱ (*ny-liargagh*), farm of
„ „ -lhergy ⎰ the slope, 167
„ „ -sloe, ?
„ „ -clybane (*cleigh*), farm of the white hedge, 172, 233
„ „ -craig, farm of the crag, 167
„ „ -geay, farm of the wind, 187
„ trim (? *chirrym*), dry farm, 244
BALL for BALLA.
Ballaspet ⎱ (*aspick*), bishop's farm,
„ aspick ⎰ 189
„ eary ⎫
„ irey ? ⎬ (*eary*), moor farm, 166
„ yrey ? ⎭
„ eigeragh (*eaghteragh*), upper farm, 239
„ ellin, Ballellan, island farm, 170
„ ingan* (St.) Lingan's farm, 214
„ injague (*injeig*), paddock farm, 172
„ jiaree* (? *joaree*), stranger's farm, 191
„ ne-*hough*,* C S (*haugr*), farm of the how, 257
„ ure (*cuar*), Yew farm, 200
Balley - Cashtal (ob), Castletown, 173, 229
Banks's how, S (*haugr*), Banks's how or headland, 256
Bannister (a corruption of Ballister),
Barna-ellan-renny (*barnagh*), Ferns' or Ferny Island gap, 171, 243
Barnagh jiarg, (? Balla barnagh jiarg,) red limpet (farm), 181, 182
Barony of Bangor and Sabal, 306
„ St. Bees, 306, 307
„ St. Trinian's, 306
„ the Hough, 307
„ The, 307
Barrick, S (*berr-hryggr*), bare ridge, 257, 300

Bastin's Close, 172, 222
BAYR, 'a road,' 155
Baregarrow (*garroo*), rough road, 241
„ beg,* little rough road, 236, 241
„ moar,* big rough road 236, 241
Barnell, Nell's road, 224
Barroose (*heose*), upper road, 239
Bayr ny *Ayra*, S, road of the ayr, or gravelly bank, 254
Bearey (? *eary*), moor, 140
Beary pairk* (? *eary*), moor park, 140, 149
BEEALL, 'entrance, mouth,' 148
Bealevayr (*y-vayr*), entrance of the road, 174
Beal-y-phurt, entrance of the port, 148
Beeal-feayn-ny-geay, wide entrance of the wind, 187, 238
Belegawn (*y-coan*), mouth or entrance of the valley, 169
Billowne, Belowne (*y-awin*), mouth of the river, 169
Begoad, Begod, S (? *ve-godi*), Godi's or priest's house, 281
Beinn-y-phot, or Penny pot, ? top of the pot, 147
Bemahague, Bemaghagg, S (? *hvamma-haugr*), slopes' or vales' how, 278
Bellabbey ?
Bemaccan, Bemecan, Bymaccan, Bimaken, Brimaken, Bowmaken, S (? *vc-maccan*), Maccan's or Magnus's house, 246, 281, 282, 308
Bendoyle, Bendoill, ? 148
Berk east ?
„ west ?
Berrag, Birrag, Ballaberrag, Berrag's farm, or (*birragh*) pointed farm, 221, 239
Bibaloe, Byballo, S (? *ve-balli*), grassy-bank house, 253, 281
„ beg,* S C, little grassy-bank house, 236, 253, 281
„ mooar,*SC, big grassy-bank house, 236, 253, 281
Bingbuie ⎱ (*binn*) 'yellow tops,' 148,
Binnbuie ⎰ 236
Bishop's barony, 306
„ court, 242
Black fort, 310

Black head, 305
,, rocks, 305
Blockeary, ? 166
Blue point, 305
Boal-na-muck (*boayl*), place of the pig or pig's stye, 164, 193
Boe Norris, Norris's cow (rock), 145
,, *The*, the cow (rock), 139
Boirrean, stony district, 140
Borrane, or Boirane - creg - lieh, stony district, or rocky ground of the gray crag, 156, 167
,, Bal*elby*, C S, stony district of Balelby, 156, 286
Bolivia, 316
Bow and arrow hedge, 229
Bracka*broom*, Brecka*broom*, ? S E, (? *brekka* 'a slope'), 272
Bradda, Braddaugh, S (*Bratt-haugr*), steep how, 300, 301
Braddan, Parish of, Skeeyley Vraddan, Braddan's parish church, 211
Braggan point ?
BRAID,. 'upland,' or 'gorge,' 139
Braid-ny-boshen (*bwoailtyn*), upland of the folds, 156, 171
,, ,, -glionney, gorge of the glen, 156, 169
,, ,, -skarrag, upland of the skate, 156
,, *The*, the upland, 139
Braids, *The*, the gorges, 139
Braust, Brausta, Ballybruste, S (? *brautar-staðr*), roadstead, roadstead farm, 279
*Breck*booiley, S C (*brekka*), slope of the fold, 272
Brerick, Breryk, S (*bruar-hryggr*), bridge ridge, 257, 280
Bretney, Bretby, S (*bratt-byr*), steep farm, 301
Bride, Parish of, Skeeylley Vridey or Vreeshey, Brigit's parish church, 210
Brither clip gut ? 315
Brondal ⎰(*Bruns, Brun*, or *Brunna-dalr*), Brown's, brown,
Brundal ⎱ or springs' dale, 274, 278, 293
BROOGH, 'a brow' (of a hill), 132
Broogh, jiarg mooar, big red brow, 143, 234
,, ny-soo, brow of the berry, 203

Broogh, *The*, the brow, 132
Brough brisht, broken brow, 244
Buggane, The, ?
Bulgum Bay, ? 316
Bully's Quarter, 224, 315
Bunghey (? *bun* ' end'), 148
Burntmill hill, 312
Bushel's house, 313
,, grave, 313
Burrow moar,* big burrow ? 240
,, meanagh, middle burrow, 240
Burrow *Ned*, Burrow *Head* (*boru-ey*), S E, bore-island head, 276
Burrow sodjey, further burrow?, 241
BWOAILLEE, (plu. BWOAILTYN), 'a fold,' 138, 150
Balthane ⎱ Byulthan (? *bwoailtyn*),
Boltane ⎰ folds, 138
Boilevell, Bell's fold, 223
Bole shoggil (*shoggyl*), rye fold, 202
Boleewillin (*mwyllin*), mill fold, 173
Bol reiy (*ree*), king's fold, 188
Bolrenny, Bulrenny (*rennee*), ferny or ferns' fold, 243, 315
Booil tramman, elder-tree fold, 199
Booiley Corage, Coraige's fold, 223
,, freoie (*freoaie*), heather fold, 201
,, bane, white fold, 233
Booldoholly (? *bwoaillee-doo-keylley*), black fold of the wood, 232
Booleyvelt, ?
Boshen ⎱ (? *bwoailtyn*), folds, 138
Botchin ⎰
Bouldaley, Daley's fold, 223
Builtchyn renny (*rennee*), ferny, or ferns' folds, 150
Bultroan (*strooan*), stream fold, 170
Buthin vane* (? *bwoailtyn*), white folds, 138, 233
Bwoaillee Cowle,* Cowle's fold, 138, 150
,, downe, deep fold, 240
,, losht, burnt fold, 150

CABBAL, 'a chapel,' 152
Cabbal druiaght, druid's or sorcery chapel, 190
,, Lingan, (St.) Lingan's chapel, 214
,, ny-*Lord* * Chapel of the Lord, 152
,, rullicky, churchyard chapel, 173

Cabbal-yn-oural-losht, chapel of the burnt sacrifice, 152, 184, 243
Caigher point, ?   316
Calf of Man, The, Manar kálfr, S, 258
California, 316
Camlork, ? S (*kamba* ?), Ridges ?, 275
    ,,   ? C (*cam*), ? crooked, 249
Cammal, S (*kamba-fjall*), Ridges fell, 275
Cardle, Cardale, Cardal, S (*kjarra-dalr*), brushwood dale, 285
Cardle veg, S C, little brushwood dale, 285
    ,,   voar, S C, big brushwood dale, 285
Carlane, *The* (see Kirlane), the sheep-fold, 174
    CARN, 'a cairn,' 138, 155
Cairn, *The*, the cairn, 138
Carmo*dil** ⎰ Carne*dale*, C S (*cairn-y-dalr* ?), cairn of the
Carmo*dale** ⎱   dale, 138, 254
Carmo*dale* beg,*C S C, little cairn of the dale, 138, 236, 254
    ,,   moar,* C S C, big cairn of the dale, 138, 236, 254
Carnageay (*y-geay*), cairn of the wind, 187
    ,, gerjoil, joyful cairn, 155, 247
    ,, lea* (*lheeah*), gray cairn, 138, 235
    ,, sharragh vane, white foal cairn, 194
    ,, *The*, the cairn, 134
    ,, vael ⎰ Michael's cairn, 138,
    ,, vial* ⎱   215, 216
    ,, vreid, hood cairn, (see addenda)
    ,, y greie ? ⎰ cairn of the sun,
    ,, y greiney ⎱   186
    CARNANE, 'a cairn' (diminutive), 158
Carnane-breck, speckled cairn, 158, 236
    ,, bedn, vedn (*vane*), white cairn, 233
    ,, *The*, the cairn, 158
Carnanes, *The*,* the cairns, 158
    CARRICK, 'a rock,' 134, 144
Carrick, rock, 134
Carrick-a-feeaih (*y*), rock of the deer 193

Carrick doan, dun rock, 234
    ,, lea (*lheeah*), gray rock, 235
    ,, nay,* S (*yn-ey*), rock of the island, 134, 254
    ,, Philip,* Philip's rock, 134
    ,, roayrt, spring-tide rock, 177
    ,, *rock*, rock rock, 144
    ,, *The*, The Rock, 134
    ,, y-voddy, rock of the dog or dogs, 194
Carrigraun, seal rock, 195
Carrin (see Karrin and Mount Karrin)
Carthure Rocks ?
    CASS, 'a foot,' 148
Cassnahowin (*ny-awin*), foot of the river, 169
    ,, ny-hawin, 148
    ,, ,, -strooan, foot of the stream, 170
    ,, ,, -stroan, stream foot, 170
Cassan kiel, narrow path, 155
    CASHTAL, 'a castle,' 152
Cashtal lajer, strong castle, 244
    ,, logh, lake castle, 170
    ,, ree *Goree*, C S, King Gorree's castle, 152, 166, 188
    ,, vooar, big castle, 152, 236
    ,, yn-ard, castle of the height, 166
Cashtall-y-Vare-vane, castle of the white road, 174
Castle Mona (modern), 303
    ,, Rushen (see Rushen), 212, 229
    ,, town, 304
    ,, Ward, Castell McWade, Ward's or MacWade's castle, 222
Castles, The, 312
Chasms, The, 312
Chester, Cheston's Croft
Chibbanagh ?
    CHIBBYR, 'a well, spring,' 153-4
Chibberbrott, broth well, 192
    ,, scayr, cold well, 244
    ,, glass, bright or clear spring, 235
    ,, harree (*sharree*), foal's well, 194
    ,, Katreeney, Katherine's well, 216
    ,, lansh, 154 ?
    ,, boghtyn* (*boght*), poors' well, 153, 185

Chibber Maghal, Maughold's well, 216

,, Niglas, Nicholas's well, 216
,, ny-cree-baney, well of the white heart, 187
,, ny-ushag, well of the bird, 196
,, oney, Roney's or Marooney's well, 216
,, Pherick, Patrick's well, 216
,, rollin, Dollin's well, 224
,, undin, · foundation well, 181
,, unjin, ash tree well, 200
,, vaill (*vayl*), Michael's well, 216
,, vainnagh (? *vainney* or *varney*), well of the milk or gap, 230
,, vastee, well of the baptism, 185
,, voirrey, Mary's well, 153, 216
,, vreeshey, Bridget's well, 216
,, y-chiarn, well of the Lord, 188
,, y-geay, well of the wind, 187
,, y-slaint, well of the health, 169, 184, 230

Chibbyrt balthane* (? bwoailtyn), folds' well, 138, 153
,, chroga (? *creggagh*), rocky well, 241

Chickens rock, The, 312

CHLEIGH or CLEIY, 'a hedge'

Chleig-ny-cuilleig, hedge of the nook, 177
,, ,, -fheeiney, hedge of the wine, 203

Chleiyrour ⎱
Clyrour ⎰ ?

Clybane, white hedge, 151

Cleigh-yn-arragh, hedge of the arrow, 229

Clougher ⎱ (? *mooar*), big hedge,
Clychur ⎰ 237

Clychur beg,* little big-hedge, 236-7
,, moar,* big big-hedge, 236-7

Clyclough, stone hedge, 168
,, een, little hedge, 160
,, na-mona, hedge of the turbary, 170

Christian's barony, 307

Citten, The city (modern)

Claare-our (*ouyr*), dun dish, 146

Claberry, ? 317

Claddagh, *The*, the water meadow, 135

CLAGH, 'a stone,' 143, 155

Claghard, high stone, 155, 240
,, bane, white stone, 143, 233
,, glass,* gray stone, 235
,, ny-dooiney-marroo, stone of the dead man, 246
,, ouyr, dun stone*, 235

Claughbane, white stone, 233
,, vane, 233
,, Willey,* Willey's stone, 224

Clanner ⎱ Glannagh (? *Balla-*
Cleanagh ⎰ *glionney*), farm of the glen, 230

Claram, ? 316

Clay head (see Eschenes and Kione cloaie), 286, 305

Clenaige ?

Cleps or Clypse, S (? *Clepps-by*), Clepps's (farm), 293
,, ,, S C, e-creer,* Creer's Clepps's (farm), 293
,, ,, veg,* S C, ? Clepps's little (farm), 236, 293
,, ,, voar,* S C, ? Clepps's big (farm), 236, 293

Clet elby, S (*klettr-ella-byr*), Elby rock, or fires' place rock, 277

Cloaie *head*, C E, Kione cloaie, stony head, 241

CLOSE, 'a paddock, close,' 149

Close-an-ellan (*yn*), close of the island, 149, 170
,, beg,* little close, 149, 236
,, buigh,* yellow close, 149, 236
,, chabbach (*cabbag*), sourdock close, 201
,, chiarn, Lord's close, 188
,, chirrym, dry close, 244
,, conley, straw close, 202
,, conning, rabbit close, 195
,, giark, hen close, 197
,, *lake,** C E, lake close, 149

Close iliam, William's close, 224
. ,,   Leece,* Leece's close, 90, 149
   ,,   managh, monk's close, 189
   ,,   mooar,* big close, 149, 236
   ,,   ny-cholbagh, close of the heifer, 193
   ,,   ,, -garey, close of the stony land, 168
   ,,   ,, -gonning,* close of the rabbit, 195
   ,,   ,, -lheaney, close of the meadow, 169
   ,,   ,, -veaynee, close of the reaper, 191
   ,,   rei, reigh, king's close, 188
   ,,   tunnag, duck close, 197
   ,,   vark, Quark's close, 222
   ,,   yn-argyt, close of the silver, or money, 204
   ,,,   y-chiarn, close of the Lord, 188
   ,,   ,,-gaur (*goayr*), close of the goat, 195
Cloven stones, The (see addenda)
Cluggid, The ?
Clyne moar ?
Clypston ?
Clytts, *The*, S (*klettar*), *The* rocks, 252
COAN, 'a valley,' 145
Coan bwee (*buigh*), yellow valley, 236
   ,,   rennee, ferns' (or ferny) valley, 145
Con-garey (? *coan-garey*), garden valley, 145, 149
   ,, shellagh, willow valley, 201
Colby, S (*kolls*, or *kolla-byr*), Koll's or summits' farm, 275, 295
Colden, Coldran, S (*kuldi-rani*), cold hill, 259, 301
Colloo, calf island, 141
Collooway, ? S or S E, calf-way, or calf-bay, 304
Commissary, S (? *garðr*), ? enclosure
Conchan, Parish of, Skeeylley Connaghyn, Connaghan's Parish Church, 207
Connehbwee (? *balla-conney-bwee*), yellow gorse (farm), 230
Connister, ?   312
Conocan (see Knockan), hillock
Contrary *Head* (? *kione-traie*), shore end, 174

COOIL, 'a corner, nook,' 135, 146
Cold clay (? *cooil-cloaie*), stony nook, 241
Coloonys, cooil-*ulist*, C S (*Ullsta'ðr*), Ull's stead nook, 300
Cooilbane, white nook, 233
   ,,   cam, winding nook, 146, 238
   ,,   *croft*, C E, croft nook, 172
   ,,   darry, oaks' nook, 199
   ,,   doo, black nook, 232
   ,,   injil, low nook, 240
   ,,   Nickal, Nickal's nook, 223
   ,,   shellagh, willow nook, 201
   ,,   slieau, mountain nook, 166
   ,,   taarnagh, thunder nook, 187
   ,,   *The*, the nook, 135
   ,,   voddy, dog or dogs nook, 194
Coolbegad ?
COR, I ? 'a round hill or cup-like hollow,' (COAR) pleasant, or S personal name.
Corbrick) S (*kora-brekka*), Cori's
   ,, breck) or Kori's slope, 253, 296
   ,, lea (*lheeah*), round gray hillock, 156, 235
   ,, monagh (*moanagh*), round turfy hollow, 156
   ,, valley (*coar*), pleasant farm, 171
Cordeman, Cornama, S (*kornhamarr*), 256, 286
Corna, Cornaa, or Cornay, S, (*korn-a*, *corne-a*), corn water or Corne's water, 285, 293
   ,, beg,* little Corne's water, 236, 285, 293
   ,, moar,* big Corne's water, 236, 285, 293
Corneil-y-killagh (*keeilley*), corner of the church, 148
Corrady, ?   156
Corrin's folly, 313
Corrony, Corna, S (*korn-a*, *corne-a*), corn water, or, Corne's water, 156, 285
Cor stack, S (*kora-stakkr*), Cori's or Kori's stack, 296
Cow harbour, 313
Crammag (*cromoge*), little cliff, 159
Cranstall, Kranstall, S (*krauns-ðalr*), Kraun's dale, 296
Cranstall Lough, Kraun's-dale lake, 296
Crawyn,* (? *Balla-crawyn*), bones (farm), 180

CREG, CRAIG, 'a rock, crag,' 134, 143

Craig-bane-y-Bill-Villy, Willy Bill son's white crag, 224, 233

,, e-Cowin,* Cowin's crag, 51, 134

,, *The*, the crag, 134

,, *The east*,* the east crag, 134

,, *The west*,* the west crag, 134

,, y-ghenny, crag of the sand, 204

Cregacable (*y-cabbal*), crag of the chapel, 172

,, adha, Hugh's crag, 224

,, bane, bedn (*bane*), white crag, 233

,, cruinn, round crag, 239

,, custane, Costain's crag, 223

,, harlot (? *Corleod*), Corlett's crag, 223

,, lea (*lheeah*), gray crag, 143, 235

,, lheeah-rio, ? hoar-frost crag, 226

,, liauyr, long crag, 237

,, Malin (? *Malane*), Magdalen's crag, 224

,, mill, or Cregg mill, rock mill, 304

,, moar* (*mooar*), big crag, 236

Cregneish, Crok-nes, S, { (*kraka-nes*), Kra-ki's ness, 296 (*króks-nes*,) nook ness, 278 (*k r a k u - n e s*), crow's ness, 284

Creg-ny-baa, crag of the cows, 192

,, ,, -crock (*cnoc*), crag of the hill, 167

,, ,, -ineen, crag of the girl, 187

,, ,, ,, thalhear, crag of the tailor's daughter, 187

,, ,, -molt, crag of the wether, 193

,, snaal* (*snafell*), snowfell crag, 141, 142

,, venagh (*meanagh*), middle crag, 240

,, voillan,* seagull crag, 197

,, vollan, carp crag, 198

,, Willysill, Willy Sell, Willy Silvester's crag, or Willy Sayle's crag, 225

,, wine* (? Quine), Quine's crag, 40, 134

Creg yn-arran { (*farrane*), crag of ,, y-arran { the spring, 177

,, ,, -chreel, crag of the basket, 182

,, ,, -jaghee, crag of the tithe, 184

,, ,, -*leech*, crag of the doctor, 304

,, ,, -vaare, crag of the summit, 166

,, ,, -whuallian, crag of the whelp, 195

Creggyn doo, black crags, 233

Cregby, S (*hryggjar-byr*), ridge farm, 273

CREGGAN, 'a crag, rock' (diminutive), used of rocky hillocks, 158

Creggan Ashen (? Cashen), Cashen's rocky hillock, 223

,, ,, Cregganatten, gorse rocky hillock, 200

,, doo, black rocky hillock, 232, 233

moar (*mooar*), big rocky hillock, 158

,, y-annag (*fannag*), rocky hillock of the crow, 196

Cregganyn, Ny, the rocky hillocks, 158

Creggans, *The*, the rocky hillocks, 158

Crogga, Ballacregga, rocky farm, 248

Cringle, S, (*kringla*), a circle, or (surname) Cringle, 251, 298

Crocreen, ripe or withered pen or fence, 151, 243, 281

Croggane (*creggan*), rocky hillock, 158

CROIT, 'a croft,' 138, 149

Croft, *The*, 138

Croit-e-Charran,* Carran's croft, 53, 138

,, e-phesson, parson's croft, 189

,, Freer, Freer's croft, 222

,, gonning, rabbit croft, 195

,, Hom Ralfe, Tom Ralfe's croft, 225

,, liannag* (*leeanag*), little meadow croft, 138, 159

,, ny-cooilley, croft of the nook, 169

,, ,, -killagh* (*keeilley*), croft of the church, 138, 151

,, ,, -moght (*boght*), croft of the poor (man), 185

Croit ny-mona (*moainee*), croft of the turbary, 170

,, ,, -quill { (? *quill* (*e*), Quill's croft, 227 / (? *cooil*), croft of the nook, 227

,, pingey, penny croft, 185

Crot-e-Caley, Caley's croft, 149

,, y-quill (? *chuill*), croft of the quill, 226 (see croit-ny-quill)

,, ,, -phurt Callow, croft of Callow's port, 171

,, ,, -vear (*bayr*) croft of the road 174

Crott-ny-gonning, croft of the rabbit, 195

,, y-vedn Bredjen, croft of widow Bridson, 222

,, ,, -daa-fiag (*feeagh*), croft of the two ravens, 196

Cromwell's walk, 314

CRONK, 'a hill,' 132, 143

Cronaback, Cronkbreck, speckled hill, 236

Cronaberry (*e*), Cronk-e-berry, Berry's hill, 273, 305

Cronkaittin, gorse hill, 200

,, airey (*aeree*), moor hill, 166

,, ard, high hill, 240

,, armyn, weapons' hill, 179

,, arrey,* watch hill, 183

,, *arrow*, ? C E, arrow hill,

,, *aust*, C S* (*austr*), east hill, 292, 293

,, ballaqueeney, Quinney's farm hill, 220

,, ballavarry, ?

,, bane, white hill, 233

,, beg, little hill, 236

,, *bourne*, C E, burn hill, 304

,, bouyr, ? deaf hill, 246

,, breck, speckled hill, 236

,, coar, pleasant hill, 245

,, collach, stallion hill, 193

,, darragh, oak hill, 199

,, derree, oaks' hill, 199

,, doo, black hill, 232

,, e-dooiney, man's hill, 155, 180

,, garrow (*garroo*), rough hill, 241

,, geayee, windy hill, 245

,, glass, green hill, 312

,, *howe*, mooar, C S C, big how hill, 257, 311

Cronkinjil, low hill, 240

,, juckley (*guilcagh*), broom plant hill, 201

,, keeill-abban, hill of the abbey church, 246

,, keeillown (*eoin*), John's church hill, 215

,, koir, chest hill, 180

,, losht, burnt hill, 243

,, moar (*mooar*), big hill, 236, 311

,, murran ?

,, mwyllin,* mill hill, 132, 173

,, ned (*yn-edd*), hill of the nest, 197

,, ne-mona (*ny-moainee*), 143, 170

,, ny-arrey, hill of the watch, 182

,, ,, -arrey-lhaa, hill of the day watch, 172, 183

,, ,, -bing, hill of the jury, 184

,, ,, -fannag, hill of the crow, 196

,, ,, -fedjag, hill of the feather, 197

,, ,, -guiy, hill of the goose, 197

,, ,, -hey (*oaie*), hill of the grave, 173

,, ,, -killane* (*keeill-ean*), hill of John's church, 215

,, ,, -lhergy (*liargagh*), hill of the slope, 167

,, ,, -mona (*moainee*), hill of the turbary, 143, 170

,, ,, -merriu, hill of the dead (men), 180

,, ,, -mucaillyn, hill of the sows, 193

,, ,, -mwyllin, hill of the mill, 173

,, ,, -shee, hill of the peace, 187

,, ,, -vowlan ?

,, renny* (*rennee*), ferny or ferns' hill, 242, 243

,, ruy, red hill, 234

,, shannagh } fox hill, 195
,, shynnagh }

,, shimmyrk (*kemmyrk*), refuge hill, 229

,, skealt (*skeilt*), split hill, 238

,, skibbylt, ? active hill, 247

,, somark, ? primrose hill, 229

,, unjin, ash tree hill, 200

,, urley, eagle hill, 196

Cronk-y-catt, hill of the cat, 195
  ,, ,, -chuill, (? *cooil*), hill of the nook ; (? *e-quill*), Quill's hill; (? *chuill*), hill of the quill, 226, 227
  ,, ,, -claghbane, hill of the white stone, 233
  ,, ,, -cliwe, hill of the sword, 197
  ,, ,, -cree, hill of the heart, 187
  ,, ,, -croghe,   Cronk - crore, Crore's hill, 217
  ,, ,, -keilleig (*keeilleig*), hill of the church enclosure, 177
  ,, ,, -killey* (*keeilley*), hill of the church, 172
  ,, ,, -leannag, hill of the little meadow, 169
  ,, ,, -marroo, hill of the dead (man), 180
  ,, ,, -scoltey, ? hill of the split, 226
  ,, ,, -sthowyr, hill of the staff, 184
  ,, ,, -voddy (*moddey*), hill of the dog, or dogs, 194
  ,, ,, -*watch*,* C E, hill of the watch, 183
Cronks, *The*, the hills, 132
Cronnag (*cronk-aeg*), little hill, 159
Cronnagyn, Ny, the little hills, 159
CRONKAN, 'a hillock,' 158
Cronkan garrow* (*garroo*), rough hillock, 158, 241
Cronkan renny (*rennee*), ferny or ferns' hillock, 158
Cronnan mooar (*cronkan*), big hillock, 158
Cront-e-Caley (*cronk*), Caley's hill, 223
Crosby, S (*krossa-byr*), cross farm, 253, 280, 281
  ,,   moar, S C,* big cross farm, 236, 253
  ,,   beg, S C,* little cross farm, 236, 253
    CROSH, 'a cross,' 154
Crosh-mooar, big cross, 154
  ,, *Sulby*, C S, Sulby cross, 154
Crossag *Bridge*, *The* (*crosh-aeg*), the little cross bridge, 159, 267, 280 ; or formerly Cros-Ivar, Ivar's cross ; Crosyvor, ob., S (*krossa-vörr*), weir cross, 267, 280, 281

Culberry Point, ?   316
CURRAGH, 'bog, fen,' 136, 147
Curragh-an-aspick (*yn*), bog of the bishop, 189
Curragh-beg,* little curragh, 136, 236
  ,,   feeagh,* raven curragh, 136, 196
  ,,   feehch, deer curragh, 193
  ,,   glass, green curragh, 147, 234
  ,,   moar* (*mooar*), big curragh, 136, 236
  ,,   *The*, the curragh, 136
Cushington, ?

Dalby, S (*dalar-byr*), dales' farm, 272
Dalenra (modern), ?   316
Daleveitch (modern), ?   316
Dalliott, S (*dalar-holt*), dales' coppice, 257, 272
Derby Castle, 311
Derby Fort, 311
Derby Haven, 297, 311
Dhoor, The (? *doo-ar*), the black water, 140
Dhrynane, ?
Dollaugh } beg (*doo-logh*), little
Dollough } black lake, 170
Dollaugh } mooar (*doo-logh*), big
Dollough } black lake, 170, 249
Doarlish-Cashen, Cashen's gap, 146
Dorlish ard (*dooarlish*), high gap, 240
Dhoon* (*doon*), close, 138
Doon, *The* (*doon*), the close, 138
Douglas (*doo-glaise*), black stream, 175, 249
Down, Balladowan, Dowan's farm, 220
Dowse, ?
Dray, ?
DREEYM, 'back' (of hill), 133, 143
Dreem beary (? *eary*), ? moor (hill)-back, 230
  ,,   faaie, paddock (hill)-back, 171
  ,,   froy (*freoaie*), heath (hill)-back, 201
  ,,   gell, Gell's (hill)-back, 74, 133
  ,,   *lang*, C E, long (hill)-back
  ,,   ny-lhergy, (hill)-back of the slope, 168

Dreemreagh, Drumreloagh (? *ny-logh*), ? (hill)-back of the lake, 230

,,　ruy, red (hill)-back, 143

,,　scarrey ⎫ (*skeerey*),　parish
,,　skeerey ⎭　(hill)-back, 271

,,　y-jees-kaig (*jees-skeaig*), hill-back of the two haw-thorns, 200

Drim reiy, ob. (*rea*), flat (hill) back (now St. Mark's), 244

Drum, *The*, the (hill)-back, 133

Dreswick, S (? *prests-vik*), priest's creek, 287

Droghad bane, ob., white bridge, 305

,,　Fayle, Fayle's bridge, 153

Druidale (modern), 315

Dubbyr veg,* little pond, 147, 236

,,　vooar, big pond, 147

Dulushtey, ? water

Duppolla, ob., S (*djup-pollr*), deep pool, 258, 301

Eairn yerrey (*jerrey*), iron end, 203

EARY, AEREE, 'a moor,' 133, 143

Eairy Kellee, or Kelly, cocks' moor or Kelly's moor, 197

,,　jora, Eairy joarey, stranger's moor, 191

,,　braid, upland moor, 230

Eary bane, white moor, 233

,,　Cushlin, Cosnahan's moor, 222

,,　glass, green moor, 234

,,　kellagh, cock moor, 143, 197

,,　Kelly, Kelly's moor, 197

,,　lhane ⎫ (*lhean*),　broad　moor,
,,　lhean ⎭　238

,,　ny-kione, moor of the end of the hill (*i.e.* of the moun-tain), 168

,,　,, -sooie, moor of the soot, 204

,,　vane ⎫ (*bane*),　white　moor,
,,　vedn ⎭　233, 234

,,　voar (*mooar*), big moor, 236

Eirey ween ?

Edd feeagh vooar, big raven's nest, 196, 197

Edremony, ob. (*eddyr-daa-moainee*), between the two marshes or turbaries, 249

Elby, S (*elda-byr*), Fires' farm, 286

Elby *Point*, S E, Fires' farm point, 286

ELLAN, 'Island,' 137, 145

Ellan-ny-foillan, island of the gull, 197

,,　,, -Maughol (*c*), Maughold's island, 216

,,　vannin, Mannan's Isle, 145

,,　vretin (*Bretin*), Britain's Isle, 226

,,　y-vodee ⎫ isle of the dog or
,,　y-voddey ⎭　dogs

Enjaigyn (see Injaigyn)

Ennaug, S (? *enna-guag*), cave crag, 274

Ennym-moar, Enin-mooar (*eanin-mooar*), big precipice, 142

Ennemona (? *moanagh*), ? boggy

Esehedalr, ob., S (*esju-dalr*), clay dale, 286

Eschenes, ob., S (*esju-nes*), clay ness, 286

Eye, *The*, S (*ey*), the island, 252, 276

Eyreton Castle, 315

FAAIE, 'a close, paddock,' 138, 149

Faaie-ny-cabbal, paddock of the chapel, 149

,,　,, -cabbyl,* paddock of the horse, 138, 194

,,　veg,* little paddock, 236, 138

,,　voar,* big paddock, 236, 138

,,　*The*, the paddock, 138

Fairy Hill, 311

Farm Hill, 315

Fheustal ? (high land by shore)

Fiddler's Green

Fildraw ?

Fire Point, or Gob-y-deigan, 227

Fisgarth, S (*fiski-garðr*), fishes' enclosure, 255, 284

Fistard, S (? *fiski garðr*), fishes' enclosure, 255, 284

Fleswick, S (*flesar-vik*), green spot creek, 278

Fochronk (*fo-yn-cronk*), under the hill, 249

Folieu (*fo-yn-hlieau*), under the mountain, 166, 249

Follit-ny-vannin, ?

Forester's Lodge, The, 313

Fort Caishtal, Castle Fort, 173

Foxdale, Folksdale, S (*Folks-dalr*), Folksdale, 287

Friary, The, 308

Gansey, S (*gands-ey*), magic isle, 288

GAREE, 'a stony place,' 'sour land,' 135, 146

Garey ashen, gorse stony place, 201

,, cheu-heese, lower-side stony place, 239

,, cheu-heose, upper-side stony place, 239

,, fluigh, moist stony place, 243

,, meen, or Garee meen, soft stony place, 146, 244

,, moar (*mooar*), big stony place, 236

,, *The*, the stony place, 135

GAREY, 'a garden'

Gara-na-chibberaugh, garden of the wells, 175

Garey feeyney, wine garden, 149, 203

,, noa, new garden, 245

Garf sheading, ? 268-271

Garraghan, ?

Gartedale, Galtedale, ob., S (*galta-dalr*) or *gallar-dalr*), Galte's dale, or hog-back dale, 274 293

Garth, *The*, S (*garðr*), the enclosure, 253, 255

Garwick, S (*geira* or *geirs-vik*), spear creek, or Geirr's creek, 261, 292, 293

Gat-e-whing, S C (*götu*, S, *whing*, C), yoke of the gate, 280

Geayllin-ny-creggyn, shoulder of the rocks or crags, 143, 167

GEINNAGH, 'sand,' 231

Geinnagh doo, black sand, 231

,, vane, white sand, 233

German, Parish of, Skeeyley Charmane, German's parish church, 161, 210

Giant's Fingers, 311

GJA, S, 'a chasm, rift,' in the Manx dictionaries, GIAU, or GHAW, 'cove, or creek,' 276

Ghaw, or *Giau* cabbyl, horse cove, S C, 276

,, ,, cam, S C, winding cove, 276

,, ,, doo, S C, black cove, 233, 276

,, ,, gortagh, S C, ? ?hungry cove, 246, 276

,, ,, jeeragh, S C, straight cove, 238, 276

Ghaw, or *Giau lang*, S E, long cove, 276, 304

,, ,, ny-cabbyl,* S C, cove of the horse, 276

,, ,, ,, -kirree, S C, cove of the sheep, 193, 276

,, ,, ,, -mooarid, S C, ?cove of the greatness, 226, 276

,, ,, ,, -Pharick (*e*), Patrick's cove, 216, 276

,, ,, Roole, Roole's cove, 218, 276

,, ,, spyrryd, S C, spirit cove, 226, 276

,, ,, veg, S C, little cove, 276

,, ,, wooar, S C, big cove, 236, 276

,, ,, jiarn, S C, iron cove, 203, 276

,, ,, yn-ow, S C S (*haugr*), cove of the how, 256-7

Gibdale, ? 316

,, Bay, ? 316

,, Point, ? 316

Gill, *The*,* S (*gil*), the ravine, 256 (addenda)

Gilgal, Guilcagh, broom, 316

Glaick, *The*, the hollow, 135

Glascoe (modern) ?

Glashen, Gylozen ?

Gleton ?

GLIONE, 'a glen,' 145

Glen altyn, mountain streams' glen, 170

,, beg, little glen, 237

,, belegawn (*beeal-y-coan*), mouth of the vale glen,* 145, 169

,, broigh, dirty glen, 242

,, cam, winding glen, 238

,, chattan (? *cassan*),* path glen, 155, 176

,, chass (? *chiass*), heat glen, 226

,, *cherry*,* C E (modern) ?

,, cooileen (*cullion*), holly glen, 200

,, corragh (*curragh*), bog glen, 170

,, crutchery, Glencruttery (*crui-tire*), harper's glen, 190

,, darragh, oak glen, 199

,, doo, black glen, 232

,, downe (*dowin*), low glen, 240

Glen drink (? *crink*), hills' glen, 167
,, duff (? *doo*), black glen, 232
,, faba ?
,,   ,, *sheading*, C S (?), 268-271
,, fessan (? *fessyn*), spindles' glen, 227
,, *gill*, C S, ravine glen, 256
,, glass, green glen, 234
,, greenaugh) (*grianagh*) sunny
,, grenagh)   glen, 242
,, *Helen* (modern), Helen's glen, 313   .
,, lough, lake glen, 170
,, may, Glenmeay (? *mea*), luxuriant glen, 247
,, *medal*, C S, * middle glen, 301
,, moar (*mooar*), big glen, 237
,, moij (see Glen may), 247
,, mona (modern), Mona glen, 243
,, ny-braid,* glen of the upland, 139, 156
,, roy (*ruy*), red glen, 234
,, Rushen* (name of sheading), Rushen glen, 160, 212, 228, 229, 268, 271, 285
,, shellan, bee glen, 198
,, tragh (*traagh*), hay glen, 203
,, truan, ? Druian's glen, 218
,, trunk (*cronk*), hill glen, 167
,, ville ? (modern).
,, y-mult, glen of the wethers, 193
Glione auldyn (*altyn*) mountain streams' glen, 170
,, crammag (*cromoge*), little cliff glen, 168
,, darragh, oak glen, 199
,, feeagh, raven's glen, 145, 196
,, glass, green glen, 234
,, Keeill Crore, Crore's Cell glen, 217
,, kerrad, S C, Garrett's glen, 222
,, kiark, hen glen, 197
,, maarliagh, thief glen, 191
,, ny-brack, glen of the trout, 198
,, ,, -goayr, glen of the goat, 195
,, shoggyl, rye glen, 202
,, thoar (*tuar*), bleach-green glen, 192
,, tramman, elder-tree glen, 199
,, y-killey (*keeilley*), glen of the church, 172

Gnebe, S (see Kneebe), 251
Goayr, *The*, the goat, 139
Gob, Gub, 'mouth, beak, point' (used of a spit of land running into the sea), 134, 144
Gob ago, ?   point
,, breac, speckled point, 144
,, creggagh, rocky point, 241
,, doo, black point, 233
,, gorrym, blue point, 235
,, lhiack, slate point, 204
,, na-roinna, point of the seal, 195
,, ny-callin, point of the body, 187
,, ,, -caashey, point of the cheese, 198
,, ,, ʼCally (*e*), Cally's or Caley's point, 223
,, ,, -cassan, point of the path, 176
,, ,, -creg, point of the crag, 167
,, ,, -creggyn glassey, point of the gray crags, 235
,, ,, -daa-slieau, point of the two mountains, 166
,, ,, -gameran ?
,, ,, -garvain (? *bayr vane*), point of the white road, 174
,, ,, -gee (*geay*), point of the wind, 187
,, ,, -Halsall (*e*), Halsall's point, 223
,, ,, -kione, point of the head, 168
,, ,, -port mooar, point of the big port, 171
,, ,, -schoot) ? (*scuit*) point of
,, ,, -skeate)   the spout, 227
,, ,, -sharrey (*sharree*), point of the foals, 194
,, ,, -Silvas (*e*), ? Silvester's point, 224
,, ,, -*sker*, C S,* point of the skerry, 134, 277
,, ,, -sloat, point of the low water, 178
,, ,, -strona (*strooan*), point of the current, 148, 170
,, ,, -traie-ruy, point of the red strand, 234
,, ,, -voillan (*foillan*), point of the sea-gull, 197
,, ,, -veinny (*beinnee*), point of the summits, 166

Gob ny-Uainaigue (*ean-aeg*), Young John's point, 223
,, *The*, the point, 134
,, y-Deigan (? *doagan*), point of the firebrand (now called Fire Point), 227
,, ,, Rheynn, point of the ridge or division, 167, 168
,, ,, skeddan, point of the herring, 198
,, ,, Stowell (*e*), Stowell's Point, 106, 134
,, ,, volley (*mollee*), point of the eyebrow, 181
,, yn-Cashtal, point of the castle, 173
,, ,, -ow, C S* (*haugr*), point of the how, 256, 257
,, ,, -ushtey, point of the water, 178
Godred Crovan's Stone, 310
Gordon, 315
Granane ?
Grange ?
Granite mountain, 312
Grauff, S (*gröf*), a pit, 251
Grave gullet, 312
Grawe, S (*gröf*), a pit, 251
Greeba, Kreevey, S (*gnipa*), a peak, 251
Greenland, 305
Greenock, Greenwyk, S (*grænn-vik*), green creek, 301
Grenaby, Grenby S, (*grænn-byr*), green farm, 301
Grenea, S (*grænn-ey*), green island, 301
Gresby, Grasby, S (*gras-byr*), grass farm, 285
Grest } Grettest, S (*greta-* or *grjöta-staðr*), Grettir's or stones' stead, 259, 294
Gretch }
Gretch heose, S C (*greta-* or *grjöta-staðr*), upper Grettir's, or stones' stead, 294
,, heis, S C (*greta-* or *grjöta-staðr*), lower Grettir's, or stones' stead, 294
,, vane, S C* (*greta-* or *grjöta-staðr*), white Grettir's, or stones' stead, 233, 294
,, veg, S C (*greta-* or *grjöta-staðr*), little Grettir's, or stones' stead, 294

Gretch voar, S C (*greta-* or *grjöta-staðr*), big Grettir's, or stones' stead, 259, 294
Groudle, Crowdale, Crawdall, ? Crowdale, 286, 305
Gryseth, ob., S (*grjöta setr*), stones' seat, 259, 286
Guilcagh, *The*, the broom plant, 139
Gullet buigh, E C, yellow gullet, 236, 304
,, chreagh moainee, EC, turbary stack gullet, 170, 176
,, ny-guiy, gullet of the goose, 197

Halland-Town (ob.), S, town of the isle, 137
Hampton's Croft, 315
Hango Broogh, S C (*hanga-broogh*), brow of the hanged, 292
,, Hill, S (*hóll*), hill of the hanged, 292, 311
Hague, *The** (*haugr*), the how, or the mound, 253, 256
Head gullet, 312
Hegnes } S (*Högna*, or *haga-nes*), Hogni's, or pasture ness, 285, 294
Hoanes }
Hæringstadt } ob., S (*Hærings-staðr*), Hæring's stead, now Kirk Michael, 294
Herynstaze }
Hillberry, Cronk-e-berry, 223, 305
Highton, Ballanard, 305
Holm (ob.), S (*holmr*), islet, 252, 253
Holm Town, Holme Town, Holm-Tun (ob.), S, or ? S E (*holma-tún*), town of the isle, 137, 260
Horalett, Haraldre, S (? *Haralds-staðr*), Harald's (stead), 294
Horse leap, 313
,, gullet, 313
Hough, *The*, S* (*haugr*), the how, or the mound, 253, 256
How, S*, how, 253, 256
Howstrake (*haugr* ?), how ? 273

'Im Leodan, or "The Heifers"' ? (as in Ordnance Map)*
Innis-sheeant, ob., Holy Isle, 145
,, Patrick ? Patrick's Isle, 205
Injeig, *The** (*injeig*, f), the paddock, 172, (addenda)

Injaigyn* (*injeig*, f), paddocks, 172, (addenda)
Intack, 318
Ippney ?
Island Close,* Close-an-Ellan, Close of the Island, 170
Island, The, 305
Ivy Cottage, 315

Johneioes, Johnnies, Johnny's, 224
Jon's Quarter, John's Quarter, 224, 315
Jurby, Jourby, Joreby, S, *Jörfa, dyra, Ivor,* or *jure (eyri) byr,* S, gravel, beasts', Ivar's, or gravelly bank farm, 205, 273, 282, 286, 295
Jurby *Point,* 205

Kallow Point, Callow Point, 315
Karrin, see Carrin (name of mountain)
KEEILL, 'cell, church,' 151, 152
Keeill abban, abbey cell, 246
  ,, Balthane, Byulthan (? *Bwoa-iltyn*), Folds' cell, 138, 151, 152
  ,, Bragga   ⎫
  ,, Breeshy   ⎬ Bridget's cell, 151,
  ,, Brickey   ⎪   214
  ,, breeshy   ⎭
  ,, cairbre, Cairbre's cell, 208
  ,, casherick, holy cell, 245
  ,, coonlagh, straw cell, 202
  ,, columb, Columba's cell, 208
  ,, colum, Columba's cell, 214
  ,, cragh, slaughter cell, 179
  ,, cronk, church hill, or hill cell, 167
  ,, Crore, Crore's cell, 210
  ,, crout, ? craft cell, 227
  ,, Katreeney,* Kathrine's cell, 216, 251, 252
  ,, Lingan, Lingan's cell, 214
  ,, Moirrey ⎫
  ,, boirrey ⎬
  ,, vorrey ⎪ Mary's cell, 215
  ,, woirrey ⎭
  ,, ny-hawn* (*awin*), cell of the river, 146, 169
  ,, own, John's cell, 215
  ,, Pharick ⎫
  ,, Pherick ⎬ Patrick's cell, 214

Keeill Pherick a-Drumma (*y-Drom-mey*), Patrick's cell, of the back (of the hill), 168, 214
  ,, Pharlane, Bartholomew's cell, 215
  ,, Ronan, Ronan's cell, 214
  ,, tushtagh, ?   248
  ,, vael ⎫ Michael's cell, 185,
  ,, vail ⎬   215
  ,, vane,* white cell, 233, 251, 252
  ,, vian, Matthew's cell, 215
  ,, vout ?
  ,, yn-chiarn, cell of the Lord, 188, 215
Killane (*ean*), John's cell, 215
Kilcrast, ob. (*Chreest*), Christ's cell, 213
,, Kellan ?
,, Martin, Martin's cell, 214
Kella ? ⎰ (*Ballakellagh*), cock (farm)
       ⎱ (*Ballakeylley*), wood (farm), 231
Kenna, or Kinna (? *kione-aa*), ford head, 230, 231
Kentraugh, Kentraie (*kione-traie*), shore end, 171
Keppell Gate, S (*kapal-gata*), horse road, 256, 283
Keristal, S (see Skeristal), 277
Kerlaine (see Carlane and Kirlane)
KERROO, 'a quarter,' 164-165
Kerroo claghagh, stony quarter
  ,, cottle, Cottle's quarter, 222
  ,, chord ?
  ,, coar ⎱ (*coar*), pleasant quar-
  ,, coare ⎰ ter, 245
  ,, creen, withered quarter, 243
  ,, creoie ⎱ (*creoi*), hard quarter,
  ,, croie ⎰   243
  ,, cruinn, round quarter, 239
  ,, doo, black quarter, 232
  ,, garroo, rough quarter, 164
  ,, glass, green quarter, 234
  ,, kiel, narrow quarter, 238
  ,, kneale, Kneale's quarter, 46
  ,, na-ard (*ny-ard*), quarter of the height, 166
  ,, ny-clough (*clagh*), quarter of the stone, 168
  ,, ,, -genny (*geinnee*), quarter of the sand, 204

Kerroo-ny-gronk, quarter of the hill, 167
„ quirk, Quirk's quarter, 52
„ valley { farm quarter or quarter-land, 164-165
Kew (? *Ballakew*), Kew's (farm), 185
Kewaigue (? *Balla-kew-aeg*), Young Kew's (farm), 221
Kilkenny (mod.), 316, 317
Kimmeragh, East?
„ West?
King Orry's Grave, 310
King William's Bank, 314
„ „ College, 313
KIONE, 'head, end,' 144, 148
Keon dowag, ? head
„ slew curragh (*slieau*), hill end bog
Kian-ny-lhane, end of the Lhen-trench, 173
Kione veg, little head, 237
„ cloaie (ob.) stony head (see Clay Head), 305
„ *dam*,* dam head, 144
„ dhoohe ?
„ doolish (ob.) (*doo-glaise*), black stream head (now Douglas Head), 144, 175
„ droghad, bridge end, 173
„ lough,* lake end, 147, 170
„ meanagh, middle head, 239, 240
„ ny-garee, end of the stony place, 168
„ „ -halby ?
„ „ -henin, end of the precipice, 168
„ roauyr, broad or fat head, 244
„ slieau, mountain end, 166
„ traie (ob.) shore end, 174 (now Contrary Head)
„ y-ghoggan, end of the noggin, 182
KIRKJA, S, 'a kirk, church,' 280
Kirby, S (*kirkju-byr*), church farm, 280
Kirk Andreas, Andrew's church, 213, 280
„ Arbory, Karbery, Cairbre's church, 208, 209, 280
„ Braddan, Bradan, ? Brandan's church, 211, 280
„ Bride, Brigide, Bridget's church, 210, 280

Kirk Christ Lezayre, Kirk Criste, Christ's church of the Ayre, 212, 213, 280
„ Christ Rushen, Kirk Christe in Sheding, ? Christ Rushen Church, or Christ's church of the little wood, 211, 212, 280
„ German, ? Coemanus's church, 210, 280
„ Lonan } Lonnan's church,
„ Lonnan } 207, 280
„ Malew, Molipa's or Lupus's church, 212, 280
„ Marown, Marooney's or Runius's church, 208, 280
„ Maughold, Maughold's church, 205, 280
„ Michael, Michael's church, 213, 280
„ Patrick, Patrick's church, 205, 280
„ Patrick of Jurby, Patrick's church of Jurby, 205, 280
„ Onchan, Kirk Conchan, Connaghan's church, 207, 280
„ Santon, Santan, Sanctan's church, 209, 280
„ Suasan, ? 280
Kirlane, The (*keyrr-lann*), the sheep fold, 175
Kitterland, S, Kitter's land, 258, 295
Kneebe, Knebe, Gnebe, S (*gnipa*), a peak, 251
CNOC, or KNOCK, 'a hill,' 142
Knockaloe, Knockaley, ? Caley's hill, 223
„ „ beg, Caley's little hill, 223
„ „ moar (*mooar*), Caley's big hill, 223
„ a-loughan (*y*), Knokloughan hill of the pond, 170
„ bane, white hill, 233
„ beg,* little hill, 142, 236
„ doo, black hill, 232
„ „ moar* (*mooar*), big black hill, 142, 236
„ e-berry* (or Cronk-e-berry), Berry's hill, 305
„ „ -doniney, Man's hill, 142, 155, 180
„ „ vriew, Judge's hill, 190
„ freiy } (*freoaie*), heather hill,
„ froy } 201

Knock glass,* green hill, 234
,, ould, ole, ? S, (*Olafr*), Olave's hill, 300
,, rule (ob.) (see Mount Rule), Rule's hill, 218
,, Rushen,* Rushen hill, 160, 211, 212, 228, 229, 268, 285
,, sharry (*sharree*), foals' hill, 194
,, shemagg ?
,, shewell, ?
,, y-nean (*yn-ean*), hill of the lamb, 193
,, ,, -killey* (*keeilley*), hill of the church, 151, 172
,, ,, -tholt (*soalt*), hill of the barn, 173
,, ,, -troddan, hill of the contest (now Castleward), 179
Knockan, hillock (now Ravensdale), 158
,, aalin } beautiful hillock,
,, alin } 158, 242

LAG, ' a ditch hollow,' also LAGGEY, 135, 145
Lagbane, white hollow, 145
,, birragh,* pointed hollow, 135, 239
,, dhoan, dun hollow, 234
,, ny-awin, hollow of the river, 169
,, ,, -chibbyr, hollow of the well, 175
,, ,, -keeilley or keilley, hollow of the church, 172, 311
,, ,, -traie, hollow of the shore, 171
,, *The*, 135
,, y-votchin (bwoailyn), hollow of the folds, 171
Lagagh moar* (*laggey*), big hollow, 135, 235
,, *The*, the hollow, 135
Lagavollough, ? hollow
LAGGAN (diminutive of *lag*), 158
Laggan *agneash*, C S,* Agneash little hollow, 285
,, doo, black little hollow, 158
,, y-dromma (*drommey*), little hollow of the (hill) back, 168
,, *The* } the little hollow,
Largan, *The* } 158

Lammall, Lambfell, S (*lamba-fjall*), lambs' fell, or Lambe's fell, 283, 296
Langness, S (*langa-nes*), long nose or ness, 258, 301
Lanjaghin (? *lann*), Deacon's enclosure, 155
Larivane, Laare vane (mwyllin laare vane) (*laare*), white floor (mill), 231
Laxey, S (*lax-á*), salmon water or river, 253, 284
Leakerroo (*lieh*), half quarter, 164
Leodan, The ?
Leodest, S (*liots-staðr*), Liot's stead, 296
,, e cowle,* Cowle's Leodest, 61, 296
,, ,, kie,* Kie's Leodest, 62, 296
Lewaigue, Lewaige (? *Balla-hlieau-aeg*), little hill (farm), 231
Leyr ?
Lezayre, Parish of, Le *Ayre*, C S, Skeeyley-Chreest-ny-*Heyrey*, Christ's parish church of the Ayre, 213, 254
Lez *Sulby*, Le *Soulby*, C S (*ny Sulby*),* ? of the Sulby, 213, 254, 298
Lhane mooar, *The* (? *lane*), the big trench, 157
LHEEANEE, ' a meadow,' 146
Lheeaney veg, little meadow, 237
,, vooar, big meadow, 237
Lheaney, *The*, the meadow, 146 (and addenda)
Lheany gibby, Gibby's meadow, 224
,, runt, round meadow (addenda)
,, *totaby*, C S,* Totaby meadow, 146, 299
Lheeanag } *The*, the little meadow,
Leenag } 159
Lhiannag }
Lheim-feeaih, deer's leap, 193
Lhen, *The* (? *lane*), the trench, 157 and addenda
Lhen mooar, *The* (? *lane*), the big trench, 157
Lhiaght-ny-foawr, grave of the giant, 185
,, -y-Kinry (*e*), Kinry's grave, 152, 223

Lhiattee-ny-beinnee, side of the
  summits, 148, 166
LIARGAGH, 'slope' (of hill), 132,
  143
Large beg,* little slope, 143, 236
  ,,   mooar } *big slope, 143, 236
  ,,   wooar }
Largee doo, 232
Largy, slope, 132
  ,,   doo, black slope, 232
  ,,   rhea* (*rea*), smooth slope,
        132, 244
  ,,   rhenny, or Lhergy renny,
        ferns', or ferny slope, 132,
        243
Lhargee ruy, red slope, 234
Lherghy clagh willey, Willey's stone
  slope, 168, 224
Lhergy colvin, Colvin's slope, 222
  ,,   *grawe*, S, Grawe slope, 251
  ,,   rhaa, Rhaa or fort slope, 173
  ,,   *The*, the slope, 132
Liargey-ny-houne (*awin*), slope of
  the river, 169
Liggea, S (*lag-ey*), low island, 254,
  301
Lingage   ?
Little London, S, (*littill-lundr*),
  little grove, 258
  ,,   ness, S (*littill-nes*), little ness,
        304
  LOGH, 'a lake,' 147
Loch *Skillicore*, ? S   ?
Lochfield ned (? modern), 317
Logh*mollo*, C S, *malar*logh, S C,
  pebbles lake, 286
Lough *cranstall*, C S, or *Cranstall*
        Lough, S C, Cranstal lake,
        296
  ,,   croute (*kruit*), harp lake, 182
  ,,   doo, black lake, 147, 232
  ,,   drughaig (*drughage*), dog-
        rose lake, 200
  ,,   *Gat*-e-whing * (farm name),
        Gat-e-whing lake, 147, 280
  ,,   na-baa* (*ny*), lake of the
        cows, 147, 192
  ,,   ny-greeagh (*creagh*), lake of
        the stack, 176
LOGHAN (diminutive of *logh*), 158
Loughan-keeill-vael,* Michael's cell
        pond, 158, 215
  ,,   ny-maidjey,   ny-mashey,
        (? *maase*), pond of the
        cattle, 192

Loughan-y-eiy or y-guiy, pond of the
  goose, 158, 197
Lonnan, Parish of, Skeeylley
        Lonnan, Lonnan's parish
        church, 207
LOOB, 'a loop,' used of 'a gulley,'
        146
Lhoob doo, black gulley, 232
  ,,   y-charran (*e*), Carran's gully,
        223
  ,,   ,, -reast, gulley of the waste,
        146, 168
Lord Henry's well, 312

Maase moar } (*balla vaase mooar*),
Mace moore } big cattle (farm), 230
Madeira, 315
  MAGHER, 'a field,' 149
Magher-a-fuill (*y*), field of the
        blood, 179
  ,,   breck,* speckled field, 149,
        236
  ,,   cabbal, chapel field, 172
  ,,   e-kew.* Kew's field, 63, 149
  ,,   glass,* green field, 149, 234,
        235
  ,,   kiel, narrow field, 238
  ,,   liauyr, long field, 237
  ,,   vane, white field, 233
  ,,   yn-ullin, field of the stack-
        yard, 151
  ,,   y-broogh, field of the brow,
        168
  ,,   ,, -caggey, field of the battle,
        178
  ,,   ,, -chiarn, field of the lord,
        149, 188
  ,,   ,, -keim, field of the stile,
        177
  ,,   ,, -ruillic, field of the grave
        yard, 173
  ,,   ,, -traie, field of the shore,
        171
Malar Logh, S C (ob.) (S, *möl*, gen.
        malar), see Logh *Mollo*
Malew, Parish of, Skeeylley
        Malew, Molipa's, or (Ma)
        Lupus' parish church, 212
Man, Isle of, 130
Manusan rocks, 317
Marown, Parish of, Skeeylley Ma-
        rooney, Marooney's parish
        church, 208
Martland   ?
Martha gullet, 315

Mary veg, S C, *Mearey* veg (*mæri*, S), little border land, 277

Mary voar, Mearey voar, big border land, 277

Maughold *Head*, 216

  ,,   Parish of, Skeeylley Maghal, Maughold's parish church, 205, 207

Maun (ob.) (now Isle of Man), 131, 251

Meayll, *The*, Mull, *The*, C (*maol*), S (*mhill*), the bare headland, or the headland, 140, 251

Meir-ny-foawr, fingers of the giant, 185

Michael, Parish of, Skeeyley Mayl, Michael's parish church, 213

Michael Sheading, S, 213, 268-71

Middle Sheading, S, Medal (*Meðal*), 301

Milner Tower, 314

Milntown, Milltown, 314

Minorca, 316

Mirescoge (ob.), S (*Myrar-skógar*), wood bog, 259, 260, 278

MOAINEE, or MOANEY, 'turbary, turf bog,' 137, 147

Moanamoght (*y-moght*), turbary of the poor, 185

Moainee mollagh, rough turbary, 147

Moaney beg, little turbary, 237

  ,,   doo, black turbary, 232

  ,,   moar (*mooar*), big turbary, 237

  ,,   mollagh, rough turbary, 241

  ,,   quill { * ? Quill's turbary, 61, 137 / ?* (*cooil*), corner turbary, 137, 146

  ,,   *The*, 137

Mooragh, *The*, the sea waste or sand bank, 134

Mön, S, Isle of Man, 131, 231

Mona, Isle of Man, 131

Mont Pelier, 317

Morest, S (*myrar-staðr*), moor stead

Mount Karrin, or Carrin, Karrin's Mount, 305

Mount Murray, 312

Mount Rule, Knock Rule, Rule's hill, 218, 305

Mount Strange, 311

Mull, *The*, S (*Mhill*), the headland or crag, 140, 251

MULLAGH, 'top, summit,' 142, 148

Mullagh-ouyr, grey or dun top, 142

  ,,   y-Sniaul, C S, top of Snæfell, 148

Mwannal-y-guiy, neck of the goose, 150, 197

MWYLLIN, 'a mill,' 153

Mullen aragher, Faragher's mill, 222

  ,,   beg,* little mill, 153, 236

  ,,   doway (ob.) (? *doo-aa*), black ford mill (now Union Mills), 170, 232

  ,,   e-Corran, Corran's mill, 153, 223

  ,,   e-Cowle,* Cowle's mill, 61, 153

  ,,   lawne, Mullin-ny-hawin, mill of the river, 169

  ,,   reneash (*rinn-eas*), mill of the waterfall ridge, 167, 170

Mwyllin-ny-cleiy, mill of the hedge, 172

  ,,   y-quinney (*e*),* Quinney's mill, 40, 153

Nab, *The*, S (*nabbi*), the knoll, 251

Naish (? *yn-aash*), the rest, 141

Nappin, *The* (*cnappan*), the little hillock, 140

  ,,   *The East*, the east little hillock, 140

  ,,   *The West*, the west little hillock, 140

Narradale, S (*Narfa-dalr*), Narfi's dale, 254, 296

Nary (*yn-aerce*), the moor, 133

Nearey (*yn-eary*), the moor, 133

Nascoin, Nascoan (*yn-eas-coon*), the narrow waterfall, 146, 238

Nassau, 316

Nay, *The*,* C S (*yn-ey*), the Isle, 252

Neb (R) (see Kneebe), 251

Nellan (*yn-ellan*), the isle, 137

  ,,   renny, the ferny, or ferns' isle, 242

Nerlough (*yn-neear*), the west lake, 241

Newtown, 315

Niarbyl, *The* (*yn-arbyl*), the tail (addenda)

Northop, S (*norð-þorp*), the north village, 267, 292

Nunnery, The, 306

Nuns' chairs, The, 314

Nuns' well, The, 314

Oaie-ny-foawr, 'grave of the giant,' 152, 186
Oatlands, 305
Ohio, 316
Olt (see Alt), mountain stream, 135
Ooig, 'a cave,' originally Ogr, S, adopted into Manx, 277
Ooig doo, S C, black cave, 233, 277
  ,, ny pheastul ?
  ,, ny-seyr, S C, cave of the carpenter, 277
  ,, veg, S C, little cave, 277
  ,, y-veeal, S C, cave of the entrance, 170, 277
*Ooig*yn doo, S C, black caves, 277
Or vooar, big verge, 144, 145
Orrisdale, Norrisdale, Orestal, S
  { *eyri*, gravelly bank dale, 272, 273
  { *ore* (Danish), forest dale, 273
  { *Orrys*, Orry's dale, 299
Ormeshan (Orme's), ? 297
Orm's *house* (ob.), S E, 14, 296
Oxwath (ob.) (*uxa-vað*), ox ford, 283

Pairk-ny-earkan, park of the Lapwing, 149, 196
Park Llewellyn,* Llewellyn's park, 149
Particles, Partical (a land division), Portions, 317, 318
Patrick, Parish of, Skeeylley Pharick, Patrick's parish church, 205
Peel, fortress, 137
Peel*town*, C E, 137
Perwick, S (*petrs-vik*), Peter's creek, 297
Pigeon's cove, The, 314
Piscoe ?
Pollock rock, The, 314
Poortown, 314, 315
  Pooyl, 'a pool,' 147
Pooil dhooie, ? kind pool, 248
Pool hilley }
  ,, vill }
  ,, villa } tree pool, 199
  ,, yilley }
Pooyl breinn, stagnant pool, 241
  ,, therriu, bulls' pool, 192
  ,, vaaish, death pool, 147, 186
Pulrose, Poolroish, wood pool, 170, 228
Priory of Douglas, 306

Purt, 'a port, harbour,' 144
Port Bravag ?
  ,, *Cornah*, C S, Cornah port, 144, 285, 293
  ,, *Cranstal*, C S,* Cranstal port, 144, 296
  ,, e-chee (*y-shee*), port of the peace, 187
  ,, e-vada (*baatey*), port of the boat, or boat port
  ,, erin, Port Iron, Phurt yiarn (*yiarn*), iron port, 203
  ,, greenaugh (? *grianagh*), sunny port, 242
    or
  ,, *greenock, greenwyk*, S (*gran-vik*), Green creek port, 301
  ,, groudle, groudale, crowdale, Crowdale port, 305
  ,, Jack, Jack's port, 315
  ,, Lewaigue,* Lewaigue port, 144, 231
  ,, ny-ding (*king*), port of the heads, 168
  ,, (or Puirt) ny-mwyllin, port of the mill, 173
  ,, St. Mary, Purt-le-Morrough, Purt-noo-Moirrey, St. Mary's port, 216, 305
  ,, skilleig, narrow strip port, 227
  ,, skillion (?)
  ,, y-vullen (*mwyllin*), port of the mill, 173
Puirt Ceabagh, cloddy port, 247
Purt Mooar, big port, 144, 237
Purt-ny-Coan, port of the valley, 169
Purt-ny-Hinshey (ob.) (*innis*), port of the isle, 171
Purt-ny-shee, port of the peace, 187
  ,, veg, little port, 237

Quarter bridge
Quarterland (see Kerroo)
Quine's hill

Rath (I), ? Raa (Manx), 'a fort'
Raa Mooar, or *The* Raa Mooar, big fort, or the big fort, 153
Rhaa, *The*, the fort, 138
Rah,* fort, ? 138
Raad-jiarg, red road, 155
Raby, S (*rár-byr*), nook farm, 279
Raclay, S (*rár-* ?), nook ?
Raggatt, S (*rár-gata*), nook path, 279

Raggey, or Racky, ?

Ramsey, Ramessay, Ramsa, Ram-
    sö, S (*hramns- á* or *ey*),
    Raven's water, or Raven's
    isle, 281, 284, 294, 295

Rarick, S (*rár-vík*), nook creek,
    279

Rauff, S (*Hrolfs ? staðr*). Ralf's
    (stead), 295

Ravensdale (modern)

Redgap

    REEAST, 'a waste, desert,' 133,
        143

Reash,* ? waste, 133

Reeast bwee, yellow waste, 236

    „   *marsh, The,* the marsh
        waste, 133

    „   mooar, big waste, 143

    „   mooar, *The*, the big waste,
        133

Regaby, Regby, S (*hryggjar-byr*),
    ridge farm, 273

Renny, Ballarenny, ferns' or ferny
    farm, 248

Rheboeg ?

    RHEYNN, 'a division or ridge,' see
        RINN

Rheyn, *The* ⎱
Rhine, *The* ⎰ the division, 133

RHULLICK, 'a graveyard, a church-
    yard,' 152

Rhullick-keeill-vael, Michael's cell
    graveyard, 216

Rhullick-ny-Quackeryn, graveyard of
    the Quakers, 152, 184

    „   y-lagg-shliggagh, graveyard
        of the shelly hollow, 169,
        242

Richmond hill (modern), 315

Rig, S (*hryger*), ridge, 253, 257

    RINN, 'a ridge,' 143

Renab, abbot's ridge, 189

    „   as, Rheneash (*eas*), waterfall
        ridge, 170

    „   cheiry, ?

    „   cullen (*cullion*), holly ridge, 200

    „   doo, black ridge, 232

    „   shent (*sheant*), holy ridge, 143,
        245

    „   skault, Renskelt (*sceilt*), cleft
        ridge, 238

    „   urling (ob.) (*urley*), eagle ridge,
        196

Rhenwyllin (*mwyllin*), mill ridge,
    173

Ronaldsway, Ranaldwath, S (*Kögn-
    valds- vagr* or *vað*), Regi-
    nald's bay, or ford, 260, 261,
    297

Ronnag (? *Ron-og*, see *Marown*)

Round Table, The, 312

Rowany, Edremoney (*eddyr-daa-
    moainee*), between two tur-
    baries, 249

Rozefell (ob.), S (*hross-fjall*), horse-
    fell, 282

Rue Point, 305

Rushen Abbey, 304

Rushen, Parish of, yn skeerey
        Rushen, Skeeylley Chreest
        Rushen, Christ's Rushen
        parish church, 160, 211,
        212, 229

    „   *sheading*, S, Russein's shead-
        ing, sheading of the little
        wood, 160, 212, 228, 229,
        268, 285

Saddle road, 310

St. Anne's Head ⎱ (*Sanctan*), Sanc-
Santon Head ⎰   tan's Head, 304

St. Germain's ⎱
St. German's ⎰ Cathedral, 210

St. John's, 306

St. Luke's, ? St. Leoc, 172, 311

St. Mary's rock, 312

St. Maughold's chair, 311

St. Michael's isle, 315

St. Patrick's chair, 314

St. Trinian's church, Ninnian's or
        Ringan's church, 214, 215

Sandbrick, Saurebreck, S (*saura-
        brekka*), sour land slope, 279

Sandall, S (*sand-dalr*), sand dale,
        275, 286

Sandwick, S (*sand-vík*), sand creek,
        286

    „   Boe, S C, sand creek cow
        (rock), 170, 286

Santon, Parish of, Skeeylley Ston-
        dane, Sanctan's parish
        church, 209

    „   burn,* C E, Sanctan's river,
        209

Santwat ⎱ (ob.), S (*sand-vað*), sand
Santway ⎰ ford, 286

Sartell, Sartfell, S (*svart-fjall*), black
        fell, 302

Scara, Skara, S (*skör*, gen. *skara*),
        edge, 252

Scarista, S (*skauris-stadr*), Skauri's stead, 298

Scarlet, Scarclowte, S (*Skarfa-kluft*), Cormorant cleft, 297 ; (*Skarfs-kluft*), Skarf's cleft, 258, 274 ; (*Skarar-kluft*), cleft edge, or edge cleft, 284

Scolaby, Scaleby, S (*skala-byr*), shed farm, 281

Scottean, ?

Scravorley (? *scrah-voalley*), sod fence, 151, 177

Scrondall, S, ?

Seal rock

Shag *rock*, *The*, the Cormorant rock, 284

Sharragh vane, or vedn, *The*, the white foal, 194, 233

Sheading, Shedding, S, 268-271

Shellag, S (*skeljar-vík*), shell creek, 261, 284

Shenmyllin (*mwyllin*), old mill, 249

  ,, rollick (*ruillic*), old church-yard, 173, 249

  ,, thalloo, old plot or land, 249

  ,, valla (*balley*), old farm, 171, 249, 275

Shonest, S (*skauns-staðr*), Skaun's stead, or meadow-land stead, 279, 298

Silver Burn, The, 305

Sir George's bridge, 313

Skard, S (*skarð*), mountain pass, 252

Skarsdale, S (*skarðs-dalr*), mountain pass dale, 273

Skeerey, 161

Skerrisdale, Skerristal, Skaristal, S (*Skauris-dalr* ?), Skauri's dale, 298 ; (*skers-dalr*, or *skerries-dalr*) skerry dale, or skerries dale, 277

Skerristal beg,* S C, Little Skauri's-dale, 236, 277, 298

  ,, mooar,* S C, Big Skauri's-dale, 236, 277, 298

Skeirrip ⎱ S (*sker-ripr*), skerry crag,
Skerrip ⎰   259, 277

Sker lea,* S C, gray skerry, 235, 277

*Sker*ranes, S C, small skerries, 277

Sker vreacy, S C, speckled skerry, 277

Skibrick, S ? (*skipa-hryggr*), ships' ridge, 281

Skinscoe, Skynneskor, S (*Skinnis-skör*), Skinni's edge, 260, 298

Skoryn, *The*, S (? *skör*), the edge, 252

Skybright, ?

Skyehill, Skyall, Scaccafel, S (*skogar-fjall*), wood fell, 180, 273, 274, 305

Sleckby ⎱ S ⎱ (*slakka-byr*), slope
Slegaby ⎰   ⎰ farm, 275

  SLIEAU, 'a mountain,' 142

Slieau, or Slieu, cairn, curn, ciarn or carn (*carn*), cairn moun-tain, 174

  ,, chiarn, Lord's mountain, 188

  ,, coar, pleasant mountain, 245

  ,, doo,* black mountain, 142, 236

  ,, eary Stane, Steen's moorland mountain, 223

  ,, lhean, broad mountain, 238

  ,, Lewaigue,* Lewaigue moun-tain, 231

  ,, losht, burnt mountain, 243

  ,, maggle (*maggyl*), testicles mountain, 195

  ,, meanagh, middle mountain, 240

  ,, meayl, bare mountain, 244

  ,, monagh (*moanagh*), turfy mountain, 243

  ,, ny-carnane,* mountain of the cairn, 142, 158

  ,, ,, -clogh, mountain of the stone, 168

  ,, ,, -freoghan, ny-farrane, moun-tain of the spring, 176

  ,, ouyr, gray or dun mountain, 235

  ,, rea,* smooth mountain, 142, 244

  ,, ree ⎱ (? *ree*), king's mountain,
  ,, reii ⎰   142, 188

  ,, whuallian (*quillian*), whelp mountain, 194

Sloc, *The* (*slogh*), the gully, 136

Sloc-na-cabbyl-screevagh, pit or gully of the scabby horse, 146, 194, 246

Smeale, S, ? (*smala-stadr*), small cattle (stead), 283

Smelt, The, 313

Snæfell, S (*Snæ-fjall*), snow-fell, 142, 256, 288

Sniaul, ob., S (see Snæfell), 141

Soderick, S (*suðr-vík*), the south creek, 289

Sodor
Sodor and Man } 289-292

Soldrick, S (*solar-vík, solar-hryggr*), sun-creek, 257, 288

Sound, The, 312

Southampton, Southampton, 315

Spaldrick, S (? *Pall-vík*), Paul's creek, 257

Spanish Head, 312

Spire Gullet, 315

Spooyt vane, white spout, 146, 233

Squeen, ?

Stack *indigo*, S E (*stakkr*), indigo stack, 274

,, mooar (*stakkr*), big stack, 274

,, *The*, the stack, or the detached rock, 253, 260

Staffland, The, 308-310

Staiden, The ?

Starvey, ?

Staward (modern), 316

Staynarhea, S, ob. (*steina - haugr*), stones' how, 275

Stockhill, (modern)

Stockfield,

Stoyl-ny-Mannanan (*e*), Mannanan's seat or stool, now usually called Mannanan's chair, 185

Strandhall, S (*strandar-holl*), strand hill, 257, 278

Strang, The, 312

Streneby, S (? *strenjar-byr*), narrow-channel farm, 279

Stroin-vuigh, yellow nose, 144, 236

STROOAN, 'a stream, current,' 158

Sornan Barowle,* Baroole stream, 158, 217

,, Rowany,* Rowany stream, 158, 249

Stroan fasnee, winnowing stream, 191

,, ny - carlane (*keyrr - lane*), stream of the sheepfold, 171, 174

,, ,, -craue, stream of the bone, 158, 180

Strooan reagh, laughing stream, 244

Struan crammag,* Crammag stream, 158, 159

Struan keeill-Crore, Crore's cell stream, 217

,, Kerry Nicholas, Kate Nicholas's stream, 225

,, ny-quill (*cooil*), stream of the nook, 158, 169

,, *snail*, ? snail stream, 158

Stuckeydoo, Stuggadoo (*stuggey*), black piece, 150, 232

Sugarloaf Rock, The, 312

Sulby, Solbee, Solveby, S (*Solva-byr*), Solva's farm, 298

Sulbrick, S (*Solva-brekka*), Solvi's slope, 298

Surby, Saureby, S (*saura-brekka*), sourland slope, 279

,, beg,* S C, little sourland slope, 236, 279

,, mooar,* S C, big sour land slope, 236, 279

Swarthawe, S (*svart-haugr*), black how, 256, 302

Tarrastack, S (? *Tarans-stakkr*), Taran's stack, 217

Testraw, Testro, ?

THALLOO, 'land' or 'plot,' 149

Thalloo-a-peishteig, land of the little worm, 198

,, Caragher,* Faragher's plot, 37, 149

,, drine, thorn-tree plot, 200

,, ,, beg, little thorn-tree plot, 200

,, kiel, narrow plot, 238

,, losht, burnt land, 243

,, Mitchal,* ? Mitchell's plot, 149, 223

,, Quayle,* Quayle's plot, 34, 149

,, Queen, ? Quine's plot, 222

,, Vell, Bell's plot, 149, 223

,, voanagh, turfy plot, 243

Thie Juan Ned, John Ned's house, 153

,, ny-hdder, house of the weaver, 191

Tholt-e-Will (*soalt*), Will's barn, 153

Thorkelsbær, ob., S (*þorkels-bær*), Thorkell's farm,

Thorkelstad, ob., (*þorkels-staðr*), Thorkell's stead, 298

Thousla Rocks, ? 304

Tobacco Gullet, 313

Tosbay, S, Totaby, Totnamby (*Toftar-as-mund* or *Toftar-mana-byr*), Osmund's or Mani's knoll farm, 274, 299

Tower of Refuge, The, 314

Towl Dick, Dick's hole,

   ,, *foggy*, C S (*fo-haugr*), under how hole, 239, 257

TRAIE, 'a shore, strand,' 144

Traie bane, white shore, 144

   ,, brisht, broken shore, 243

   ,, cabbage (*cabbag*), sourdock shore, 201

   ,, coon, narrow shore, 238

   ,, cronkan,* hillock shore, 144, 158

   ,, curn, cruin,* (*cruinn*), round shore, 144, 239

   ,, dullish, seaweed shore, 202

   ,, foalley, treacherous shore, 248

   ,, *fogog*, C S* (*fo-haugr*), under how shore, 239, 257

   ,, lagagh* (*laggey*), hollow shore, 135, 144

   ,, ny-earkan, shore of the lapwing, 196

   ,, ,, -feayney, shore of the wine, 203

   ,, ,, -foillan, shore of the seagull, 197

   ,, ,, -fuilley, shore of the blood, 179

   ,, ,, -*gill*, S, shore of the ravine, 256

   ,, ,, -Halsall* (*e*), Halsall's shore, 223

   ,, ,, -sloat, shore of the small pool, 178

   ,, ,, -uainaigue* (*ean-aeg*) (*e*), Young John's shore, 144, 224

   ,, ,, -vollan, shore of the carp, 198

   ,, vaaish, death shore, 186

   ,, vane, white shore, 233

Treein, treen (a land division), 161, 162

Treljey, Treljea, ?

Tremmissary, Tremesare, S (*bramar-setr*), seat edge, 276

Trinian's, St., St. Ninnian's, 214

Trollaby, S (*trolla-byr*), trolls' farm, 288

Trollatoft, S (*trolla-toft*), trolls' knoll, 260, 288

Tromode, Tremott (*bramar-holt*), wood edge, 275, 276

Tynwald, Tinwald, S (*bing-völlr*), Parliament-field, 261-266

Tinwald *Hill*, S E, Parliament-field hill, 261-266

Ughtagh-breesh-my-chree (*brishey*), Break-my-heart hill, 143, 188

Ulican, Oolican* (? *ulla*), 298

Ulist, S (*Ulls-stadr*), Ull's stead, 298

Union Mills, 170, 232, 314

Ushstairs ? (small rocks in the sea)

Vaish ? (*balla-vaase*), cattle (farm), 230

Virginia, 316

Voney ? (*balla-voaney*), turbary (farm), 230

Walberry, ?

Warfield, Wardfell, S (*varða-fjall*), Beacon Fell (now South Barrule), 287

Whallag, The   }
Wollag, The   } ?

Whing, *The* (*quing*), the yoke, 141

White Bridge, 305

White Hoe, S (? *hvit-haugr*), white how, 301

White House, The

White Strand, 305

Wigan, 316

Yn *ow*,* C S (*yn-haugr*), the how, 253, 256

Yiarn jerrey, Iron End, 186

Yn scregganagh, the rocky place, 141

Yons quarter, John's quarter, 224

Y slogh, the pit, or the gulley, 136

ADDENDA.

SURNAMES.

SCANDINAVIAN.

CRIGGALL [1754] seems to be a late corruption of CRINGLE (see p. 86). It is very uncommon.

EXOTIC.

COSNAHAN [1614]. The name of four vicars of the parish of Santon, from whom all the COSNAHANS in the island appear to be descended. It is probably derived from an Irish place-name, *Cosna-abhann* (*oun*), 'foot of the river.' It is now very uncommon. (See p. 222.)

NAMES OBSOLETE BEFORE WRITTEN RECORDS.

The recent discovery at Corna (see p. 285) gives us the well-known Irish name MALACHY, and the curious Scandinavian name SAUÞAR IUAN (correctly Sauðar), '*Sheep's John.*'

PLACE-NAMES.

SIMPLE NAMES (CELTIC).

The following should be under the above heading: *The* ARD, 'the height' (p. 167); *The* LHEN, 'the trench' (p. 157); *The* LHEANEY, 'the meadow;' *The* INJEIG, 'the paddock,' and IN-JAIGYN, 'paddocks' (p. 172). The name of *The* NIARBYL, the long, low promontory near Dalby, is probably a corruption of *Yn-arbyl*, 'the tail.'

COMPOUND NAMES.

Aah, 'a ford ;' in AAH-NY-LINGEY (p. 145).

SUBSTANTIVAL AFFIXES.

Kellag, in BALLA KELLAG and AIREY KELLAG, perhaps from surname (p. 68).

Doubtful.—BREBAG (Cr), 'a kiln,' not known in colloquial Manx ; in BALLA-BREBBAG. BREID, 'a hood,' possibly in CARN-VREID.

Renniagh, 'fern,' may possibly occur as an affix (p. 242).

ADJECTIVAL AFFIXES.

Runt, 'round,' probably a corruption of the English word ; in LHEANEY RUNT, 'round meadow.'

Doubtful.—Kelly gives ' *Brooee* (a), abounding with sand-banks or hills, as Balley-brooee.' There are two places called BALLA-BROOIE.

Cosnec, 'gainful, profitable ;' possibly in BALLACOSNEY.

SCANDINAVIAN NAMES (SIMPLE).

The GILL, 'the ravine,' (p. 256).

ENGLISH NAMES.

CLOVEN STONES, THE, probably so called because the only two stones now remaining have, superficially, the appearance of having been originally one. Feltham gives, in 1798, a representation of the place where these stones are, showing a small stone circle with a kistvaen in the centre.

ERRATA.

Page 91. *Scarff* is now obsolete.
,, 137. *Alt* is also found in a compound name (see p. 167).
,, 148. The words ' (d) Position,' should be above *beinn,* on p. 147, not at p. 148.
,, 150, line 17, for *Fold,* read *Folds.*
,, 159, for *cromage,* read *cromoge.*
,, 180, for *bone slope,* read *Grawe slope* (farm name), see p. 251.
,, 191, for *Farsee,* read *Fasnee.*
,, 192, ,, *Maskey,* ,, *Mashey.*
,, 203, Scandinavian derivation referred to in error.
,, 220, for *Guinney,* read *Quinney.*
,, 227, ,, *Fers,* ,, *Fess.*
,, 230, ,, *Vainey,* ,, *Varney.*
,, 239, line 19, for *Heese,* read *Heose.*
,, 259, for *Stadr,* read *Staðr.*
,, 260, ,, *Stakkr,* ,, *Stacka.*
,, 260, ,, *Troll's,* ,, *Trolls'.*
,, 296, ,, *Lamb's,* ,, *Lambe's.*
,, 305, ,, *Carine,* ,, *Carrin.*

LIST OF SUBSCRIBERS.

AGNEW, Mrs., 11, Devonshire Terrace, Lancaster Gate, London, W.
Allen, Thos. (H.K.), Bellevue, Maughold, I.O.M.
Anderson, Col. (The Receiver-General), Balla Cooley, Michael, I.O.M.
Andrews, Miss G. M. R., 12, Charleville Road, Dublin.
Archer and Evans, Messrs., Victoria Street, Douglas, I.O.M.
Armstrong, Edgar, 37, Cannon Street, Manchester.
Arnison, Major W. B., Penrith, Cumberland.
Arthur, The Rev. P. (M.A.), Tortworth Rectory, Falfield, R.S.O., Glos.

Backhouse, Thos. J., York Cliff, Blackburn.
Bardsley, D. W., 89, Egerton Street, Oldham.
Bardsley, John W. (The Lord Bishop of Sodor and Man), Bishops' Court, I.O.M.
Barnsley, Ed. W., 6, Reservoir Road, Edgbaston, Birmingham.
Beddoe, Dr. John (F.R.S.), The Manor House, Clifton, Bristol.
Bethell, W., Rose Park, Hull.
Bishop of Moray and Ross, Eden Court, Inverness, N.B.
Black, Dr. Ernest, Sydney Mount, Douglas, I.O.M.
Black, Geo. F., Museum of Antiquities, Edinburgh.
Blakeley, Robert Platt, Church Croft, Whalley Range, Manchester.
Bonaparte, His Highness Prince Louis Lucien, 6, Norfolk Terrace, Bayswater, London, W.
Bradbury, Dr. Jos., Laxey, I.O.M.
Brearey, Arthur W., 5, Windsor Terrace, Douglas, I.O.M.
Brereton, Major-General (J P.), Riversdale, Ramsey, I.O.M.
Bridson, John Ridgway, Bridge House, Bolton-le-Moor.

Browne, Rev. G. F. (B.D.), St. Catherine's College, Cambridge.
Brown, James and Son, Times Buildings, Douglas, I.O.M. (50
    copies).
Brown, John A., 14, Victoria Road, Douglas, I.O.M.
Brown, Rev. T. E. (M.A.), Clifton College, Bristol.

Cain, W. J. (Sen.), Woodburn Square, Douglas, I.O.M.
Cain, W. J. (Jun.),   „   „   „
Cain, W., Anderson Street, South Yarra, Melbourne (4 copies).
Caine, Hall, Hawthorns, Keswick.
Caine, John, 70, Carisbrooke Road, Walton, Liverpool.
Callow, F. G. (Advocate), Hawthorn Villa, Onchan, I.O.M.
Campbell, Rev. E. (M.A.), Millom, Cumberland.
Cannell, Claude, Douglas, I.O.M.
Carine, Mark, 8, Belgrave Terrace, Douglas, I.O.M.
Christian, Edward, Glendale, Queen's Co., New York, U.S.A.
Christian, Major Hugh H., Bitton Lodge, Portobello, N.B.
Christian, George B., 105, Cedar Avenue, Cleveland, Ohio, U.S.A.
Christian, Robert,   „   „   „
Christian, Mrs. J. H., 18, Mansfield Street, Portland Place, London,
    W.
Christian, Stephen, Fogg Lane, Didsbury.
Christopher, H. S., The Green, Castletown, I.O.M.
Christopher, Captain A. C., c/o H. S. Christopher, The Green,
    Castletown, I.O.M.
Clague, Wm., Ballavale, Walkley, Sheffield.
Clarke, Archibald, 2, Osborne Terrace, Douglas, I.O.M.
Clarke, Rev. B. P. (M.A., R.D.), Marown Vicarage, I.O.M.
    (3 copies).
Clarke, Sam., Allesley House, Moseley, Birmingham.
Colbourne, G. F. (M.A.), King William's College, I.O.M.
Clay, Mrs. Alfred, Darley Hall, Matlock.
Cleator, John, 47, Cheltenham Street, Barrow-in-Furness.
Clucas, Rev. G. P. (M.A.), Repton, Burton-on-Trent.
Corlett, Rev. John, St. John's Parsonage, I.O.M.
Corlett, Robert (H.K., J.P.), The Craige, Andreas, I.O.M.
Corlett, Richard E., Athol Street, Douglas, I.O.M.
Cosnahan, James, 11, Cambridge Terrace, Douglas, I.O.M.
Cowell, John T., Rose Lodge, Douglas, I.O.M.
Cowin, L. Beecher, 1, Highbury Hill, London, N.
Cowin, James, Belvedere, Douglas, I.O.M.
Cregeen, J. N. (Dr.), Silverburn, 2a, Prince's Road, Liverpool.
Cregeen, Hugh Stowell, 42, Freeland's Road, Bromley, Kent.

Crellin, Miss A. M., Orrysdale, Kirk Michael, I.O.M.
Crellin, J. C. (H.K., J.P.), Ballachurry, Andreas, I.O.M.
Crennell, Rev. John (M.A.), Beamish Vicarage, Stanley, R.S.O.,
    co. Durham.
Cubbon, William, 65, Buck's Road, Douglas, I.O.M.
Curphey, Peter. 40, Derby Square, Douglas, I.O.M.
Curphey, Jos., 64, Berkley Street, Liverpool.

Dawkins, W. Boyd (F.R.S.), Woodhurst, Fallowfield, Manchester.
Dickson, H. H. W. (B.A.), King William's College, I.O.M.
Daltrey, Rev. Thos. W. (M.A., F.L.S.), Madeley Vicarage, New-
    castle, Staffs.
Derby, The Earl of (K.G.), Knowsley Hall, Prescott.
Dixon, Rev. Canon R. (D.D.), St. Matthew's Vicarage, Rugby.
Drinkwater, G. (M.A.), (H.M. Crown Receiver), Kirby, I.O.M.
Dutton, John, Mona Cliff, Douglas, I.O.M.

Ellison, T. P., Bucks Road, Douglas, I.O.M.

Faraker, W. Cregeen, 71, Wickham Road, Brockley, London, S.E.
Faraker, Rev. Robt. (M.A.), 37, Fernhead Road, London, W.
Fargher, J. C., 186, Ramsden Road, Balham, London (2 copies).
Fargher, Wm., La Porte, Indiana, U.S.A.
Fell, Dr. James Kennedy (M.R.C.S., F.S.A.), 1, Harley Street,
    Barrow-in-Furness.
Ferrier, Rev. E. (M.A.), Castletown, I.O.M.
Frowde, John, Free Public Library, Barrow-in-Furness (2 copies).

Gasking, Rev. Samuel (M.A., F.L.S.), 8, Hawthorn Terrace,
    Liscard, Cheshire.
Gawne, Rev. R. Murray (M.A.), Reymerston Rectory, Attle-
    borough.
Gell, Miss Elizabeth M., Anfield Hey, Douglas, I.O.M.
Gell, James S., Sandy Mount, Castletown, I.O.M.
Gell, Sir James (The Attorney-General), Castletown, I.O.M.
George, Rev. Beauchamp (M.A.), Maycroft, Douglas, I.O.M.
Gill, J. Fred. (The Deemster), Douglas, I.O.M.
Gill, John, New Road, Laxey, I.O.M.
Godlee, J. Lister, 3, New Square, Lincoln's Inn, London, W.C.
Goldie-Taubman, J. S. (S.H.K., J.P.), The Nunnery, I.O.M.
Gray, Rev. J. H. (M.A.), Queen's College, Cambridge.
Greensill, Frank, Marina Road, Douglas, I.O.M.
Guest, W. H., Arlington Place, 263, Oxford Road, Manchester.

Hall, Rev. J. W. (M.A.), South Baddesley Vicarage, Lymington, Hants.

Hall, John, The Grange, Hale, Altrincham, Cheshire.

Harrison, Rev. S. N. (M.A.), May Hill, Ramsey, I.O.M. (2 copies).

Haviland, Dr. Alfred (M.R.C.S.E.), Clarence Terrace, Douglas, I.O.M.

Heaton, R. W., King's College, Cambridge.

Hebblethwaite, John W., 17, King Street, Liverpool.

Heyes, Charles B., Hawarden Avenue, Douglas, I.O.M.

Holmes, Mrs. Annie, Sea View Villa, Port Soderick, I.O.M.

Howland, John T. (C.E.), Mona Cottage, Laundry Road, Fulham, London, S.W.

Howson, William, Victoria Street, Blackburn, Lanc.

Hughes-Games, Rev. J. H. (M.A.), Handsworth Vicarage, Birmingham.

Hughes-Games, Rev. Dr. J. (LL.D.) (Archdeacon), The Rectory, Andreas, I.O.M.

Hutchinson, W. A., Castle Fields, Rastrick, Near Brighouse, Yorks.

Inglis, Rev. David (M.A.), 39, Derby Square, Douglas, I.O.M.

Isle of Man Natural History and Antiquarian Society, P.M.C., Kermode, Ramsey, Hon. Sec.

Johnson, W. D., 104, West Fifty-fifth Street, New York, U.S.A. (2 copies).

Johnson, G. and R. (Printers), 12, Prospect Hill, Douglas, I.O.M.

Joyce, Dr. P. W. (LL.D.), Lyre-na-Grena, Leinster Road, Rathmines, Dublin.

Kaighin, Mrs. M., 8, Schott Street, Cleveland, Ohio, U.S.A.

Karran, J. J., Thornton, Douglas, I.O.M.

Karran, James, 8, Finch Road, Douglas, I.O.M.

Kermode, Rev. W. (M.A.), Ballaugh Rectory, I.O.M.

Kermode, Philip M. C. (M.B.O.U., F.S.A.), Sea Bridge Cottage, Ramsey.

Kermode, Evan, 10, Kingswood Grove, Douglas, I.O.M.

Kerr, E. C., Dumbell's Bank, Ramsey.

Kerruish, W. S., Cleveland, Ohio, U.S.A.

Kinvig, T. H., Arbory Street, Castletown, I.O.M.

Knapp, Prof. W. I. (Ph. D., LL.D.), Yale College, U.S.A.

Kneale, Wm. (Bookseller), Victoria Street, Douglas, I.O.M.

Kneen, Thos., The Glencrutchey, Nr. Douglas, I.O.M. (2 copies).

Laughton, Mrs., Ballaquane, Peel, I.O.M.
Leece, Rev. C. H., Ballamona, Port Soderic, I.O.M.
Leece, Thos., Stanley Villa, Derby Road, Douglas, I.O.M.
Lewis, W. E. (M.A.), King William's College, I.O.M.
Library, The, Jesus College, Oxford.
Library, The, King William's College, I.O.M.
Little, James W. (J.P.), Strand, Barrow-in-Furness.
Lupton, Rev. B. J. S. (M.A.), St. Mark's Parsonage, Ballasalla,
    I.O.M.

Mackinnon, Prof. Don, 1, Merchiston Place, Edinburgh.
Maclagan, R. C., 5, Coate's Crescent, Edinburgh.
Macnish, Rev. Dr. Neil (M.A., LL.D.), Cornwall, Ontario, Canada.
Macqueen, Capt. Alexander, 1, Taubman Terrace, Douglas, I.O.M.
Maitland, Dalrymple, Brook Mooar, Union Mills, I.O.M.
March, Dr. H. Colley, 2, West Road, Rochdale.
Marsden, Joseph T., 50, Belgrave Road, Darwen, Lancashire.
Maxwell, Sir Herbert, Bart., M.P., Monreith, Whauphill, N.B.
Moore, James, Victoria Street, Douglas, I.O.M.
Moore, Mrs. W. F., Cronkbourne, Douglas, I.O.M.
Moore, W. F. (J.P.),   ,,   ,,   ,,
Moore, Miss E. E.,   ,,   ,,   ,,
Moore, Rev. F. J. (B.A.), Kirk Braddan Vicarage, I.O.M.
Moore, Miss S., 9, Belmont Terrace, Douglas, I.O.M.
Moore, Lucas E., New Orleans, U.S.A.
Moore, Thos. H., Andreas, Kingsmead Road, Birkenhead.
Moore, James, Bombay.
Morfill, W. R. (M.A.), 4, Clarendon Villas, Oxford.
Morris, Rev. W. (M.A.), Ramsey, I.O.M.
Morrison, Miss, Athol Street, Peel, I.O.M.
Mylrea and Allen, Duke Street, Douglas, I.O.M. (2 copies).
Mylrea, J. A. (H.K., J.P.), Crescent, Douglas, I.O.M.

Newton, Rev. A. S. (M.A.), Grammar School, Ramsey, I.O.M.
Nicholson, C., Well Road Hill, Douglas, I.O.M.
Nicholson, J. M., 2, St. Thomas' Walk, Douglas, I.O.M.

Okell, W. H., Glen Falcon, Douglas, I.O.M.

Patterson, Geo., The Studio, Ramsey, I.O.M.
Pearson, J. L. (R.A.), 13, Mansfield Street, Portland Place,
    London, W.
Pearson, F. L., 13, Mansfield Street, Portland Place, London, W.

Pearson, Rev. Henry, Lambley Vicarage, Nottingham.
Penfoid, Rev. J. B. (M.A.), King William's College, I.O.M.

Quayle, Mrs., Bridge House, Castletown, I.O.M. (5 copies).
Quayle, G. H. (H.K.), „ „ „
Quayle, Miss, „ „ „
Quayle, Miss E. „ „ „
Quayle, T. C., Erie Street, Cleveland, Ohio, U.S.A.
Quine, Rev. John (M.A.), Grammar School, Douglas, I.O.M.
Quirk, Jos., Braddan School House, I.O.M.

Radcliffe, E., Kingswood Grove, Douglas, I.O.M.
Radford, Mrs., Farm Hill, Douglas, I.O.M.
Ralfe, P., 8, Woodburn Square, Douglas, I.O.M.
Ready, Col. J. T., Ellerslie, Hawkhurst, Kent.
Reynolds, Llywarch, Old Church Place, Merthyr Tydfil.
Richman, Alfred L., 9, School Lane, Liverpool.
Ring, G. A., Alexander Road, Douglas, I.O.M.
Rixon, A. W., 10, Austin Friars, London, E.C.
Robinson, Joseph, 5, Falkner Square, Liverpool.
Roddam, R. J., Roddam Hall, Wooperton, R.S.O., Northumber-
    land.
Roney, Richard, Frances Villa, Laureston Road, Douglas, I.O.M.

Saunderson, F., 9, Earl Terrace, Douglas, I.O.M.
Savage, Rev. Ernest B. (M.A., F.S.A.), St. Thomas Vicarage
    Douglas, I.O.M. (2 copies).
Seckham, Mrs. B. T., Thorpelands, Moulton, Nr., Northampton.
Sherwen, Rev. Canon William, Dean Rectory, Cockermouth.
Stephen, R. S. (M.A., H.K., J.P.), Spring Valley, Douglas, I.O.M.
Stowell, Thos., 132, Buck's Road, Douglas, I.O.M.
Sutherland, James M., Clifton, Nr. Douglas, I.O.M.
Sutton, Charles W., for Free Public Libraries, Manchester.
Swinnerton, Charles, The Studio, Port St. Mary, I.O.M.
Swinnerton, Fred, „ „ „ „ „
Swinnerton, Robert, Selbourne Road, Douglas, I.O.M.

Tarbet, Thomas, 804, Wilson Avenue, Cleveland, Ohio, U.S.A.
Taylor, Rev. Canon (Litt. D.), Settrington Rectory, York.
Teare, William, 24, Mona Street, Liverpool.
Tellet, Dr. F. S. (F.G.S., C.P.), Ramsey, I.O.M.
Tupper, William, New Road, Laxey, I.O.M.
Tyson, F. and E., Mona Cottage, Crescent, Douglas, I.O.M.

Walpole, Spencer, Dr. (LL.D., His Excellency the Lieutenant-Governor), Government House, I.O.M. (5 copies).

Walsh, the Rev. Father Edmund, St. Mary's Rectory, Douglas, I.O.M.

Walters, the Rev. F. B. (M.A.), Principal of King William's College, I.O.M.

Ward, the Hon. James Kewley, Box 1818, P.O., Montreal, Canada.

Whiteside, R., Brunswick Road, Douglas, I.O.M.

Wood, G. W., Ballagawne, Riggindale Road, Streatham, London, S.W.

Woodd, Mrs. Robert B., Woodlands, Hampstead, London, N.W.

Wren, A. P., Messrs. Wren and Sons, 7, Fen Court, London, E.C.

Young and Sons, Henry, 12, South Castle Street, Liverpool (2 copies).